By Nicki Bennett

Always a Bridesmaid
Christmas Travel Advisory
Comfort and Joy
Evan's Heaven
Flight
Home for Christmas
New Traditions

DREAMSPUN DESIRES
The Cattle Baron's Bogus
Boyfriend
Bad to the Bone

With Ariel Tachna
The Escape Artist
Rocky Road to Love
Under the Skin
Wellspring

ALL FOR LOVE
Checkmate
All for One
Stronghold

HOT CARGO STORIES
Hot Cargo
Something About Harry

EXPLORING LIMITS
Exploring Limits
No Limits

OUT AND ABOUT
Out of Bounds

Published by DREAMSPINNER PRESS
www.dreamspinnerpress.com

By Ariel Tachna

Best Ideas
Château d'Eternité
With Nessa L. Warin: Dance Off
Fallout
The Guardian of Machu Llaqta
Her Two Dads
Highland Lover
Home for Chirappu
In Search of Fireworks
The Inventor's Companion
Knit Two Together
The Matelot
Music of the Heart
Once in a Lifetime
Out of the Fire
Overdrive
The Path
Popcorn Garlands
Rediscovery
Revelations in the Dark
A Rose Among the Ruins
Seducing C.C.
Stolen Moments
A Summer Place
With Madeleine Urban: Sutcliffe Cove
Revelations • Talking in Code
Testament to Love
Why Nileas Loved the Sea

AT YOUR SERVICE
At Your Service • Service with a Smirk

DREAMSPUN DESIRES
LEXINGTON LOVERS
Unstable Stud
A Matchless Man
Stage Two
Rebuild My Heart
Home and Away

GAMES LOVERS PLAY
Amorous Liaison • Best Behavior
Ride 'em Cowboy

HOT CARGO
Healing in His Wings
With Nicki Bennett: Hot Cargo
Something About Harry

LANG DOWNS
Inherit the Sky • Chase the Stars
Outlast the Night
Conquer the Flames
Cherish the Land

PARTNERSHIP IN BLOOD
Alliance in Blood • Covenant in Blood
Conflict in Blood • Reparation in Blood
Perilous Partnership • Crossroads in Blood
Reluctant Partnerships • Lycan Partnership
Partnership Reforged • Partnership Reborn

With Nicki Bennett
The Escape Artist
Rocky Road to Love
Under the Skin
Wellspring

ALL FOR LOVE
Checkmate • All for One • Stronghold

EXPLORING LIMITS
Exploring Limits • No Limits

OUT AND ABOUT
Out of Bounds

Published by **DREAMSPINNER PRESS**
www.dreamspinnerpress.com

Wellspring

Nicki Bennett
Ariel Tachna

Published by

DREAMSPINNER PRESS

8219 Woodville Hwy #1245
Woodville, FL 32362 USA
www.dreamspinnerpress.com

For Connie Bailey, who gave us the idea in the first place.

Acknowledgments

Our sincere thanks to Trisha, whose fantastic beta comments added so much depth to the story.

CHAPTER ONE

Galveston, 1867

AMERICA.

The land of opportunity.

The land of freedom.

Erick von Hellermann knew better than to believe that unquestioningly. He might never have set foot on these shores, but he had traveled extensively in Europe and knew that reputation rarely conveyed the reality of a place. Even so, he hoped to lose himself in the vast expanses of the Texas plains. In all that open space, there was surely room for one man who wanted nothing more than to leave his past behind.

The ship docked, and the passengers made their way off slowly, through the port authority where they gave their names, professions, and country of origin. Erick struggled with the unfamiliar accents. He read English fluently, having been schooled on Shakespeare and other classics, but he had seldom had an opportunity to speak it, and the drawled speech full of words he did not recognize now overwhelmed him. When his turn came, he gave his name as Erick Heller, listing Bremen as his home. A new name for a new start, and the ship had sailed from Prussia. If Bremen was not his true city of origin, no one here would be any wiser, and perhaps the changes would slow down anyone who might come looking for him. He didn't think his cousin would send anyone, since his return would keep the other man from inheriting his title and estate, but Erick was not entirely sure his mother would accept his decision. The baroness had been most disconcerted at his decision to leave home after the death of his wife and son in childbirth. Regardless of what his mother said, that stage of his life was over. He hoped the one in front of him would be better than the one he left behind.

"Your profession, sir?" the harbor master asked.

Erick smiled. "Cowboy."

The man looked at the cut of Erick's suit and the quality of his shoes in surprise, but he inscribed "cowboy" on the page next to Erick's name.

Exiting the office, Erick paused on the edge of the docks to take in the bustling port. In that respect, it reminded him of the port in Bremen, but the resemblance ended there. Instead of the brisk, almost cold breeze of winter, the wind off the ocean here was already warm and humid, making Erick's shirt cling uncomfortably to his sides beneath his jacket and his cravat feel stifling around his neck. The sun beat down overhead on unfamiliar plants and trees, on dusty streets and rough-hewn wooden houses. He saw none of the familiar pale stone that characterized the buildings of his former home.

The sound of a horse screaming wrenched his attention from his vague thoughts back to the present. The animal in question reared up on its hindquarters, front hooves pawing the air as its voice cut through the noise of the harbor again. It was a beautiful black horse, but its handler obviously had no idea how to work with it. Not pausing to consider his actions, Erick strode toward the scene, all too aware of the crowded docks and the damage a frightened or enraged horse could do in a crowd if it escaped the man's control.

Reaching the handler's side, he grabbed the lead rope as it flew free, letting the horse rear once more but catching the cheek strap of the halter when its hooves hit the ground again. He crooned soothingly in German, the calm tone of his voice far more important than the words themselves. The horse fought him, but Erick held on, using the full weight of his body and all the strength of his will to bring the animal under control. The next attempt to rear was half-hearted, though the horse still pawed menacingly at the ground. Erick kept up the gentle murmurs, an oasis of calm in the chaos of the docks. The horse responded slowly, the wild look fading from its eyes as it focused on him. Erick continued talking, his free hand moving to stroke the animal's neck and withers. They quivered beneath his touch but settled when he kept the contact light and soothing. The horse truly was magnificent. He only hoped it belonged to someone who would appreciate it.

"That's quite the touch you got there."

Erick glanced up to see who had spoken, his mind racing to make the drawled words translate in his brain.

"He is afraid," Erick said slowly. "I am not. He knows that."

"You ain't from around here, are you?" the other man asked.

Erick shook his head, trying not to stare. In his travels, Erick had met people of enough nationalities not to be surprised at the sun-bleached hair brushing the man's shoulders or his tanned skin, but it was not at all typical of his home—*his former home*, he reminded himself. Nor were the heavy work pants and open-collared shirt the other man wore, a scarf tied loosely around his neck, or the thin braid interwoven with small, colorful beads that dangled at one temple from below his wide-brimmed hat. Erick suspected he had just met his first cowboy. "No, I am from Prussia. Erick Heller at your service."

"Cade Webster." The cowboy pulled off a thick leather glove to offer Erick his hand. The calluses confirmed Erick's supposition that this man was no stranger to hard work. "Shall we see if we can find this boy's owner?"

"He ain't got no owner." The sailor came back to the horse's side now that it had calmed. "His owner died during the crossing. He'll be sold at auction."

"I will for him now pay," Erick said. "I will a horse need, and he is perfect."

"He's got a nasty temper and is too strong for his own good," the handler disagreed, "but that ain't my problem. See the captain about a price."

"Has he a name?" Erick asked before the man could walk away.

"Not that I ever heard anybody use."

"If you want to speak with the captain, I'll watch the horse until you come back," Webster suggested.

Erick hesitated, not sure if he could trust the offer.

"Look, mister," Webster said. "Around here, the fastest way to get shot is to mess with someone else's horse. I'm gonna make sure he don't wander off or get scared again. That's all."

"My apologies," Erick said with a sharp bow. "I am… unfamiliar with customs here. I will with the captain now speak."

CADE WATCHED the man walk up the gangplank of the ship that the horse he was now holding had come off of. It was no surprise the horse was restless. It smelled freedom after weeks of being confined in the hold of a ship with probably moldy hay for food and who knew what for water. All things considered, the animal was in pretty good shape, although Cade suspected Heller would have a fight on his hands getting the horse used to listening again. If he hadn't seen the masterful way Heller dealt with the beast—calm but firmly in control—he would have said the man wasn't up to the task, but now he wasn't so sure. He might look like a European dandy, but he had a way with horses if nothing else.

As he stroked the horse's neck, he wondered what brought Heller to Texas. Cade had seen plenty of men arrive in Galveston with little more than the clothes on their back and maybe a trade with the hope of building a new life for their families. He'd seen it work a time or two as well, but Heller didn't have the same air of desperation. The cut of his clothes and the way he had simply assumed he had the resources to purchase the horse spoke of a privileged upbringing and some degree of continuing wealth.

That only added to Cade's curiosity. It would be his downfall, Nadua, his adoptive mother, always told him, but he wanted to find out more about the mysterious stranger. Heller had obviously arrived only minutes ago. Cade could offer to show him around, help him find a boarding house and maybe even a restaurant for dinner if the boarding house didn't include meals. He could ask a few of his questions and learn a little bit more about the man.

Heller returned a few minutes later, the horse's papers in hand.

"Did you get it all taken care of?" Cade asked, though he already knew the answer.

"It is done," Heller said in his funny accent. He clearly knew what he was saying, but the pronunciation was a little off, bringing a smile to Cade's face. He handed the rope back to Heller.

"Good. Could the captain tell you anything about him?"

"The captain said Thunder is his name. This is not for a horse a good name."

There it was again, Cade thought. The awkward turn of phrase that wasn't quite right. It reminded Cade a little of when he'd had to get used to speaking English again after speaking Comanche for so many years. "Why not? He certainly made a lot of noise earlier."

"Names are important," Heller said. "With a name like that, everyone expects a loud, difficult horse, and so they make him one. Much better would it be to give him a name like…. Butterfly. Then everyone will a quiet horse expect, and so he will one become."

"Just like that?" Cade asked incredulously. He'd worked with his share of horses and had known more than a few who were completely misnamed.

"*Nein*," Heller said, "not 'just like that' but with work and patience and time, *ja*. Yes."

"So his name's Butterfly now?" Cade asked.

"Perhaps not Butterfly," Heller conceded. "I will on the proper name for him think. Now I must a stable find."

"If you'd like, I can show you where I kept my horse the last time I came to town," Cade offered. "It's run by a German couple, actually. You might enjoy meeting someone from home."

Heller's face tightened at the offer, making Cade wonder what he'd said wrong. "Texas is home now. Prussia is in the past, where it will stay."

"There is another stable," Cade said, "but I don't think it's as clean or as well-run as the one where I kept my horse."

"Clean is important," Heller said slowly.

"I could take him there for you," Cade said, not sure why he suddenly cared so much about not letting this man out of his sight. "That way you'd know he was taken care of without having to be reminded of ho—where you came from."

Heller hesitated a moment longer, clearly torn. "*Nein*," he said finally. "There is no reason to avoid others from Prussia."

It seemed an odd concern. Cade took any opportunity he could to visit with Comanche when he came across them, but he didn't know what had driven Heller across an ocean, so maybe their circumstances were different enough to explain it. "Come on, then. I'll show you where the stables are."

"First must I for supplies arrange," Heller said.

"That'll mean a few days in Galveston," Cade observed. "Let's get your horse settled and then we'll see if we can't work out the rest."

"Why are you me helping?" Heller asked suddenly as they walked down the street toward the stable. "You know me not."

"Because you have a way with horses." Cade gave Heller the acceptable part of the answer. He kept his growing fascination to himself. "My boss is looking for a couple of new hands, including a new bronc buster, on the ranch. I thought you might be interested."

Heller stayed silent for so long that Cade worried he'd committed some kind of breach of etiquette when Heller finally looked at him again. "I might be interested."

Chapter Two

Erick sat at the table in the saloon across from his new friend, not quite sure how they had gotten there. He had expected to need time to find his footing once he arrived in America, but events since he stepped off the ship in Galveston had moved so quickly that he felt a bit like a leaf swept in the wind. How much worse would it have been had he not been fortunate enough to meet Webster? He hadn't been managed so thoroughly since his mother arranged his presentation at court when he was sixteen. Webster had shown him around town, helping him settle his new horse and find a boarding house with an empty room. The boarding house only served breakfast, so Webster had promptly offered to buy him dinner. Erick had almost refused on the grounds that he was already beholden to the man for his help, but Webster had insisted he accept, saying it was only fitting to welcome Erick to Texas.

The beans and rice the saloon girl brought to the table were spicy, unlike anything Erick had ever tasted in Prussia, but he found himself eating more even as his eyes watered from the heat of the dish.

"You okay over there?" Webster asked.

Erick nodded and took another deep swig of beer. It wasn't Prussian beer, but it was drinkable and it quenched the fire in his mouth, at least until he took another bite. "The food at home was not so spicy." He smothered a frown at the slip. *Texas is home now*, he reminded himself.

Webster laughed. "I had the same problem when I first arrived. You get used to it."

"You were not in Texas born?" Erick asked, curious to learn more about the man sitting across from him. Webster's muscular physique proclaimed him man, not boy, but beyond that, Erick could not determine his age. Somewhere over eighteen, somewhat less than Erick's own thirty-three years. His blue-green eyes sparkled with delight and mischief at times, but he had taken appropriate care in helping Erick find accommodations for both his new horse and himself. The cowboy might appreciate a good joke now and then, but he could be serious when such behavior became necessary. All in all, a delightful companion.

Best of all, a companion with no ulterior motive. Erick was used to people cultivating his acquaintance for his connections, his title, his name, or his wealth, but those things had no meaning here. Yet Webster had spent some hours with him today for no apparent reason beyond desiring Erick's company. Dare he think he had made a friend? He was quietly pleased that Webster would see in even so obvious a newcomer someone worth investing time in.

"I hail from Kentucky originally," Webster said, "but my parents were dirt poor—their land wasn't worth shit. When Texas joined the Union, they decided to take their chances out here. It didn't go so well for them—they died before they ever got here—but I turned out okay."

The casual vulgarity surprised Erick less than his companion's seemingly casual attitude toward his parents' death, both reminding him he was no longer in the rarefied salons of Europe. He wondered how old Webster was at the time—young enough to soften the loss, but capable enough to have survived it? He did not know the other man well enough to ask. "I am sorry for your loss," he said quietly. "But I am glad you turned out okay." He stumbled over the unfamiliar word, frustrated with the lapse. He hated sounding uneducated.

"It was a long time ago," Webster replied. "I barely remember them, to be honest. Either way, I'm happier working with animals than I ever woulda been trying to grow things. Animals like me. Plants, not so much. And the ranches out here that run cattle always need hands to take care of them."

As much as he would like to know more about Webster's background, Erick didn't push. He was no more eager to talk about his own past. "Cowboys," Erick murmured instead, the stories he'd read in Prussia coming back to him as he imagined days and nights spent in the saddle, out on the open plains with nothing around but the herd of cattle and his fellow riders. After the stilted manners and stifling etiquette of his childhood and youth, it sounded like heaven.

The saloon girl reappeared at their table, batting her eyelashes in Erick's direction. He answered her question without giving any outward sign of noticing her charms. Even if he had been interested, his mother had taught him better than that. As it was, he had left that life behind, and he had no intention of starting his new one with any kind of ruse.

When she had left again, Webster leaned closer. "If you decide you want some… friendly company, just say the word and I'll scoot. You were cooped up on that ship for a long time. I understand if you need some relief."

"Your company is far more congenial than hers could be," Erick replied with a warm smile. The overly painted woman held no appeal for him. If he needed relief, he could make do with his own hand as he had for the duration of the voyage and indeed much of his life. If his mind's eye conjured an image of a tanned, long-haired cowboy, no one would ever know. "What will we tomorrow do?"

"The first thing I have to do tomorrow is meet the shipping agent at the wharf," Webster said. "My boss ordered a shipment of furniture from England for his wife before he went and got himself killed falling off a horse. Miz Roarke sent me to pick it up, even if she thinks it's a bigger waste of money now than she did when old man Roarke first ordered it."

Erick smothered a chuckle as Webster rolled his eyes. "You gotta meet her to understand. She ain't the type to just make house. She's as strong as most of the ranch hands and knows more about running the ranch than all of us put together, 'cept maybe Payne. She inherited the land from her pa as his only child, after he raised her like he would a son. Anyhow, she would have canceled it if she could, but Roarke had already paid for the order, and a letter wouldn't have reached England before it was already on the ship. I met the shipping agent today to let him know I was here. I have an appointment tomorrow morning to pick up the furniture. Once I have it, it'll be time to head back home."

"Think you she will be willing another hand to hire?" Erick tried without success to imagine his mother managing a cattle ranch, although she was well-accustomed to expecting her commands to be followed. Webster seemed to admire Frau Roarke, though, which implied an open-mindedness too uncommon in Erick's life to this point.

"That'd be up to Payne—he's the foreman, and Miz Roarke don't let nobody onto the ranch without his say-so—but I don't see why he wouldn't. You speak English well enough—he won't hire anyone he can't talk to himself—and you know your way around a horse. I can teach you how to toss a rope and the rest you can learn on the job," Webster replied. "But if you're coming with me, we'll need to get some work clothes for you. That suit you're wearing wouldn't last a week on the ranch. And you'll need a bedroll and camping gear for the nights out on the range, plus enough supplies to make it back to Wellspring—that's the name of the ranch. Assuming Payne hires you, you'll eat and bunk with the rest of the hands."

"And if he does not?" Erick asked. Once again Erick was glad of his mother's insistence on a complete education. He knew his speech sounded foreign to Webster's ear—even he could hear the differences between his diction and the other man's—but Webster didn't seem to have any problem understanding him. Hopefully that would be enough to get him a job at Webster's ranch. "I am willing to learn and to do other tasks until I do. I can stables clean if nothing else."

"You'll do that too," Webster said. "We all do. But there's plenty of other work. Have you ever broken a horse?"

Erick frowned, not understanding the question. "Why would I a horse break? It would not of any use be if I did."

Webster laughed, the sound coiling in Erick's gut. "Not that kind of breaking," he said. "Training, teaching."

"Why did you not say that?" Erick asked. "Yes, I have trained horses a saddle and bridle to take."

"Then I know you'll have a job." Webster's confidence convinced Erick of his assertion. "Besides the cattle, we round up wild mustangs that we break for the hands to use or to sell to other ranches. That's how Roarke died. He got thrown and broke his neck, and we haven't found a new bronc buster to take over. Some of the other hands have a bit of experience with young horses, but that's not the same as working with the wild ones. Plus Payne needs us all on the range with the cattle, not back at the ranch house working with the mustangs."

"I will my best do if he hires me," Erick promised. The thought of having one familiar task in a land where everything was new reassured him immensely. He had refused to dwell on the future during the passage, not wanting to work himself into a panic over something he could do nothing about, but now that he had arrived, his uncertainty returned full force, both eased and augmented by the time he had spent with the handsome cowboy across the table from him. Webster had done everything he could to make Erick's transition easier, but his demeanor, his comportment, everything about him proclaimed the differences between Erick's old life and his new one.

"Let's see how you do with Butterfly as we ride west," Webster said. "If you handle that brute as well on the trip as you did on the docks today, I'll have all the proof I need to convince Payne to hire you."

CADE WALKED slowly back to his hotel, having left Heller at the boarding house where he'd taken a room for the few days they would be in Galveston. His mind raced as he pondered their conversations over the course of the afternoon and evening. Heller still looked like an aristocrat, but Cade had seen no signs of the kind of high-handed behavior he associated with that breed. The man had asked questions, taken instruction, and generally been a pleasant companion all evening. And his talent with the horse he'd acquired still amazed Cade. Every time the stallion got skittish, Heller had calmed him with a touch or a word. If the two had been together for years, that might not have been so impressive, but Cade knew exactly how long they had known each other—as long as he himself had known Heller. And that made Heller's feat impressive indeed. If that carried over to the wild horses on Wellspring, Payne would be a fool not to hire Heller on the spot. And Zeke Payne was many things, but no one had ever accused him of being a fool.

Cade hoped it would work out because in the few hours they'd already spent together, he had grown to like the man. Heller's face wasn't weathered the way Cade was used to, more proof that he'd had a life of some privilege before leaving Prussia, so Cade couldn't peg his age as easily as he could with another cowboy, but he would guess the man was somewhere around thirty-five with brown hair, fair skin, and the most striking blue eyes Cade had ever seen. The skin would darken and the hair lighten under the harsh Texas sun, but those eyes….

Cade knew he'd dream of them tonight and probably for many nights to come, especially if Heller got the job and stayed around to fuel Cade's fantasies. He resisted the urge to adjust his pants as he neared the hotel. He could wait until he got inside and could take them off in private.

The desk clerk nodded at him and handed him his key as he came inside. Cade returned the nod politely and climbed up to his room under the eaves. It was the cheapest room in the hotel, but it was still nicer than a lot of the boarding houses, although the one Heller was staying in had been respectable. If he hadn't already paid for the night at the hotel, he'd have seen about getting a room at the boarding house where Heller was staying.

That thought elicited a soft groan. Cade locked the door behind him, tossed open the garret windows to let out the warmth of the day and hopefully catch some of the breeze off the ocean, and stripped down to his union suit. He unbuttoned the top half of the long underwear as well, baring his chest and shoulders. Flopping down on the bed beneath the open windows, he let his mind wander back over the day.

One moment stuck in his thoughts: Heller's reaction to the girl in the saloon. Her intentions couldn't have been much more obvious unless she'd draped herself across Heller's lap, but he had paid even less attention to her than Cade had. It was the man's words that struck him hardest, though. *Your company is far more congenial than hers could be.* Cade told himself not to get his hopes up, but unless the man was so clueless he didn't realize the girl was offering him sex, Heller's comment bordered on suggestive.

Closing his eyes, Cade summoned the image of the Prussian in his proper suit as he came down from leaving his trunk in his room at the boarding house, bowler hat under his arm, his hair brushed neatly, his jacket dusted off and his shoes polished. He was the wet dream Cade never knew he had.

He let the fantasy spin out, imagining Heller was coming down to meet him for an outing, the pressed and proper appearance intended to entice Cade rather than because his upbringing dictated it. Aware of the public setting, Cade did not embrace Heller but instead settled for a discreet brush of his hand against the other man's. Heller—Erick— understood, though, his smile softening the stern lines of his face and giving a special glow to his already brilliant eyes. That smile held a promise for later, a promise Cade fully intended to make good on.

In the way of dreams, the setting dissolved around them, coalescing instead to the waterfall and quiet pool he had found while riding with the herd, deep in the back country at Wellspring. As far as he knew, none of the other ranch hands knew it was there since it was a two-day ride from the main house, giving him and Erick the assurance of privacy as they spread out on the blanket for their picnic lunch.

Alone with Erick now, Cade did not have to hold back, leaning over to press a kiss to the side of Erick's mouth. Erick laughed and turned his head so their lips met. Cade leaned into the kiss, deepening it by degrees. His pulse pounded as Erick pressed him to the blanket, straddling him so their bodies rubbed together provocatively.

Cade slid his hand over his underwear, mimicking the friction of body against body from his fantasy. He groaned, imagining Erick's body pinning him down, Erick's lips stealing his breath, Erick's hands driving him wild. He tweaked his nipples with his free hand as he stroked his cock more deliberately through the cloth, striving for release now to the thought of Erick rutting against him, driving them both to climax. Cade wasn't usually a passive lover, but it felt so right to give in to his dream lover that he didn't resist, letting the heat of his climax build low and deep as he imagined Erick devouring him. With a startled shout, he found his pleasure, his body pulsing with the rapture radiating through him. He collapsed on the bed, his hand sticky with his release. He would need a bath in the morning and a trip to the laundry before returning home. He had a clean union suit in his bag, but unless he wanted to wear that one all the way back to the ranch, he'd need to get some washing done.

For now, he settled for stripping bare and slipping between the sheets. He would deal with the rest—and with Heller—in the morning.

CHAPTER THREE

THE REMAINDER of the night passed in restless, sweaty dreams, leaving Cade feeling terribly unrefreshed the next morning. He ordered a bath and dropped his clothes off at the laundry before heading to the boarding house where Heller was staying to meet him. It did nothing for his composure when Heller rose to greet him wearing a similar suit to the one he had worn yesterday and the one Cade had spent all night imagining peeling off him. "I need to go to the warehouse to pick up the furniture," he said gruffly. "Once I've done that, I'm all yours for the day."

The moment the words left his mouth, Cade wished he could call them back because the images they conjured were far too disconcerting for his peace of mind. Heller seemed to take them in stride, though, no surprise showing on his face.

"I will with you come," Heller offered. "That way will we already together be."

"You know…." Cade hoped his advice would be taken the right way. "… it would sound less foreign if you said, 'I will come with you' instead of putting 'come' at the end of the sentence."

"Only come or all actions?" Heller asked.

Cade breathed a quiet sigh of relief that he hadn't offended the man. "All actions."

Heller nodded sharply. "I will come with you. We will accomplish more that way. Is that correct?"

"Yes, that's right," Cade said. "You ready to go, then?"

"I am ready," Heller confirmed.

"I've got to get the wagon," Cade said as they walked toward the warehouse district.

"I will with—" Heller stopped and shook his head. "I will help you with the horses."

"Thanks," Cade said. "I left them at the livery here at the docks, but we still have to hitch them up, and that will go faster with two rather than one."

They found the stable and hitched the four draft horses to the ranch's big covered wagon. Cade noticed the stolid animals reacted as comfortably to Heller as the high-strung stallion had done the day before. Cade grinned at the reaction of the other cowboys if Heller showed up on the ranch still calling that brute Butterfly. He'd try to suggest something a little less feminine as they rode west. Once the horses were hitched, Heller swung up on the seat next to him.

Cade drove the team with practiced ease down to the warehouse. He tied them to a hitching post and unlashed the back of the wagon, dropping the rear gate as well. "This would be so much easier if she'd let me bring the buckboard," Cade muttered.

"What is the difference?" Heller asked from where he hovered at Cade's elbow, obviously willing to help but not knowing how.

"It doesn't have the canvas across the top for one thing," Cade said. "And it's lighter and only requires two horses to pull. But the weather is unpredictable in the spring, and since the money's spent, she didn't want to risk any damage to the furniture. Not to mention the weight of the furniture might be too much for the smaller wagon."

Heller nodded. "It seems I have much to learn."

"Don't worry." Cade flashed a grin in Heller's direction. "I'll teach you."

ERICK'S FACE tightened at the innocent comment, not because of anything Webster said but because of his own inappropriate reaction. He had spent the night tossing and turning in his lonely bed, a novel sensation for a man used to sleeping alone, but Webster had planted the idea of congenial company in his mind at dinner, and Erick had not been able to weed it out. The cowboy had haunted his thoughts until he fell asleep and his dreams for the rest of the night.

Waiting for Webster to arrive this morning had been hard enough, but then they had started work and Erick had pushed aside his inappropriate thoughts.

Until now.

Now he was assailed by thoughts of everything Webster could teach him, not on the range, but between the sheets. Erick's social standing and the realities of acquiring amenable companionship had resulted in a certain sameness to all of his amorous encounters. With a cowboy for a lover, Webster or someone else, his social standing would count for nothing, and perhaps he could finally experience the other side of lovemaking. He suspected Webster could give him a good ride if the man was willing.

Unfortunately, he had no indication that Webster shared his preferences, much less was interested in him. He couldn't stop the spike of desire, though. "I will learn gladly whatever you wish to teach me."

Erick saw a spark light Webster's eyes, but he had no way of telling if it meant what he wanted it to mean. Stifling the urge to run his fingers through his hair, a habit his mother had spent years trying to break him of, he turned his attention back to the bustle around them. "The shipping master will meet you here?"

"He said he'd be here at nine." Webster pulled out a pocket watch. "We're a few minutes early, but I'd rather that than miss the appointment. I'm getting anxious carrying around the money Miz Roarke sent for the final expenses."

The shipping agent arrived before Erick could think of a reply. He opened the warehouse and showed them the six crates that contained the furniture Webster's employer had ordered from England. He didn't quite catch what Webster muttered under his breath, but he could tell from the man's face that it was not complimentary. Pushing back his sleeves, he looked at his new friend. "The sooner we start, the sooner we can be finished."

Webster nodded, looking at the crates for a moment. "Let's get the smaller ones in first, up near the front. We'll save the big one for the back, right over the axle. It'll have more support that way, plus we won't have to move it as far."

The smaller ones were hardly small as far as Erick was concerned, but he saw the logic of what Webster suggested. It took both of them, the shipping agent, and one of the warehouse workers to move even the smallest of the boxes from the warehouse onto the wagon, and Erick was sweating by the time they had it aboard. By the time they loaded the last crate, he had done more hard labor than the rest of his life put together.

It felt wonderful.

"We've ruined your suit." Webster climbed onto the box seat of the wagon next to Erick. "I'm sorry. I'll buy you a new one to replace it."

"*Nein*," Erick replied immediately. "My new life is not suits but clothes like yours. It does not matter if the suit is ruined. I would have no reason to wear it anyway. I will donate the others to a local church before we leave for your ranch."

"That would be a shame," Webster blurted, the color staining his cheeks visible even beneath his tanned skin. Erick allowed himself a moment to hope it meant Webster had noticed his appearance. "You should keep one of them so you'll have something to wear if you meet a gal you want to court."

Erick shook his head. "I left that behind when I buried my wife in Prussia. There will be no more… gals for me."

"You don't know that," Webster insisted, though his voice had an odd tone to it that Erick didn't know how to read. "I'm sorry to hear you lost your wife, but you're still young. You could fall in love again."

"I did not say I loved her," Erick pointed out, his voice dry. "Our parents arranged our match. She managed the house while I managed the estate. We had a partnership, not a love affair."

"Just like Miz Roarke, but she's made a new start. You can too." Webster slapped the reins on the horses' rumps to start them moving toward town, the tension that had invested his compact frame as they discussed his marriage gone now. "You want to have options if you meet the love of your life."

Images filled Erick's mind of a life spent on the range with a cowboy much like the one sitting beside him, a campfire burning next to them as they snuggled into a bedroll for warmth. "I will think of something should I meet such a person. I lived in a world where nothing mattered but meeting the expectations of others in behavior and in dress. I am happy to leave that world behind."

"I can see that." Webster pulled to a halt in front of the local mercantile. "We should be able to get the gear you need here. If we can, we could leave for the ranch first thing tomorrow morning."

"I would like that." Erick said. "I would like to see your home." If fortune favored him, perhaps it could become his home as well.

CADE HAD done many difficult things in his life, leaving behind the Comanche who had adopted him after his parents' death being one of them, but standing in the Galveston mercantile watching Heller come in and out of the dressing room trying on new clothes had to rank up there near the top. The entire morning had been fraught with tension to the point that Cade was almost convinced the other man shared his preferences if not his attraction. That only made it harder because he caught little hints to suggest interest, but nothing so blatant it couldn't be a simple misunderstanding or difference in cultures. Without his jacket to hide Heller's lower body, the pants they had selected visibly hugged his thighs and backside, outlining muscles hard from riding. That and the hint of hair he could see at the open shirt collar were enough to feed another night's fantasies and more. All he needed were boots and a hat and he'd be dressed for the trail.

"It fits?" Heller stretched and turned to try to see himself in his new clothes.

"They fit perfectly." Cade swallowed hard around the lump of desire in his throat. "Now we need to get your trail gear and we'll be ready to hit the road."

After setting Heller's new garments and boots on the counter, they spent the next hour picking out a bedroll, saddle bags, a Western saddle and bridle to replace the English ones Heller's horse came with, a mess kit, and a hat. They also added more tins of beans and a packet of beef jerky. Cade had brought enough food for himself, but not for both of them.

"You'll want to pick out a gun as well," Cade said as Heller stacked his purchases on the counter. "You never know what kind of varmints you'll meet out on the range."

"Varmints?" Heller repeated.

"Bad things," Cade said, not really sure how to explain the word. "Rattlesnakes, coyotes, horse thieves. You need to be able to defend yourself. Plus, when we're out on the trail for weeks at a time, being able to hunt for fresh meat is useful as well." Cade hunted with a bow and arrow rather than a rifle, but he didn't figure Heller would want to learn that particular skill. And he carried a rifle too, because he never knew when having one would be useful.

"I can hunt," Heller said. "I hunted on my family's land in Prussia, although I did not bring my rifle with me."

"Have you ever used a pistol?" Cade patted the Colt on his hip.

Heller shook his head. "Do I need one?"

Cade shrugged. "It has certain advantages over a rifle. Most of the other cowboys on the ranch carry one, but I don't think it would be a deal-breaker if you didn't. I can teach you how to use it if you want."

"You will be much teaching me," Heller observed with a wry smile.

"I don't mind if you don't," Cade replied with a wink. So maybe it was a risk, flirting with Heller so openly, but he'd done it anyway. He needed to know if there was any hope of his interest being returned.

Heller's smile changed so slowly and so subtly that Cade was still not entirely sure of what he was seeing. "I do not think I will mind at all." He set a rifle and a pistol on the counter. "What else do I need?"

Cade looked over the pile of goods, trying to see what they might have forgotten. "A holster and ammo, but I think that's everything. Settle up here and we'll get some grub. It's too late to head out tonight, but this way we can get an early start in the morning."

Heller nodded and waited for the storekeeper to tally his purchases. Cade blanched at the total, although given everything Heller had purchased, it wasn't an unreasonable price.

"I have only Prussian money," Heller said apologetically.

The shopkeeper shrugged. "As many ships as we get in and out from there, I can use it to pay off my next shipment of goods. The bank on Commerce Street could exchange the rest for you."

Cade shook his head at one more proof of the life of privilege Heller had obviously left behind to come to Texas. He couldn't help but wonder why. It was a question that would have to wait, though, because the other man had already proven uninterested in talking about his past. Cade tipped his hat to the shopkeeper as they left.

They loaded Heller's gear on the wagon along with the furniture, then drove back to the boarding house, where Heller took only a few things to secure in his saddle bags. "The innkeeper has offered to donate the trunk and suits to his church. I will have no need of them any further."

Cade had left a life behind to start over twice, but he had never cut himself off as completely from the old one as Heller seemed desperate to do. It made Cade all the more determined to help him find his feet in the new one.

Letting none of his thoughts show on his face, he flashed Heller a grin. "Let's go exchange your money and then find one more good meal before we hit the road and have to live on hardtack and jerky."

THEY MET the next morning, after Cade picked up his laundry, at the stables where Heller had boarded his horse. The owner glared at Heller, saying something in German that Cade could not understand. Heller replied, clearly apologetic, and fetched the horse from inside.

Cade climbed down from the wagon to hold the horse's head while Heller put the new saddle and bridle on the recalcitrant animal. "If you aren't planning on breeding the monster, you could geld him once we get to the ranch," Cade suggested. "It might make him a little easier to get along with."

"We will see how the trip goes," Heller replied. "If he cannot learn to behave, we will take other measures, but we will give him the chance first."

Cade couldn't stop his smile at the repeated use of "we." Whatever was going on in Heller's head, he clearly planned to include Cade in his near future. "A good run's the first thing he needs," Cade said. "Once we're out of town, you can let him wear himself out a bit."

"*Ja*," Heller said. "Yes. That will be good for him. And for me. It has been many months since I have ridden hard and fast."

Cade knew what Heller meant, but the words conjured another image entirely in his lust-addled brain. Heller could ride him hard and fast any time.

Chapter Four

THE RIDE out of Galveston was a revelation for Erick. He knew Texas would be different from Prussia, but he was unprepared for the magnitude of the difference. Everywhere he looked he saw something new, from the trees with moss hanging in graceful, haunting lines from their branches to the birds to the warmth, so different from early spring in Prussia. He couldn't seem to stop gawking like an uneducated child, but he wanted to see and understand everything all at once. Fortunately his companion seemed happy to answer his questions, explaining about the live oak trees with their Spanish moss and the seagulls and pelicans and the fact that this was typical weather for early March but would get much warmer soon. It did cool off in the fall and winter, he assured Erick, sometimes even snowing in the hill country and farther north. The last was a relief as far as Erick was concerned. He didn't care as much about the snow as he did about knowing there would be some break from the heat and humidity.

The first half of their day's trip involved the not so simple task of getting off the island. Erick kept a tight rein on his horse despite the animal's clear desire to run, not knowing where they were going and too worried about all the traffic, pedestrians and carriages, carts and wagons like the one Webster drove, to allow the horse its head. Not to mention, the saddle he currently occupied fit his body completely differently than what he was used to. Rather than keeping him perched atop the horse, back straight, body poised perfectly, this saddle rose high in front and behind him, leaving him with the odd feeling of being surrounded, cradled even. It would definitely take some adjustment.

They ate lunch on the road, Webster passing Erick a couple of ham biscuits, shortly before they crossed a bridge over brown, silty water to the mainland. If Erick expected a city like Bremen or even one like Galveston, he was mistaken. They passed a few weathered wooden buildings surrounded by unfamiliar greenery as the road branched off north and south, but they continued west, and before long Webster's wagon was the only conveyance heading toward the lowering sun. Erick's horse clearly took issue with the plodding gait of the draft horses, tossing its head in frustration as Erick tightened his grip on the reins. He wondered how long it would take them to reach their destination at this slow pace. He was about to ask when Webster brought the wagon to a halt.

"Is there a problem?" he asked.

"No," Webster replied, "but we'll need to make camp eventually, and it's never too early to start looking for a good spot. It'll be two days before we reach Houston, and the only towns between here and there are too small to have a hotel. And we can't just pull off the road anywhere we feel like it because of the marshes. We also might want to think about hunting something up for dinner. We can eat jerky and beans from a can, but if we can get fresh meat, I'd rather have that."

"I can hunt," Erick offered. "I cannot help find a campsite, but I can handle a rifle."

"Ducks make good eating," Webster said, "or turkey if you see one. If you ride your brute through the brush, you might scare up a rabbit or two. The wagon makes too much noise for us to find a deer, probably, but we don't want that much meat anyway. It would go bad before we could finish it all."

"My 'brute' still needs a run," Erick said. "Perhaps I will give him one and see if I can find anything for dinner at the same time."

"If I find a campsite, I'll wait within sight of the road until you come back," Webster replied. "We'll pull farther off the road before we make camp, but I'll stay where you can find me easily."

"I would be a fool to lose you." Before he could say more, Erick loosened his hold on the reins and gave the horse his head. It took off with a speed that pushed Erick back in the unfamiliar saddle. For a few minutes he let it run free, reveling in the breeze cooling the day's sweat from his skin. He marveled at the freedom his new clothing allowed him. He would not miss his suits and cravats with this as the alternative. As the sun continued to sink, though, he reined in to a more reasonable pace to explore the brush surrounding the road. He debated dismounting, but Webster had warned him of snakes, so he retrieved the rifle he had secured behind the saddle and scanned the ground around him. Not far from the road something startled from the scrub, and he sighted the rifle almost by instinct, bringing down a fair-sized hare.

He scouted the area a bit longer without rousing anything else, so before the sun could set completely, he returned to the road. Fortunately he hadn't gone far before he spotted the wagon pulled into a slightly less overgrown plot beneath a tree dripping with the strange Spanish moss.

"One rabbit only," he said as he dismounted. Webster had removed his hat and jacket and rolled up his shirtsleeves, revealing muscular forearms. The evening sun caught on the beads woven into the braid of hair that hung from his temple, making them sparkle. "I hope you know better than I how to cook it. I learned how to dress the animals I hunted in Prussia, but never how to cook one."

Webster laughed and reached for the rabbit. "Yeah, I can cook it. The… people who adopted me made sure I could take care of myself out here."

Erick handed it over and watched as Webster skinned it with an economy of movement (and a wickedly sharp knife) that suggested much practice. When he was done, he tossed it in a black pan that looked heavy enough to use as a weapon if necessary and hung it over the fire.

"This will take a bit to cook if you want to get your bedroll set up. I toss mine out under the wagon in case it rains during the night, but you can spread yours wherever you want."

"I cannot judge the weather here, so I will follow your lead." Erick retrieved his bedding from inside the wagon and crouched to unroll it, settling it to one side to allow space for Webster's. He wouldn't let himself dwell on the prospect of the two of them lying beside each other in the dark, focusing instead on the hard, rock-studded ground. *Best grow used to it*, he told himself. *You may not always have even a wagon to block the rain.*

Webster looked skyward, at stars that were familiar and yet not quite right to Erick's eye. "We probably won't get wet tonight, but you never know, this close to the coast. Storms can blow in faster than you can blink. Did you get that hard, fast ride you'd been missing?"

"Fast, but not hard." Erick settled himself on the ground in front of the fire, wondering if the innuendo in Webster's query was intentional. He didn't know the cowboy well enough to guess, despite what he might wish it to be. "Whoever named him Thunder knew not how to handle him. He ran as smoothly as a spring zephyr." He shifted position, feeling the effects of the new saddle. "Perhaps that is the name for him—Zephyr."

"I don't rightly know what a zephyr is," Webster admitted, "but it sounds better than Butterfly, that's for damn sure."

"Perhaps I have not the word right." Erick hoped the growing darkness hid his flushed cheeks. "I meant a gentle breeze."

Webster huffed a laugh, the quirk of his lips and twinkling eyes only adding to his attractiveness. Despite his frustration at expressing himself, Erick felt Webster was laughing with him, not at him. The other man's face held too much kindness for it to be anything else. "Still don't know if it's the right word. 'Round here, we call a breeze a breeze, but I like the name." He poked at the pan and flipped the meat before returning his attention to Erick. His gaze warmed Erick more than the fire. "Not too long now. I'll let it cook a little more. In the meantime, there's coffee if you want some. It cools off fast once the sun goes down."

Erick poured himself a cup of the strong brew and sat again, trying to copy Webster's easy slouch. He still had so much to learn, but he couldn't imagine a better teacher.

Cade woke up the next morning as the sky started getting light. Heller snored lightly in the bedroll not far away, but Cade didn't disturb him. He allowed himself a moment to study the other man. Nocona would scold him for being so obvious about it, but Heller slept deeply, so Cade felt no need to hide. In slumber, Heller's features lost their controlled expression, making him look… softer. Cade wondered what he'd have to do to see that expression when Heller was awake. Scolding himself for a fool, he pushed to his feet and rose. He was used to being on his own. He should get the fire lit again and put coffee and beans on for breakfast. They'd finished off the rabbit the night before, so there wouldn't be any meat this morning, but Cade was used to that too.

When the fire was going again and both pots hung over the flames, Cade went to check on the horses. The draft horses regarded him with their usual placid stares, too used to him and being outdoors to care, but Zephyr was a different story. He didn't rear or fight the way he'd done at the docks, but he was definitely nervous. Cade clucked at him as he approached and, when he was close enough, stroked his flank soothingly. Zephyr whickered softly and butted Cade's chest with his head.

"You're all bark and no bite, aren't you?" Cade ran a hand over the stallion's velvety nose. The horse snorted in reply and knocked Cade backward a few steps before shaking out his mane and going back to grazing on the grass at his feet.

Cade laughed and left him to it. Heller could check his hooves for stones before they rode out after breakfast. Cade wasn't going to give the horse the chance to take a bite out of his ass. Now if Heller wanted a bite….

He pushed that thought away and focused on breakfast, not on how Heller had looked riding Zephyr yesterday, all prim and proper, not slouched in his saddle like a cowboy. Then again, he didn't imagine Heller had ever spent all day working on horseback either, not if the cut of his suit was any indication.

Except Heller wasn't wearing a suit now. No, he was wearing heavy denim and leather, much like Cade was, only newer and less dusty. That would change when they got past Houston and into drier, open land, but for now he was as shiny as a new penny.

Rustling from the direction of the wagon caught his attention and he glanced over to see Heller crawling out ass-first. Cade tried not to stare as Heller stood and stretched, his shirt riding up above the waistband of his dungarees and giving Cade a glimpse of pale skin. He bit his lip as he resisted the urge to bite that patch of skin instead. When Heller bent again to tie up his bedroll before tossing it into the wagon, Cade had to force his gaze away from the curve of his ass outlined perfectly in his snug jeans before he did something he wouldn't be able to take back. Like grope the hard muscle. Heller might have led a life of some luxury in Prussia, but he'd ridden enough to have a rider's legs and butt.

"Morning," Cade said. "Coffee should be just about hot if you want some. Beans'll take a little longer."

"How did I survive before this without coffee?" Heller squatted to pour himself a cup.

Cade laughed. "You think my coffee is strong, wait until we get back to Wellspring. The cook there makes it even stronger."

"Wellspring? This is a fountain, a water source, yes?"

"No. Well, yes, but not in this case. Wellspring Ranch. When we get out farther west, it used to be mostly open range, though fences are becoming more common. So each ranch has its own brand so we know which livestock belongs to who." He pointed to the draft horses still tethered nearby. "Most of the time, it's a letter for the rancher, but maybe on its side or with a curved bar under it. Lazy H or Rocking S or something like that. Our ranch was founded by Miz Roarke's grandfather, Wells was his name, and there's a source on the land, so that's where the name came from. Then for the brand, he had one made special, with two wavy lines, almost a W but also a stream. Here, I'll show you."

He got up and offered Heller a hand, pulling him to his feet when he took it. The skin was smooth against his, something that would change before long, even if Heller wore gloves most of the time. He came right up into Cade's space, so close their bodies almost touched, meeting his gaze for one long, fraught moment before taking a step back and waiting for Cade to lead him toward the horses. Cade brushed away the mud that had accumulated on one of the horses' hips so Heller could see the brand. "Wellspring."

Heller studied the mark, reaching out a finger to trace the lines. "Will Zephyr need to be branded thus?"

"Not unless you want him to be," Cade replied. "He's your horse, not a ranch horse. Nahnia, my horse, doesn't have the Wellspring brand, but a lot of the others use horses that belong to the ranch, and a few, like Payne, have the brand on their horse so no one can argue where they belong. Nobody cares about a cowboy like me, but half the county hates Payne. They'd love an excuse to accuse him of stealing a horse, so it's safer for him to have the brand on his gelding, even if it does belong to him."

"Why do so many hate this Payne?" Heller asked, frowning.

"'Cuz they don't like seeing a black man doing better than them," Cade replied honestly. If Heller was going to have a problem working for Payne, better to find out now, when Cade could leave him in Houston or Austin rather than after they reached Wellspring. "Although if they rode half as well or knew half of what he does about running a herd, maybe they'd have a better chance of doing as well. He's a hard man, and don't let anyone tell you different, but he's fair and he's honest and he'll keep his word, which is more than I can say of a lot of men. Wellspring ain't the first outfit I've worked for, but it's damn sure the best."

Heller smiled. "Then I am doubly fortunate to have met you. I am sure most would look at me and judge me deluded to imagine myself a cowboy. I can but hope I will learn enough before we reach Wellspring and meet Herr Payne."

"Just Payne. The only person who calls him anything else is Miz Roarke." And the less said about that, the better. Because while the neighboring ranchers might resent Payne's role as foreman, they'd lynch him in a minute if they knew the rest. "We better get on the road. It'll take us a month as it is to reach Wellspring. We don't need to make it longer."

"So long?" Heller's surprise didn't sound displeased, but maybe Cade was just reading his own feelings into the question. He wouldn't mind spending the time with the new hand. Because he'd need the time to get used to life on the range, that was all.

"The wagon is heavy and the horses can only cover so much ground. It's not like there's real roads, most of where we're going. Dirt tracks, yeah, but they're rutted and uneven, and if we push too hard, we run the risk of a broken axle or a lame horse, and that would slow us down even more," Cade explained. "And it's a good four hundred miles. You ain't never seen any place that's big like Texas."

"I did not realize your home is so far. From one border of Prussia to the other is less." Heller nodded his head. "*Sehr gut.* I will have much time to grow accustomed to my new country."

Cade didn't know what had prompted Heller to leave his old country, though perhaps losing his wife and child had something to do with it, but he'd take the attitude of embracing the new one over resentment any day. "Breakfast should be hot by now. Eat plenty. Lunch will be cold jerky on horseback unless you want to take a turn driving the wagon. Then it'll be cold jerky on the wagon bench."

Cade wouldn't ask for a turn on Zephyr, although if Heller offered….

Heller didn't smile, but the corners of his eyes crinkled. "Do I dare trust you to handle Zephyr? He is too strong and has a nasty temper, after all."

Cade snorted. "I've spent more of my life on horseback than I have with my feet on the ground. I think I can handle him. But he's your horse. And if there's one rule everyone respects out here, it's not to get between a man and his horse."

"I must remember that, then. If you will trust me to handle the wagon, I will trust you with my horse."

Cade served up two plates of beans and handed one to Heller. "Ever driven a team before? If not, you should learn. It's a useful skill to have on the range."

Heller settled the plate on his crossed knees as if he'd been eating from a dented tin plate all his life. "I am familiar with driving a team, though not a vehicle such as this, or one with four horses."

Cade didn't know what kinds of wagons or carriages they had where Heller was from, but the draft horses were placid and the wagon sturdy enough that he didn't see how Heller could do any damage as he figured out the differences between two horses and four. "Then you can take a turn when you want a break from the saddle."

Chapter Five

A week after setting out with Webster, Erick realized how vastly he'd underestimated the demands of his new life. He'd thought the flimsy cot on the ship from Bremen had inured him to the loss of his soft feather mattress, until he'd tried sleeping with nothing but a thin bedroll between him and the hard and often rocky soil. When it rained, the ground was damp even beneath the protection of the wagon. When it was cold, no doubt he'd shiver, though at present he more often sweltered in the unaccustomed warmth and humidity. He still ached from spending most of the day in an unfamiliar saddle, though adopting the looser posture he'd observed in Webster seemed to help. Instead of lavish banquets, his meals consisted of beans and jerky and whatever game he or Webster could manage to hunt. He hadn't been able to bathe since he'd left the boarding house in Galveston. He had only Webster's belief that his employers would offer Erick a job at the end of their journey.

He was used to being in control of his life, of knowing his role in society and among his peers. Leaving that rigid, stifling formality had seemed a grand adventure, but he hadn't foreseen being so out of his depth. In truth, he wondered how he would have fared had he not had the good fortune to fall in with Webster on his arrival. He'd learned so much already through watching and doing his best to echo the cowboy's actions.

"It's getting late," Webster called from his place on the wagon seat, dragging Erick from his spiraling thoughts. "Let's find a place to stop for the night and I'll see if I can find us some meat. If you don't mind me borrowing Zephyr."

"Even though you have not yet trusted me with your wagon, I suppose I must trust you with my horse," Erick said wryly. He was learning to recognize the fauna in his new home, but there was no question that Webster was the better hunter.

"There's no must about it, not with a man's horse," Webster said. "The wagon and draft horses are ranch property. Anyone can use them. A man's horse, though, that's different. Fastest way to get yourself shot is to mess with another man's horse. So if you don't want to let me borrow him, I won't. I'll hunt on foot. It certainly wouldn't be the first time." He pulled a bow from beneath the wagon bench and rested it across his knees. "Maybe we'll get lucky and scare up some game while we're looking for a campsite."

This wasn't the first time Webster had made a point about the sanctity of a man's horse. He clearly hadn't taken the remark the way Erick had meant it. Another aspect that apparently didn't carry over to his new life. He drew up the reins and dismounted. "I meant no offense," he said formally. "I know Zephyr will come to no harm with you."

Webster grinned, cocky and yet shyly pleased, a combination Erick had not known was possible until he saw it cross the cowboy's face. It was an expression he would gladly elicit more often. "Thanks, Heller. I'll take good care of him, and I'll find us something good to eat tonight." He slung the bow over his shoulder and jumped down from the wagon seat to take the reins Erick offered him. "When you find a good spot, get a fire started. I'll find you."

Before Erick could ask how or anything else, Webster had swung up onto Zephyr's back, dug his heels into the horse's side, and raced away with a loud whoop.

He spent a moment watching man and horse fly down the dusty road before climbing into the wagon. Webster gave himself over to the experience the way he'd given himself over to everything Erick had seen him do—wholeheartedly and without hesitation. It made Erick wonder if he would make love the same way. The thought made him blush, even though there was no one there to see it. "*Mach schon*," he murmured, flicking the reins over the team's backs. They lumbered forward, and he smothered a pang of regret for the matched pair of bays he'd left behind along with the rest of his former life. This was his life now, and looking back served no purpose. He could only move forward.

CADE GAVE Zephyr his head and reveled in the wind whipping against his face and through his loose shirt. He'd left his jacket in the wagon. He'd be glad for it when the sun went down and the temperatures dropped, but already in mid-March, the Texas sun was warm enough to make him take it off during the day. He sank deeper into the saddle, letting his body adapt to Zephyr's smooth gait. Heller had lucked out when he found the stallion. Cade had ridden his fair share of horses, and this one was as good or better than any of them. Not that he'd tell Nahnia that.

When Zephyr slowed of his own accord, Cade wrapped the reins around the saddle horn, set an arrow loosely to the string of his bow, and settled in to hunt. Zephyr was well-trained enough to respond to nudges from Cade's legs and shifting weight.

A deer sprang across the path in front of him. Cade raised his bow out of habit, but they had no way to preserve the meat, and the two of them wouldn't eat it fast enough to keep it from going bad. Cade had learned many lessons from the tribe that raised him, but the most basic had been to take only what he needed. Greed was a white man's crime.

The young hog that ran across his path, on the other hand, was the perfect size. Enough for dinner tonight, breakfast tomorrow, and they could smoke the rest for the next few days. He drew and fired with barely a second's pause. The animal did not even have time to squeal as the arrow pierced its eye. Cade dismounted smoothly and slit its throat, giving silent thanks for its sacrifice the way he'd been taught. Then he tied the limp body to the back of the saddle and turned Zephyr around the way they'd come, scanning the horizon as he did for signs of smoke from the campfire. Hopefully Heller had found somewhere to set up camp.

His sharp eyes caught the uneven puffs against the darkening horizon. Behind him the sun was still lighting the sky in dazzling colors, but to the southeast, back toward Galveston, it was edging toward black.

"Let's go, Zephyr. We don't want to get lost in the dark before we find the campsite."

Zephyr understood the way he leaned forward in the saddle, if not the words themselves, and took off at a ground-eating canter. Less than twenty minutes later, he rode up to the campsite to find the horses unhitched and brushed down, both bedrolls laid out under the wagon, and a pot of coffee on the fire.

And Heller, hatless, stripped down to his shirt with the sleeves rolled up to his elbows, revealing strong forearms dusted with the same dark hair that covered his head and peeked out of his open collar. With each mile they put between Heller and his old life, he seemed to relax that much more, shedding another layer of his past. Cade wondered how many more layers he could convince the man to shed before they reached Wellspring.

"You're efficient," he commented to Heller as he untacked and settled Zephyr.

"It needed done, and now we can prepare what you have brought." Heller raised a brow when Cade untied the hog and dropped it beside the fire. "A fine shot indeed. I have hunted boar, and they are cunning prey."

"This one was too young to be savvy, but thanks," Cade said with a shrug. "We'll eat well for a few days at least. Then it'll be back to beans and jerky unless we get lucky again. Probably not quite what you're used to, back home."

It wasn't exactly subtle, but Cade had grown up with people who valued forthrightness over subterfuge. He'd reintegrated in the white man's world for the most part, but he still had no patience with double-speak.

"It matters not what I was used to." Heller pulled the knife from his belt and began to expertly gut the hog. "This is home now."

And that right there—the mystery all wrapped up with unexpected demonstrations of skill—were enough to drive Cade crazy. Maybe if he talked about his past a little, Heller would be more willing to open up? "I know that feeling. It's happened to me twice, in fact. Once after my parents died and the Comanche took me in, and a second time when I left them. It takes a brave man to leave behind everything he knows to start a new life."

"You lived with the Comanche?" After carving a portion from the hog's belly, Heller set it on the fire to roast. "I know little of the native people of this land save what I have read, and I suspect it is more sensationalism than fact."

"Scaremongering, anyway," Cade replied. He took the rest of the meat Heller had already carved and strung it over the fire, high enough to smoke it without exposing it directly to the heat of the flames. "Each tribe is different, and anyone who tells you otherwise don't know what they're talking about. White men brand them as savages because their ways are different, but they took in an orphaned child whose parents died of starvation or disease, leaving him wandering alone, all of six years old. That's more than I can say for most white men. I don't have a lot of memories from before, but I remember at least one wagon driving by and ignoring me, even though I begged for help. The Comanche family that adopted me treated me the same as the rest of their children, even though I obviously wasn't one of them by birth."

"That is how you came by your skill with the bow?" Finished dismembering the hog, Heller wiped his knife on a kerchief before replacing it in his belt. "It is most impressive."

"Yeah, they taught me to hunt and ride and cook and how to live with the land instead of exploiting it," Cade replied. "What about you? Where'd you learn your skills?"

Heller hesitated for a moment, then shook his head. "Hunting was an expected pastime. Certainly one I preferred to frivolous balls and soirees." As he paused again, a vision of him in fancy dress flashed through Cade's mind, and for one impossible second, Cade imagined himself in the scene, joining Heller on the dance floor, but he barely belonged in the world he lived in now. He would never fit in the world Heller had left behind. "In Prussia, my life was constrained by social status and expectations. My marriage was arranged, as I told you, for reasons of status and finance. When my wife died and our son with her...." He drew a breath. "The expectation was that I would wed again, to provide an heir. I would not take part in such a sham a second time. I signed the estate over to a cousin and embarked on a new life, one in which I can make my own way."

Not many men of Cade's acquaintance—white men, anyway—would have been as forthright. They would have claimed a great love affair as a reason not to marry again, even if they'd been in Heller's exact situation, because it would gain them sympathy. That Heller would choose honesty over sympathy only added to his attractiveness in Cade's eyes, not that Heller needed much help in that regard.

"Social status don't mean much out here unless you got the money to buy a big tract of land. A cowboy is a cowboy, unless you're a black man or were raised by Indians. Then people get all twisted up about you, but the Wellspring outfit don't care about that. They can't rightly, with Payne in the lead," Cade said. "I *am* sorry about your wife and son, though. I know what Nadua, my adoptive mother, went through when my brother Pahayoko died. Even if it was an arranged marriage, it must have been hard to lose them."

He didn't mention that Pahayoko's death had been the trigger that eventually led Cade to leave the tribe. That was a story best saved for another time.

"Enough to make me realize how purposeless was my life. Here I will earn through my own efforts what I need." Heller flipped the pork belly and settled back. "Your story is of far more interest than mine. How long were you among the Comanche?"

Cade wasn't sure his life was all that interesting, but he let it go for now. He'd have more time to ask Heller questions. "Fifteen years," Cade said. Fifteen wonderful years. "It's been another ten since I left, and I still miss them every day." He might have found something like a new family at Wellspring, but it didn't keep him from missing Nadua and the braves who had been brothers to him. He'd made a point after he left the tribe to make sure his remaining brother knew where to find him, even if he didn't always know where to find them.

Heller held his gaze long enough to make Cade wonder what he saw in his expression. "You give me hope that I may weather my changes as well as you have surmounted yours."

Cade summoned a smile that didn't feel too forced. "You've done pretty damn well so far. You just have to remember that where you are don't change who you are."

And that was as philosophical as he was willing to get. "Think that roast is done yet?"

Chapter Six

Erick pondered Webster's words as they continued their journey westward. Time would acclimate him to his new surroundings, he knew. The question was whether he knew any longer who he was. He had prided himself in doing the best for his estate and the tenants and servants he held responsibility for. While being responsible for no one but himself had seemed appealing, he was honest enough to admit that at present he was dependent on Webster, and it left him unsettled. Of what value was his ability to manage an estate, to keep books, to blend in to society, in this new life? He could only hope that once they reached their destination, he would have absorbed enough skills from observing Webster to earn a place for himself.

Not for the first time, Erick marveled at his good fortune at falling in with Webster. The cowboy was everything that appealed to Erick—handsome, strongly built, capable, and kind enough to share his skills and experience with a stranger. Surely most men wouldn't spend time showing him how to form a lasso and practice roping tree stumps with it. At times Erick thought he saw a hint of returned interest from Webster, but that could just be his reading what he wished to see into Webster's innate friendliness. If he were to give in to the fantasy of tangling his fingers in Webster's long hair and pulling him close, he could find himself abandoned far from anywhere or, worse, staring down the barrel of Webster's gun.

A sudden scream tore Erick from his thoughts. Zephyr bucked beneath him, knocking Erick forward in the saddle. He tightened the reins automatically, but that only made Zephyr rear up instead. Erick leaned forward, gripping hard with his thighs, but the Western saddle wasn't made that way, and the change in position pulled Erick's boots from the stirrups. A second buck shook him loose from the saddle completely and he went flying through the air to land on the dusty ground with a hard thump.

Feeling foolish—he hadn't been thrown from a horse since he was a green youth—he rolled to his side to push up onto his elbow when he found himself face-to-face with a coiled snake at least as thick as his arm. The snake reared up, its forked tongue flickering out and a rattle sounding as it shook its tail. Webster had warned him of venomous snakes, but he'd thought to confront them in the underbrush, not the middle of a road. He reached slowly for the pistol at his belt, but the snake swayed ominously and he froze.

At the angle he lay on the ground, he had little hope of drawing, aiming, and firing faster than the snake could strike, and if it bit his face, he would surely die from it. He could only hope if he stayed motionless, the snake would decide he was no threat and slither off. The constant rattle suggested the likelihood of that was indeed small.

Crack!

The report of a pistol rent the air and the snake's head exploded, surely no more than an inch from his face, showering Erick in blood and gore. Erick collapsed onto his back, trying to slow his pulse and breathing. Only now that the danger was past did the full impact of his peril grip him, and he had to breathe deeply through ribs bruised by his fall to stop from shaking. Webster had surely saved his life.

Webster knelt beside him, breathing almost as heavily as Erick was, and Erick accepted his hand to help him to his feet. Fighting the urge to throw himself into Webster's strong arms, a lifetime of training forced him to rein in his racing emotions. "Again, a most impressive shot," he managed before pulling out his kerchief to wipe his face.

"I couldn't let the damn thing kill you." Webster glanced down and rubbed the back of his neck, obviously uncomfortable with the praise. It was a good thing he hadn't said everything he wanted to, Erick thought, because he would never wish to make Webster uncomfortable. But it also made him determined to look for more instances to let him know how much Erick admired his skills. Surely there could be no harm in that. "Sorry about the mess. An arrow wouldn't have splattered like that, but I couldn't reach my bow in time. We'll find a stream or a pond or somewhere and make camp early tonight so you can wash up properly. And maybe wash your jacket and shirt too. I'm afraid the blood got everywhere."

Erick couldn't hold back a chuckle. "You saved my life—a little blood is a small consequence. It is I who should apologize to you for letting my attention lapse. I do little to recommend myself as a horse trainer, I fear."

"Everyone gets thrown sometimes, and anyone who says otherwise either hasn't ridden a horse or is lying through his teeth," Webster replied. "Although getting distracted out here probably ain't the best idea. And you'd have done the same for me if the situation had been reversed."

"I would certainly try, though I could not have made the shot you did." Webster flushed again, but there was no denying his skill, however thrilling Erick found it. "Let us continue on. I find the prospect of cleaning myself appealing."

Webster stooped to pick up the snake carcass and toss it into the wagon. "Can't let this go to waste—rattlesnake makes good eating."

In his panic over the snake, Zephyr had bolted down the road, Erick saw now. "Come on," Cade said. "Climb up and we'll get him as we drive by. No use chasing him on foot."

Erick climbed onto the seat of the wagon, keenly aware of the heat of Cade's body next to him. Fortunately Zephyr didn't seem inclined to keep running once he was safely away from the snake, and they caught up to him within a few minutes. He mounted Zephyr and guided him to keep step with the draft horses. After his scare, he preferred to stay close for now.

They didn't talk as they continued, but the silence was easy between them. He didn't know what Webster was thinking, but Erick kept reliving the moment after Webster's incredible shot, when the cowboy sank to the ground beside him, nearly as shaken as Erick himself. What would have happened if he'd turned and kissed Webster as his emotions had screamed at him to do? Probably nothing good, especially when his face was covered with snake gore, his rational side insisted. Webster hadn't done anything he wouldn't have done for anyone. Erick needed to keep reminding himself of that.

That afternoon—around four if Erick could judge the time from the height of the sun—they came across a shallow river. "Let's make camp here," Webster said. "You can wash up and I'll get a fire started for dinner."

Erick unsaddled Zephyr and left him to graze before walking to the river. He kept an eye out for any more snakes as he unbuttoned his shirt—he would not risk losing Webster's opinion any more than he already had—but the grass gave way to a bare, rocky bank. He knelt to gauge the water's temperature, far warmer than a Prussian river would be at this time of year. For a moment he debated stripping completely.

He would give much to feel fully clean, but the channel didn't look deep enough to submerge even to his waist. He pulled off his boots—they were too new to ruin the leather—and hung his hat from an overhanging branch. Wading into the water, he shrugged the shirt off his shoulders, opened the top several buttons of his union suit, and bent to splash the cool water over his face and chest. Even that much was refreshing.

"Heller," Webster, already hatless, called from behind him. When Erick straightened and turned, Webster grinned. "Catch."

Erick lifted his hands automatically and caught a thin cake of soap.

"You didn't buy any for yourself in Galveston, and since it's my fault you're all bloody, I figure the least I can do is share." As he spoke, Webster peeled off his jacket, pulled his shirt over his head, and started to unbuckle his belt.

Feeling his face heat, Erick quickly turned back to the water and worked the soap to a lather. He'd imagined what Webster's body might look like beneath his work clothes, of course, but he couldn't risk betraying his body's reaction to the planes of strong muscle that defined Webster's chest through the thin fabric of his undergarment. Wishing the river were colder, he dunked his head below the surface, holding his breath as long as he could before straightening to shake the water from his hair. He could—he would—master his impulses. He couldn't risk Webster's revulsion, or worse, if he discovered the truth.

"I didn't save you from that snake for you to go drowning yourself," Webster joked when Erick reached for his shirt.

Even that was enough for him to catch a glimpse of Webster kicking aside his union suit, which landed directly on his boots, enough for him to appreciate that Webster's strong legs and backside were equally muscled. Clearly the idea of washing fully appealed to Webster too. Before the cowboy could turn, Erick dunked his shirt into the water and scrubbed the soap over the splashes of blood. "I can swim," he answered, wondering how helpless he appeared, since it would take serious effort to drown in the sluggish river. He rinsed the shirt quickly. That would have to be clean enough, because he wasn't about to put himself through watching Webster wade into the shallow water. He squeezed out as much wetness as he could and set the soap on the bank, then stood. "I will the fire start for dinner." Hoping Webster was too engaged in washing to watch him flee, he pulled the damp shirt around himself. The fire would help it dry.

CADE SMOTHERED a sigh of disappointment when Heller left the river without even taking off his pants. He'd spent enough time in the white man's world not to hope Heller would strip all the way down like Cade did without thought, but he'd hoped for a wet union suit to give him a hint of the body beneath Heller's clothes.

The Comanche hadn't named him Wolf for nothing, though. Even as a young child, he'd seen more than most, and in his peripheral vision, Cade had soaked up the sight of Heller's bare chest. He might claim to have lived a life of fairly idle luxury before coming to Texas, but his body said otherwise. He wasn't bulky, but the muscles he had were well-defined—lean and wiry rather than bulging. And the pelt of hair on his chest....

Having grown up among smooth-chested warriors, the hair on Heller's chest was both exotic and alluring to him. He wanted to run his fingers through it and see if it was soft or wiry.

And that thought would have to wait, because in his current state, there'd be no hiding his reaction to the image. Instead he focused on getting his clothes clean. He hadn't brought his spare pants to the river, and he wasn't about to change into them when he got back just to sleep, so Heller would just have to deal with the sight of Cade in his union suit until morning. He hoped Heller appreciated his consideration. He wouldn't have bothered for most people.

When his clothes were as clean as he could get them without a washboard, he carried them back to the wagon and pulled on a clean union suit. "I'm dressed again, so you don't have to look elsewhere all the time."

"Most men would not appreciate being stared at." Erick gestured toward the snake carcass he'd retrieved from the wagon, still not meeting Cade's eyes. "You will have to show me how to prepare rattlesnake."

Cade wasn't most men. He'd grown up in a different culture with a different set of values, but now wasn't the time to discuss it. He didn't know if there would ever be a good time to discuss it, although he'd jump at the chance if he could be sure he was reading the few signs of interest he thought he'd noticed correctly. Unfortunately some white men's ways still confused him, and Heller was even worse for being a foreigner. "Fried," he said instead. He grabbed the cast iron skillet and a dollop of lard. "We'll let the fat get good and hot and then we'll fry it up. If we had a jalapeño or two, we could add some extra bite. You ever had jalapeños?"

Heller's posture relaxed slightly at the change of subject. Most people might not have noticed it, but Cade knew how to read subtle cues. Nudity made Heller uncomfortable. Cade would have to remember that he came from a much more formal culture, though he'd have to adapt eventually. He'd get an eyeful at the Wellspring bunkhouse.

"It is a vegetable?" Heller asked. "It is not one I am familiar with, though the food in Galveston was pleasingly spiced."

"It's a Mexican vegetable, but I wouldn't recommend eating them by themselves until you get used to them. They're pretty strong. But they add a good flavor to things. The cook at Wellspring, Trujillo, is part Mexican, so we eat a lot of grub from there. And what he can do with beans and rice will make it so you can't eat anyone else's." Cade licked his lips just thinking about it. Heller's gaze followed the motion.

Now wasn't that interesting? Maybe Heller's discomfort was about more than just nudity. The mixed signals frustrated Cade, but that could be as much about his ability to understand white men as it was about the signals Heller was—or wasn't—sending. He had learned patience along with marksmanship from the Comanche. He could bide his time and see what other signals Heller sent. And maybe send a few more of his own.

Chapter Seven

THE SKY grew steadily darker as they rode along, the air hanging thick and heavy on Erick's skin. "Rain soon," Webster said from the wagon seat. "Good thing. It'll cut down some of this dust."

A streak of lightning brightened the sky, touching the horizon to the west. Seconds later, thunder cracked, making Zephyr dance beneath him. Erick tightened the reins, murmuring softly in German until the stallion settled. The first drops of rain hit his skin, warmer than he'd expected. Another bolt of lightning flashed, the peal of thunder louder, and with no more warning the heavens opened. Erick's clothes were instantly drenched, and Zephyr nickered and shifted uneasily. The sky darkened to an unhealthy greenish tinge, and the sudden sheets of water blurred the road in front of him.

"Well, fuck," Webster said. He slapped the reins against the horses' backs to urge them to move faster, but when they reached the bottom of the hill, the lowest point Erick could see, Webster pulled them to a halt and set the brake on the wagon before jumping down from the seat, water running off the brim of his hat and down his back to soak his clothes. Erick might have taken a moment to appreciate the sight if it weren't for the frown on Webster's face and the urgency in his voice. "Hobble Zephyr and help me get the draft horses unhitched. And pray to whatever god you believe in that we just get rain and not a twister. We're sitting ducks out here if a twister blows in."

Erick wasn't sure what a twister entailed, but if it was worse than the deluge currently battering them, he could live without experiencing one. He dismounted and led Zephyr to the side of the wagon, then pulled a strip of leather from his saddlebag. Once he'd secured the stallion's front legs to keep him from bolting, he moved to the opposite side of the wagon from Webster to release the other two draft horses from their traces. The animals didn't seem troubled by the heavy rain, unlike Zephyr who flinched and neighed at each crack of thunder.

"I'll put their hobbles on," Webster said. "Get in the wagon before you get any more soaked."

Erick did as Webster said because he'd already hobbled two horses and had the leather for the other two in his hand. He grabbed his saddlebags and shook the water from his hat before climbing into the back of the wagon. A moment later, Webster climbed in after him and dropped the oilcloth across the entrance, enclosing them in near—but dry—darkness.

"I was hoping for a spring shower, not a heavy storm." Webster pulled a blanket off one of the boxes, tossed his hat onto the box, and used the blanket to wipe the water from his face. He pulled his shirt off with a wry twist of his lips and laid it out across the wood, then peeled his union suit down to his waist. "Not that it's going to dry much until the rain stops, but at least I can get dry myself. I've got an extra shirt if you want. I don't know how waterproof your saddlebags are."

Even in the dim light of the cramped wagon, Erick's gaze couldn't help but be drawn to Webster's broad, bare chest and powerful arms. He swallowed past a suddenly dry throat and looked down at his own sodden shirt. There was certainly no comparison, but it was foolish to sit in wet clothes and risk catching a chill. He wrestled the buttons free and, following Webster's example, pushed the shirt and the equally wet undergarment beneath it to his waist. He reached for the blanket Webster had used to dry himself, his forearm brushing against the cowboy's torso, solid and warm against his chilled skin. Suppressing a shiver, he drew his arm back quickly and scrubbed at whatever he could reach, not meeting Webster's eyes.

Webster either didn't notice or was too polite to react, because he simply dug in his gear until he pulled out a shirt, which he offered to Erick. "You don't want to catch cold."

Erick reached for it before realizing that Webster made no move to retrieve a second shirt for himself. "No need," he answered, pulling the blanket around his shoulders. "I would not wish you to catch cold either."

"Suit yourself." Webster set the shirt on the wooden shipping container and bent to pull off his boots. He grimaced as he poured water from them to seep between the floorboards of the wagon. He tossed the boots aside and undid the buckle on his belt. "I'd offer you a pair of pants, but I don't think mine will fit you. You're taller than I am."

Judging that sitting in wet boots was a poor idea, Erick bent down to grasp one just as Webster thrust his dungarees and undergarment to the floor. Finding himself with his nose almost brushing Webster's manhood, he sat up abruptly, the interior of the wagon suddenly steaming.

Webster seemed completely oblivious to his distress, drying off with another blanket before digging in his pack to pull out a dry union suit. He stepped into the legs but only buttoned it as high as his waist. Erick was more grateful than ever for the lack of light. Surely Webster wouldn't be able to see his reaction under the circumstances.

After Webster sat down, Erick bent again to remove and drain the water from his own boots. He set them to the side but didn't dare undress any further. He pulled the blanket down to cover as much of himself as he could and hoped fervently that the storm would pass quickly.

Webster leaned back against the nearest crate and closed his eyes, apparently content to wait out the storm in silence, but the stillness weighed on Erick, pressing in from all sides and leaving him feeling like he had nowhere to look but at Webster's bare chest and barely covered legs. He allowed himself a few moments to give in to temptation before he forced himself to close his eyes also. He didn't need to stare at Webster. The image of his body was burned into Erick's mind. He couldn't stop himself from imagining every way he would touch and taste and lavish pleasure on Webster—on Cade—even though he didn't dare hope the other man felt the same.

CADE FELT Heller's gaze on him like a touch, but he held himself still, his eyes closed to mere slits, so much that it would appear to most people that they were closed completely, and let Heller look his fill. He'd settled that way so Heller could change in relative privacy if he wanted to get out of his wet pants. Even if his saddlebag wasn't completely waterproof, the clothes inside would be drier than the ones he was wearing now, but all he'd done was take off his boots and stare at Cade. No matter how foreign Heller's ways, that couldn't be simple curiosity, could it? That had to be genuine interest.

Cade's cock stirred inside his union suit, but unless he got fully hard, it wouldn't be noticeable beneath the loose fabric. If Heller said anything, Cade could always spin a tale he'd find acceptable about who Cade was thinking about and why. Heller never had to know Cade was reacting to him. Unless he wanted to know....

Cade pushed the thought aside, but once it had occurred to him, he couldn't unthink it. Heller was watching him. Maybe that was a question of being jammed into a cramped wagon soaking wet during a Texas thunderstorm, but Cade didn't think so. He could have stared at the roof of the wagon, at the shipping crates, hell, at a spot over Cade's shoulder. But he wasn't. He was staring directly at Cade.

Oh, he didn't linger for more than a few moments before he closed his own eyes and feigned sleep, but Cade didn't need more than those few moments for hope to bloom in his chest, as tenacious as the scrub grass that grew around the ranch house at Wellspring. Cade shifted under the guise of getting more comfortable and stretched in a way that would put his muscles on display.

Was Heller watching? He couldn't tell without opening his eyes far enough to give himself away if Heller *was* watching through lowered lashes as Cade was doing.

Before Cade could risk a longer glance, a shrill equine shriek snapped Heller's eyes open. He tossed the blanket aside, pulled on his boots, and pushed his way under the oilcloth and out of the wagon faster than Cade had ever seen him move. Cade slid to the entrance and nudged the oilcloth aside enough to see outside—what he could see through the sheets of rain.

Heller had grasped Zephyr's head and was murmuring to him, words Cade couldn't understand—probably German—but the tone was calm and confident. The horse tried to pull away, and Heller held on, his biceps straining with the effort to hold the big head still. Slowly Zephyr stopped shaking and pawing at the muddy ground. Heller tugged at the shirt that still hung around his waist and spread it over Zephyr's eyes, securing it by tying the sleeves under the horse's jaw. He stroked Zephyr's neck until he stood quiet, then quickly untacked him. With a final pat to the horse's flank, he slung the saddle into the wagon and climbed back inside.

Cade didn't bother trying to hide his appreciative stare as Heller got settled again. Living with the Comanche, he had learned to live in harmony with nature rather than to view it as the enemy, something that was all too lacking in the world he now inhabited. Seeing Heller risk his own safety to reassure his horse appealed to Cade in far deeper, more powerful ways than just an attractive body—not that there was anything wrong with Heller's body. "I don't guess he saw a lot of storms like this in Prussia, or wherever he was before he got on that ship," Cade said, because he had to say something. He might not be hiding his stare, but he was not quite ready to ask Heller to hold him in the same solid embrace he'd used on Zephyr. He didn't want to drive Heller back out into the rain.

Heller bent to pull off his boots again, now liberally coated with mud. "Once he knows it will not harm him, he will go better." He glanced at his muddy hands, then raised an eyebrow and wiped them on the thighs of his dungarees. Cade wasn't sure why, but the incident seemed to have given Heller back some of his confidence. At least he hadn't swaddled himself up in the damn blanket again. "We will both need to accustom ourselves, will we not?"

"You're doing just fine," Cade replied. "Hell of a lot better than I did when I first left the Comanche and had to get used to what passes for civilization around here. Let me tell you, it ain't always very civilized." Heller made it a damn sight better than it had been before, although if Cade was honest, Wellspring wasn't as bad as most of the ranches where all that mattered was making a buck, not the land or the people who might be hurt in the process.

A corner of Heller's mouth twitched. "Perhaps not so different than what passes for society in the 'civilized' world. At least the dangers here are more direct."

Cade laughed. "Yeah, there ain't nothing veiled about a rattler or a twister, although we got our share of hidden dangers too. Out on the range, might makes right more than it should, and the strong take what they want if there's no one stronger to stop them, even if what they want ain't theirs to take. The people at Wellspring ain't like that, but without old man Roarke around anymore, the neighboring ranchers are like vultures, waiting for the slightest sign of weakness. They can't imagine Miz Roarke is strong enough to run the ranch on her own because they've got their own wives so far under their thumbs that they can't make hide nor hair of an independent woman."

"'Might makes right' is a philosophy not limited to your range." Heller slicked the water from his chest, then smoothed down his windblown and water-soaked hair. "In my experience, not showing weakness is seldom enough. The strong must protect those who cannot protect themselves."

Cade had been right in his snap decision that Heller would be a good fit for Wellspring. "Just don't assume, even for a minute, that Miz

Roarke can't protect herself. Sure, we all watch out for her, but we watch out for each other too. She'd have our hides if we even suggested she needed it more than someone else."

The wind picked up, shaking the oilcloth covering the wagon. Cade frowned when the flap over the entrance blew back. He pushed to his knees and scooted past Heller to secure it in place. The tight space gave him the perfect excuse for brushing against his bare arm as he passed. His skin was cool to the touch, making Cade want to warm him up.

If he were still with the Comanche, if the Army had never come and Payahoko hadn't been killed, if he had the freedom to act according to his desires rather than according to rules that would never truly make sense to him, he would pull Heller into his arms, rub their bare skin together until heat sparked through them both. He'd pull the blanket around them and strip them both bare, bring them pleasure in any and every way Heller would let him. Hands, lips, ass. He'd give it all right there in that drafty, damp wagon to a man who'd dashed outside to calm a frightened horse without thought to his own comfort or safety and talked about the strong protecting those who couldn't protect themselves like it was the most obvious thing in the world.

But the Army had come and Cade had left and he didn't have that freedom. And Heller lived by the white man's strange rules, so Cade did none of those things.

Heller shivered at the slight touch, but Cade let the moment pass. He lived in the white man's world now.

Chapter Eight

As they continued on, Erick's confidence that he had made the right decision gradually strengthened. He'd grown comfortable with his new saddle, his hunting success improved as he learned to recognize palatable game, he took his turns driving the wagon almost as often as Webster did. Since the day of the storm, it seemed he'd earned the man's approval, if not yet his respect. And if he sometimes hoped Webster's gaze softened from approval into appreciation, well, the fantasy harmed no one.

After days of seeing nothing but scrubland on either side of the road, they began to pass stretches of cleared field, with here and there a building in the distance. Shortly after they'd stopped for lunch, they came across several grazing cattle with the largest horns Erick had ever seen. Despite knowing they'd reach ranchland eventually, his pulse quickened at his first sight of the legendary Texas longhorns.

"If we push a little, we should make it to Austin tonight," Webster said. "We can sleep in real beds and eat food someone else prepared. And even take a hot bath, if you want one. And if you're real lucky, you might find friendly company for the evening."

Erick couldn't imagine finding company more agreeable than Webster, but after two weeks on the road, no doubt Webster was looking forward to spending time with someone other than Erick. "A bath sounds most appealing," he admitted. "Being soaked in the rain is a far inferior substitute."

Webster laughed, a sound Erick had become addicted to for all its rarity. "It's a luxury, that's for sure. Course, in the summer you'll be wishing for a good soaking in the rain to cool things off. At least at Wellspring, we have the creek so we don't run short on water, but that don't much help with the heat."

It had already grown warm enough for Webster to roll up the sleeves of his work shirt, baring forearms corded with muscle that might have featured in more than one of Erick's daydreams. To his dismay, Erick had learned that his pale skin burned far too quickly under the strong sun. He'd taken to wearing the hat he'd bought in Galveston and keeping his sleeves buttoned whenever the sky was clear. He supposed he'd have to deal with Webster stripping off his shirt completely when it grew truly hot, baring even more of his golden skin and broad chest. "You are fortunate to have a source of water. We have passed few enough on our way."

"Miz Roarke's grandfather claimed the land when it was still part of Mexico, back when they first invited Americans in to settle," Webster explained. "It's the oldest ranch in the area, although not the largest."

Erick ignored the pang in his chest at the thought of generations of von Hellermanns who'd made up his family's legacy. He had left for the chance to be free of its strangling expectations, but some part of him would always miss it. He'd deeded the inheritance to his cousin, who he could only hope would care for the estate and its families as they deserved. Still, it felt good to think he could play a part in preserving another family's legacy.

Webster slapped the reins along the draft horses' rumps to urge them to a faster pace, eagerness clear in his expression and in the way he scanned the horizon constantly. Erick had come to appreciate the sharpness of Webster's vision over their time together, so while he had no hope of seeing as far as the other man, he looked the same way, curious to what he would see next.

At first it was nothing more than a smudge on the horizon, but as they continued on, the smudge resolved into a collection of buildings, smaller than Galveston, which surprised Erick since he understood it was the Texas capital. It wasn't Bremen or Berlin, but it was a decent-sized city with brick and stone buildings and wide, if dusty, streets.

After so long being the only travelers on the road, Zephyr was inclined to take offense at the increasing number of carts, drays, carriages, and other riders they encountered. Keeping the fractious stallion under control through the turns Webster made as they wove deeper into town claimed much of Erick's attention until the wagon drew to a stop in front of a three-story brick building with a limestone facade.

Webster set the brake and jumped down from the wagon. "I'll see about getting us rooms if you want to take Zephyr to the stable around back. I don't imagine he'll stay tied to the hitching post."

Erick nodded and nudged Zephyr into a walk. It took longer than he'd expected to get the stallion settled—he was not pleased to be shut into a small wooden stall and made his displeasure loudly known before

Erick was able to calm him (and hope nothing happened to set him off again before morning). By the time he passed the stable hand a coin for his trouble and walked back to the front of the building, he found Webster pacing in the lobby. His tension was unusual enough to make Erick wonder if he had spent too long in the stables.

"There you are," he said when he caught sight of Erick. "I was only able to get one room. By the time I paid for stabling the horses, baths, and board, I didn't have enough left for a second room. I'm sorry."

The words came out in such a rush Erick had a hard time following them, and a harder time understanding why it would make Webster uncharacteristically tense. He could probably afford to pay for a second room himself, if it would make Webster more comfortable, but until he hired on at Wellspring (assuming he was hired) and began earning a salary, he felt it prudent to conserve what funds he had left. He didn't object to spending them for good cause, such as the clothes and supplies he bought in Galveston, but after weeks of sleeping on the ground, any bed would be a luxury. He didn't need a room to himself—in fact, the idea of sharing that minor intimacy with Webster appealed, even if lying beside him with nothing more than a sheet between them would demand all his restraint. Keeping his hands and lips to himself when faced with the powerful temptation of Webster's near-naked body beside him would be delectable torture, especially if he was not misreading the hints of interest he thought he had seen more frequently since the day of the storm. That hope made him bold enough to risk a daring comment. "There is no need to apologize. After all, we have been sleeping together for weeks, have we not?"

The clouds shadowing Webster's face broke beneath the force of his smile. Dare Erick call it a leer? "We sure have. Why don't you get the key while I get the wagon settled? Dinner after that, and then it'll be our turn in the bathing rooms."

Erick followed Webster to the desk where a clerk consulted a register with Webster's name written in, and next to it, an X in place of a signature.

He masked his reaction through long practice while the clerk handed him a key and Webster headed out the front door. He had not suspected Webster could not read or write, though given the upbringing he'd described with the Comanche, perhaps it was not surprising. He wondered how Webster managed, though he clearly could recognize the different values of currency, and perhaps knew enough to make out common signs such as "hotel" and "stables". It was harder for Erick to imagine a life without the pleasures of reading. He had a few well-loved books stowed in his saddlebags, though there had never been enough leisure time in their trip so far to bring one out. He had thought he might read tonight, though he would not want to discomfit Webster by doing so.

It only took a few minutes for Webster to return from the stables. Erick followed without comment as he led them up a flight of stairs to their room.

The room wasn't large, nor was the bed, though after sleeping on the ground for weeks any mattress would be welcome. Erick set his saddlebags down in one corner as Webster tossed his in another and hung his hat neatly on the hat and coat rack near the door. "I don't know about you, but I could eat a whole steer, I'm so hungry."

Erick might have preferred to bathe before dining, but he settled for brushing the dust from his clothes as best he could. "Anything we do not have to catch and cook ourselves will be welcome."

Webster grinned brightly. "And after we take our baths, I'll show you the best saloon in town. Best whiskey you'll find in the city. And the prettiest girls too."

Because of course Webster would know where the prettiest girls in town could be found. Even so, Erick wasn't immune to the power of his smile and found his lips twitching in turn. "I put myself in your capable hands."

"You won't regret it," Webster promised. "But first, a steak dinner like nothing you've had before."

They ate in the hotel's dining room, and while Erick enjoyed the meal, he enjoyed even more watching how much Webster enjoyed it. At his first bite of steak, he closed his eyes and moaned in pleasure, making Erick glad there was a table between them and a napkin across his groin. "I would think that steak would be a common meal on a cattle ranch," he observed when he trusted his voice not to break.

"We have it sometimes," Webster replied after he swallowed, "but we only get paid for the cattle we drive to the railhead in the fall, so we don't butcher all that many. We hunt, like we've been doing, and we raise pigs and chickens for meat and eggs."

After that, Erick let Webster enjoy his meal without unneeded conversation. It felt comfortable, even if they were in a room full of other diners rather than sitting around the campfire eating beans or grilling whatever game they'd brought down that day. When Webster had mopped up his plate with the last biscuit, he smiled at Erick again and bounded to his feet. "Ready for a bath?"

Erick had been ready since they left Galveston, the dip in the river notwithstanding. "Show me where to go."

Webster led him up to their room first to gather clean clothes, then down to the main floor and toward the back to a row of numbered doors. "Now we wait for one of the rooms to be empty," he explained. "Someone from the hotel will bring clean water and then we can go in."

"We?" slipped out before Erick could censor himself. He'd been looking forward to this bath all day, but while he'd imagined Webster fully naked ever since his first tantalizing glimpses of the cowboy's body, the thought of Webster seeing him naked wasn't nearly as appealing. Especially since his reaction could lead to his being punched or worse.

Webster blushed. "You can go first. I'll take the second one to be free. I'm used to the dust of the trail."

Before Erick could process that Webster was blushing, a door opened and a housemaid slipped out. "Water's hot, sir, and clean towels on the sideboard. Enjoy your bath."

Erick glanced at Webster, but he'd recovered his usual aplomb and waved Erick on. "I've got the next one. You heard the woman, enjoy your bath."

As soon as the door closed behind him, Erick began to strip out of his clothes. Apart from the rare wash-up in a creek, he hadn't felt clean in weeks. He folded the garments more carefully than their begrimed appearance deserved, but he wasn't sure there would be time to have them washed before they left Austin.

The bath wasn't especially hot, but it felt heavenly to submerge his body into even tepid water. Erick dunked his head and used the bar of soap the hotel provided to wash his hair, then slicked it back from his forehead and scrubbed the bar across his arms and chest. Despite his hope, exposure to the sun hadn't done more than add to his unfortunate array of freckles. An image of Cade's tanned torso—because he couldn't think of him as Webster here, like this—flickered behind his closed eyelids, and his cock began to stir. Erick closed a soapy hand around it. He hadn't indulged himself since leaving the rooming house in Galveston—he hadn't dared with Cade sleeping just beside him beneath the wagon or across the fire when the skies were clear. And since they'd be sharing a bed tonight, it would be best to slake any inappropriate urges now.

He stroked slowly, drawing out the memory of taking refuge from the storm inside the wagon, Cade leaning back half-undressed, body still glistening with rainwater. As the pleasure built, it wasn't Cade's broad chest that filled his thoughts, but his kindness in taking a stranger under his wing; not his corded arms, but his generosity in sharing his expertise with an ignorant newcomer. As Erick spilled into the dingy bathwater, Cade smiling at him across the dinner table was all he could see.

This is dangerous, Erick reminded himself as he finished his ablutions. He dried quickly and changed into his only other set of clean clothes, then folded the towel and draped it over the lip of the tub, forcing himself to breathe slowly and deeply. He could find himself in a world of trouble if his attraction were not returned. Fortunately Cade was no longer in the hall, giving Erick more time to regain his composure. Imagining Cade reclining in his own bath wasn't helping in that regard.

Chapter Nine

Cade sighed with relief when Heller disappeared into the bathing room. Fuck, he'd come close to letting more show than he meant to, but Heller had this way about him that made Cade want to throw himself at Heller's feet and beg for his attention. Oh, he knew what kind of attention that would gain him from most men—a kick to the balls if he was lucky, a bullet to the head if he wasn't. But nothing stopped him from wanting.

When a second room opened up, he hurried inside and stripped down. He sank into the tub and let out a groan as he relaxed against the tin rim. If the water wasn't as hot as he'd get at Wellspring, it was still hotter than the Brazos or the rain shower had been. More importantly, it was private and he could indulge his fantasies. He'd seen the way Heller stroked Zephyr's soft nose. If he was that way with his horse, how much more care would he show a lover?

Damn, what Cade would give to find out! He jerked his cock quickly, knowing others were waiting for a bath and that Heller would probably be waiting for him outside. He briefly entertained the thought of Heller coming in to look for him and finding him like this. He'd watch at first, unsure of his welcome, but this was Cade's fantasy, and in that fantasy, he'd dare what he couldn't outside his thoughts and let Heller know just how welcome he was. And once he knew, all hesitation would disappear, and Heller would take charge, kneeling down beside the tub and replacing Cade's hand with his own, stroking and rubbing until he found the perfect rhythm to bring Cade pleasure. The thought, brazen as it was, tipped him over the edge.

He was lucky no one from the ranch could see how bad he had it. Chel would laugh her ass off if she were here. Then she'd kick his for falling for someone he couldn't have.

With a sigh, he pulled himself out of the tub, dried off, and got dressed. A drink was sounding better and better. If he couldn't lose himself in Heller's arms, he'd lose himself at the bottom of a bottle instead.

He walked out to see Heller waiting as he'd predicted. "Fancy a drink?"

Heller's face wore the bland expression Cade hadn't seen since the early days in Galveston, making Cade hope he hadn't shouted Heller's name without realizing it, but Heller only nodded. "Lead on."

THE LUCKY Penny looked a lot better these days than it had the first time Cade had seen it, lost and alone in the white man's world days after leaving the Comanche. He hadn't been interested in the saloon girls, just in losing himself at the bottom of a bottle, but Chel hadn't let him pass the point of no return, insisting he eat and bathe and eventually he'd found his feet again. He'd returned the favor a few years later when she'd traded the life of a saloon girl for that of a cowhand. Cade couldn't take any credit for the saloon's improvement other than having cleared the way for a management change. He pushed through the swinging doors and smiled. The room was busy, most of the tables full of rowdy cowhands, but the floor was clean, the chandelier bright, and the girls smiling as they served drinks and enticed the men out of their hard-earned pay.

He walked up to the bar and leaned forward casually. "Got a whiskey for a thirsty cowboy?"

The bartender was reaching for a bottle when a sultry voice stopped him. "The good stuff for this one, Rudy."

"You're looking fine, Abby." Cade ran an appreciative eye over the tall, auburn-haired woman in the stylish dress, its higher neckline and silky material distinguishing her from the rest of the girls.

"Miss Roth," she corrected him. "Have to keep these buckaroos in line nowadays."

"Miss Roth," Cade repeated, unable to stop his smile.

"That'll be a nickel," Rudy said as he set the whiskey on the bar.

"A nickel?" Cade repeated. "That's highway robbery, *Miss Roth*."

"That's good whiskey, Mr. Webster," Abigail replied. She turned to the bartender. "His drinks are on the house."

"And my friend's?" Cade asked. "You aren't going to make him drink the cheap swill, are you?"

"I can pay for my drink," Heller protested from where he stood a few steps away from the bar.

"His too." She waved them toward a table. "Anything else, you'll both have to pay for, just like anyone else."

"I wouldn't dream of denying your girls their hard-earned money," Cade said. Not that he'd be doing anything with them for them to earn any of his money, but he wasn't going to say *that* out loud. Heller might be interested, after all. Watching Heller walk up the stairs of the Lucky Penny with any of Abigail's girls, knowing he was interested in them, not in Cade, would mean he'd misread everything since leaving Galveston. If ever there was a reason to get drunk, that would be it.

"Pick your poison, Heller." Cade gestured to the array of bottles behind the bar. "Miss Roth stocks a fine selection."

"Perhaps a brandy, then." Once the bartender poured Heller's drink, Cade pulled out a chair and settled in at the table Abigail indicated.

"Business seems good," he commented while Heller followed and took his own seat.

"Better now that Farrell's gone." A commotion at a table across the room drew her attention, and her expression hardened. "They never learn. Enjoy your drinks, gentlemen." She stalked away toward the ruckus, leaving Cade sure that particular cowboy would never be welcome at the Penny again.

Sure enough, she had the brawl settled and the offending cowboy tossed out in a matter of minutes. Cade took a sip of his whiskey and smiled at Heller. "That is one hell of a woman."

"You know her well," Heller said, his expression blank and his voice neutral.

"Pretty well," Cade replied. "I helped her and the girls out a couple years back, nothing any decent man wouldn'ta done. Abigail shows her gratitude with free drinks when I'm back in town."

Heller raised an eyebrow, but before he could say anything, one of the saloon girls dropped into Cade's lap and threw her arms around his neck "Cade!" she squealed. "It's been forever since you came around!"

"You know me, Millie." Cade pulled the dark-haired girl in the low-cut gown into a tight hug. "I go where the wind takes me. Or where Miz Roarke sends me, anyway."

She pouted at him and pressed a smacking kiss to his cheek. He rubbed at it and grimaced when his fingers came away covered in her lipstick. "Did you have to get rouge all over my face?" he asked.

"I could help you wash it off," she purred with a coquettish smile.

Heller took a sip of his drink and grimaced. Probably wasn't up to the standard he was used to, Cade supposed, though anything he'd find once they left the Penny would be even worse.

"C'mon, Millie, don't hog Cade all to yourself," another girl protested. She caught Millie's arm and pulled her to her feet, promptly taking her place in Cade's lap. "He'd much rather spend time with me anyway."

"Now, girls, you know you're all my favorites," Cade protested, because if he didn't, he'd end up in real trouble. To prove his point, he shifted so Izzy was sitting on one knee and patted his other thigh for Millie to come back. She did with a flounce and a squeal that made Cade want to wince. "Say hi to my friend Erick, girls. He might appreciate some love too."

Even if he hoped Heller wouldn't take them up on it.

"Hi, Erick," the girls chorused, though neither of them made a move off Cade's thighs.

Heller didn't seem distressed at their indifference, or at Cade's use of his first name. "Ladies." He rose to his feet with a small bow.

"Ooh, a gentleman!" Millie sidled over to Heller's lap as soon as he sat again. "Don't get many of them around here, do we, Izzy?" She wrapped an arm around Heller's neck, and damn, but Cade shouldn't find the blush that bloomed in his cheeks so arousing. Izzy squirmed closer, so at least Cade would have an excuse if Heller happened to notice.

Not that Heller was looking his way. Before he could say anything to Izzy, who was running a finger down his cheek, another saloon girl wriggled her way onto Cade's empty thigh.

Cade wrapped his arm around her waist automatically. He might see the girls here more as sisters than anything else, but their attention still felt good. He didn't get a whole lot of human contact out on the range. He might insist he'd only done what any good man should have done when he shot Farrell after he caught the man trying to abuse Chel, but everyone at the Penny insisted it made him a hero—their hero, anyway. "You're looking better than the last time I saw you, Ruby."

Ruby hadn't been there when Farrell was still in charge. Abigail had taken her in after she'd been beaten half to death and abandoned. That didn't seem to matter, though. She fawned over Cade the same as all the other girls. And he adored her right back.

"I could show you how much better." She ran a hand down Cade's chest, and Izzy pouted.

"No one would dare raise a hand to anyone in here after what you did for Chel." Not to be outdone, she slipped open a button of Cade's shirt and slid a hand inside. "How is Chel, anyway? We haven't heard from her since you took her away."

"She's doing good," Cade said. "Miz Roarke don't stand for any nonsense on the ranch." Cade suspected Chel had taken a lover once or twice from the other men in the outfit, but it had been on her terms, not anyone else's, and if he'd noticed her spending more time with Trujillo, the outfit's cook, recently, well, that was her business and he was keeping his nose well and truly out of it.

"Give her our love when you see her again." Before Millie could say more, Heller put her off his knee—gently, not that Cade would have expected him to shove her off, no matter how uncomfortable he clearly was at her attentions.

"I think I shall return to the hotel. The chance to sleep in a real bed is appealing." Heller flushed again and drained his glass of brandy. "Ladies, it was a pleasure to make your acquaintance," he said as he stood.

Cade started to rise as well. "Do you know the way back? I can come with you."

Heller shook his head. "I can find my way. I would not want to take you away from your... friends."

Cade heard what Heller didn't say, but the girls here *were* his friends—nothing more, perhaps, but no less important for being friends, not lovers—and he didn't see them often. "Good night, then," he said as he sat back down.

His movement had displaced Izzy and Ruby enough that his lap was momentarily empty. Momentarily because Millie took advantage of the opportunity to reclaim his attention.

ERICK FOUND his way back to the hotel easily—he had been paying attention on the way to the saloon, despite the distraction of a clean and freshly dressed Webster walking beside him. Cade—he was Cade in Erick's thoughts now, at least—had obviously wanted to impress the girls at the saloon. Any hope that Cade might possibly return his interest was well and truly dead now, and all for the best. The way the saloon girls were hanging all over him, and Cade plainly welcoming their advances, made his preferences all too clear.

Not that he should have expected anything different, Erick acknowledged as he let himself into their room and stripped down to his union suit. He'd let a few sidelong glances and his own attraction feed his imagination. Well, he knew better now. Cade could have any one of the girls who'd thrown themselves at him. Judging from what they'd said, he'd already taken one of them back to the ranch with him. Whether she was a wife or merely a lover, he was clearly still open to taking up with others in her absence.

It's none of your business, he told himself as he slid beneath the sheets. He had no right to judge the other man's actions, no claim on him at all, much as he might wish otherwise. He fell into a restless sleep, waking at any noise from the hall outside as other guests made their way to their rooms. As the night wore on and Cade didn't return, Erick tortured himself imagining in him one of the saloon girl's beds. Though why only one? Cade was strong and virile—he could take his pleasure more than once. Or maybe they'd share him. A vision of Cade sprawled naked across a mattress and surrounded by fawning women refused to be banished. Erick groaned and took himself in hand, imagining himself in the saloon girls' place while damning himself for an attraction he'd have to fight all the harder to keep hidden.

CHAPTER TEN

CADE LET himself into the hotel room the next morning, in charity with the world. Abigail had found an empty bed for him the night before—after demanding to know why he was asking her for a bed when every girl in the place would have willingly shared hers. Abigail had taken one look at his burning cheeks and seen right through his excuses. *If that tall drink of cool water doesn't appreciate you, he's not worth your time.*

After Heller's disinterest in Millie and the other girls, Cade actually hoped he might have a chance. Or maybe it was just saloon girls Heller wasn't interested in. But if Heller was too snobbish to want them because they earned their living that way, he'd lose all the respect he'd earned in Cade's eyes by treating them so courteously.

"Did you sleep well?" he asked when he saw Heller still in bed, despite the later than usual hour. He'd hoped to give Heller some space and let him have the bed to himself since it was a small room and even smaller bed. As much as he would have enjoyed spending the night so close to Heller, he doubted either of them would have gotten a good night's sleep if he had.

"The bed was comfortable. And you?" Heller asked, not meeting Cade's eyes as he rose to dress.

"I always have a good night," Cade replied with a cocky grin to hide his reaction to the intimacy of watching Heller dress.

"That I do not doubt." Heller straightened his collar and gestured toward the door. "Shall we go to breakfast, or do you care to refresh yourself first?"

"Abby let me wash up there this morning before I came back," Cade replied easily. "I keep telling her she don't owe me anything, that I just wanted to save Chel, but she don't listen."

Heller didn't respond, just opened the door and headed down to the dining room, leaving Cade to follow. *What bug crawled up his ass?* Cade wondered when Heller's face remained an impassive mask throughout being seated and placing their orders.

Deciding he didn't want to ask, no matter how much he wanted to know, Cade applied himself to his coffee in silence. He'd planned to spend two or three days in town, as much to show Heller around as to take a break from the road and stock back up on supplies, but if Heller was going to keep acting like this, he could show himself around.

The waitress had just dropped off their meals when a voice at the next table caught his attention.

"Stupid uppity bitch, thinking she can run a ranch by herself. It's about time someone taught her a lesson."

Cade risked a glance sideways and stifled a groan when he recognized Johann Reichardt, the owner of the JR, the largest ranch outside of Eldorado. He only hoped Reichardt lived up to his reputation for not paying any attention to hired hands because if he recognized Cade, he'd shut his trap, even if he didn't do anything else, and Cade needed to know what he was planning if he was talking about who Cade thought he was.

"What do you suggest?" Otto Ulrich, the owner of another neighboring ranch, the Bar U, asked.

Heller's cocked eyebrow was the only indication he'd heard the comments too, but to Cade's relief, he didn't ask any questions that might alert the two ranchers.

"The simplest solution would be to marry her," Reichardt replied. "Then when her land is under my control, it won't matter how much she protests. The water will be ours to use as we please. She's comely enough. I wouldn't mind having her in my bed for a few years." *Miz Roarke would geld you first*, Cade thought, clenching his jaw to hide his anger. "If she's fertile, she'll even give me an heir for my empire. And if not, well, as her husband, her land is mine anyway, and no one would think twice if she had an unfortunate accident."

"And if she refuses to marry you?" Ulrich asked.

"Then there are other ways of getting what we want," Reichardt replied.

"Over Payne's dead body," Cade muttered under his breath, though in truth, it would be over the dead body of every man and woman in the Wellspring outfit once Cade told them what he'd just heard. He just had to get back to Wellspring before Reichardt could get to Miz Roarke. On horseback and without a wagon full of furniture to slow him down, Reichardt could travel faster than they could. Miz Roarke wouldn't agree to marry him, he was sure of that much, but she needed to know about the rest of his threats.

Heller didn't say anything as the two men left, though Cade wasn't sure if he understood something was going on or was just still pissed for some reason. The eggs, biscuits, and gravy tasted like sawdust to Cade, but he wolfed them down. As soon as Heller placed his fork on his empty plate, Cade grabbed Heller's arm and all but dragged him back to their room.

"Since you invoked Herr Payne, I surmise those blackguards were speaking of your ranch?" Heller asked once the door closed behind them. Cade had to admire Heller's quick mind for figuring out the situation and having enough sense to keep quiet until they were alone.

"Yeah, they own most of the ranchland that surrounds Wellspring," Cade said. "They want the water source on Miz Roarke's property. The creek runs through their land, but if we have a dry summer, that isn't always enough for them. Then they start coming with their threats. Let their cattle graze on our land or they won't let us cross through their ranches to get to town for supplies. Oh, they aren't that blunt about it, and up until now, old man Roarke dealt with them, but he's gone now, which means they think they can pressure Miz Roarke into a new arrangement. They got another think coming, let me tell you. She's nobody's fool, and there ain't a man or woman at Wellspring who wouldn't fight for her."

"Then we should get word to her about their plans as quick as we may, should we not?" Heller was already placing his belongings into his saddlebags as he spoke.

"Hell yes," Cade said as he jammed his own gear into the appropriate pouches. "Can you hitch the team while I go to the general store? If we're going to push hard enough to get back to Wellspring as soon as we can, we won't have time to hunt. We'll be riding from sunrise until it's too dark to see and up again at first light. It's another two-week drive, but we'll have to find a way to make it faster than that."

Heller nodded and was out the door as Cade took one more glance around the room. He'd hoped to spend at least one more night in Austin before they hit the trail again, but he couldn't risk Reichardt or Ulrich getting to Miz Roarke before they could warn her. He'd just have to hope Heller was up to the demanding hours.

By the time Cade got back from the general store with a sack of jerky, canned beans, and coffee—no way was he riding dawn to dusk for days on end without its stimulant—Heller had the draft horses hitched to the wagon and sat astride Zephyr as cool as you please. Maybe he'd be able to keep up after all.

Cade tossed his purchases into the wagon, climbed onto the seat, and slapped the reins to get the horses moving. He'd keep them to a walk or trot until they cleared the city, but as soon as they didn't have to worry about traffic, he'd push them as hard as he dared. Damn, he wished Heller knew where Wellspring was. He'd send him ahead on Zephyr or take Zephyr and leave Heller to get there with the wagon and team when he could. But neither of those was an option under the circumstances. He'd just have to drive the draft horses as hard as he could.

TEN DAYS of riding as hard as they could push the horses didn't allow much opportunity for conversation, and Erick was grateful. It was too difficult to try to talk while moving at speed. They didn't even stop for a midday meal, just chewed a handful of jerky in the saddle or on the bench of the wagon, and when it grew too dark to continue safely, they pulled off the road, opened a can of beans, and then slept until sunup. Erick took advantage of the time to anticipate what his life would look like once they arrived at Wellspring. Assuming Payne agreed to take him on, he'd be working with the horses and Webster—he needed to stop thinking of him as Cade—would be riding the ranch minding the cattle. Any free time he'd no doubt prefer to spend with his girl Chel, judging from what he'd heard at the saloon. Erick would be lucky to see him at mealtimes if Cade was near enough to the bunkhouse. There would be little to feed his hopeless attraction. The sooner he accepted that, the better.

If only his attraction would listen to reason.

Late afternoon on the next day, Cade—because Erick's mind refused to go back to thinking of him as Webster, even though he no longer dared hope for anything more than friendship—drew the wagon to an unexpected halt. Erick looked around for any threat, but all he could see was a puff of dust down the road. He glanced at Cade, who had a hand on his pistol.

"JR land." Cade spat the words as if they were a curse. "They haven't wanted to spark a range war, so they haven't refused to let us through, but they never make it pleasant."

Sure enough, the puff of dust resolved into a group of half a dozen riders, all with rifles resting across their laps. "Webster," the lead rider said when they reached the wagon. "What're you hauling?"

Erick knew nothing about the other man other than the tension he could read in Cade's shoulders, but he bristled at the way the man jerked his horse to a halt, the bit tearing at the sides of the animal's mouth. The sun glinted off wicked-looking spurs, and that was all Erick needed to see. Any man who treated his horse that way deserved none of Erick's respect.

"Supplies for Wellspring," Cade replied, his voice tight. "Not that it's any of your business, Carter."

"You're on our land now," Carter replied. "It's my business if I say it's my business."

Erick didn't care for the odds, but he reached behind him to free his rifle. His pistol was easier to handle, but he was more accurate with a rifle, and accuracy would be called for if the confrontation turned violent.

"Who's this?" Carter sneered, his disparaging gaze flicking over Erick. "Wellspring must be desperate if this is the kind of hands you're hiring now."

Erick bit back the retort that sprang to his lips. He didn't need to intensify the situation, but he met Carter's gaze and cocked the rifle, holding it steady against his saddle horn.

"I'd take Heller over any dozen of your men," Cade retorted. "Looks can be deceiving. Yours certainly were."

Carter's hand twitched on the butt of his rifle. Erick wanted to intervene, but Cade knew the situation far better than Erick did. He just hoped Cade would hold his temper.

"Fuck you," Carter spat.

"Not if you were the last man left alive," Cade replied. "Now are you going to let us through or are you going to start a range war?"

Carter looked as if he were giving it serious consideration before pointing his rifle barrel up to the sky. "Tell Miz Roarke if she expects to cross JR land, she best be ready to pay the price. Our generosity won't last forever. Reckon the bill's gonna come due soon." He lashed his reins across his mount's neck, and the group of them turned and rode off.

"Prick," Cade muttered. By the time Erick refastened the rifle behind his saddle, Cade had the team back to a trot. He urged Zephyr to catch up, refusing to let Cade's retort mean what it implied.

"Carter used to work at Wellspring," Cade said when Erick reached him. "He's a violent, abusive ass. Payne fired him after he tried to corner Chel a couple of times. She got away before he could do anything, but I'll never forgive him for it."

That reminder was enough to smother the arousal Cade's bravery had sparked. His comment that he wouldn't fuck Carter if he were the last man alive was meant to insult him in the worst way possible, nothing more. It was a reminder Erick needed to take to heart for his own safety.

Chapter Eleven

Cade drove on until well after dark, but since he hadn't spoken since the confrontation with Carter, Erick didn't question him. Fortunately the night was clear enough that the rising half-moon provided sufficient light to avoid any overt dangers. Finally, after passing a large outcrop of rock, Cade drew the team to a halt.

"Sorry for pushing so hard, but I wouldn't spend the night on JR land. We just crossed onto Wellspring property."

Erick patted Zephyr's neck, but the horse hadn't worked up a sweat. "We can continue if you wish to reach the bunkhouse tonight."

The first smile since they'd left Austin lit Cade's face, making Erick realize how much he had missed them. "It's another half-day's ride to the ranch buildings. Wellspring runs a hell of a lot of land."

"You know the land and the situation better than I," Erick said. "If you wish to continue, I will follow. Or we can camp tonight and make the remaining journey tomorrow morning."

"As much as I want to sleep in my own bed, there's rough terrain between here and the ranch house, and Payne would have my head for risking the horses. Unless Reichardt is already at the house, he won't beat us there in the morning."

"Then let us find a place to make camp."

Cade gave him another luminous smile and hopped off the wagon. "Here is as good a spot as any. The outcropping gives us a bit of shelter, not that the weather is bad, and it'll hide our fire from JR."

"Are you that worried about what they might do? You said this is Wellspring land." Erick dismounted and began unsaddling Zephyr as they talked.

"Call it being careful," Cade replied. "I don't *think* they've gotten desperate or stupid enough to attack us openly on Wellspring land, but I'd rather be safe than dead." He unhitched the team and hobbled them nearby.

"That seems a reasonable course of action." Erick got Zephyr settled and began building a fire so they could heat up more beans and fatback for dinner. While he understood and supported Cade's caution, he would be glad for a bit more variety in their diet.

"Just wait until your first meal at Wellspring," Cade said as he pulled the pans from the wagon. It wasn't the first time Erick noted how their minds traveled the same paths, though perhaps Cade was just as hungry as Erick was. "Javier is a wonderful cook, and there's always plenty for all the hands."

"Javier?" Erick stumbled a little over the unfamiliar name.

"Javier Trujillo, our cook. I don't rightly know how we got lucky enough to keep him since his family are Mexican hidalgos. He don't talk about why he left, but it's our win."

It seemed he was not the only one leaving a family behind to start anew at Wellspring. Assuming he would have that chance. "You are confident Herr Payne will take me on?" Erick hoped his uncertainty wasn't reflected in his voice. He'd agreed to Cade's offer to accompany him to Wellspring because he had no other option, but over the journey he'd grown to hope he'd find a place—a home—there.

"You've more than proven yourself to me on the way here." Cade opened a can of beans and dumped them in the pan over the fire Erick had started. "He'd be a fool not to hire you on, and Payne may be a lot of things, but he ain't nobody's fool."

Erick held that approbation to his heart. If he could have nothing more, at least he'd earned Cade's respect.

"And if the JR outfit really does start a range war, we'll need all the help we can get," Cade added as he stirred the beans. "I hope it won't come to that, but I wouldn't put anything past those bastards."

"You hate them so much?" Erick asked.

"They don't have no respect for anyone who don't think or act exactly like they do," Cade explained. "They hate Payne because he's black. They dismiss Miz Roarke because she's a woman. I'm trash because I lived with the Comanche as a child. They'd give you a chance because you're a white man, but only if you shared all their attitudes, which you don't or you wouldn't be coming with me. And as far as they're concerned, if you don't fit in with what they think, you're worthless."

"Then let us hope your opinion of my chances is correct, because though I have no wish for conflict, it would be my pleasure to prove them wrong." He didn't know the others Cade had named yet, though he was sure once he did, he would share Cade's esteem. But he would not allow anyone to think of Cade as trash.

As THEY rode the next morning they passed scattered clusters of cattle, and once a cowboy rode by, raising a hand in greeting but not stopping to speak with them. The sun was directly overhead before Erick caught sight of buildings in the distance. Cade gave a whoop and cracked the reins over the draft horses' backs, coaxing them to their top speed. Erick let Zephyr continue to canter, uncertain of his reception despite Cade's assurance.

A small crowd had gathered outside the ranch house by the time Cade—and shortly after, Erick—reached it. "Bringing home strays again?" a big man dressed entirely in black drawled when Erick reined Zephyr to a halt. He didn't need Cade to tell him this must be the ranch foreman; his tall, confident stature and the air of authority with which he spoke made that clear.

"You know me, boss. I can't resist," Cade replied as he threw a wink over his shoulder at Erick. "Erick Heller, meet Zeke Payne, foreman of Wellspring Ranch. Payne, Heller's got a way with horses. I was thinking he could work with the mustangs until we can teach him the finer points of driving cattle."

Payne ran an appraising eye over Erick and Zephyr. "If he can manage that stallion, I might be convinced to give him a chance."

"Not only managed but tamed him. He was a screaming brute until Heller took him in hand." Cade's exaggeration made Erick uneasy, but he'd just have to prove to Payne that he was as capable as Cade implied.

He dismounted and offered Payne his hand. "I will work hard for you if you will have me."

Payne frowned but took his hand in a rough clasp. "We need a new bronc buster, and Webster's as good a judge of character as anyone I know. We got two rules around here. Do your best and tell someone if you fuck up. Well, and don't mess with the women. Fastest way to get your ass fired is unwanted attention to any of them. Other than that, we're easy to get along with. Stow your gear in the bunkhouse and welcome to Wellspring," Payne said.

The women had nothing to fear from him, but Erick wasn't about to admit that to Payne. He glanced toward Cade, who had climbed out of the wagon and was surrounded by people clapping him on the back and welcoming him home. *He's already done more for me than most men would*, Erick told himself. *He has his own duties now. I can't expect him to always guide me by the hand.* He gathered his few things from the back of the wagon, took Zephyr by the reins, and led him toward the long building Payne had indicated as the bunkhouse.

CADE GREETED everyone who'd gathered to welcome him home, but he kept one eye on Erick—he'd become Erick in Cade's head when he'd backed Cade up during the confrontation with Carter—the whole time. He wasn't at all surprised Payne offered Erick a job, but he wanted to be the one to show Erick around and help him get settled, so when Erick started toward the bunkhouse, Cade pulled free from his friends, grabbed his own bedroll, and fell in step beside Erick.

"Told you he'd hire you. Let's get you and Zephyr settled. Javier is making chicken enchiladas, and we don't want to miss that!"

"I must not keep you from your work," Erick protested, but Cade thought he caught a glimmer of pleasure, or maybe just relief, in the other man's expression.

"I could use your help unloading the wagon in a bit. But for now, let's get you settled in." The interior of the bunkhouse was dim and cool after the bright sunlight outside. Cade glanced around, looking for an unclaimed bunk. Unfortunately the beds on either side of his were both taken. It would have to be Carter's old bunk, then. He led the way toward the back of the long row of cots, one bed atop another to double the number of hands it could house. "You can stow your things in here." He indicated the chest at the foot of the bed. "It don't lock, but no one will mess with your gear."

Erick set his saddlebags on top of the chest and tucked his bedroll under the bunk. It wasn't much, but Cade hoped Erick would see the thin mattress as a step up from sleeping on the ground.

"Thank you. For everything," Erick said.

"It was nothing special," Cade demurred, embarrassed at having attention drawn to his actions. "Just helping out a friend in need. You'd have done the same if our positions were reversed."

"I will hope for the opportunity to repay you," Erick insisted. "I cannot afford to take my only friend for granted."

Cade hoped his face wasn't flushing. He didn't need repayment for basic human decency—not that he'd complain about a kiss like the girls at the Lucky Penny insisted on giving him every time he dropped by— but he would miss having Erick all to himself. "That won't last long. I'll introduce you around to everyone at dinner."

"If you will show me where I may stable Zephyr, I will help you unload the wagon," Erick offered. "Then you or Herr Payne can instruct me on what else needs done."

"Just Payne," Cade reminded him, though he thought he'd miss Erick's quaint formality. "C'mon, I'll show you where you can get Zephyr settled."

Erick followed Cade back out of the bunkhouse, both of them blinking against the harsh sunlight. Cade adjusted the brim on his hat, but it only did so much to protect his eyes. Erick grabbed Zephyr's reins while Cade fetched the draft horses someone had helpfully unhitched for him. "The barn's this way, although most of the time, we leave the horses in the paddock. Probably can't do that with Zephyr, though. We don't want him picking fights and Payne deciding he needs to be gelded."

"He will need to accept other horses in time, but perhaps not this first day. Especially if there are mares near their time," Erick said. "Though if Payne is looking to increase the herd, he will not want to deprive Zephyr of his assets." He led Zephyr inside the barn as Cade released the draft horses into the paddock. By the time Cade followed him inside, he already had Zephyr in a stall and was brushing him down, murmuring to him softly. "I am sorry to have pushed you so hard, but you will have time to rest now."

"At least until tomorrow," Cade said with a smile. "After that, it'll depend on what Payne has you doing around here. If you're working with the mustangs, it'll be mostly here near the house, but if he has you out on the range with the rest of us, Zephyr will have to get used to long hours, although we don't usually have to push as hard as we did the past few days."

He stepped inside the stall to stroke Zephyr's nose. "But you're up to it, aren't you, fella? You're a big strong stallion."

"He will do what he must." Erick gave Zephyr a final pat and set the brush on a ledge. "You are away from the ranch most days?" Cade could almost imagine he sounded disappointed.

In the close confines of the stall, Cade breathed in the scent of leather and sweat—and horse, though that wasn't nearly as alluring. Erick met his eyes, and Cade swallowed before he realized he hadn't answered his question. "Yeah, unless there's work to be done on one of the buildings, most days I'm riding with the cattle." Though Payne had been talking about digging a well to tide them over when the creek ran low, and didn't it just say something if that backbreaking labor sounded appealing if it meant he'd be able to spend more time around Erick?

"I NEED to talk with Miz Roarke and Payne." Cade nudged Erick in the side once he had Zephyr settled. "They'll want to hear what you have to say too."

Erick didn't know why his account would carry any more weight than Cade's, but he followed Cade up the porch of the house Payne had greeted them in front of.

To his surprise, Payne answered the door when Cade knocked on it. "Webster?"

"We need to talk to you and Miz Roarke," Cade said. "We overheard some things in Austin that you both need to know about."

Payne opened the door wider. Cade removed his hat and cleaned the worst of the caked dirt off his boots before going inside, so Erick made sure to do the same. The inside of the ranch house was simple but clean, and when they walked into the kitchen, the woman sitting there—Frau Roarke, or rather Mrs. Roarke, he had to become used to the American honorifics—rose to greet them. She wore a plain cotton gown that didn't hint at the kind of wealth that could afford to ship a full set of furniture from Europe to Galveston, and her stern expression didn't change when Cade greeted her.

"This is Erick Heller. I met him in Galveston and he helped me on the trip back." Again, Cade made his contribution seem larger than it was, but Erick bowed slightly and received a nod in return.

"Now what's so important that you need to interrupt us?" Payne demanded.

Cade didn't show any reaction to the pronoun, starting into an explanation of the conversation they'd overheard at the hotel in Austin. "Reichardt and Ulrich are up to no good. They were talking about trying to pressure Miz Roarke into marrying one of them so they could take over the ranch, but that's not the worst of it. They said if she wouldn't, they'd find other ways to get her land."

Mrs. Roarke sighed. "How many times do I have to tell them they'll take my land over my dead body?"

"That's the problem, ma'am," Cade said. "I think they're starting to believe you, because they said once you married one of them, they'd have control of the land and it wouldn't matter if something happened to you."

"You're not marrying anyone," Payne spat, surprising Erick with his vehemence.

"Of course I'm not," Mrs. Roarke replied. "But we still have to deal with them when we go into town or when it's time for the cattle drive. I can't just order them shot the second they set foot on Wellspring land."

Payne seemed inclined to argue that, but she laid a hand over his, silencing him. "If we had a sheriff worth a damn, we might expect some help there, but—"

"But Lutz is so far up Reichardt's ass he can spit out of his belly button," Cade finished for her. "So what can we do, ma'am?"

"Not the way I would have worded it," Mrs. Roarke replied without blinking an eye. Erick's estimation of her went up another notch. "As for what we can do, nothing until they act on it. Talking isn't illegal, even if they're making threats. But forewarned is forearmed." She turned to Payne. "No one out on the range alone, ever. And double the night shifts because however they decide to put pressure on us, they'll do it at night—sabotage, trying to steal our cattle or horses, even outright attacks." Then she looked at Erick. "I don't imagine this was what you had in mind when you signed on here. If you've changed your mind, I understand. But if you stay, I need to know you'll fight as hard as the rest of us to protect the ranch."

Erick had to admire her determination. "This is my home now. I will defend it as long as I draw breath." Even if he had not already given his loyalty and respect to Cade, the reception he received at Wellspring earned his allegiance.

There didn't seem to be much to say after that. Mrs. Roarke smiled grimly and Payne scowled but nodded his approval. "Thanks for the warning, Webster. Heller, get settled this evening so you're ready for work tomorrow. We start early around here. I'll see you in the barn at six. You can show me whether you're as talented as the last stray Webster brought back with him."

Payne must be referring to Chel, though surely he could not be alluding to the position she was engaged in before she left Austin? "I shall do my best." He bowed his head toward Mrs. Roarke before following Cade out.

"That went over about as well as I expected," Cade said when they were alone. "At least Payne didn't start cussing. Course he's probably in there turning the air blue now, but that's better than cussing at me."

Chapter Twelve

The dinner bell rang just as they were leaving the ranch house. "It's chow time," Cade said, his stomach rumbling at the thought of Javier's cooking. "We'd better hurry so we aren't at the end of the line. Javier always makes plenty, but if we're at the front of the line, we'll be done first so we can go back for seconds."

Erick laughed as they joined the other hands crowding toward the collection of rough-hewn tables and benches that served as the dining hall whenever the weather allowed. They all squeezed into the actual dining hall when it was raining or cold, but it was usually more comfortable under the shade of the live oaks than it was in the mess hall. As soon as they'd secured their place in line, Cade began introductions.

He wouldn't have chosen to start with Burke, but he was the one closest in line. "Erick, meet Ned Burke, our blacksmith and all-around jack of all trades. He can fix pretty much anything."

"You trying to staff Wellspring all by yourself?" The smith thrust a grease-stained hand in Erick's direction. "First Chel, and now this one? Not as easy on the eyes as Chel, but as long as you don't break anything I'll have to fix, I guess I can work with you."

"I would ask if you could look at the shoes on my horse, when you have the time," Erick said. Cade gave him points for not wiping his hand on his jeans after they shook. "He has ridden hard from Galveston, and I am not sure the shoes he had when I acquired him will suit for this country."

"Sure, Hoss, give me more work to do your first day," Burke grumbled.

"Save your sarcasm—and your attempts at humor—for someone who appreciates them." Cade elbowed Ned in the side, but he knew Burke would check Zephyr as soon as he finished eating. "As for staffing Wellspring, I just meet interesting people."

"I'm interesting," Burke protested.

"Like a rattlesnake is interesting," Cade muttered. He smiled at Erick. Now that their news was delivered, he had two weeks of neglect to make up for, pushing from sunup to sundown, too focused on getting back to Wellspring to give Erick much attention, and while he couldn't reach out and hold Erick's hand the way he wanted, he could usher him through the meal and meeting the rest of the outfit in other ways. "Moving on. Now that you've met the worst we have to offer, meet the best. Javier Trujillo, ranch cook. Javier, this is Erick Heller. He's just off the boat, so warn him before you feed him anything too spicy, okay?"

"Of course." Javier handed them each a plate. "The enchiladas aren't spicy by my standards, but if they're too much for you, let me know, Heller. I'll keep it in mind for future dishes."

"I have eaten enough beans and jerky to enjoy anything you put before me," Erick said. "Ca—Webster has praised your cooking, so I look forward to learning to appreciate a new cuisine."

"You hear that, Burke? Cuisine," Javier called to the table Ned had taken a seat at. "I think we'll get along just fine, Heller."

Cade ignored the byplay between Javier and Ned, used to their banter. No, he was focused on what Erick had said—or almost said. Erick had started to use his given name rather than his last name. It wasn't much, but combined with Erick's insistence in the barn that Cade was indeed his friend, it was enough to leave his palms sweaty and his skin tingling as he hoped against the odds. Whether that friendship could turn into an interest to match Cade's own remained to be seen, but Cade was more determined than ever to find out.

CADE GUIDED Erick to a seat at the table Ned Burke had claimed, so Erick assumed the taunting between the two of them was not as serious as it sounded. The cook, Trujillo, had sniped at Burke also. It seemed that mocking comments were a common form of interaction, one he would have to accept if he were to fit in here. He very much wanted to shed the "just off the boat" image Cade had used to describe him. And as much as he appreciated Cade taking the time to introduce him to the rest of Wellspring's hands, he needed to shed his dependence on Cade for everything.

"Hoss, Wolf Boy," Burke acknowledged them as they sat. It seemed Erick had acquired a new title, at least from Burke, but—"Wolf Boy?" He glanced between the smith and Cade.

Cade took pity on his confusion. "My Comanche name is Tʉtaatʉ Isa. It means Little Wolf. Burke here decided that gave him the right to call me Wolf Boy. He gives everyone nicknames. It's annoying as hell"—Cade aimed a glare at Burke—"but we put up with it because he's good at what he does."

Before Erick could reply to that, a woman's voice interrupted. "You're finally back, I see."

Cade jumped to his feet and pulled the woman into a tight embrace. Erick dropped his gaze to his plate, granting them privacy in their reunion. This must be the Chel he had heard referred to so often. Burke rolled his eyes and muttered "Get a room," loudly enough for Cade to hear him.

"Fuck off, Burke," Cade replied, although his voice held no heat. "Come on, Chel. I have someone I want you to meet."

So he had been right. Erick pasted a smile on his face, prepared to meet the woman who had what he dreamed of. His stomach fell when he got a good look at her. She was beautiful—brown hair pulled back in a loose braid that fell to the middle of her back, fair skin that didn't seem at all affected by the sun, and perfect curves beneath the pants and vest she wore—and to judge by the way she held herself, she was not "just off the boat" despite the hint of accent in her voice. An ideal match for a cowboy like Cade.

Cade sat back down and pulled her down to sit next to him. "Chel, this is Erick Heller. I met him in Galveston. Payne just hired him to work with the mustangs. Erick, this is Michele Bessette, Chel to her friends."

Erick rose and bowed over her hand. He ignored Burke's snickering. Just because she was dressed like any other cowhand was no reason to forget how a woman should be treated. "Fräulein Bessette." He hoped it was Fräulein, but if she and Cade had married, surely she would have taken his name?

"Herr Heller," she replied easily. *"Schön, Sie zu sehen."*

He had expected many things, but not her replying in his native tongue. "You speak German?" he asked in English, out of respect for the others around him who didn't speak the language.

"Only a little, but enough to bid you welcome. Please, call me Michele. I know what it is to be a long way from home, surrounded by a language you have only studied but never truly spoken," she said. "If Cade saw fit to bring you here, I would be pleased to know you, but I have been riding all day and have not yet eaten. I will return when I have a plate."

Erick sank back into his seat. He'd been prepared to resent "Chel" on sight, but she was as charming and gracious as she was beautiful, and if appearance was anything to judge by, she held her own working among the men. Of course Cade would be drawn to her. Smothering the hopeless feelings that clawed at his heart, he picked at his plate of food. He couldn't say if it was too spicy since he didn't taste any of it.

He looked up when Cade let out a soft whoop next to him and murmured, "About damn time." Confused, Erick looked around, only to see Michele standing next to the cook, Trujillo… who had his arm around her waist. He looked over at Cade sharply, but Cade's expression showed only happiness and relief, no jealousy, no concern, no indication that he was in any way bothered by what he was seeing.

Which made absolutely no sense, unless Erick had misinterpreted everything he'd heard about the woman from the moment her name first came up. When she leaned closer into Trujillo's side and Cade's smile only widened, that conclusion seemed more and more like the right one.

When Cade scooted over to make room for her, Erick didn't even complain about being jostled. "You finally listened to me," Cade said before Michele was fully settled. "I told you Javier was a good man."

"Time will tell," Michele retorted, but she sounded teasing, not cynical.

"At least you'll be sure of eating well," Burke commented, but even his tone was less grating, and Michele didn't dignify his comment with a response.

Conversation was abandoned in favor of their meals, and Erick had to admit to enjoying the unfamiliar food once he could taste it. He still wasn't sure what to make of Cade's relationship with Michele, but for whatever reason, it did not seem to be a romantic one. He wouldn't allow that to give him any hope.

"Anyone else for seconds?" Burke asked as he scraped the last sauce from his plate.

"The only reason there are seconds to offer is because Kit and Olav are out on the range," Cade said as he stood. "Erick, you still hungry?"

"Our last full meal was nearly two weeks ago in Austin," Erick said. Michele glanced at him with an expression he couldn't interpret, but he picked up his plate to follow Cade. "You did not underestimate Mr. Trujillo's skill. I find his food most pleasing."

"Man compliments me like that, he's got to call me Javier." Trujillo—Javier—slid another serving onto his plate.

"Then you must call me Erick." The familiarity felt odd, but it reinforced Cade's assurance that he wouldn't remain Erick's only friend for long.

Cade bumped his shoulder as they returned to the table and their food. "Told you you'd find your place here. After dinner, I need to check on Nahnia, if you want to meet him. I didn't take the time earlier, what with needing to talk to Payne and Miz Roarke. Or you can go back to the bunkhouse with the others. You don't have to stay with me if you'd rather settle in and get some rest."

Erick knew he couldn't hang on Cade's coattails forever, but he was loath to give up what might be a last opportunity to share time together before Cade was swept back into his duties on the range. "I would be pleased to meet Nahnia. I should be sure Zephyr has settled in as well."

The bright smile Cade sent him assured him he'd given the right answer, and that warmed something inside him. He might be adrift in this new and ever-changing landscape, but amidst it all, he had Cade, and Cade wanted Erick at his side. In what capacity, Erick didn't know, and that left him frustrated with himself and the situation, but at least Cade desired his companionship. Even if it never became anything more, Erick would cherish it.

"Then finish up and we'll go."

After they'd cleaned their plates for a second time, Cade stood to drop his utensils in the bucket at the end of the food line. Erick nodded in farewell to his tablemates and followed his example. "Thank you again for a most enjoyable meal, Javier," he told the cook, who broke into a smile.

"Finally, someone with manners. Cade, you could learn something from our new friend."

Cade flushed and rubbed at the back of his neck, a gesture Erick was coming to love and hate in equal measure. "He has praised your abilities from the moment we met," Erick interjected before Cade could reply. "Perhaps he does not always remember to tell you, but he appreciates you nonetheless."

"Javier is right. We all take him for granted," Cade said. "Thanks for dinner, Javi. I'll try to remember to tell you more often. Let's go check on the horses."

Rather than leading Erick to the barn, Cade went instead to one of the paddocks that surrounded it and whistled sharply. A cream gelding with black mane, tail, and lower legs cantered up to them and butted Cade in the chest. "Hey, Nahnia. I missed you too."

"He is a most unusual color," Erick observed as he reached up to stroke Nahnia's forelock. "What do you call a horse with such markings?"

"He's a buckskin," Cade explained. "If he were more gray, he'd be a dun. And then there's the paints, the ones with the big white and brown patches, and the appaloosas, with the almost solid brown or black heads and spots on their hindquarters. All four of them are pretty common among mustangs. I've had Nahnia since he was a foal."

"I must become familiar with horses such as this if I am to work with them." Nahnia bumped Erick's hand with his nose, clearly soliciting more petting.

"They won't be attention hogs like this one," Cade said, fondness clear in his voice. "But he's been alone for over two months, so I guess he's due some extra loving."

The images that conjured made Erick long to confess that he'd been alone far longer, but he bit his tongue. Just because Cade wasn't involved with Michele didn't mean he wanted the relationship Erick ached for. "Did none of the other hands ride Nahnia while you were gone?" he asked instead.

"Chel took care of him for me, of course—and anybody else woulda done the same—but remember those conversations we had about a man's horse and the difference between ranch horses and a cowboy's personal horse? Nahnia's my horse, and nobody would ride him without my permission except in an emergency. Fortunately we didn't have any emergencies while I was gone, so nobody rode him," Cade replied. "Which means tomorrow, he'll be a handful when we get out on the range. But he woulda hated being tied behind the wagon all the way to Galveston and back too. At least here, he had the run of the paddocks." He gave Nahnia's nose another stroke. "Let's go check on Zephyr."

The big stallion appeared every bit as greedy for caresses as Nahnia was, but he had settled into his stall and seemed as prepared to make his home at Wellspring as Erick was. After paying him the attention he took as his due, Erick turned to Cade, wishing he could be as open as the horses about needing Cade's affection.

"Ready to get some shut-eye?" Cade asked. "Payne wasn't kidding about how early we start. We gotta take advantage of every minute of daylight."

Erick had never slept in a communal setting like the bunkhouse before, but the long days of riding had left him tired enough that he doubted any noise the other men might make could disturb him. If he regretted no longer having Cade to himself, he was not about to admit it. "I would be well rested to begin my first day as a true cowboy."

"Don't worry. You'll do fine. Payne's a hard man—he's had to be to get this far—but he's fair, and I saw what you did with Zephyr," Cade said as they walked into the bunkhouse.

Men milled around in varying states of dress, some with bare chests, others in just their union suits. A few were gathered around the central table playing cards. Another sat on his bunk darning a pair of socks. And on the bunk above Cade's, Michele was sharpening a wicked-looking stiletto. Cade flopped on his bunk, pulled off his boots, and tossed his hat to catch on the hook attached to his bedpost. "Make yourself comfortable," he told Erick. "We don't stand on ceremony in here."

He let out a sharp whistle, drawing the attention of everyone in the room. "For anyone who hasn't met him yet, this is Erick Heller. He signed on just before dinner. Also, the JR boys are up to their old tricks. We overheard Reichardt and Ulrich making threats in Austin, and we ran into Carter on our way in, and he wasn't exactly subtle, so be careful over the next few weeks. I don't know what they'll try, but I know they'll try something."

Among the grumbling about JR and Carter, several men nodded in greeting to Erick as he made his way to his bunk. He was glad Cade hadn't introduced them all individually, as Erick was sure he'd never remember their names until he began to interact with them. When he reached the bunk where his saddlebags rested on the chest at its foot, he was startled to see the blacksmith, Burke, lounging on the lower bed.

"Couldn't resist my charms, Hoss? I'll have you know I'm spoken for, so your foreign wiles will be wasted on me." Erick clenched his jaw to keep it from dropping in shock at the crude comment. Had his affection for Cade given away his inclination? Though Burke seemed more amused than appalled…. Before he could decide how to respond, Burke pointed a thumb toward the upper bunk. "New guys go topside. Don't worry, I'm pretty sure they deloused the bedding after Carter left."

"Shut up, Burke," Michele said from across the room. Erick surely hadn't expected to find her here, rooming with the men, but no one seemed to find it extraordinary for her to be dangling her legs from the bunk above Cade's, dressed in a sleeveless shirt and knee-length drawers as utilitarian as any of the men's. "Stop trying to scare Cade's friend. He has few enough of them as it is. We don't need you running off a new one."

Cade squawked indignantly from his bunk, making Erick's lips twitch as he tried not to smile. Michele met his eyes and nodded, so he wasn't sure if he was successful or not. Her manner was much less formal in this setting than it had been at dinner. He hoped she would eventually be comfortable enough to speak with him the same way. He would have to temper his own ingrained formality, he suspected, if he was to fit in. Then she leaned down so she could stare at Cade. "You should have let me kill the fucker instead of just letting Payne fire him. That would be one fewer bastard to worry about."

"And watch you hang for it? Not likely," Cade retorted. "If he'd attacked Miz Roarke, maybe, but you know the good people of the town wouldn't give two cents about the virtue of a 'former whore.' Like that gives Carter an excuse to try to rape you."

"He didn't succeed, did he?" She sheathed the knife and tucked it under her pillow with a sharp grin. Erick had no difficulty believing that none of the other men would offer her any unwelcome advances. Life at Wellspring was definitely nothing like the world he had left behind. He unpacked his few changes of clothes into the chest, slid the saddlebag underneath with his bedroll, and studied the bunk, debating how to reach the upper bed without encroaching on Burke's space.

"Boots off before you climb up. The slats at the foot will hold your weight." Burke smirked. "And you might want to strip down first. Let us all see what's got Cade so worked up he brought you back with him."

Erick froze, hoping he wasn't flushing at Burke's insinuation. He had kept his proclivity hidden for nearly twenty years—how had he given himself away so quickly? He took a step toward the trunk that held his belongings, wondering if he had time to saddle Zephyr and ride away before the situation became ugly.

"I will hurt you, Burke," Michele said, the smile that had accompanied her earlier threats gone and her eyes cold. "Shut the hell up before I shut you up."

Cade didn't glance Erick's way, but his gaze on Burke was as sharp and deadly as his arrows. Erick had often heard the expression *if looks could kill*, but he had never seen it so vividly portrayed as now on Cade's face. "Fuck off, Burke. Some things aren't funny. Even from you."

Burke scooted deeper into his bunk and mimed sewing his lips shut. Around the room, the other hands chuckled and resumed their card games and other pastimes as if the interplay with Burke was nothing out of the ordinary, which made Erick wonder. He had expected, feared even, that he would have to hide here as he had hidden in Prussia, but Burke's comments seemed to imply a different attitude. Either way, he wasn't about to strip with a woman in the room, no matter how casually she or the other men were dressed, but he did tug off his boots and remove his shirt. His pants and union suit were staying right where they were.

There were no further comments as he clambered into his bunk and settled onto the flimsy mattress. Despite the light and noise around him, he was asleep as soon as his head hit the pillow.

Chapter Thirteen

Cade dragged out of bed the next morning before the sky had even started to lighten. He needed a little privacy, and this early in the morning was pretty much the only time he could guarantee no one else would be out back using the outdoor shower Burke had rigged up. It was, in Cade's opinion, a stroke of genius, proving the value of his fancy degree from some big school back east—Harker, Harlem, Harvard? He couldn't ever remember the name, but Burke bragged about it from time to time, like it was supposed to mean something. He'd come to Wellspring at the end of the war, but even with the haunted look in his eyes, he'd been an asset from the moment he stepped foot on the ranch. He'd created a system to gather water in rain barrels on the roof of the bunkhouse and then pipe it through hoses to a small wooden enclosure, where the hands could stand underneath the flow and get clean without the work of hauling water. Burke had even managed a tank to heat it, but most days, it was hot enough that Cade preferred the water cold.

He stripped and turned his face into the flow, letting the cool water wake him the rest of the way up as well as rinse away the dirt and sweat that had accumulated since they left Austin.

Thinking about Austin led to thoughts of Erick, not that he was ever far from Cade's thoughts these days. It was a damn shame Burke was so good at what he did—the outdoor shower was just one example of his genius—because Cade was tempted to shoot him after his comments the night before.

He didn't need both feet to work as a blacksmith, did he? Cade could shoot him there and it wouldn't keep him from working. Just take off a toe or two, enough to teach him a lesson.

Cade sighed. Miz Roarke would never go for it, no matter how much Cade wanted to. He'd just have to hope Erick wasn't too offended, or worse repulsed, by Burke's implication. Cade wouldn't be lucky enough for Erick to return his interest. He'd started to hope, really hope, after the storm, but then things had gone south in Austin. If he'd been less focused on getting back to Wellspring, maybe he'd have been able to think about it, work out what had gone wrong between them and get things back on track, but there hadn't been any room for anything other than figuring out how to squeeze one more mile out of the daylight they had until they'd finally made it home. Maybe Erick had thawed a little last night, but Cade couldn't be sure, and that went back to his luck. He'd used up his allotment of luck and more the day the Comanche found him. It was one of the reasons he never gambled or played other games of chance.

He looked skyward to see the stars fading. He'd spent so much time thinking about Burke that he hadn't taken the time to see to his more personal needs. Maybe it would be easier today since Erick would be staying here to work with the mustangs while Cade would be out on the range, unless Payne had other plans for him. Without Erick's constant proximity, Cade might actually manage to think about other things besides how much he'd like to take Erick to bed.

He finished up, dried off, and dressed for the day. As he left the shower, he heard Javier ring the bell announcing breakfast. He hoped Javier had made flapjacks, but Cade would settle for his fluffy scrambled eggs after weeks of trail food.

He grinned when he got close enough to smell fried dough. He looked around to find Erick, warmth blooming in his gut at having him near to hand again, and dragged him toward the mess tables. "You're in for a treat. Javier made flapjacks this morning. We gotta get in line before Logan and Svensen do, or there won't be any left."

Erick looked rumpled and bleary-eyed and absolutely adorable as far as Cade was concerned. He followed Cade toward the food line. "I would give them my share in place of a cup of coffee."

Cade pointed toward the huge pot at the end of the table. "That's one thing that's never in short supply, especially mornings. I should warn you, though, Javier makes it strong enough to put hair on your chest." He resolutely didn't think about the intriguing patch of hair on Erick's chest. Instead he swiped a hand over his shirtfront. "Not that it worked on me."

Erick's cheeks pinkened just enough for Cade to notice, and that was even more intriguing than the hair on his chest that didn't need any help from Javier's coffee. "I think I will manage to survive it." He accepted a plate of flapjacks and hightailed it to the coffee pot, returning to the table with a cup filled to the brim. Cade could see his gaze sharpening as he sipped the dark brew.

Cade would get a cup of his own later, but for now, he dug into the flapjacks, unable to stop the moan of delight that escaped him at the light, fluffy texture. "Even more than sleeping in my own bed, this is how I know I'm home," Cade told Erick when he'd swallowed.

Logan plopped down on the bench next to Cade, looking like he hadn't slept in days, dark circles under his eyes and tension lines around his mouth. "Here." Cade fetched a cup of coffee and put it in front of Kit. "You look like you could use this."

Kit grunted and drank the entire cup without pausing. Cade refilled it before he could ask. "Bad night?"

"Bad month," Kit replied. "We hit the two-year anniversary of Mac losing his leg. I keep thinking he's dealt with it, and it keeps coming back to bite us in the ass."

Cade hummed in sympathy. He couldn't even imagine what MacRae had gone through, losing half his left leg to a Confederate bullet at the battle of Palmito Ranch just two weeks before the war finally ended.

"Oh, sorry, Erick. You didn't meet Kit last night. Kit Logan, Erick Heller. Erick came back from Galveston with me," Cade said.

If he didn't know Kit was devoted to Mac, he might have felt a flare of jealousy at the way Erick's eyes widened when he shook the bigger man's hand. "Svensen take off already?"

"Soon as we got back," Kit confirmed.

"Olav Svensen and Kit were on night watch," Cade explained. "Svensen's sweet on the schoolmarm in Eldorado. Payne always arranges for him to have weekends off so he can spend them in town with Miz Sarah."

"Be glad, it means two more nights without listening to him snore." Kit chuckled. "Second-best thing about me and Mac having our own cabin."

Cade laughed. "Yeah, yeah, rub it in. Look, if you need to stay close for a while, I'll take your night shifts until Mac's doing better. I know the nights are the worst."

"I might take you up on that," Kit said. "He won't complain, but it's easier when we're both on the same schedule."

Erick finished the last of his flapjacks—how did he manage to eat so quickly without shoving them into his mouth the way Cade did, he wondered—and drained his coffee. "I would not be late my first morning. It was a pleasure to meet you, Mr. Logan."

Cade frowned and resisted the urge to run after Erick, but he wasn't a lost puppy desperate for attention. (Chel might disagree, but Cade wasn't planning on sharing that observation with her.) Still, he'd wanted to spend a little time with Erick at breakfast since he wouldn't have a chance again until dinner. Oh well, too late now. He finished his own meal and clapped Kit on the shoulder. "I'll tell Payne I offered to switch shifts with you."

He started to get up when Payne's shout cut through the morning bustle. "Listen up, everyone. Webster probably told most of you about the newest threats from the JR last night, but in case you didn't hear it, Reichardt and Ulrich are up to no good. Until further notice, no one goes out of sight of the ranch house alone, and keep your rifles handy and your pistols handier. We won't start anything, but if they choose to start it, we will damn well finish it. Is that understood?"

A chorus of "yes, sir" and "got it, boss" rang out in reply.

"Webster, Bessette, take the herd northeast of here today. Chiles and Beaufort, you keep an eye on the southern herd. Logan, get some sleep. And when Svensen gets back, tell him the rule applies to him too. If he wants to go into town to make cow eyes at Miss Dawson, he'll have to find someone to go with him. I'm not risking him riding through JR territory by himself, no matter how much he fancies the schoolmarm."

When Payne had finished issuing his orders, Cade walked up to him. "Hey, boss, Logan says MacRae has been having a hard time of it recently. I told him I'd take his night shifts as well as my own until MacRae is doing better again."

"That's damn generous of you, Webster."

"Logan would do the same for any one of us if our positions were reversed. I figure it's the least I can do after being gone for so long." He gave Payne a nod and headed back to the bunkhouse to get his hat and pistol so he could meet Chel and head out north.

By the time he made it to the barn, she already had Nahnia saddled along with her own horse, Chanteur. "About time you got your lazy ass in here," she said as she tossed him the reins. He tried to catch one more sight of Erick. Discreetly. He didn't need Chel hassling him about it, but he'd be out on the range all day. A final glimpse to hold him 'til dinner wasn't too much to ask, was it?

"Someone woke up on the wrong side of the bed this morning," Cade quipped to distract her. "Or is it that you woke up in your own bed instead of in Javier's?" Javier had his own cabin because he had to wake up so much earlier than everyone else and often went to sleep earlier as well. Cade didn't actually know if things had progressed to that stage between the two of them, but Chel would wonder what was wrong with him if he didn't give her just as much shit as she gave him.

That didn't even earn him a glance. "If you're looking for your *amant*, he's already in the paddock so you might as well get to work." Chel mounted and kneed her horse into a gallop, leaving Cade scrambling to follow her.

"He's not my anything," Cade protested when he'd caught up. He didn't know what the word Chel had used meant, though he could make a good guess. If only she were right, but for once, her instincts had missed their mark.

"You want him to be," she retorted. "Though volunteering for double night shifts is not going to help you with that."

Cade shrugged. "It was the right thing to do. Mac needs Kit around, especially at night. That's more important than maybe starting something with Erick, assuming he's interested, which is a big assumption."

He could say it to her, the things he would never say to anyone else, the things he couldn't even say to Erick, the person he most *wanted* to say them to. She would never judge. She might chide him for not guarding his heart. She might scold him for falling for someone unattainable. She might tell him love was a fairy tale. But she would never judge.

"Cade, *petit loup*, I know men. What La Fleur blanche did not teach me, working at the Lucky Penny did. Trust me, he's interested. But if a month on the road together was not enough to show him you're not averse to a relationship with another man, how are you to do it now if you are never together at the same time?"

"It's not forever. Just until Mac is doing better again," Cade said, even though he would miss time spent with Erick. "And it's not like we'd be together all the time anyway. He's up in the paddock working with the mustangs while I'm out here keeping an eye on the herd. I'll still see him at breakfast and dinner, even if I'm on night shift."

Chel rolled her eyes and muttered something in French under her breath.

Payne wasn't in the barn when Erick arrived, making him wish he'd taken the time for another cup of coffee. He walked down the line of stalls, stopping to greet Zephyr with a pat on the nose and a promise to check back with him later. The far end of the barn opened onto a fenced-in field where a half-dozen horses grazed. He leaned against the fence and watched them for a few moments. They were smaller than the horses he was familiar with, but their bodies looked strong.

One of the horses, a chestnut mare with irregular white markings, lifted its head and stared at Erick. He held its gaze, and it slowly walked toward the fence. They'd been handled enough to become accustomed to people, then, at least somewhat. That would make his job easier. He should have picked up a lead rope before approaching the horses, he realized.

"Making friends already?" Payne strode through the barn, a lead rope in hand. The paint nickered but held its ground. Moving slowly, Erick took the lead from Payne and clipped it to the halter. The horse tossed its head and danced in place. He'd have to remember to pocket some sugar cubes from the coffee fixings tomorrow to use as treats.

"It seemed a wise way to start," Erick replied. "These horses, they have been handled some already, yes?"

"Yeah, we cut them from the herd a few months ago and been working with them when we have time, but while they'll come up to us easily enough, we've never even gotten a saddle on most of them. Just not enough time. The mustangs were Roarke's project. We talked about dropping it after his death, but they're a steady source of income between cattle drives, and we need that," Payne explained. "That one's the only one we've tried to ride since his death, but it didn't go so well. We sent the one who killed him back to the herd."

Erick reached between the rungs of the fence and let the paint approach his hand. Once it decided he didn't seem dangerous, he gently touched the side of its neck. The paint shook its head but didn't back away. Before long Erick was running a palm down its nose and combing his fingers through its mane. When he stopped, the horse nickered and took a step forward, as if chasing after his touch.

"Good girl," Erick murmured. "Be patient a moment." Tomorrow he would be better prepared, he told himself as he returned to the barn for a blanket and saddle, but this was his opportunity to show Payne what he could do and that Cade's faith in him was justified. He set them over the top rail and resumed petting the paint until it settled, then hoisted himself over the fence into the paddock.

He wouldn't have been surprised if the horse backed away, but it stood its ground. "*Ach*, you are a brave one. Let us hope the others follow your lead." He took a step closer, smoothing the paint's mane and moving down its neck until he could stroke its side. For several minutes he did nothing but caress the horse, slowly increasing pressure as he accustomed it to his touch.

"I'll give Webster one thing," Payne said from where he stood by the fence. "You've got a way about you."

"A horse should be your partner, not your servant," Erick said. He held the paint's gaze as he walked around it to stroke its other side. "If you gain its respect and trust, it will always bring you home." When the horse stood still under his strongest touch, he reached for the saddle blanket and settled it over its back. The paint's ears twitched, but it made no move to shake it off. Erick resumed his stroking, murmuring praises to the horse in German, eventually leaning against its side and reaching over its back with increasing pressure.

"Now we will see." Erick gathered the saddle and set it atop the blanket. When the paint didn't buck, he petted its head, letting it grow used to the added weight. The most dangerous step came next—reaching beneath the horse to cinch the saddle. To his relief, the paint made no move to kick or bite, twitching a little but letting him tighten the girth. He used his best estimate to adjust the stirrups and then let the horse settle for a few moments, stroking its flank.

For some horses that might be enough for one day, but the paint hadn't balked yet, so Erick pressed on. He grasped the saddle horn and jumped as if to leap into the saddle, getting it used to his movement. Then he put a foot into the stirrup and stood, leaning his weight against the horse's side. He repeated this several times, gradually leaning farther across the saddle. Through it, the paint held its ground. "You do so well," he crooned as he mirrored the actions on the horse's other side. In an emergency, being able to mount from the left could mean surviving or not.

He glanced at Payne, who stood watching with his arms crossed. He rested against the paint's neck, gauging its temper. It inclined its head into his touch. Deciding it was worth the risk of being dumped on the ground to impress the boss, he caressed the paint's neck with one hand and grasped the saddle horn with the other. "Now, my brave one." Taking a deep breath, he stepped into the stirrup, swung his other leg over the paint's back, and settled into the saddle.

To his intense relief, the paint stood, accepting his weight. He leaned forward against its neck, combing his fingers through its mane. "Bravo, *Kleine*. You make me proud."

"I'll be damned," Payne said from the edge of the paddock. "Welcome to Wellspring, Heller."

Erick didn't try to hide his smile. Cade was right—it seemed he had found a home after all.

Chapter Fourteen

THE DINNER bell surprised Erick when the sun was directly overhead. He hadn't been sure the cook would make a meal with most of the hands out working, but he was not the only one still near the ranch house. He had heard the occasional clang of the blacksmith's hammer, and the men who had been on the previous night's shift might be awake and hungry by now. He unhooked his rope from the mustang he'd been working with and headed toward the outdoor tables, wishing vainly that Cade could be there and hoping he would know someone besides Burke. He didn't need to listen to any more comments like those from the night before.

"Mr. Heller, get a plate and join me," Mrs. Roarke said when he neared where she sat.

Erick wiped his hands on his kerchief and accepted a plate with a sandwich and beans from Javier. He took off his hat and seated himself across the table from Mrs. Roarke, knowing that he had passed one test with Payne but that he still needed to prove himself to his true employer. He couldn't let any failure on his part reflect poorly on Cade. "You are most fortunate in your cook." He waited for her to begin eating before he would bite into his sandwich. "I have quite enjoyed the fare since my arrival."

"Trujillo is a genius, there's no doubt," Mrs. Roarke said. "He can turn even the simplest ingredients into a feast. Did you get settled in the bunkhouse last night?"

"The accommodation is most comfortable." Not that Erick had anything to compare it to, but he could imagine far worse. "I look forward to making the acquaintance of more of my fellows."

"I imagine Webster introduced you to Bessette already, and I'm sure you met Burke, because he's a terrible busybody and can't stand not being the center of attention. And Trujillo, of course." She glanced over to where a dark-haired man sat alone, bent over his plate. "Did you meet MacRae?"

Erick shook his head, hiding a smile at how well she had characterized his bunkmate.

"I'll introduce you to him in a few minutes, but first, tell me more about yourself. Webster was so full of other news that I didn't have the chance to ask for your story last night."

"I had just arrived on the ship from Bremen when Ca—Mr. Webster was kind enough to take me under his aegis. It is due to him that I find myself leading the life I had only read about." He hoped his slip had gone unnoticed, but her keen-eyed glance told him otherwise. Surely the weeks they had spent together were excuse enough for the informality? He cautioned himself to keep a closer guard on his tongue.

"Webster has a kind and giving heart, even if he tries to hide it beneath a brash exterior. I'm not surprised he offered to help you." His new employer was a discerning woman, to see Cade's qualities so clearly. "Bremen is in Prussia, if I'm not mistaken? Texas is a far cry from there. What made you decide to leave?"

"Tales of the frontier have always fascinated me." He weighed what more to tell her. Cade already knew his story, and he sensed Mrs. Roarke would see through any prevarication. "My wife and son died in childbirth. I wished for a new start, where I could make my way through honest effort." All that was true, even if he'd left out as much as he admitted.

"I'm sorry for your loss, but I'm glad you found your way to us," she said. "Although women are scarce out here. You'll have to go to Austin at least if you want to find yourself a new wife. There are only a few unmarried women between here and there, and Svensen is courting one of them. As for the others, I'm not sure what's going on at the moment between Burke and Miss Hart, the owner of the general store in town, but however much they fight, anyone with sense can see they belong together."

Interesting that she didn't include herself or Michele in that category, though Erick wondered if it was because she was uninterested in marrying again. If her only options were men like Reichardt or Ulrich, he could not fault her. "I am not in search of another wife." He hoped she would not prove to be a matchmaker. He'd had more than enough of that before leaving Prussia. And his heart was already claimed, futile though it might prove to be. "I have upturned my life enough already, I think."

"I can only imagine," she said with a light laugh. "But life as a cowboy is a far cry from anything you could have known there, I would think. Your manners and your English skills, and the fact that you read tell me you're an educated man. You could surely find a trade more suited to your past experience."

"But not to my desires," he admitted. "As for my experience, I do not know what trade it would qualify me for. Do Americans hire others to manage their estates?"

"It depends on what you mean by managing an estate," Mrs. Roarke replied. "And what kind of estate you're talking about. I'm sure some of the big industrialists in the East have people to do that kind of work. Out here, it's the foreman who runs the herds and usually it's the rancher who does the rest, but not everyone has a head for figures, and knowing what supplies to order and in what quantities is as much an art as is it a science. Payne runs the outfit just fine, but the rest came to me along with the land when my pa died."

Erick nodded. Other than his skill with horses, it was the only part of his former life he took any pride in. "It is a heavy responsibility to have fallen on you. But from what Mr. Webster has told me, you acquit yourself admirably."

"He's a good man." Movement drew her attention. "MacRae, come meet our newest cowboy."

Hearing her name him so gave Erick a flush of pride. Though he hadn't earned the title yet, he vowed to prove himself until he did.

The dark-haired man Erick had noticed startled like he'd been shot, but he approached the two of them warily. As he neared, Erick could see his left leg ended in a wooden foot. "Ma'am."

"Sergeant John MacRae, Erick Heller."

MacRae nodded politely and offered his hand. Erick shook it. "It is nice to meet you, Sgt. MacRae."

MacRae shook his head. "I ain't been a sergeant since the war ended. It's just MacRae, or Mac, if you like." He tipped his hat to them both. "I'd best get back to work, ma'am."

Mrs. Roarke waved him off kindly and turned back to Erick. "MacRae came back to Wellspring with Logan after the end of the war," she explained. "It's rare to see one without the other unless Logan has been on night shift."

They might be together more often since Cade had volunteered to take Logan's night shifts, though after meeting MacRae, he could appreciate the kindness behind the offer. The man was as skittish as the horses Erick was taming. Maybe Payne hadn't told her about the change, since she admitted he ran the outfit. "Wellspring is staffed with good men, from what I have seen this far."

"We don't keep any other kind around," Mrs. Roarke said, her gaze turning hard. "Every member of my outfit has to be able to rely on the others when the cards are down. There isn't any room for doubt or disloyalty out here. It's too dangerous otherwise." She paused, glancing deliberately toward MacRae's retreating back. "Even when the rest of the world would condemn a person for his background, the color of his skin, his infirmity, or the leanings of his heart."

"Such beliefs do you honor." Erick wondered how deeply she had seen into him. "They are sadly all too rare in the world."

"I'm glad we understand each other. I'll let you get back to work." She stood before Erick could reply and strode back toward the house.

Erick finished his sandwich, marveling at his good fortune at finding such tolerance. No, he admitted to himself, fortune had nothing to do with it. His presence at Wellspring was due wholly to Cade Webster.

CADE GAVE Nahnia's nose one last stroke and headed to take a shower. Chel had already disappeared in the direction of Javier's kitchen, so he didn't worry about stripping down outside the enclosure and walking inside, even though the water was already running. The men all tried to maintain some degree of modesty in Chel's presence, but they didn't bother when she was elsewhere. He'd taken two steps inside when his brain caught up with his eyes.

Erick stood beneath one of the faucets, his face tipped up to the stream, buckass naked.

And what an ass it was, if Cade said so. Tight and firm and round and—

Erick yelped when he turned to wet down his hair and spotted Cade. His gaze burned over Cade, eyes wide, before he turned again to face the wall. Maybe Chel was on to something. Yeah, Erick had turned away, but only after he'd looked, and hard. Maybe Erick wasn't so much uncomfortable himself as trying to keep Cade from finding out something that might make *Cade* uncomfortable. And if that was the case, maybe the time had come to show his hand. "My apologies," Erick muttered, head down as he edged toward the towel he had tossed on the bench. "I had not thought—"

"Hey, no," Cade said. "Don't apologize. I'm so used to barging in as long as I know where Chel is that I didn't even check to see who was in here. I can go if you want." He didn't want to, not when staying meant stealing more glances at Erick, but he would if Erick asked.

Erick hesitated, but he had clearly not finished washing up yet. "Not if you should not object? I would not come to dinner without washing. I had not expected to exert so much effort the first day."

Cade didn't object. Hell no, he didn't object. "Why do you think I'm in here?" He let a little of his appreciation seep into his tone as he turned on the second spigot and angled himself into the spray. If he treated being naked in the shower together as the commonplace event it was, maybe Erick would relax too. "You're lucky I'm the first person to barge in on you. Course it ain't that hot yet, not like it will be in a couple of months. Then there'll be a line to get in here before dinner."

"Another aspect of my new life I must accustom to." Erick dropped the towel on the bench and moved under the water again, keeping his back turned to Cade. Not that he minded a longer view at that sweet ass. "You must think me foolish."

"None of that," Cade insisted, trying to catch Erick's expression, but he kept his back firmly to Cade. Protecting his tender underbelly in more ways than one. "I think you're incredibly brave to come here and start over like you have, especially since I know your life in Prussia wasn't like it is here. You've got class and book learning and shit I never had the chance at. I think you're a lot of things, Erick Heller, a real gentlemen and a real catch for whoever's lucky enough to catch your eye, but foolish definitely ain't one of them."

His heart pounded in his chest as he spoke, his whole body tensed as he waited on Erick's reaction. Chel better be right, or he could be risking not only Erick's affection but his friendship. And even if he couldn't have one, he couldn't bear losing the other.

Erick glanced over his shoulder at Cade, his cheeks pinker than the lukewarm water could account for. Cade hoped that was a good sign and not the result of a day spent working in the sun and heat. Had Erick remembered to wear his hat? Keeping his gaze fixed on Cade's face, Erick said, "You have something much more valuable than mere 'book learning,' Cade. You have taught me so much since I arrived in America. I would be honored should you allow me to share what knowledge I have with you in return."

Well, he hadn't driven Erick off with the compliment. That was a start. Not that he knew what to do with the return compliment. Still, he recognized an opportunity when he was handed one. "You'd do that? Miss Dawson, the schoolmarm, offered once, but I don't have time to ride into town for lessons. My only other option was Burke, and no, I'd end up shooting him before we finished a single lesson."

The corners of Erick's mouth curled up, the equivalent of a wide grin from anyone else. "I would be happy to help you."

Cade wanted to cross the space between them and lick the crease at the edge of Erick's lips caused by that little half smile. He smiled back, elated. He still wasn't completely convinced Chel was right, but he had a way now to guarantee Erick's time and attention. "Maybe we could start after dinner. If you're not too tired?"

"Of course. We can spend an hour or two each night, if you wish." Erick turned his attention back to washing up, but he seemed more relaxed. "I will hope to finish several lessons before you are tempted to shoot me."

Cade snorted as he turned back to his own shower. "There's exactly one thing you could do to make me want to shoot you, and since I doubt you'll ever decide to insult my Comanche family, you're probably safe."

"I would enjoy hearing more of your time with them, if you should not object to speaking of it."

"Careful what you wish for," Burke said as he swanned into the shower area and tossed his towel over the enclosure walls. "If you get him started on them, you'll never get him to shut up."

"Fuck off, Burke," Cade snapped. He had the worst timing. Not that Cade could tell him to leave. The shower was public space unless Chel was using it. Still, he resented anything that intruded on what little private time he could find with Erick, though the offer of lessons would give him more. "Like you aren't just as bad about the things you come up with."

"At least 'the things I come up with' are useful," Burke retorted. "This shower, for example. Or trying to come up with a better prothesis for Mac's leg. Not like your old stories."

And that, Cade thought, *is why we put up with his sorry ass. Because he cares enough to do shit like improve Mac's broken-down peg leg.*

"They are not old stories to me," Erick said. "I can appreciate both your devices and Cade's adventures. It was tales such as his that drew me to America."

Burke rolled his eyes but didn't keep the conversation going. Cade shot Erick a grateful look, quietly pleased that Erick would defend him, and finished up. If it was just the two of them, he'd linger as long as he could, but he didn't have any desire to give Burke any more fodder for his commentary. Last night's comments had been bad enough. He slung his towel around his waist and ducked out of the shower enclosure. He hadn't stopped to get clean clothes on the way from the barn, but fortunately the back door to the bunkhouse was just a few steps away, and no one would blink twice at him coming in with just a towel on.

He pulled on drawers and pants—it was already too hot for a union suit—but didn't bother with a shirt. He'd have to put one on before dinner, but he had a little time still before then.

Erick entered a few minutes later. He must have brought clean clothes to the shower with him, since he was dressed and carried his soiled clothes under one arm. He opened the chest at the foot of his bed to stuff them into his saddlebag.

"There's a basket over there you can put your laundry in." Erick flushed again as he looked up at Cade. So what if he flexed just a little? He'd worked damn hard for those muscles, and he hoped the blush meant Erick was appreciating them. "Miss Sarah's sister Annie comes to the ranch a few times a week to do the washing. Just be sure to put your initials on them so you get them back."

Erick pulled a pencil from the saddlebag and marked inside each piece before dropping them into the basket. "I am glad you told me before I ran out of clean clothes."

"Not that anyone would complain about seeing you naked," Burke commented as he dropped his own load of clothes on top of Erick's. "What?" he squawked when Cade elbowed him. Burke made everything sexual about everyone, but Erick was different. In part because he was new and didn't understand yet that Wellspring was a safe place for everyone, but mostly because Erick was *his*. Except it would take more than an elbow to stop Burke from running his mouth. "I've got eyes, haven't I? Hoss is a better nickname than I thought."

Erick's face turned nearly as red as Javier's chiles, making Cade wish he'd gotten as good a view of Erick's front as he had Erick's back. He'd have to add that to his list of things to do next time he ran into Erick in the shower—which would be as often as he could arrange it without being obvious.

CHAPTER FIFTEEN

THE SUPPER bell saved them both from any more of Burke's innuendos. Cade stood up and pulled a shirt on, because Miz Roarke insisted on proper attire at the tables. If they left off their shirts while they were working, that was their business, but not at meals.

"How'd the first day with the mustangs go?" Cade asked Erick as they waited in line for their food.

"I think Payne was pleased." Erick accepted a bowl of chili and a slab of cornbread from Javier with thanks. "The horses are quite intelligent, which is not surprising in wild creatures. Once they are used to being handled, training them will be a pleasure."

"That's great! I knew you could do it," Cade said. He hadn't doubted Erick's skills after watching him with Zephyr, but a little vindication was good for the soul. And he suspected Erick needed the validation too. "I'll have to come watch, the next day I have here at the house instead of out on the range."

"You spend most days on the range," Erick observed. Cade thought he sounded regretful, but that might be wishful thinking.

"Five days on, two off, 'cept when we're driving the herd to market. One night out of the five, or two while I'm covering for Kit while Mac needs him." Cade claimed his own food and led them to a table where Chel was already seated. She nodded a greeting but kept eating. "Payne usually puts them on the same schedule, but Mac's leg's been bothering him enough to keep him from riding, and there's not much work needs done here at night."

"If Reichardt is really a threat, we might need a night watch on the ranch as well as the herd." Chel scooped up the last of her chili with a piece of cornbread and popped it in her mouth. "Mac might not be up for riding, but he's still a damn fine shot."

"I feel that is something of a requirement," Erick observed.

"With a pistol, Mac's almost as good as I am," Cade said. "Now he just needs to get used to that new leg from Burke so he can get his balance. It's throwing off his aim with a rifle. But he's too damn stubborn to practice."

"My aim is better with a rifle than a pistol. Perhaps we could set up targets and practice together," Erick offered. "I do not know if your friend is competitive—"

"Oh hell yes. Make it a challenge and he'll be on it like fleas on a dog."

"Tomorrow, perhaps?" Erick said. "If there is time amidst all the other tasks we must accomplish?"

"Tell Payne what you're planning and he'll give you the time," Cade assured him. The solution wouldn't have worked from anyone but Erick because Mac would see right through it, but an outsider like Erick…. Mac would fall for it in an instant. And Erick in all his generosity had the thought and made the offer without hesitation. As if Cade needed another reason to admire him. Even if a small part of him hoped it wouldn't impinge on their time to spend alone together. "The mustangs are important, don't get me wrong, but with the JR threatening, having everyone able to shoot is more important. I can talk to Payne if you want me to."

"Perhaps you could ask your friend Mac? You can tell him it is for my benefit. I would not want him to think it an impertinent suggestion from someone he does not know."

"I'll tell him, and I'll introduce you too. That way it ain't awkward tomorrow. I'll tell him you need practice with the pistol, and then you can mention you're better with a rifle after he's shown you just how good he is," Cade suggested, even as he admired Erick's cleverness in devising a way to help Mac without wounding his pride and his kindness in thinking to do so in the first place. "I'll mention it if he comes to dinner tonight, and if not, I'll drop by his and Kit's cabin after we finish eating."

"He doesn't always feel up to dealing with people," Chel added by way of explanation.

"If he must deal with Burke, I believe I can understand." Erick didn't smile, but the corners of his eyes crinkled in the way Cade was learning meant amusement. He reveled in the little signs no one else picked up because no one else bothered to look. He'd told Erick Wellspring would welcome him, would offer him a new home, and seeing Erick's amusement now made his heart light to know he'd been right. "Mrs. Roarke introduced us today at lunch."

Cade may have spent too long studying Erick's face, because Chel elbowed him in the ribs as she stood. "Smart man," she told Heller. "I am going to shower," she added to Cade before stalking away.

"Not that anyone would bother her, but I'll warn off anybody else until she's finished."

Cade half hoped Erick would follow him as he took up his sentry position at the corner of the bunkhouse where he could see both the dinner tables and the path to the showers, but Erick stayed where he was. Cade told himself that was good, that Erick needed to meet other people and that it was a sign of his respect for Chel's privacy, which definitely added to his good opinion of the other man. But he really wanted Erick to himself for a few minutes, and with Chel headed to the shower, no one would come bother them until she was back in the bunkhouse.

Not that he was staring at Erick or anything, but he was surprised when Erick picked up the empty plates from their table and returned them to Javier. He watched them speak for a few moments, wondering what Erick was saying. Then Javier wrapped a wedge of cornbread in a napkin and handed it to Erick. Instead of walking toward the bunkhouse, Erick turned in the opposite direction. It took Cade a moment to realize that he must be heading toward the paddock.

Chel was finishing her shower when Erick returned, minus the cornbread that Cade realized he must have fed to the horse he was training.

"Did you make friends?" Cade asked before Erick could go into the bunkhouse. He really ought to let the man go in and put his feet up, but Cade was feeling greedy for his attention. And yeah, Erick had said they'd start reading lessons tonight, but he could have changed his mind.

"The paint worked hard today. Good behavior should always be rewarded."

Chel chose that moment to come out of the shower enclosure, scrubbing a towel through her hair. "Maybe you can teach that to Cade too."

"Hey, I'm good," Cade protested.

"That's what all the boys say." Chel arched an eyebrow at him. "And yet so few of them live up to their claims."

"Does Javier?" Cade retorted.

Chel's eyes narrowed, but Cade didn't back down. "Javier is a man, not a boy. He doesn't need to boast of his abilities."

"I have not heard Cade boast, though I judge his abilities most impressive," Erick interjected. Cade felt his ears redden, and Chel snickered. He elbowed her in the ribs before she could make another smartass remark.

"You said you'd start teaching me to read and write," he reminded Erick.

Erick must have seen something in Chel's expression—okay, he was watching Erick, not Chel, so what?—because his eyes crinkled and the corners of his lips turned up. "You are welcome to join us, if you wish. It will help me to improve my English as well."

"That is kind of you, but Javier has been teaching me a little," Chel replied. "And you will have your hands full with Cade. I wouldn't want to be in the way."

Cade looked at Chel sharply. She hadn't mentioned anything about reading lessons with Javier, although it would be just like her to keep it a secret until she had mastered it. Or she could be deflecting for reasons of her own. Still, he wouldn't complain about having Erick's attention all to himself. "You're never in the way, Chel."

"Please join us whenever you wish," Erick offered. "I believe you are more experienced at handling Cade than I am."

"I have been known to manage him on occasion," Chel replied slowly, "but I'm quite sure he'd rather you handle him than me."

Cade bit back the yelp at Chel's blunt speech. Sure, he'd definitely rather Erick "handle" him, but Chel didn't need to be that obvious about it. "I've seen how you handle men. Javier is one brave son of a bitch. I'll definitely take my chances with Erick."

"I am unsure if that warrants my thanks." Cade didn't know how much of the implication Erick understood, though he'd started it, in a way. "Perhaps you should join us if only to evaluate my handling."

The look Chel shot Cade was as clear as day—if Cade didn't act on the opening she'd just handed him, she'd beat him. "Another time," she replied. "I already have plans for the evening. You should have your lesson down by the spring. It will be quieter there than in the bunkhouse, and you should still have at least an hour until it starts to get dark."

Oh yeah, she was going to beat him bloody if he messed up the opportunity she was creating. Too bad he wasn't as convinced as she was that Erick would be interested. "What do you say, Erick? Want to walk down to the spring? It's only about ten minutes from the house."

"Let me gather what we will need."

As soon as Erick was in the bunkhouse, Cade turned on Chel. "Could you be any more obvious? The spring at sunset? It's a good thing he doesn't understand what you're trying to do."

"If I am being obvious, it is because you are too blind to see what is right in front of your face," Chel replied serenely. "You should thank me for giving you the perfect opportunity to be alone with him. Do not waste it."

"Chel," he protested.

"You don't have to fuck him—or let him fuck you—tonight. I can be reasonable in my expectations. Just promise me you will be open to the possibilities."

Her words were a punch to the gut, blunt as only she could be, as she would only be when it was just the two of them. But he wanted. Oh, how he wanted what her words conjured up—Erick's beautiful body over him, riding him hard, or under him, ridden to a lather. He'd take either in a heartbeat, even as his heart yearned for more than just a quick tumble. He shook his head to clear the image away. He was going down to the spring for a reading lesson, nothing more, nothing less. "Fine, but you're going to owe me so big if you're wrong."

She shrugged. "If you wish. But I'm not wrong."

Erick rejoined them, every inch a Texan in his dungarees and work shirt, hat on his head, boots on his feet. The only thing missing was a gun belt around his waist, but they were only going to the stream in the heart of Wellspring's territory, and Cade had his pistol if needed. None of that helped lessen his lingering reaction to Chel's words. Cade only hoped Erick was too preoccupied with the small bundle in his hands to notice. "Let us take advantage of the remaining sunlight."

"Have fun," Chel sing-songed as she headed toward Javier's cabin.

Cade glared at her back before turning to Erick, his expression softening. However annoyed he might be at Chel, Erick wasn't the cause, and her meddling had the benefit of an hour or more alone with Erick. "This way."

They walked through the scrub around the ranch house down toward the spring, the one place on the ranch that never completely succumbed to the heat. Even on the worst days, the water was cool and the air fresher than anywhere else on the spread. Miz Roarke's father had built a hanging swing for his wife, and Cade sat there now. Erick joined him immediately. Even in the warm evening, Cade could feel the heat from Erick's thigh barely brushing his. He almost scooted closer, Chel's insistence ringing his ears and dovetailing with the glimmers of hope he'd gained from Erick's words and actions, but fear held him back. He already had so much more of Erick than he'd imagined possible. Could he really risk losing that? "This is one of my favorite spots on the ranch," he said. Most of the hands came down to the spring at one time or another, but Cade had never deliberately come down to the spring with someone, not with the idea of seeking privacy, not like a courting couple. "Maybe in the world. What I've seen of it, that is."

"It is most pleasant," Erick agreed. He glanced down, his cheeks pink. "I have not many supplies," he apologized. "I brought only a few favorite books with me, but they are in German. Perhaps one day I may go into town. You mentioned Svensen is courting a schoolteacher. She may have some books we could borrow. For today, I have a journal and some pencils. I thought we could begin reviewing your letters."

"Anything," Cade said, his voice a little too raw, but he couldn't fix it now. "My ma had started teaching me my letters before she died, but that was a long time ago. I probably forgot most of what I learned."

He didn't think of his parents often—he'd been so young when they died and so loved with the Comanche—but the few memories he had were good ones. How his mother always smelled of lavender, even after days on the road. How his father never had a cross word for anyone, even when everything went to shit and they had no real choice but to leave for Texas. The memories drew him back from the knife's edge of arousal he'd been walking, and the very real desire to learn what Erick could teach him returned full force.

"You may remember more than you think." Erick wrote out for a few moments in the journal, then handed it to Cade. "I have made both the capital and lowercase letters. Can you read them out to me?"

Cade took the paper and studied it, trying to remember what he'd learned at his ma's knee, but most of the lines jumped and blurred together, nothing decipherable. "That's a C," he said, pointing to it. "And I know the W. And that's maybe an S?"

Erick didn't scoff the way his ignorance deserved. He considered for a moment and then handed a pencil to Cade. "Let us try this. I will tell you the name of each letter, and you copy it out. That may help fix them in your memory."

With no judgment forthcoming for his struggle, Cade took the pencil and put his faith in Erick's care. He copied each letter painstakingly as Erick said them aloud. When he was done, he repeated them back to Erick again. "That was easier." He looked down at his shaky letters. "Although I may need some practice writing them. Yours are a lot neater than mine."

"That will come with time," Erick assured him. The promise of more lessons, of more of Erick's gentle tutoring and his simple assumption that Cade *could* do this, was as heady as the *wokowi* the shaman had given him during his coming-of-age quest. He had never been allowed to become addicted to the *wokowi*, but he could easily become addicted to having Erick treat him like an equal. "I will leave you some paper and pencils so you can practice whenever your duties permit." He turned to a fresh sheet of paper. "Can you write your name?"

"I never learned how to spell it," Cade said. "Although I could try."

"Take your time and sound it out. Your name is not hard," Erick encouraged.

Easy for you to say, Cade thought, though Erick's patience gave him the courage to try. He focused on the sheet of letters and what he thought each sounded like and slowly wrote out his name.

"Excellent, though your name has a final E to make the long A sound. Without it you would be a cad, and you are anything but that." Bringing a smile to Erick's face was Cade's new goal in life. "For names, the first letters are capitals and the rest are most often lowercase. Try again that way, please."

Wanting Erick to smile at him again, Cade worked his way through his name a second time, checking the sheet each time to make sure he had the letter formed correctly. His handwriting was still shaky, but he thought the letters looked a little better than they had the first time. Feeling confident, he tried Erick's name next: *Erik.*

"This is where language makes fools of us all." Erick took the journal and wrote *Erick.* "To be honest, I do not know why there need to be both a C and a K in my name, and in other languages it might be spelled with only one or the other, but so it is."

Cade rather desperately wanted to kiss Erick for his kindness, his patience—who was he kidding? Because Erick was hot as hell— but Chel's assurances aside, he couldn't quite believe a man like Erick Heller would be receptive to his interest. And he'd rather have the quiet comfort of more lessons like this one than take the chance, find out he was wrong, and lose even that. He fought the desire to lean into Erick with the sun setting behind them, to slide his arm around Erick's waist in the hope Erick would put an arm around his shoulders and draw him closer, would brush their lips together in a kiss as kind and patient as the lesson in letters had been. It would make every dream he'd had since he first dreamed of another boy to love him come true if Erick felt the same. If he didn't, he would lose not only the dream his spirit quest had promised him, but also the chance at Erick's friendship and at learning to read. No, he couldn't take that chance, no matter how he yearned for the man sitting so near. Instead of giving in to his desire, he thanked Erick, copied his name carefully, and said, "What about Chel?"

Chapter Sixteen

"Thank you for allowing me to ride into town with you." Erick sat next to Javier on the buckboard, while Burke rode beside them on his horse, Napoleon. "Svensen assures me that Miss Dawson will have primers she will let me borrow."

"She lent me one to help teach Michele," Javier confirmed. "Besides, I'll appreciate your help loading the groceries, since whatever excuse Ned made to go into town, he'll spend all his time trying to sweet-talk Miss Hart into stepping out with him."

"Miss Hart will just have to do without me today," Burke said from the saddle. "I have actual business with the blacksmith. I am running low on good iron to work with, but does that stop the horses from throwing a shoe or the cowboys from breaking tools? Let me assure you, it does not. And now we've got Hoss here getting more of the mustangs ready to sell, and that means even more horseshoes."

Erick had trained himself not to blush at Burke's ridiculous nickname. "The devil makes work for idle hands," he countered instead.

"And he'll spend five minutes at the blacksmith and the rest distracting Lizzie from filling my order at the mercantile," Javier added.

"Just for that, Javi, I won't help you unload when we get back to Wellspring," Burke said. "Now, spill, Hoss. Where have you and Webster been sneaking off to after dinner every night? Hmm? We can build another cabin, you know. Wellspring is a safe place for anyone who needs it. We don't judge."

"I will steal your hammer and hide it where you will never find it," Erick threatened. He wasn't ashamed of the time he spent tutoring Cade, but he didn't want to open him up to Burke's mockery. And if he spent too many nights in his bunk after their sessions imagining just the kind of thing Burke was implying, imagining what Cade's muscles would feel like under his palms, what his skin would taste like under his lips, it was no one's business but his own.

"He's helping Cade learn to read and write, like I am with Michele," Javier said. "Not everyone had the chance for an education the way we did, Ned."

"Uh-huh, Javi," Burke drawled. "Reading and writing is exactly what you're doing, all those evenings alone in your cabin with no one around to see."

"I will beat you with your hammer after Erick steals it if you don't show Michele the respect she deserves," Javier growled, his body tensed and eyes flashing. Erick had never seen such a reaction from the generally mild-mannered cook, but he was pleased that Javier's feelings for Michele seemed genuine. Once he had gotten past the jealousy he now believed was unfounded, Erick had grown to like and admire Cade's friend for her honesty and capability.

"And that assumes Cade does not, how did he put it? Shoot your ass full of arrows?" Erick said.

"I was joking," Burke wheedled, although Erick was not so sure it had been a joke until Javier had not taken it as one. "You both need to lighten up a little. This is what happens when you don't get your needs satisfied regularly. And you can't even tell me there aren't any interested partners around now since you're seeing Chel—and since Wolfie drools every time he looks at you, Hoss."

"I'm sure Lizzie would be happy to know your only interest in her is to get your needs satisfied," Javier countered. It seemed he wasn't quite ready to forgive Burke yet. Erick wasn't either, though he'd learned quickly enough to discount the majority of Burke's remarks. While he'd noticed Cade smiling at him more often, there was certainly no "drooling." Their responsibilities kept them from seeing much of each other except at mealtimes and their evening lessons, but those moments of having Cade all to himself were the highlight of Erick's day. He was not at all surprised that Cade was proving to be an excellent student. It warmed Erick's heart every time Cade recited the alphabet or succeeded in spelling out a new word. As much as the evenings meant to Erick, as much as Cade seemed to appreciate them, he couldn't risk letting himself hope they meant more to Cade than the chance to practice his letters.

Deciding it would be better to defuse the tension if he could, Erick turned to Javier. "Who else should I know in town? Miss Dawson, of course, and Miss Hart. And I believe Cade mentioned Miss Dawson has a sister. But I am sure they are not the only people in town whose acquaintance I should make."

"Well, there's James Murphy, the blacksmith, though everyone just calls him Jock. And Doc Lillard—he's also the undertaker when needed. Bobby Meier and his brothers, Billy and Tommy, run the only drinking establishment in town, the Lone Star—the only place to get a meal too, if you're satisfied with fried eggs and bacon, and they have a few rooms upstairs they hire out if anyone needs to sleep off a drunk. Robert Graff runs the sawmill. The ranch gets all their lumber from him. And of course there's the sheriff, Randall Lutz." If Erick hadn't already heard Cade's opinion of the lawman, the way Javier spat out his name told its own tale. "Oh, and Reverend Smithson, if you're the religious sort."

Erick wasn't, particularly, but he also understood the importance of seeing and being seen at Sunday services. He would attend with the other cowboys if they went but would not insist on it if they did not. "I will endeavor to remember everyone's names. And I believe I shall reserve my dining for back at the ranch. Your cooking far outstrips fried eggs and bacon."

It was clearly the right thing to say, because Javier's fists unclenched slowly as they talked.

"There's no bank in town," Burke added. "You have to go to Austin for that, but Lizzie has a locked room in the back of the mercantile that people use to store things sometimes."

"And if you need to send mail or a telegraph, you have to deal with Henry Tatum in the sheriff's office." Javier didn't seem to think much of that idea, so it was fortunate Erick didn't anticipate having need of either. The last thing he wanted was for anyone in Prussia to track him down in America. Given how remote Wellspring was, Erick had few worries now that it could happen.

The first straggling buildings of the town came into view as they talked. Neither Galveston nor Austin had compared to the European cities Erick was accustomed to—not that he missed their grime and overcrowding—but Eldorado would scarcely qualify as a village. There were perhaps a dozen structures along the intersecting main streets. He could pick out the smithy by the paddock with several horses inside, what he presumed was the saloon by the larger number of horses tethered outside, and the tiny church by its steeple. Wooden signs identified others as they passed. Javier drew the buckboard to a halt in front of the building that proclaimed itself "E. Hart Mercantile," while Burke continued on to the blacksmith down the street.

Javier hopped down from the buckboard, so Erick did the same and followed him inside. A woman in a simple dress stood at the counter inside, but the simplicity of her attire aside, she would not have been out of place in any of the salons in Europe with her poise and commanding demeanor. "Javier," she said with a smile. "You've brought someone I don't know with you today."

"Lizzie," Javier tipped his hat as he returned her smile. "This is Erick Heller, Wellspring's newest cowboy. Erick, Miss Elizabeth Hart."

It gave Erick a thrill every time someone referred to him as a cowboy, even though he still felt like a greenhorn. He removed his hat and bowed. "It is a pleasure, Miss Hart."

"*Vielen Dank*, Herr Heller," she replied with a smile, confirming Erick's guess that she was a woman of culture. "I thought I heard a hint of Prussian in your voice." He wondered what had led to her running a mercantile in a tiny Texas town, and hoped he would have the chance to know her better. "Oh, please tell me he's setting a good example for Ned, Javier."

"Whether Ned will profit from his example is another question entirely," Javier replied. "Here's our list for the week, Lizzie."

"If you have any carrots, I would like to purchase several pounds worth," Erick added. At Javier's questioning glance, he explained, "They are treats for the horses. I find rewards much more effective than switches, and I would not take from the provisions you need for meals."

"If you're using them for training, they'll go on the ranch account. I'll square it with Payne," Javier said.

"I have some I was afraid I would have to throw out, but they will still be fine for the horses," Miss Hart replied. "And I wish more men shared your opinion on rewards and switches. The world would be a much more peaceful place if they did."

"Thank you. And then do you know where I might find Miss Dawson? I am hoping to borrow some books from her," Erick said.

"At this time of day, she'll be at her desk having lunch," Miss Hart said. "The schoolhouse is next to the church."

"I believe I can find the church on my own," Erick said with a smile. "I will be back shortly to help load the wagon," he told Javier before walking the short distance down the dusty street. Two small buildings sat beside the steepled sanctuary. One was likely the Reverend Smithson's residence. The other, windows open and a handful of children of varying ages playing outside, he judged to be the schoolhouse. Several of the children stopped to gape at him as he removed his hat and walked inside.

"Miss Dawson?" he asked the dark-haired woman behind the largest desk. "My name is Erick Heller. I am employed at Wellspring Ranch, and Mr. Svensen told me you might be willing to lend me a primer and perhaps some other books for beginning readers."

"Come in, Mr. Heller. Olav told me you would probably come by," Miss Dawson said. "It's nice to meet you. I set aside a few books for you to choose from." She rose and crossed to a small wooden bookcase where she gathered a pile of books held together with a leather tie. "See if any of these will suit for you."

"It is most kind of you." Erick selected several books, one slightly more advanced than the other. "I will return these in a few weeks in exchange for others, if that is acceptable."

"I wish we had more of a library to offer. Unfortunately we must rely on donations for what little we have."

Erick thought wistfully of the library he'd left behind, four walls covered floor to ceiling with bookshelves. He determined to make a donation to Miss Dawson's library fund once he received his first pay from Wellspring. "I am grateful for what you have to share."

"You're quite welcome," she said. "And, in case no one has said it yet, welcome to Eldorado."

"Thank you. I am most happy to be here." With a final bow of thanks, Erick carried the books back to the wagon and stowed them carefully under the seat. He was just in time to help Javier load a surprisingly large number of boxes, barrels, and sacks into the back of the buckboard. Perhaps not so surprising, now that he'd seen how much Logan, Svensen, and several of the other hands could eat. His own appetite had grown as he settled into his demanding daily duties.

"Herr Heller, I packed the carrots you asked for on the top of this box so they won't be crushed," Miss Hart told him with a smile.

"You must call me Erick, please," he asked her.

"His first name is Hoss." Burke dismounted and tossed his horse's reins over the hitching post. "Ask me why we call him that."

"Please don't," Erick implored. "No one but you calls me that in any case."

"I know Ned well enough to know I don't want to know. And please, call me Lizzie."

"If you wish…. Lizzie," Erick said. "Thank you for the carrots." He tipped his hat and then turned to Javier. "Is there anything else you need to do while we're in town?"

"Only check to see if there's mail for the ranch," Javier said. "Then we can start back. Ned can catch up with us when he's done visiting with Lizzie."

Erick followed Javier to the sheriff's office that doubled as a post office. After Cade's and Javier's comments, he was disposed not to trust the man, but it never hurt to know all the players. Javier greeted the lawman with a short nod and a curt "Lutz." Erick made no effort to introduce himself. Unless Lutz asked, he'd just keep to himself.

"Well now, you must be the new cowboy I've been hearing about," Lutz said as he rose from his desk. "Hellman, was it?"

It took Erick a moment to remember that Cade had mentioned his name to Carter when they'd crossed JR land to reach Wellspring. So Cade's comment about Lutz being Reichardt's man seemed to be accurate, though Erick didn't know why he would warrant such notice, or why Lutz calling him a cowboy felt somehow mocking. "Heller," he corrected with a brief nod. He wouldn't offer his hand unless Lutz did.

"Good to put a face with a name," Lutz continued, not acknowledging the correction. "It's always useful to know who belongs around here and who doesn't. And what brings you to a place like Wellspring?"

"I heard it was the best outfit in the state," Erick replied calmly. Lutz's eyes narrowed before an artificial smile spread across his face.

"You must have been talking to Burke," Lutz said, his tone dismissive. "Everything he touches is the best or biggest or brightest, to hear him tell it. They're a decent outfit, don't get me wrong—a few squeaky wheels like Burke or Payne aside—but Texas is an awful big place."

"Which means plenty of land for everyone," Javier broke in. "I've got the mail. Let's head out." He brushed past Lutz with a frown, so Erick just nodded again and followed the cook out the door.

"I don't trust Lutz as far as I could kick him," Javier said as they headed back to the wagon. "Somehow any time there's a ruckus in town, it's never any of the JR outfit to blame, according to him. You'd do best not to get on the bad side of him."

"Since I have no plans to engage in any 'ruckus,' it should not be an issue." Erick wasn't exactly sure what a ruckus involved, but since the only time he'd be in town would be to exchange books for Cade's tutoring, it seemed a safe promise to make.

Javier chuckled. "If we actually started it, it would be one thing, but since the JR hands inevitably goad one of our resident hot heads into being stupid, it's not as easy to avoid as you'd think."

They reached the wagon and Erick climbed onto the seat of the buckboard next to Javier. "Do you want to drive home?" Javier asked.

"Should we wait for Burke first?"

"He knows the way, and I don't want to put up with his bad mood if Lizzie shoots him down again," Javier said. "So no."

"I have not driven this pair before. It will be good for them to get to know me." Erick took the reins and snapped them to start the team moving. Javier wasn't the most talkative hand, so Erick spent the trip back to the ranch anticipating Cade's next reading lesson and wishing he were bold enough to simply claim what he desired. As soon as the thought rose, he rejected it. He had never been that type of man, even when he did not feel what he felt for Cade. And he was not even brave enough to admit to those feelings, on the very real chance that he was reading what he wanted to see into Cade's natural friendliness. Better to accept what he had, even if he longed for so much more.

Chapter Seventeen

Erick didn't see Cade until dinner the next day, their respective duties and the extra night shifts Cade had taken on for MacRae keeping them busy on different parts of the ranch, but Cade was all smiles and a friendly clap on Erick's shoulder as he put down his plate of something Javier called *arroz con pollo*. Erick had never seen rice quite that yellow before, but none of the other hands seemed surprised by the color, and everything Javier had served so far had been delicious, so Erick was willing to give it a chance.

That train of thought derailed completely when Cade left his hand on Erick's shoulder as he hopped over the bench and took his seat. Erick told himself Cade had just needed to keep his balance and Erick's shoulder was at a convenient height to lean on, but Cade had never seemed to need help before, displaying nearly acrobatic grace in everything he did.

"I hear you met Lutz in town," Cade said when he was settled. "At least it sounds like he was almost polite."

"He knew my name, or some version of it, so your assumption that Carter or someone from JR is in contact with him proves true," Erick answered. "Though his only complaint was to refer to Burke and Payne as 'squeaky wheels.'" He missed the warmth of Cade's hand, though they needed both to cut into their chicken, which proved as delicious as every other meal Javier made. "Miss Dawson was so kind as to lend several books for our lessons," he added.

Cade leaned into him enough to bump their shoulders together. "After dinner? I mean, if you don't have anything else planned?"

Erick forced himself not to shift even closer to Cade in return. "I have it on Javier's authority that Burke will be particularly unpleasant tonight since Miss Hart refused his advances." Erick hoped it wasn't obvious how much he longed to spend time alone with Cade under any pretext. "Leaving the bunkhouse seems prudent."

"We can always go down to the spring," Cade said with a soft smile, so different than the smirk he directed at most of the other hands. "It's cooler there anyway."

The other cowboys continued to insist it would get hotter over the summer, but as far as Erick was concerned, it was hot enough already. Cooler sounded good to him. And it meant not having to conduct their lessons in front of the other hands, though in fairness no one but Burke had mocked Cade about them, and mockery seemed his default reaction to everything. Michele had even joined them on the nights she didn't spend with Javier. *Admit it,* he scolded himself. *You don't want to share him with anyone else.*

"And I've been practicing my letters. I took the notebook with me and studied them while I was watching the herd yesterday and today. Not a lot to see out there, most days," Cade added, his expression so eager that Erick couldn't help but praise him.

"You have made excellent progress with your writing. Now that we have books, we can begin lessons in reading as well." Cade approached everything with enthusiasm, whether it was their lessons or Javier's meals or the cows who had just calved for the first time. It was such a refreshing contrast to Erick's former contemporaries who considered any display of emotion vulgar.

Cade's smile turned shy, but he bumped Erick's knee with his own and dug into his meal with his usual gusto. A number of the other hands nodded or spoke as they got their own dinners and sat down to eat, but none of them joined Cade and Erick, making Erick hope he hadn't done anything to offend them—or to betray his interest in Cade beyond teaching him to read. Even Michele, practically a fixture at Cade's side, stayed near the serving line with Javier rather than join them as she usually did. When Cade had wolfed down everything on his plate, he patted his stomach. "Do you want more or can we go now?"

"Let me get the books from the bunkhouse. I can meet you at the stream if you like?"

"I'll go with you so we can walk together." Was it Erick's imagination that Cade walked a step closer to him than he had before? His warm smiles, the nudges of shoulder and knee, the speed with which he finished his meal, all tempted Erick to hopes he knew he shouldn't entertain. He retrieved the books from his bunk and started down the path that led to the creek, trying not to indulge his fancies. Cade was excited about learning to read, not about the person teaching him.

It would have been easier if the back of Cade's hand didn't brush against his occasionally. Each time it happened, Erick expected Cade to pull back or apologize or brush it off, but he did none of those things. He never did more, but he did nothing to keep the random touches from happening again.

Erick was careful not to react in any way that might appear to be discouraging.

When they reached the hanging swing beside the spring, Erick sat and opened the primer Miss Dawson had lent him. Cade settled beside him, so close their hips and thighs pressed against each other. Erick swallowed down the urge to wrap an arm around Cade's shoulders when he leaned forward to study the book.

"You know the letters by now." Erick pointed to the first page, where the capital and lowercase A were illustrated by a ripe red apple. "Can you sound out the words?"

Cade's brow furrowed. "It's an apple, but that's not reading. That's looking at the picture." He huffed a bit and looked at it again, clearly committing the letters and sounds to memory. "Okay, apple. Got it. What's next?"

"Perhaps I should hide the pictures," Erick said with a smile as he turned the page to a drawing of a bell. "If you know the word, read me the letters that spell it."

"Bell," Cade said. "B-E-L-L, bell." He reached for the next page just as Erick did and their fingers tangled against the sheet.

Erick felt his cheeks heat and prayed Cade was too intent on the book to notice as he turned the page. "I have seen one of these in the barn. Payne insists it is only to keep mice out of the hay, but I saw him petting it one morning." The page showed an illustration of a large orange tabby.

Cade laughed. "That's Biscuit. The one in the barn, I mean. His name's Biscuit. Cat. C-A-T, cat. And don't let Payne hear that you saw him. He once threatened to fire Burke for claiming Payne liked Biscuit. Of course he threatens to fire Burke at least once a week, so maybe it would be different if someone else said it."

"I am not sure which is worse, the threat of Payne firing me or the idea of being linked with Burke in his mind." The next page showed a long-eared hound. "Packs like this were common for hunting, though I preferred to rely on my own skill rather than run my prey down until it was too weak to escape."

"The Comanche hunt with dogs sometimes," Cade replied. "We've had hounds at times since I've been here, but there ain't any hanging around right now. D-O-G, dog. Do you miss your home? You rarely talk about it, but when you do, it seems like you have good memories."

Erick gave the question the consideration it deserved. "Not so much, no. There were very rigid expectations of proper behavior, especially within my own family, which I found stifling." He wasn't brave enough, or perhaps foolish enough, to admit struggling in particular against the expectation of marrying again to provide an heir. "I respect my family's heritage, but I did nothing to contribute to it."

"It makes me glad I live out here," Cade said. "Apart from being polite to women and chewing with my mouth closed, nobody much cares how I act. Not as long as I don't break any laws, anyway. For what it's worth, I'm glad you ended up here."

Erick could no longer imagine what his life might have been like if he hadn't had the good fortune to meet Cade, but until he met Cade, his life had been ruled by the dictates of society, the first being never to flaunt one's emotions. He found it harder to leave that rule behind than he would like. "I find myself glad to be here as well. In Prussia I had peers and acquaintances. Here I hope I am beginning to prove myself enough to make true friends." Hoping he did not sound too much like a stiff prig, he turned the page, trying to return Cade's attention to the book rather than personal revelations he found uncomfortable to discuss.

He nearly jumped out of his skin when Cade rested a hand firmly on his knee. "I can't speak for anyone else, but I'd call us friends."

And that is enough, Erick insisted. *It must be.* "If not for your friendship, I would still be in Galveston hoping to find someone willing to take on a raw immigrant." And that did not bear thinking about. He tapped the book's image of a large bird with a white head.

"Naw, you'd have found something by now for sure. You're too smart and too good with horses. E-A-G-L-E. I know that's an eagle, but why is it E-A? Why not just E?"

Erick very carefully did not move his leg where Cade had left his hand. He might have to resign himself to only Cade's friendship, but that didn't mean he'd be the one to pull away when Cade touched him.

"E by itself has a different sound," Erick explained. "Think of egg, England, Eldorado—even Erick," he said, feeling daring at calling attention to himself. "E and A together sound like east, ear, eat." He watched Cade's lips as he formed the words silently, flushing again when he realized Cade had stopped and he was still staring at his mouth.

Before he could think of an excuse or even a deflection, Cade leaned in suddenly and pressed their lips together. He pulled away so quickly Erick didn't have time to kiss him back, then Cade was on his feet and running like the hounds of hell themselves were on his heels.

Erick was too stunned to react before Cade disappeared, and as much as he longed to chase after him and demand to know if the kiss meant what he hoped, he needed to ask Cade in private, not in front of a crowd of interested cowhands. Alone in the growing dusk, he traced a finger over his lips, reliving the press of Cade's mouth. For once he didn't deny the hope that warmed his heart. Perhaps his dreams were not so impossible after all.

STUPID, STUPID, stupid. How could he have been so stupid, kissing Erick like that completely out of the blue? He was lucky Erick hadn't punched him in the face, but he could forget about more reading lessons, more dinners sitting side by side, more anything. He'd given himself away.

He just hadn't been able to help himself. Erick had been so kind and patient and had looked so handsome in the soft light. And he hadn't pulled away from any of Cade's touches, even the ones that pushed the limits a bit.

Cade stormed into the bunkhouse, grabbed his bow and quiver, and stormed back out. He couldn't deal with people right now, not even Chel, who quirked an eyebrow at him as he blew in and out. He had to calm down, and the only way to do that right now was to shoot. At this hour, no one else would be out on the impromptu shooting range Payne had agreed to let them set up on the far side of the main house. No one would want to run the risk of angering Payne or Miz Roarke with the sound of gunfire, but Cade wasn't planning on using a gun, and his bow didn't make enough noise to carry into the house.

He pushed his turbulent thoughts aside and focused on the easy draw and release of shooting until the rhythm of it overtook the chaos in his mind and he could see things with more perspective.

Erick *hadn't* pulled away from any of Cade's touches, not even when Cade set his hand on Erick's knee and left it there. The touch itself could have meant anything or nothing, but Cade hadn't moved his hand. Surely Erick would have said something if he hadn't welcomed it.

Or would he have? He was still getting used to the way things were done on the range. Maybe he thought it was normal for Texas and hadn't wanted to stand out as a foreigner. Though if Cade found out anyone else had been touching Erick that way, he'd make sure they lost a few fingers for their trouble.

Erick hadn't punched him for the kiss, not that Cade had really given him time to react. It had been enough for Cade to feel the prickle of a day's worth of beard, though. Enough for him to register the dry heat of Erick's lips.

Enough for him to know Erick hadn't kissed him back.

Fuck. He was going in circles.

"Of course you'd be here." Cade didn't know how long Chel had been watching him, another sign—as if he needed it—of how fucked up he was. "You're so predictable, Cade. What did you do now? Erick was worried about you."

"He was just making sure I wasn't around to throw myself at him again," Cade said bitterly. He shot another arrow without looking her way.

"Oh, Cade." Great, now on top of screwing his friendship with Erick, he'd disappointed Chel too. "What did you do, *louveteau*?"

Cade lowered his bow and rubbed a hand over his face. "I kissed him," he mumbled.

"And Erick was so scandalized that he punched you in the face?"

"He's too much of a gentleman to do that. Not that I hung around long enough to give him a chance," Cade admitted. "Nobody will notice if I toss my bedroll under the trees out here, right?"

"He didn't look scandalized when he came back to the bunkhouse," Chel mused. "Concerned not to find you there. Wondering where you might be. You wouldn't want to worry him further by not coming back. The poor man probably wouldn't sleep all night."

Cade sighed and leaned against the fence that marked the border between Miz Roarke's garden and the firing range. "Did he say anything?"

Asking made him pathetic, but not knowing was worse.

"Would you want him to, in front of everyone?" Cade shook his head. "Believe that I know enough about men to tell that he wasn't angry, or disgusted, or whatever other ridiculous reaction you're imagining. Cade, that man thinks you hung the moon."

"You think so?" Cade asked, desperate for a sliver of hope that he hadn't fucked up the best thing to ever happen to him.

"How can someone with the vision of a wolf not see what's right in front of him?" Chel took the bow from Cade's hand and tilted his head up to meet her gaze. "Talk to him, Cade. Not tonight," she added at Cade's panicked flinch. "Figure out a way to get him alone and tell him what you want. I think you'll find he wants the same thing."

"Is that what you did with Javier?" Cade knew the question would probably earn him bruised kidneys, but that was preferable to the squirmy feelings in his chest at the moment. He didn't get good things in life—or if he did, he didn't get to keep them.

"Javier is a man, not a frightened little boy." Chel linked her elbow around his, the rare touch somehow settling his jittery nerves. "Come to bed, *petit loup*, before Erick comes looking for you."

Cade couldn't decide if he wanted to bristle at the jab or curl into her side. The insult was better than bruised kidneys, even if it was a little too on-point for comfort. He let her draw him back toward the bunkhouse, though, because he couldn't face a private conversation with Erick right now, no matter what she said. At least in the bunkhouse he could see that Erick was okay with his own eyes. He'd work up his nerve to talk to him tomorrow. Or the next day. Or never.

Judging by the look Chel shot him, he wasn't going to get away with never.

Chapter Eighteen

Erick accepted the plate of *migas* from Javier and carried it to the table where Mrs. Roarke sat, trying to rein in his irritation. Since the night Cade had kissed him, they hadn't had the chance to exchange a word. Cade had returned to the bunkhouse with Chel from wherever he'd disappeared to and climbed into his bunk without meeting Erick's eyes once, and Erick's heart had sunk. Was he regretting the impulsive act? Was he upset that Erick hadn't kissed him back? Did he think Erick wasn't interested? He had spent so long fretting before falling into an exhausted sleep that when he finally woke up, Cade's bunk was already empty. Erick hoped to catch up with him at breakfast, but Payne had pulled Cade, Logan, and Michele aside and sent them off to gather a part of the herd from the far pasture. He'd watched them ride off, bedrolls strapped to their saddles. That was two days ago and they hadn't returned yet.

"You seem out of sorts this morning, Heller," Mrs. Roarke said as he poked at his food. "Is something bothering you?"

"The mustangs are all accepting a saddle now and will soon be ready to ride. Perhaps it is time for me to learn to work with cattle as well as horses." There was no guarantee that Payne would agree, or that he would send Erick out with Cade, but it was at least a chance to spend more time together than their reading lessons, assuming Cade would even want to continue them.

"That's good news," Mrs. Roarke said. "I'll see how many Zeke wants to keep on hand and put the word out in town if we have some left for sale. And tell him it's time to round up a new batch. You should ride out with him, or whoever he sends, to bring them in. Since you'll be working with them."

He tried to look enthusiastic at the prospect. He loved working with the horses, but unless Payne sent Cade with him to round up more, it wouldn't give him a chance to spend more time together. After the weeks of travel to Wellspring, having Cade all to himself, even these few days without seeing him ached like a missing limb.

"In the meantime," she continued without seeming to notice his lack of enthusiasm, "I was hoping you would take a look at the ranch ledgers with me. I don't usually have problems making them balance, but I can't seem to find my mistake this month. You did say you'd managed an estate in Prussia."

"Of course," he said with a bow of his head. Another task that would keep him away from Cade, but he couldn't begrudge the chance to contribute the only other skill he had to offer. "I can review them after our meal, if you like."

"Yes, please. The sooner we can get the books to balance, the sooner you can get out on the range. I know you're eager to learn, but while I wouldn't trade any of our hands for all the gold in the world, most of them don't have the skills necessary to help me," Mrs. Roarke replied.

"I am honored by your trust in me." Erick had just stood to return his empty plate to Javier when a cloud of dust down the road caught his eye. For a moment he hoped it might be Cade and the others returning, but they'd be riding for the barn, not up to the front of the ranch house. By the time they drew to a halt and dismounted, he identified the man he and Cade had overheard in Austin—Reichardt, Cade had named him. He didn't recognize his companion, but by the frown on Mrs. Roarke's face, she wasn't pleased to see either of them.

"Mr. Reichardt, Mr. Sanders," she said noncommittally. "What brings you to Wellspring?"

"To see you of course, madam," Reichardt replied as he dismounted, with a smile that set Erick's teeth on edge. They might very well be there to see her, but that wasn't their only mission. Erick wished he'd thought to pick up his gun before he left the bunkhouse that morning, but he still wasn't used to wearing it for no reason.

Movement to the left caught his eye and he glanced toward it to see MacRae lounging indolently against the bunkhouse, one hand resting on the hilt of his pistol. Erick still hadn't found the time to witness MacRae's shooting, but he trusted Cade's assessment. That was one gun against two possible assailants, but it was better odds than before.

"You've seen me, now if you'll excuse me, some of us have to work for a living," Mrs. Roarke said, her voice cold.

"Mrs. Roarke…. Grace, a beautiful woman like you shouldn't have to work herself to the bone running a place like this," Reichardt barreled on as if she hadn't spoken. "If you'd just consider my offer… with our combined spreads, you could live like a queen."

"I am quite content with what I have, thank you." It was clearly a dismissal, but Reichardt paid no attention.

"But you could have so much more." Reichardt's gaze slid over her simple cotton dress like a snake slithering up to its next meal. "French gowns, a maid to attend to you. You'd never have to lower yourself to consort with the hired hands."

"Miz Roarke said she wasn't interested," MacRae drawled. "You'd best be on your way."

Reichardt frowned, and his companion took a step closer, his hand falling to his own sidearm. It was time to defuse the situation, or at least get Mrs. Roarke out of danger before it escalated.

"If you please, we can review the accounts now," Erick said in his most authoritative voice. It bought him enough time to take Mrs. Roarke's arm and lead her into the house. Surely Reichardt wasn't bold enough to force his way inside.

"This isn't over," Reichardt shouted.

Spotting a rifle leaning against the wall. Erick stepped back onto the porch and cocked it. MacRae had drawn his pistol, and the two of them were enough to discourage the JR owner from whatever his next action might have been.

"You'll regret this," Reichardt spat as he remounted his horse, the other man following his lead.

"Not as much as having anything to do with you." Mrs. Roarke moved beside Erick on the porch, her own pistol raised. "Now get off Wellspring property before I have my men escort you off."

Erick stayed where he was, rifle at the ready, until he could no longer see even the dust trail left by the two men's horses.

"Hellfire and damnation," Mrs. Roarke said when she finally lowered her pistol. "I did *not* need that this morning. Or any morning for that matter. Zeke will be livid when he hears about this." She took a deep breath and squared her shoulders. "MacRae, stand watch and alert us if there's any sign of them returning."

"Ma'am," he said with a tip of his hat.

Erick followed her into the house and waited as she opened the door to a well-appointed office. Indeed, it was nearly a match for his office at his estate in Prussia.

"I regret I was not better prepared," Erick said. "I thought it best not to be armed when working with the horses, but I will carry a pistol with me henceforth."

"Keep it within reach," Mrs. Roarke said. "You're right not to wear it if you're in a situation where you might get thrown, but near enough that you can grab it if needed. I hate that it's come to that, but I don't trust Reichardt as far as I can spit."

It didn't take long for Erick to familiarize himself with Wellspring's ledgers and identify where a transposed entry had prevented them from balancing. It was no slight to Mrs. Roarke's bookkeeping, as he had been frustrated by the same sort of issue in his own accounts. "A second set of eyes can be helpful in preventing this type of error, if you would care to have my assistance, Mrs. Roarke," he offered.

"If you're going to be my assistant accountant, I think you can call me Grace," she said.

"If Herr Payne would not object," he answered. The foreman refused to let anyone call him anything but Payne, but it felt disrespectful to refer to him so informally, whatever his relationship was with Mrs. Roarke—Grace.

"I'm my own woman," Grace replied. "I decide how I wish to be addressed and by whom, Heller. Zeke respects that or we'd have parted ways already."

"Then you must call me Erick," he answered, "Grace."

Grace smirked at him. "If Webster will not object."

Erick's cheeks flamed, but before he could babble an excuse, Grace's smile softened. "You have nothing to fear here. You've seen how Logan and MacRae are treated. The others may joke and tease at first, but they will not judge you for following your heart. Heaven knows they'd have left already if they were the type to judge, what with my relationship with Zeke."

Once again Erick gave silent thanks to any power that was listening for his good fortune at meeting Cade and finding a home at Wellspring. "There is nothing for Cade—Webster—to object to," he admitted, hoping his regret was not reflected in his voice. "I had been aiding him to improve his literacy, that is all." And he still wasn't sure whether even that would continue.

"That is between you and him," Grace said. "But if those reading lessons turn into something more, you are still safe and welcome here, Erick."

Erick offered her the same formal bow he would have made to a princess. "I will do all in my power to keep you safe as well," he vowed.

CADE TOSSED his bedroll under his bunk and flopped down on the mattress. After three days in the saddle and sleeping rough, it felt like heaven. Before he could settle, Chel kicked the bottom of his boot.

"I'm done with the shower. Get in there and get cleaned up before you stink up the whole bunkhouse. None of us want to smell you."

Cade closed his eyes and ignored her. He just wanted a few minutes to rest. He'd take a shower before dinner. Or maybe he'd take one during dinner so he could put off seeing Erick a little longer.

Chel kicked him in the shin this time. "Oww!"

"Shower. Now."

Before she could lame his other leg as well, he pushed himself to his feet and shuffled toward the shower building. He could hear water running as he stripped out of his dusty gear and tossed it on the bench. *Probably Kit*, he thought as he walked into the humid space, only to find himself face to wet, naked ass with the one man he'd been trying to avoid for nearly a week.

He almost turned around and walked right back out, Chel be damned, but he wasn't quite that much of a coward. He cleared his throat. "Um, hi, Erick."

Erick spun around in surprise—he obviously hadn't heard Cade come in. For a moment Cade thought he was going to turn his back on him again, but Erick stood his ground, swallowed, and met Cade's eyes. "Welcome home, Cade."

Cade forced himself to keep his gaze fixed on Erick's face rather than let it wander the way he wanted. "Thanks. It's good to be home. I… um, well, I missed our reading lessons."

He'd missed a hell of a lot more than just their lessons, but that seemed the safest thing to focus on. And maybe if they could start their lessons back, he could find a way to talk to Erick about what he really wanted to say.

Erick's posture eased and a corner of his mouth twitched up. "We yet have most of the alphabet to get through. Perhaps after dinner, if you are not too tired."

"After dinner would be great," Cade said. He stepped under the spray of water and let it cool the burning excitement inside him. "Did I miss anything interesting while I was out on the range?"

The tense posture was back. "Indeed you did. Herr Reichardt and one of his men. He tried to importune Grace, and threaten her when she would have none of him. I am afraid he did not take her rejection well."

Grace, is it? Cade didn't think she let anyone but Payne call her by her given name. It would seem things had gotten more than a little interesting in his absence. "Better not let Payne hear you call her that. He might decide to 'importune' you. As for Reichardt, I hope she shot him in the ass."

"I am assured that Grace decides how she wishes to be addressed and by whom." That was definitely a twinkle in Erick's eyes. Cade only wished he'd been the one to put it there. "There was no shooting, though it took Grace, MacRae, and myself threatening it to convince them to depart."

Cade let out a low whistle. "If MacRae was involved, you're lucky it didn't end up a full-blown shootout. He's on a hair trigger anyway, but the one thing guaranteed to set him off is someone threatening a woman."

It was the reason Cade trusted Mac. He'd come to Chel's defense in town without knowing who she was or what had led to the argument. He simply couldn't stand to see a woman in danger.

"It is fortunate Payne was not present, or I would not have been able to prevent it," Erick admitted. "I know Grace will warn him, but I also know men of Reichardt's kind. I fear much worse is to come."

Cade was afraid Erick was right about what was coming, but he'd gotten one thing wrong. "Payne won't start anything, no matter the provocation. He can't. They'd have him lynched before we could do a thing to stop them. No, he'll defend himself and Wellspring, but he won't fire the first shot. MacRae, now… he might. Hell, I might if they push me the wrong way. But Miz Roarke would beat me like a rented mule if I did."

Erick finished rinsing and picked up the towel he had slung over the shower wall. He wrapped it around his waist and turned back to Cade. "I will see you at dinner, then?"

Cade turned to face him fully, giving Erick a chance to look if he wanted to. "I wouldn't miss it."

"That is good." Erick's eyes didn't wander the way Cade hoped they might, but his lips curved in a shy smile. "I missed you, Cade." Before Cade could reply, he was gone.

Well, fuck. How was Cade supposed to interpret that? He couldn't stop the glimmer of hope in his chest. He'd have to hope reading lessons tonight weren't all Erick was willing to share with him.

He finished washing up quickly and headed back to the bunkhouse. He definitely didn't want to be late to dinner tonight!

Chapter Nineteen

Cade had just slipped into place at Erick's side when Payne stood up and gave a sharp whistle. Conversation ceased completely and everyone turned their attention to the ranch foreman.

"Trouble's brewing," he said without preamble. "Reichardt and Sanders came sniffing around this morning, and when Miz Roarke wasn't amenable to their propositions, they got belligerent. MacRae and Heller ran them off." He stopped and gave a tip of his hat in Erick's direction, then one in MacRae's. "But they left spewing threats. Now I'll be the first to call Reichardt a windbag, but he has the men, the money, and the firepower to back up those threats if he chooses to. He wants Wellspring. He'll take it legally by forcing Miz Roarke to marry him if he can, but if he can't, he'll try to take it illegally."

Cade grimaced and looked around at the others. Every one of them wore an expression of grim determination. The JR owner would find no easy marks at this table.

"They're dirty sidewinders," Payne continued. "They'll try any sneaky underhanded trick they can think of to make it look like we're the ones who started a range war, and they'll use that to have Lutz throw us in jail to weaken the protection around the ranch. Do not let them goad you into starting anything. If they fire first, shoot back and shoot to kill, but *only* if they shoot first."

"But it would be our word against theirs," Jesse Beaufort protested, generating a murmur of agreement.

"That's why no one goes anywhere alone," Payne reiterated. "There will be a witness to anything that happens. Of course Lutz will argue that we'd lie for each other, but he'd have to prove it." Payne cut through the angry muttering with another whistle. "There will be at least three hands on guard here at the ranch at all times. Everyone will be armed unless you're sleeping. Trujillo, Burke, Heller, I know you don't usually wear sidearms, but we can't take any chances. If Reichardt thinks he can get to Miz Roarke against her will, we will put the motherfucker in the ground."

A chorus of "hell yes" and "damn right" echoed around the tables.

Cade leaned into Erick, forcing himself not to react as the heat from Erick's body seeped through their shirts and into Cade's skin. The situation was too serious to allow for any distractions, even one as damn-near perfect as Erick. "Are you okay with carrying your Colt?"

"Yes, although… would you mind if instead of a reading lesson tonight, you could take me to your range so I may practice? I am not as accurate with a pistol as I may need to be."

Cade bit back his disappointment at the request. He'd hoped for the privacy of the spring to pick back up where they'd left off in the shower. Still, at the range he was in his element, and he wasn't opposed to a chance to show off. And no matter how much he wished otherwise, they would need every advantage they could get in a fight against the JR, so Erick's suggestion was a reasonable one. "Of course I don't mind. We can go as soon as we finish eating."

"I WILL feel like a true cowboy wearing a six-gun," Erick said when they had retrieved his Colt and gun belt from the bunkhouse. Cade kept the thought that no cowboy would carry his gun rather than wear it to himself. When they reached the range, Erick buckled the belt around his waist and bent to tie the strap to secure the holster around his thigh. "Though I am not sure I have done this properly."

"Let me check," Cade offered before he could think better of it. He ran his hand along the edge of the gun belt until he could get his fingers beneath it and tug a little, but it stayed right where it belonged. Then he grabbed the holster and tried pulling it away from Erick's leg, because no matter how tempted he was to reach between Erick's thighs to check the knot, that was one step too far without an actual conversation between them. The holster didn't budge, so Cade decided that was as good as it was going to get. "It's fine. You aren't going to be in a showdown with them anyway, so it's not like you have to worry about a quick draw. Fire a couple of shots to get used to the feel of it."

Erick slid the gun into the holster and took a few steps, stopping a fair distance in front of the target. He drew the gun and sighted carefully before firing. The shot hit the outer edge of the circle ringing the center. It was a more than respectable first shot, but Erick frowned and fired two more, closer but still outside the center ring.

"You're pulling to the left." Cade came to stand behind Erick. "Here, let me help." He reached around Erick to adjust his aim minutely. The position put them close enough that their whole bodies touched. He wanted to take advantage of the situation, to rub against Erick so he'd know just how much Cade wanted him, but anyone could show up at the range and probably would. The sound of gunshots usually drew an audience pretty quickly.

"Really, Webster?" Mac drawled from behind them. "That's the tactic you choose?"

Cade nearly jumped out of his skin—he hadn't expected the audience quite that fast—but he didn't back away from Erick. "Try it now," he said.

Erick's next three shots buried themselves in the center ring. He turned his head enough to meet Cade's gaze and there, there was the twinkle Cade would do anything to put in Erick's eyes. "I imagined aiming at MacRae," he murmured before stepping away to reload.

It was hope, pure and simple, that shot through Cade's chest. Why would Erick imagine aiming at Mac if he didn't resent the interruption as much as Cade did? And why would he resent the interruption if not for how close they were standing?

"Show us what you've got then, MacRae," Cade said. "Since you think you're hot shit."

"Never said I was hot shit." Mac limped closer to the shooting line. "Not with this bum leg, anyway. But I need to be able to shoot a rifle again." He sighted down the gun, but his stance wobbled before he fired, the barrel arching up and the shot missing the target entirely. "Fuck!"

"Hold it again, like you're going to fire," Cade said, "but don't pull the trigger yet."

Mac did as Cade instructed. Cade stood behind him and studied Mac's stance. "You're standing lop-jawed on that leg." He looked around until he found a small, flat rock. "Lift up." He slid the rock under the foot of Mac's prosthetic. "Try it now."

Mac fired again. The barrel—and his stance—stayed stable, although the shot still only hit the outer edge of the target. Mac grumbled under his breath.

"Hey." Cade bumped their shoulders together. "I bet you didn't do that well the first time you shot a rifle when you were a kid. Give yourself *some* credit."

"Not much to take credit for when a greenhorn with a pistol can outshoot me," Mac muttered, though his next shot hit several rings closer to the center.

"In fairness, I have shot a pistol before," Erick observed. "I have not had much cause to use one before now, but it is easier to carry than a rifle."

Cade had spent a pleasant evening showing Erick how to use his pistol on their way back from Galveston, but then they'd had to be careful not to use up all their bullets, so once he was sure Erick could use the pistol in an emergency, they'd stopped.

"Unless you're riding herd and need to hit something at a distance." Mac stepped back to reload again, ceding the target to Erick, who fired off several shots that all hit the center ring. "Not such a greenhorn at all, I reckon."

"Then you'll just have to keep practicing until you can beat him," Cade goaded. "As good as you are with a pistol, it won't take you long. Then you and I can give it a go. If you think you can take me."

"Ain't looking to get into a pissin' contest with you. Just want to be able to ride with Kit again. Once I get used to this contraption." Mac's next shots edged the inner ring. "Burke may be a pain in the ass, but he does have his uses."

Since getting Mac back on shift with Kit was Cade's primary goal as well, he'd go along with anything that reached it. "Amen to that. And that shot woulda taken out anything you'd need to hit on the range. A rattler or any other varmint, animal or human. Just in case you weren't sure if you were ready. Now we just have to get Heller here ready."

"I do not think Payne intends me to work with the herd." Was that regret in Erick's voice? "I would welcome the opportunity, but Grace—Mrs. Roarke—mentioned bringing in more horses. And there must be enough hands to guard the ranch should JR men attempt to make good on Reichardt's threats."

Cade stifled his disappointment at the thought of not getting to spend the days with Erick. "Even if you're at the house most of the time, when it comes fall and we have to drive the herd to Abilene, we'll need all the hands we can get. And if you are guarding the house, it's all the more important that you're ready. MacRae, go bother Logan and leave us to practice."

Mac gave him the stink eye but slung his rifle over his shoulder. "Is that what you're calling it now?" he asked as he limped away.

Fortunately Erick didn't seem to catch what Mac was implying. He hit the bullseye with his remaining shots before sliding the pistol into its holster. With MacRae gone and Erick's aim improving, Cade was free to admire the way the holster clung to Erick's thigh and had to force his attention back to what Erick was saying. "… see you use your bow. I had little opportunity to watch you hunt with it on our journey here."

Cade never said no to a chance to show off with his bow, but the request meant more from Erick. With anyone else, it was one-upmanship, a chance to prove the skills he'd learned from his Comanche family had as much value as their bullets. With Erick, it was more, a chance to prove he could protect and provide if called upon to do so. And sure, he'd done both on the trip from Galveston, but then it had just been practical. It meant something now. Oh, he knew Erick could provide for himself just fine. He'd done his share of the hunting on their trip. And he'd just shown he was capable of protecting himself. That didn't change the values Cade's family had instilled in him.

He set his pistol aside, settled his quiver over his shoulder, and picked up his bow. "The advantage of the bow is that it's silent," he said as he drew and fired. "Or close enough. There's no retort to alert your target to your presence."

He took a step and fired again, the fletching of the second arrow brushing against the first one in the center ring.

"That is… most impressive." Erick reached out to run his fingers down the wooden curve, stopping short of Cade's hand. "You learned this from your adoptive family?"

"Yes." Cade turned his hand so their fingers touched. "Although these days some of them use rifles too, when I was a kid they still hunted using the old ways. Erick, I…."

Erick drew in a breath. "Cade, if I have misjudged, forgive me, but…." He leaned forward and brushed his lips against Cade's, feather soft, then looked up to meet Cade's gaze.

"Nothing to forgive," Cade choked out before diving back in for another kiss. He tried to keep it as soft as the one Erick had given him, but he wanted too much after fearing for so long that Erick wouldn't feel the same way. He forced his hands to stay at his sides, but he couldn't stop the hungry groan that escaped his throat at the way Erick's mouth felt beneath his, sweet and supple, and just as eager for more.

"Perhaps this would do better without weapons?" Erick's eyes twinkled but his breath came faster as he removed his gun belt. His fingers brushed against Cade's, stoking a flare of heat as he imagined the gentle touch on other parts of his body. "And where others might not join us?"

Cade snorted inelegantly. "Why d'ya think Mac and Kit have their own cabin?" He stole a kiss from Erick's lips, unable to resist a moment longer. "Nowhere's really private. Too many busybodies."

Erick removed the bow from Cade's clasp and set it on the ground, then settled his hands on Cade's hips and drew him closer. "I would prefer no interruption, but Grace assures me I will find no judgment here. That alone is worth any risk." The kiss this time was firmer, coaxing Cade to part his lips and let Erick's tongue trace them.

Cade sucked Erick's tongue deeper into his mouth and pressed a thigh between Erick's legs so he could grind their hips together. Erick was as hard as he was, and it drove Cade wild. He wanted to throw caution to the wind, bear Erick to the ground, and fuck him—or get fucked by him—right there, but common sense won out. It was nearly dark, they weren't anywhere private, and who knew whether any JR hands were prowling around? Or the usual predators for that matter. "We have to go back," he murmured against Erick's lips.

Erick rocked against him and slid a hand to the back of his head, pulling him into a kiss that was hard and wet and claiming. "*Lieber Gott,*" he panted when he finally let Cade breathe. "I have longed for this since we met."

Cade groaned. "I wish I'd known." He nuzzled Erick's jaw, stubbled at the end of the day the way it never was in the morning. "All those nights on the trail with no one within a hundred miles…." They'd never manage that kind of privacy on the ranch unless they rode two days south to the waterfall. He rutted against Erick's thigh as he imagined all they could get up to there. "I wanted you the minute I saw you calm Zephyr down." He turned and kissed the hand that still rested on his shoulder, the hand that had caught the rope and calmed Zephyr with such a masterful touch. "And it's just gotten stronger the more I've gotten to know you."

"If we had not already showered…." Erick arched against him, the jut of his erection riding the crease of Cade's thigh. "Perhaps I will sleep in the barn tonight. I would not have to listen to Burke's innuendo, and I would have privacy, even if I cannot share it with you."

Sparks danced up Cade's spine, sorely tempting him to join Erick in the barn, but if he did that, someone would come looking for them, and he refused to have their first time together ruined by interruptions. "So you'll just make me listen to Burke's innuendo alone." He gave Erick another kiss, desperate for more contact, even if kisses were all he would get tonight. "Sleep in the barn if you'll be more comfortable there tonight. I'd join you if I thought I could get away with it without someone coming looking for us."

Erick's smile was positively wicked. "I would much prefer to have you join me, but now I have more than imagination to satisfy myself."

Cade suddenly realized why Erick wanted privacy, and the idea of his pleasuring himself to the memory of their kisses made his cock jump. "Fuck, Erick, you can't say something like that when I have to go sleep in the bunkhouse alone."

"Tomorrow we will find somewhere after dinner," Erick promised. "We could make some excuse to ride back to town, if it is the only way to be together."

"Let me think about it." Like he'd be thinking about anything else. "If I can't come up with a better idea, we'll do that." And listen to everyone give them shit for it, not that they'd get any less for going off alone on the ranch, to the waterfall or elsewhere, because no matter how subtle they tried to be, Chel would see through them for sure and Mac already had—or at least thought he had.

That didn't bother him nearly as much as it probably should.

At the moment, he found it didn't bother him at all. Erick wanted him. Erick wanted him so much he was going to sleep in the barn tonight so he could take himself in hand to the memory of touching and kissing Cade. Erick *wanted* him. No, tonight nothing in the whole fucking world could bother him.

"We will find a way." Erick pulled him into another searing kiss. Cade would absolutely have to find a place to jack off before returning to the bunkhouse. There was no way he'd be able to sleep, as hard as he was now. "Anticipation makes the moment sweeter, so they say. *Gute Nacht*, Cade."

CHAPTER TWENTY

"Go on with you, Biscuit," Erick chided. "Just because I let you sleep with me last night does not mean you can help with the horses. You might be trod on." If the cat could talk, it would no doubt express that it found the suggestion highly insulting, but it jumped to the top of the fence rail and began to clean itself as daintily as a large orange tabby could.

Shaking his head, Erick unsaddled the chestnut paint he'd dubbed Rosy and slipped her a carrot from his pocket. In truth, most of the mustangs were as ready as he could make them, but with Reichardt's threat looming, he doubted Payne would want to take hands from the ranch to corral more. It also made him reconsider his suggestion of riding into town. As much as the prospect of a night alone with Cade tempted him, it would mean two fewer hands to defend Wellspring if Reichardt made good on his threats.

"If I'd needed more than Webster's word to take you on, which I didn't, mind you, Biscuit taking to you like she has would have done it. That cat is a better judge of character than any man I've ever met," Payne said. "She hated Adam Carter on sight. I should have fired him the moment she hissed at him."

"Why didn't you?" Erick asked before he could think better of it.

"Because the last thing I need is word getting around that I'm fucking crazy," Payne replied. "Bad enough I'm a freed slave. That keeps a lot of men away. I don't want to run off the ones willing to give me a chance. I fired him as soon as he gave me a reason."

"I understand he made untoward advances toward Miss Bessette."

"If that's a fancy way of saying he tried to rape her, but she's no one's bitch." Payne ran an eye over Erick appraisingly, making Erick wonder what Payne saw when he looked at him. "I almost felt bad not patching him up before I kicked him off Wellspring property. I'd have done something about it sooner if it had been up to me, but while Roarke was alive, he made those decisions."

"I am surprised Cade let him live," Erick replied.

Payne snorted a laugh. "It took four men to hold him back. Not that she needed the help since she damn-near gelded Carter. The only reason he's still alive is because Miz Roarke reminded them both that killing him would get one or both of them hanged."

"But it makes him the more dangerous now."

Payne nodded. "Most of Reichardt's men like the paycheck or they'll only work for a white man or they're bullies who get off on pushing around people who can't stand up for themselves. Carter is one of those, but it's personal now too. He wants revenge, and he'll find a way to get to Bessette. He'll rape her if he can, because that's what she denied him before, but if he can't, he'll kill her. And yes, she can take care of herself, but a bullet from a distance can take out even the best fighter. The thing about the hands here at Wellspring… we all look out for each other."

"I have promised Grace the same. I would do more than train horses." Erick gestured to the mustangs in the paddock. "Four of this group are ready for the hands or for sale. I welcome whatever other duties you may assign to me."

Payne raised an eyebrow when Erick used Grace's given name, but he made no other comment. Apparently Grace's insistence that she decided to whom she gave leave to use her name was correct. "We can start the hands mixing the ones you've got ready in with the horses they usually ride to give them some experience. We'll need two or three horses per hand when we make the drive to the new railhead in Abilene. Normally I'd send you and a few of the boys to get another batch of mustangs before then, but I don't want anyone that far away from the outfit until we see how things are going to play out with Reichardt. Which means you're going to get your wish. As soon as you get the last two ready to ride, I'll add you to the rotation with the herd."

It was tempting to ask to be put on the same rotation as Cade, but Erick was not ready to push Payne's goodwill any further. "Thank you. I will not fail your trust in me."

"If I'd had any doubt, I wouldn't've hired you in the first place. Now get to work. The barn is filthy." Payne stalked off, leaving Erick shaking his head. Mucking stalls was the next task on his internal list anyway, but now he had more than just the anticipation of seeing Cade that evening to make the grueling job easier to bear. He was going to be a true cowboy!

"FUCK!" CADE said as he scanned the horizon. From the valley where they kept watch on Wellspring's herd, the hills rose up to the border of their property with JR land. And at the top of the hill—far enough up to be on JR property, but visible where usually there was no one—was a group of riders.

"Cade?" Chel looked in the same direction.

"At the top of the hill. JR hands." Cade peered closer. "Six total. They aren't doing anything. Just sitting there watching. And they're on their side of the fence. But dammit, I had plans for tonight that involved Erick and a room in Eldorado, and now there's no way in hell we can leave the ranch."

"And why would you need to leave the ranch?" Chel grinned wickedly.

"We don't all have cabins like Javier when we want some privacy," Cade grumbled.

"You have managed privacy for your lessons."

"When that's all they were, yeah, but last night changed everything. And sure as shit, the first time we try for anything more than a few kisses, Burke will come up with some urgent reason to have to go to the spring for one of his inventions, and I'd have to kill him."

"That would make Payne unhappy. I can make sure you are undisturbed," Chel offered.

Cade eyed her warily. He had no doubt she could and would do it, but favors from Chel usually came with strings attached. "What's the catch?"

"Can I not do a favor for a friend?" She batted her eyelashes innocently.

She hadn't been innocent since the day she entered La Fleur blanche. "Not usually," he replied.

"Cade, I owe you my life. My life at Wellspring, if not my entire life. There is no catch," Chel said with a sigh. "Except maybe to give me first crack at Carter if he's stupid enough to attack Wellspring."

Cade grinned at her ferally. "Only if you're right there beside me. Otherwise, no promises."

"Deal. Now, you keep an eye on our spies. I'm going to warn the others. And don't do anything stupid. You have *plans* for after dinner."

Chel spurred her horse and rode off before Cade could think up a suitable retort. Besides, she was right. He did have plans. Wonderful, sexy, intimate plans with a wonderful, sexy, gorgeous man who somehow seemed to find Cade just as attractive. He couldn't wait for it to be time to head back for dinner so he could tell Erick about Chel's offer. He was *so* getting lucky tonight!

ERICK TRIED not to keep looking over his shoulder for Cade as he picked at his dinner. No doubt it was another of Javier's flavorful creations, but he was not tasting a bit of it. After working with the mustangs all day, he'd cleaned himself thoroughly in the shower, hoping fruitlessly that Cade might again join him. He'd dressed in the best of his limited selection of clothing and dawdled as long as he could in the bunkhouse before he needed to join the other hands for dinner. Cade and Michele arrived as Erick was getting his plate and pulled Payne aside into a low-voiced discussion. Just as Payne headed toward the ranch house and Cade and Michele lined up for food, Burke dropped into a seat at the table.

"So tell me, Hoss. MacRae says you and Wolf Boy were looking pretty cozy while you were shooting last night. Is there something we should know about?"

"You should know that MacRae's new leg needs some adjustment. It leaves him off balance and difficult to aim his rifle"

"Don't try to distract me, Hoss. Mac and I worked on that this afternoon. When do you think he told me about last night? I'm not judging. I don't judge. Ask anyone. I don't have any room to judge. So tell me. What's going on between you two?"

"Nothing that is your business, Burke." Before he could continue, Cade slid onto the bench beside him and dropped a hand on his shoulder.

"Are you bothering my… friend, Burke?" The heavy pause in his voice conveyed what his words did not.

Burke blinked once. "Nope. Not at all. Not me. No, sir. Wouldn't think of it." He picked up his plate and moved to another table.

Erick turned to Cade. "That is a skill I need to learn."

Cade laughed. "He's seen me shoot and he's convinced I'm just crazy enough to shoot him if he pushes me too far. That's all there is to it."

The idea of being with Cade was too new for Erick to want to share it with anyone else. At least not before they had exchanged more than a few stolen kisses. He'd spent the previous night imagining baring Cade's body to his view and touch, and now he could look forward to the privacy they needed. "I have some news," he said instead. "Payne is going to add me to the rotation to ride out with the herd as soon as I finish training the last two mustangs."

"That is good news." Cade's smile lit up his face. He leaned in closer so he could speak without being overheard. "I have good news too. Chel has offered to stand lookout when we go for our reading lesson tonight so we won't be disturbed."

"Then you should finish your dinner." Erick turned to his own plate with newfound hunger. "I am sure tonight's lesson will be quite comprehensive."

Cade's pupils contracted, making his eyes seem even bigger and brighter than usual, and his gaze grew hot before he turned his attention to devouring his food. "Give me ten minutes to take a shower," he whispered when he had finished eating. "I'll meet you at the spring."

Erick forced himself to remember the last respectable noblewoman his mother had tried to interest him in so his own eagerness would not be apparent. He thanked Javier for the meal when he returned his empty plate and then stopped at the bunkhouse to pick up the books he'd borrowed, even if he was sure they would not be opened. Michele was waiting at the head of the trail that led to the spring, though he was grateful she did no more than nod to him as he passed. Then he had nothing to do but wait in growing anticipation for Cade to join him.

CHAPTER TWENTY-ONE

IT TOOK less than the promised ten minutes, though it seemed an eternity to Erick, before Cade came hurrying down the trail, his blond hair still dripping water onto the collar of his shirt, and threw himself in Erick's arms. He kissed Erick like his life depended on the contact of their mouths, a kiss Erick returned with all the longing he'd kept bottled up since his first sight of Cade on the docks in Galveston. When Cade finally pulled away, panting into Erick's shoulder, he gasped out, "Oh God. Fuck me now."

Erick had spent most of the day and the previous night imagining just that, but with Michele's assurance of privacy, there was no need to rush. Not before he'd gotten his hands on the magnificent body he'd fantasized about. "You are too fine a gift to partake in haste." He unbuttoned Cade's shirt—an easy task since half the buttons were already undone—and leaned forward to kiss a path down Cade's throat.

Cade's head fell back, giving Erick full access to his skin, golden and smooth in the gathering dusk. "You… and your… fancy… words," Cade panted. "You know I'm… a sure thing… right?"

"That does not make you unworthy of being appreciated as you deserve." Erick didn't know how much experience Cade had, but he was determined to drive the memory of any other lover from Cade's mind. And cherishing Cade would give Erick as much pleasure as it did Cade. He ran his hands beneath the shirt panels to caress the strong planes of Cade's back and continued to press kisses across the wealth spread before him. He could sate himself on the taste of Cade's skin, cool from the shower but heating beneath his touch.

Cade arched into the caress, shrugging his shirt off completely before wrapping his arms around Erick's shoulders. He ran one hand into Erick's hair, dislodging his hat. Erick paused to see if Cade would guide him, but the touch stayed light, encouraging but not directing.

Erick wished he had thought to take the blanket from his bunk, though that would open them to too many questions when they returned.

Instead he sank slowly to his knees, unfastening Cade's gun belt and setting it on the ground before moving to the buttons on his dungarees.

"Eriiick!" Cade's knees trembled and almost gave out on him. Erick grabbed his hips to help steady him until Cade managed to lock them straight again. He gave a throaty chuckle. "If you're gonna suck me, I either need a tree or a place to lie down."

His mouth already watering at the prospect, Erick maneuvered Cade to the swing and managed to work his fly open before sitting him down. Cade's cock sprang free, thick and ruddy, and Erick lapped his tongue over the tip before taking it as deep into his mouth as he could. This was a pleasure he had only dreamed of, and he intended to savor it to the fullest.

Cade spread his legs as wide as he could with his pants hampering his movements, slid his hips forward to the edge of the seat, leaned his head against the back of the swing, and gripped Erick's shoulders tightly. "Fuck, that's good," he groaned. "Almost as good as fucking you will be." Then, as if he realized what he'd said, he lifted his hands and his head and looked at Erick. "If you'd want that, I mean. Some day."

"What have I done to deserve you?" Erick pushed up to reach Cade's lips, the hunger in his kiss at the thought of taking what Cade offered an answer in itself. But that was for later. Tonight was for Cade. To leave no doubt, he added, "I would want that very much. But just now I have weightier matters to attend to." He stole one more quick kiss before kneeling back down to resume his most pleasant task.

Cade's groans fell like raindrops on Erick's ears. He kneaded Erick's shoulders and rocked his hips slightly in time to the up and down motion of Erick's head, but beyond that, he gave himself completely into Erick's care. His trust redoubled Erick's determination to lavish all the pleasure on Cade that he deserved.

Wrapping one hand around the base of Cade's cock, Erick reached the other up to flick over a peaked nipple. It took a few moments to synchronize the motion of the swing and the rocking of Cade's hips and his own slide up and down the delicious length to keep from choking, but he found the perfect rhythm at last, to judge from the increasingly frantic sounds he was wringing from Cade.

"Cl-close," Cade choked out, pushing at Erick's head. "Wait. Stop. I want you inside me."

Erick was tempted to continue, to savor Cade's taste on his tongue, but the thought of feeling Cade around him made his cock jump, and he hoped to have many more opportunities to experience bringing Cade to completion. He pulled off with a final kiss to the glistening tip. "How are we to do this? I will know better to bring a blanket in future, but…." Their surroundings, while private, were not best suited to lovemaking. "Perhaps I could sit on the swing, and you could…."

"Ride you like the stallion Burke compares you to?" Cade said with a lascivious grin. "I can do that." He stood up, toed off his boots, and dug into his pocket for a jar of lotion before dropping his pants to the ground. "Get comfortable, because I intend to take you for a long, *hard* ride."

Erick could feel his cheeks heating, but Cade's suggestion sounded almost perfect. He made quick work of removing his gun belt to set beside Cade's and stripping his clothes. Tossing them over the back of the swing, he sat and beckoned to Cade. "Let me prepare you, and then you may judge how adept a rider I am."

Cade set one foot on the edge of the swing, opening himself to Erick's hands and gaze. "I thought I was the one doing the riding," he said.

"This time." Erick pulled Cade between his spread legs. "Lean down so I may kiss you." As fiercely as Cade plundered his mouth, Erick couldn't say which of them controlled the kiss, but he was not one to argue with such heady results. He somehow managed to uncap the jar and dipped his fingers inside, rubbing the lotion between them before tracing them along the crease between Cade's cheeks. He teased around the pucker and slid a finger inside slowly to gauge Cade's reaction.

"Feels so good," Cade groaned. "Not as good as you're going to feel when I finally get on your lap, but still good."

"Let us see if I can make it feel better still." Erick added a second finger, circling until he found the spot he was searching for.

"Fuck!" Cade's gasps of pleasure were hard for Erick to resist, but he needed to be sure Cade would feel nothing but joy when he finally slid inside him, so he worked in three fingers and spread them until Cade was moaning to stop fucking around and just fuck him already.

Erick scooted to the front of the swing to give Cade as much space to put his legs as possible. "Can you climb on?"

Cade grinned at him before stepping onto the swing and lowering himself into a squat that ended with him hovering directly over Erick's cock. "You'll have to guide me the last little bit. I can't quite see where I'm going."

Erick wiped what was left of the lotion from his fingers over his cock, a gasp escaping at the sensation. He squeezed around the base as he aligned himself, determined to give Cade the long, hard ride he'd promised. "Ease down," he murmured, holding on with one hand as he grasped Cade's shoulder with the other.

Cade sank down, taking Erick in all the way to the root. His eyes closed, his lower lip caught between his teeth, his face was the picture of ecstasy, and Erick had to bite his own lip to stop himself from finding completion at the sight of Cade's bliss and the tight heat surrounding him. Cade's shout when Erick pushed up into him, pressing just that little bit deeper, was surely loud enough to be heard back at the bunkhouse, making Erick glad Michele was guarding their privacy.

Planting his feet to brace them, Erick caught Cade's head and pulled him down into a kiss that stole both their breaths. When he could bear to tear himself away, he nuzzled Cade's ear. "Ride 'em, cowboy."

Cade let out a sharp bark of laughter that nearly unseated him from his perch on Erick's lap. "Really, Erick?" he asked even as he began to post on Erick's cock.

"I have always wanted to say that." Erick slid his palms down Cade's chest and caught his hips, pushing up as Cade bore down, settling them into a perfect gait. As much as he longed to draw out the moment, to heighten Cade's pleasure, it was too intense to last. "I am close," he groaned, clasping Cade's cock and hoping he could hold out long enough to see the flush of climax on Cade's face.

"Then you better fuck the come out of me now," Cade ground out. "Come on, Erick. Make me feel it tomorrow."

"I would rather make you feel it now," Erick gasped. There was no lotion left on his hand, but Cade was leaking enough to ease the friction as Erick stroked him fast and hard. "Now, Cade, now!" He held on just long enough for Cade to stiffen and cry out, spilling hotly through his fingers, before his own release tore through him and his eyes fell closed on the vision of Cade's face suffused with pleasure.

Cade slumped forward against Erick's chest. "Damn, I needed that. It's been too long." He nuzzled Erick's jaw and worked his way across for a kiss, which he lingered over. "You're a good ride, Erick Heller. Even better, you're a good man."

Erick bit off a moan as Cade pulled back enough to slide free and dropped beside him on the swing, slinging his legs over Erick's. He ran his palms against the burr of stubble on Cade's cheeks and turned his head to claim another kiss. "Perhaps next time you will let me take the saddle."

"Time and place, sweetheart. You name them and I'll be there," Cade said.

Tomorrow wouldn't be too soon for Erick, but he didn't suppose they could rely on Michele's kindness to stand watch for them every night. "You would know better than I where might be safe. Perhaps Payne will schedule us both to herd duty on occasion."

"Hey, none of that. It's not a question of safety here at Wellspring." Cade bumped his shoulder against Erick's. "Only of whether we'll be interrupted. We all walked in on Kit and Mac at one time or another before Payne moved them into the foreman's cabin, and yeah, we gave them shit for it, but that's all. It's more that it's private. Hell, if we told the others we were going to the barn and to leave us alone, they would. We'd just hear about it later. So when I said time and place, I meant it. I want to be with you, even if that means putting up with their teasing."

Erick swallowed down the swell of emotion warming his chest. Cade's acceptance, the acceptance of everyone at Wellspring, was everything he had scarcely allowed himself to dream he'd find when leaving his old life behind. "I have always had to hide my desires," Erick admitted. "I had hoped to find more freedom in America, though it is still hard to trust I have found such tolerance. I fear I may be slow to overcome my instinct to concealment. But if the worst we have to endure is Burke's comments, it is a small price to pay."

Cade pressed a kiss to Erick's lips, the movement tugging the drying hairs on his belly. "We should clean up before we head back. No need to give Burke any more ammunition. The stream shouldn't be too cold—race you!" Considering the unfair advantage Cade had by being on top, Erick allowed himself to enjoy the view of his magnificent buttocks before rising to join him.

They rinsed and slicked themselves dry as best they could before dressing. Erick picked up the unopened schoolbooks with one hand and, after only a moment's hesitation, extended the other. Cade smiled and threaded their fingers together as they headed back toward the bunkhouse.

Michele met them at the head of the trail with a raised eyebrow when she saw their joined hands. "See, *louveteau*. I told you all would be well. Do not make me play matchmaker again. It doesn't suit me."

Cade shot Erick an affectionate smile. "I don't think that'll be necessary."

"I thank you for your assistance, Michele," Erick added, though he didn't release Cade's hand. "You must let me know how I can repay you."

"Just keep this one happy. It grows tiresome to listen to him whining."

"I don't whine!" Cade protested.

"But what if he doesn't like me?" Michele said. "But what if he isn't interested in me like that? But what if he just wants to be friends?"

"I didn't say any of those things," Cade objected.

"Perhaps not, but they were certainly implied in the things you *did* say," Michele replied imperiously. She turned to Erick. "I trust he knows where he stands in your esteem now?"

"If he does not, it will be my mission to convince him," Erick assured her. They had reached the bunkhouse, and though Erick drew a steadying breath, he did not release Cade's hand. It was time to prove that the acceptance he'd been assured he would find among the hands was real. Cade squeezed lightly, and Erick opened the door. What was the worst anyone could say?

"Hoss! And Wolfie! I didn't think you had it in you." Next to Erick, Cade glared at Burke and headed toward the table in the center of the room, not letting go of Erick's hand. "Then again, neither one of you's walking funny, so maybe you didn't have it in you."

"Ha ha, Burke. You're so funny. What's next? Going to ask for all the gory details? You're just jealous because unlike some of us, you're not getting any and have to get your jollies through those of us who are."

Before Erick could say anything, another hand sat up from his bunk. Matt Chiles, Erick thought his name was—he hadn't had much interaction with him since he and Jesse Beaufort often rode the herd together. "Hey now, can't we just be happy for Cade and Erick? I for one will be glad for anything that improves Cade's mood." His wide smile took any sting from the words.

"Indeed," Svensen boomed from across the bunkhouse, "any bond that ties us more deeply to one another must be celebrated, although

I doubt Payne would appreciate us breaking out the whiskey when JR threatens. Still, we must encourage this new development."

"I was just joking," Burke grumbled. "They know that. Right, boys?"

Cade looked mutinous, but Erick set the books on the table and gave Burke a level stare. "Perhaps you should reserve your attempts at humor for those who appreciate them. Though I am not certain whom those may be." He gave Cade's hand a final squeeze before releasing it to walk to his bunk. "In any case, I must sleep. I have two more horses to finish training before Payne will allow me to ride with the herd."

Erick stretched out on his mattress as Cade swaggered from the table to his own bunk, the sway of his hips bringing back the memory of Cade riding him. He rested his hands behind his head and smiled. While he was hesitant to believe what he and Cade had shared could grow into the relationship he dreamed of, at the moment he was quite satisfied.

Chapter Twenty-Two

Boom!

The echo of a rifle shot tore Cade from a sound sleep. He grabbed for his gun belt as he rolled from bed, sticking his feet in his boots as he stood. He had the belt fastened around his waist before he was fully upright and his bow in his hand and his quiver on his back before anyone else had even gotten out of bed.

Crack! Crack!

"That's gunfire, you idiots! Hurry up!" he shouted as he raced for the barn. Things had been quiet with JR over the past two weeks, but it seemed their luck had run out. He whistled for Nahnia, left in the paddock for the night, glad again that he'd trained the horse with and without saddle and bridle. The moonlight glinted off the buckskin's hide, his mane and tail all but invisible in the darkness, as Nahnia cantered toward him. He opened the paddock gate to let Nahnia out, swung onto his back, and dug his heels in, driving him to a full-out gallop toward the northeast, where Kit and Mac kept the night watch. Chel and Olav were guarding the southern pastures, too far away for a gunshot to be heard from the bunkhouse. The others would follow as they could. Cade wasn't leaving his friends without backup for any longer than necessary.

Cade was impressed to see Erick alongside Chiles and Beaufort riding toward him. Like Cade, Erick hadn't taken the time to saddle Zephyr; he was riding one of the mustangs he'd been training, with only a rope halter. No saddle meant no place to holster his rifle, so he was armed only with the pistol at his hip. He'd shown himself nearly as accurate with the smaller weapon, though Cade sincerely hoped this didn't turn into a gunfight.

With a nod to Beaufort, Chiles took off in the opposite direction Cade was riding, leaving Erick to join him as if he'd been part of their team for far longer than just over a month. Erick didn't speak, letting them both focus on trying to hear or spot the source of the gunfire.

Fortunately the moon was waxing, giving them some light to see by. Even better, no more shots rang out, so whatever had caused the initial gunfire had not led to a full-on shootout. Cade sat back, the shift in his weight causing Nahnia to slow to a trot and then to a walk. Erick followed suit when Cade raised a hand to indicate caution. The herd was in sight, but he saw no sign of Mac or Kit. He gestured to the left, indicating they should ride that way since Jesse and Matt had gone to the right. They would cover more ground if they split up, but Payne didn't want anyone riding out alone, and given the gunshots they'd already heard, Cade understood the wisdom of those orders.

A few moments later they heard hoofbeats approaching. Cade nocked an arrow and Erick had his hand on his pistol, but by the time the rider neared Cade could recognize Kit's horse, Scout. "Was that you shooting?" Cade asked.

"No, but it might have been Mac. We take turns riding the perimeter so we can both get some rest. He was bedded down a bit farther this way." Kit spurred Scout on, leaving Cade and Erick to follow. Cade couldn't hear anything other than their horses' hoofbeats, so whatever had led to the gunshots seemed to be dealt with. He only hoped nothing had happened to Mac. Kit wouldn't take it well if Mac had been injured again—or worse.

The sound of more horses approaching had Cade reaching for his bow again before the shadows resolved into Beaufort and Chiles. "Have you seen MacRae?" Cade asked when they were within earshot.

"No, should we have?" Beaufort replied.

"His bedroll is here," Erick called from where he'd ridden slightly ahead.

Cade frowned as they joined Erick. That wasn't a good sign. He turned toward the fence between Wellspring property and JR land, scanning for any movement, but a cloud blew across the moon, obscuring his vision. "Well, shitfire. I guess we're going to have to do this the hard way."

Before Cade could dismount, intending to track Mac on foot, Beaufort raised his rifle and fired into the air. "That should get his attention, if he's—" Kit glared, and Beaufort shrugged. "—within earshot," he finished.

There was no return fire, but Kit jumped the fence before even Cade could see anything in the darkness. He wondered if Kit's vision was really better than his, or if he was just that attuned to Mac, who

Cade finally spotted riding toward them with something draped across the saddle in front of him. Too small to be one of JR's men, at least.

"What the hell, MacRae?" Beaufort shouted. "You woke the whole ranch! What were you shooting at?"

"Saw something moving outside the fence line." MacRae urged his horse over the fence and flung a carcass on the ground. "Thought it might have been one of Reichardt's pricks, but it was just a coyote."

"Next time maybe look a little closer *before* you shoot and give us all conniptions?" Cade suggested. "I was having a good dream." Not to mention riding bareback at full gallop on a freshly fucked ass—he had found Erick working shirtless in the tack room and hadn't been able to resist temptation—wasn't exactly comfortable. He hadn't noticed it when his emotions were running high, but now that his pulse had settled, he could feel it and was planning a slower ride back to the bunkhouse.

"Sure, I'll just sneak up on any intruders and give them a chance to take a shot at me instead of picking them off from a distance, just to protect your dreams," Mac replied, his voice laden with sarcasm. "Because those are my top priority."

"Look, you know I didn't mean it that way," Cade said, because he wasn't actually a selfish prick. "But you gave us all a scare over nothing."

"No harm done," Matt interceded before Mac could spit back an angry reply. "Mac didn't know what was out there, and with Reichardt's threats, it's a natural reaction to be safe rather than sorry. But we might want to think about some way to let the night hands know if any of us have to approach them. We wouldn't want to shoot one of our own by mistake."

"One of our own wouldn't be prowling around outside the fences in the dark," Mac muttered, but he edged his horse closer to Scout after the bay jumped back onto Wellspring land. "Sorry, Kit. Didn't mean to cause a big stink."

"Don't apologize." Cade felt bad. Mac had been doing his job, even if it had turned out to be nothing. "You reacted to what you saw as a threat, despite what I said a minute ago. As for a signal, there's any number of bird whistles we could use." He ran through a couple he'd learned from the Comanche. "We can discuss it tomorrow and decide on one. For now, I vote for going back to bed."

"Jesse and I will round everyone else up," Matt volunteered. "We're on shift at the ranch tomorrow, not out with the herd, so we have an easy day. You and Heller need your rest more than we do—especially since Heller's riding the range for the first time tomorrow," he added with a grin.

Cade waved his thanks and turned Nahnia back toward the bunkhouse at an easy lope that wasn't too rough on his ass. "Nothing like a little excitement to liven up the night," he said to Erick as they rode back.

"I prefer our earlier excitement to this," Erick replied dryly, and Cade couldn't help but laugh. "Though I anticipate tomorrow may hold its own excitement. I look forward sharing my first experience tending the herd as a true cowboy with you."

"Yeah, me too. But we'll have time to ourselves again tomorrow. Ourselves and a few hundred head of cattle, anyway."

IT FELT like he had barely closed his eyes before the clang of the triangle announcing breakfast woke Erick from his sleep. The sun was scarcely high enough to cast any light into the bunkhouse, so he scrambled into his clothes, spotting Cade shrugging his quiver over his shoulder before he headed out the door with a wink. Erick resisted the urge to hurry after him, though he didn't resist the smile that spread across his face at Cade's sauciness. As much as he wanted to spend every possible moment with Cade, he could not ignore the threat to his new home. Erick buckled on his gun belt and retrieved both the pistol from beneath his pillow and the rifle from beneath the lower bunk. After a moment, he opened the storage chest and drew the knife from inside and slid it into one of his boots. He hoped he wouldn't need any of his weapons, but with the tension gripping everyone at Wellspring, he decided to err on the side of caution.

Breakfast was a tense, somber affair, as if the middle of the night gunfire had been more than a false alarm, making Erick wonder if the news had not made the rounds that it had been just that, or if something else had happened that he was unaware of.

"Is aught amiss?" he asked Javier when it was his turn to fill his plate.

"Kit and Mac haven't checked in this morning," Javier replied. "They could simply be waiting for you and Cade to relieve them, but usually they'd be back for breakfast."

"We will eat quickly and go to find them," he promised before spotting where Cade was sitting. He slid into the space beside him, some of his tension easing as Cade leaned against his shoulder. As eager as he was to experience his first day as a true cowboy, this was not the way he would choose to begin it. Could something have happened to the two hands after they left them? Still, with Cade at his side he felt he could face anything. "Do you know that Logan and MacRae have not returned?" he asked.

"Yeah," Cade said grimly. "After a night shift, Mac's ugly mug is usually first in line." He gulped the last of his coffee. "Are you riding Zephyr or the paint today? I'll get the horses ready while you finish eating."

Erick stuffed the last piece of bread on his plate into his mouth and swallowed it quickly. "Zephyr, but I will saddle him. He has not been handled as much since I started working with the mustangs, and I would not want him to kick or bite you." He had hopes of getting his hands on Cade's body again later, and letting his horse injure him would hardly be conducive to those plans.

"Let's go, then. It's probably nothing, but I won't sit easy until I see them safe with my own eyes."

They headed to the barn and readied their horses with an economy of movement that spoke of their agitation and then they were on their way, retracing their route from the night before at almost the same speed.

They found Logan and MacRae in the same place they had left them. "You weren't at breakfast," Cade said, half observation, half question.

"Sorry to worry everyone, but we saw riders on the fence line just before dawn and didn't want to leave the herd unattended," Logan said. "Now that you're here, we'll head back in and let everyone know we're safe and what happened. I know you always do, but keep a sharp eye out today. I've got a bad feeling."

So did Erick, but he kept it to himself, nodding at MacRae and Logan as they mounted and rode away. He turned his attention to Cade, who sat at seeming ease on his horse, but Erick had come to know him well enough to sense the coiled tension beneath his calm mien. "You must instruct me in what to do." He brought Zephyr to a walk beside the smaller buckskin.

"Depends on whether Kit's bad feeling is right," Cade replied. "If it isn't, we keep each other in sight and keep an eye on the herd. If it is, we deal with whatever happens the best we can. And we hope like hell Kit's wrong because even if his bad feeling is a stampede instead of JR hands causing trouble, two of us against several hundred head of cattle is pretty bad odds."

Erick regretfully set aside his hope of sharing any intimacy with Cade. Perhaps another day they might steal some time together, but he would not put Cade or the herd at risk by contributing anything but his full attention to their surroundings.

Fortunately the morning was quiet. They spotted a section of downed fence tie, but it did not appear that any of the cattle had jumped the sagging rails, and Cade was able to repair it with a few nails and a small mallet from his saddlebag. They dismounted long enough for a quick lunch of sandwiches Javier had provided to Cade. Instead of sitting across from Erick as he'd done during their trip to Wellspring, Cade sat down close enough that their thighs touched, bringing back thoughts of the day before. Erick leaned into Cade's side as they ate, relishing the opportunity to be close to Cade with no one around. The eager way Cade lifted his face for a kiss only reinforced Erick's delight at the chance. Sooner than he would have liked, Cade sighed and rose. Erick followed, duty reasserting itself, and they were riding again.

The dry, flat land all looked the same to Erick, but Cade pointed out features like the line of scrubby trees that marked the creek's path and described a remote waterfall on the south side of the ranch where he promised to take Erick one day. He also showed Erick the mounds of dirt thrown out from the burrows of prairie dogs. To Erick's delight, one of the creatures popped out of its hole to chitter at them, and Cade laughed at his excitement.

"Not enough meat to make 'em worth shooting," he said. "Just be careful your horse don't step in one of their holes. It could bust a leg."

Erick wouldn't wish that on any horse, and especially not on a horse like Zephyr, so he kept an eye out for the holes as they continued their ride. While Cade still had so much to teach him, he delighted in being able to ride with him as a near-equal.

He couldn't have said, later, what set off the knot of cattle grazing a little way off from the rest of the herd, but one minute all was quiet and the next, half a dozen cows and calves had bolted. Before Erick could react, Cade spurred Nahnia forward, unspooling a long whip from a hook on his saddle. Its crack rang out across the whole valley as he snapped it over the heads of the runaway animals. Nahnia raced toward them, Cade moving in concert with him, and then to the side. The whip cracked again, and the cows veered away from it, beginning to turn back toward the rest of the herd.

Cade's "hyah" could be heard even over the pounding hooves as he leaned closer over Nahnia's neck. If anything, the cow pony seemed to pick up speed as he passed the cattle. Cade spun Nahnia almost on his heels to face the oncoming rush and cracked the whip again. The cows shied away from it, and Cade drove forward, sending them back toward Erick and the rest of the herd.

Erick didn't have a whip, and couldn't wield it with Cade's expertise if he did, but he didn't need to watch helplessly either. He dug his legs into Zephyr's side, urging him forward to circle the runaway cattle on the opposite side from Cade. For a moment he thought the stampeding cows would overrun him, but he stood his ground and echoed the "hyah" Cade had shouted as loudly as he could. The cows veered away and, bracketed by Cade on one side and Erick on the other, began to trot back toward the rest of the cattle.

The herd mooed and shifted as the runaways rejoined them. "Thanks for catching them," Cade said, panting slightly from the exertion of the hard, fast ride. "You slowed 'em enough they didn't set off the whole herd. That woulda been a mess, with just two of us out here trying to stop them. Let's hope that's the worst of Kit's bad feeling."

"I could not let you face them alone," Erick answered, "though I do not doubt you could have managed them without my help. You were magnificent. Are all cowboys as proficient with a whip as you are, or is that another skill you learned from your adoptive family?"

"No, that's a skill I learned after I left home," Cade replied. "The Comanche stampede bison, but they don't use whips. They'll shout and wave hides and things to scare them, and then ride alongside to herd them, but that's all."

"There is so much I must still learn." If he could hope to attain half the abilities Cade seemed to embody innately, he would deserve to consider himself a true cowboy. Still, Cade said he'd had to learn to use a whip, no matter how effortless—and arousing, if Erick were honest with himself—he made it appear now. With effort, Erick could aspire to become nearly as adept.

"You will." Cade's utter confidence resonated in his voice. "Nobody was born knowing all this shit. We all learned it, and you will too."

Cade drew Nahnia alongside Zephyr, so close his leg brushed against Erick's, and leaned across the remaining distance. "Anything you need," Cade said before pulling Erick into a soft kiss.

Erick leaned into the kiss, grateful for the solitude that allowed them this intimacy. "With that incentive," he asserted, "I will be sure to do so."

Late in the afternoon, Cade tensed and reached for his bow. Erick unhooked his rifle and set it across his lap as he scanned the horizon to see what had set Cade off. It took several moments of searching before he finally found the black specks on the horizon that resolved into riders.

"I'm tired of them watching us," Cade said. "Let's go see what they want."

"Is that a good idea?" Erick asked.

"Probably not, but as long as we stay on our side of the fence and don't draw first, they can't say we started it." Cade spurred Nahnia into a ground-eating canter. Erick sighed and urged Zephyr to follow.

They rode within a cautious distance before the four riders on the other side of the fence drew their pistols. Cade reined Nahnia in, and Erick halted Zephyr beside him. He recognized one of the riders as Adam Carter, and another as the man who had accompanied Reichardt the day he'd appeared at Wellspring to try to coerce Grace into accepting his suit. He'd been too on edge at the time to remember the man's name.

Cade had his bow in hand but no arrows, although Erick knew how fast he could put one to the string and shoot. He would bet the JR riders didn't, but that wasn't particularly reassuring at the moment. He kept his hands on the reins, taking his cues from Cade for now.

"Did you fellas need something?" Cade asked. "We been seeing you on our fences for a few days now."

"Just checking the lay of the land," Carter replied. "Gotta make sure nobody's going where they don't belong."

"Does that go both ways?" Erick asked. "Or does that only apply to Wellspring riders crossing onto JR land?"

Cade shot him a surprised look, but Wellspring was Erick's home now, and he was as protective of it as he'd ever been of his estate in Prussia.

"Buncha mutts and bitches got no right squatting on land that oughta be part of the JR." The rider Erick had seen at Wellspring spat a stream of tobacco juice over the fence, barely missing Cade. Erick's hand dropped to the rifle in his lap, but Cade shook his head.

"We don't want to be the ones starting anything," he said quietly, then raised his voice to address the JR riders. "Miz Roarke is the lawful owner of Wellspring, and if we catch any of you trespassing on her land, we'll have the law on you."

"You do that," the man called out, laughing. The whole group of them seemed to find Cade's threat funny. "I'd like to see Lutz and our crew bash a few of your heads in. Nobody'd miss a few injuns and colored and furriners, would they, boys?"

"Clean the place up for people with the right to run it," another agreed.

"I'd take any one of those 'bitches' and 'mutts' and free black men and proud immigrants over any ten of you in a fight any day," Cade said. "As for Lutz, he ain't the only law in Texas, just the closest. You'd do well to remember that."

"You're one of the first I'd take out, squaw," the first man retorted.

Erick really needed to learn the lout's name, because he was going to have a reckoning with him one day. "You are so sure of what you mean to do. Have you taken over from Reichardt, then?"

"Who the fuck are you?" he blustered. "Just off the boat, aintcha? Oughta know better than to take up with trash like this redskin."

"My name is Erick Heller," he answered, knowing his accent marked him as an immigrant, as worthless as Cade or the others he had denigrated in the JR hand's view. "What is yours, my friend?"

"Frank Sanders, and I'm no friend of anyone working for Wellspring."

"Be assured that your sentiments are wholly reciprocated." Sanders seemed to be working on whether that was an insult or not. Erick glanced at Cade. "We should check the rest of the herd, perhaps?" He knew he had no right to give Cade orders, but if he had to listen to Sanders's ignorant ranting any longer, he was likely to do something he'd regret later.

Cade tugged on Nahnia's reins, making the horse take a step backward without turning from the fence. Erick would have to teach Zephyr that trick, as it let Cade continue to keep watch while moving away.

The JR outfit jeered, but Erick did his best to ignore them. Then Sanders pulled his pistol and fired a shot into the ground inches from Nahnia's hooves. The horse twitched but didn't rear. Cade looked over at Erick with a subtle shake of his head as he angled his bow. "Get ready to run like hell," he muttered out of the corner of his mouth.

Erick tensed in the saddle, waiting for Cade's signal. Almost faster than his eye could follow, Cade grabbed an arrow, drew, and fired, the shot knocking the pistol from Sanders's hand.

"Go!" he shouted to Erick, wheeling Nahnia and spurring him into a full gallop. Erick leaned low over Zephyr's neck and did the same.

Shock at Cade's shot kept the JR outfit from returning fire immediately, but it didn't take long before shots rang out behind them. Erick ducked even lower, bracing for the possibility of the burn of a bullet in his back, but their adversaries seemed not to have Cade's aim, fortunately.

Once the gunfire ceased, Erick slowed Zephyr to a walk and glanced over his shoulder. None of the JR hands had jumped the fence line, though they hadn't moved off either, continuing to shout taunts and laugh raucously. Erick's instincts insisted he do something to drive them away, but unless they crossed onto Wellspring land, he could take no action. Swallowing his frustration, he resecured his rifle and turned his attention to a much more agreeable sight, his gaze raking Cade's body for any sign he'd been injured and breathing in relief when he confirmed he was unharmed.

"A most impressive shot. I could not have made it even with a rifle. I assume you meant to hit his gun, of course," he added, holding back a smile.

"Oh, if I'd meant to hit Sanders, he'd be dead," Cade said with a tight grin, "but then we'd have a range war on our hands, and Miz Roarke would fire my ass. As it is, all I did was disarm someone who shot at me first. And I even left him all his fingers. Which, maybe I shouldna done. Maybe I shoulda shot a couple of 'em off, just to teach him a lesson."

"That would make you no better than they are, and you are a finer person than that." Erick respected how well Cade had reined in his temper when he'd come so close to losing his own. He bit back a sigh. "I like this not. They will not be satisfied with insults and close shots much longer, I think."

"Kit and Mac will tell Payne about the riders, and we can let him know things have escalated when Chel and Jesse come to take the next watch." Cade ran a hand through his hair and settled his hat lower on his head. "But you're right. Things are going to get ugly soon."

Erick was afraid Cade was right, but there was nothing either of them could do to defuse the situation. They would simply have to stay vigilant and do their best not to inflame matters.

Chapter Twenty-Three

THE REST of their watch passed quietly, and Michele and Beaufort arrived exactly on time. Cade explained quickly what had happened. They reacted with grim-faced anger, as Erick had expected, before sending Erick and Cade back toward the ranch house.

Once they got their horses settled, Cade turned to Erick. "I have to find Payne and tell him what happened, but you can head to the shower and start cleaning up for dinner if you want."

"Perhaps you would care to join me?" Erick had been riding a low thrum of desire since watching Cade's prowess with his bow, and while they couldn't count on Michele to stand guard for them, he found he didn't care. Cade had assured them that no one would go beyond teasing if they saw them together, and Erick was willing to take that risk. "I can gather clean clothes for us both while you speak with Payne."

Heat flashed in Cade's eyes as he grinned. "I'd love to join you. Make sure someone sees you getting my things as well so they'll know to leave us alone. There are limits to what we can get up to in the shower, but I'm sure we can come up with something."

"I have confidence in your resourcefulness." Erick glanced around the barn, but there was no one but Biscuit and the horses to see them. He pulled Cade into a quick kiss, far shorter than he wanted, but they would have time to indulge in the shower. And for him to get his hands over all the parts of Cade's body he hadn't been able to linger over—until now.

Cade licked his lips, testing Erick's resolve, but before he could move in again Cade swatted his seat. "Stop tempting me. I can't report to Payne with a hard-on. Get our clothes and I'll meet you there." He grinned over his shoulder as he headed out of the barn. "Besides, I'm a sure thing."

Erick admired his backside as he sauntered out—he was fairly sure Cade was swaying his hips knowing Erick was watching—and took a few breaths before heading to the bunkhouse. He didn't need to provide any more ammunition for banter by appearing visibly aroused himself. If he was fortunate, most of the hands would already have left for dinner.

Fortune was not with him. Burke was changing into a fresh shirt when Erick walked in. Erick ignored him as he pulled out a set of clean clothes, but when he bent to the chest at the foot of Cade's bunk, the blacksmith cackled.

"Hoss!" Burke exclaimed. "Going through Wolfie's things already? You're moving fast there, my friend. I'd better start designing that cabin for you."

"Why do you not build one for yourself?" Erick asked. "Surely it would be more peaceful for everyone."

"Because if I did that, I'd miss out on all the good gossip," Burke replied with an insouciant shrug. "And then how would I get what I need, hmm? No, this way I hear everything and people cooperate with me to shut me up or to learn what I know."

Erick's gut clenched at the thought of who Burke might tell about him and Cade and what might happen as a result. Burke blustered right on as if he hadn't just scared a decade off Erick's life.

"Only here at Wellspring, of course. Those JR bastards don't have anything I want and couldn't pay me enough to get anything I have, knowledge, skills, or finished products."

"I fear payment is not in their plans." Erick had not considered it until now, but Burke's resourcefulness could prove of value to JR's owner. "We were fired upon today. They stayed outside the fence, but had we not ridden off, they might well have done serious harm." The memory of the insults Sanders had hurled angered Erick as much as his bullets. "Cade is informing Payne, but it would do well for everyone to be more vigilant. They may not respect Wellspring's boundaries much longer."

Burke sobered and picked up a gun belt from the table to strap around his waist, the first time Erick had ever noticed him wearing a pistol. "They won't find Wellspring an easy target, not even the ones who aren't usually fighters. And take your time cleaning up. I'll make sure you and Webster aren't disturbed."

The change in demeanor startled Erick, and he nodded sharply. As annoying as Burke could be at times, he was clearly loyal to Wellspring and, despite his sometimes crude comments, loyal to his fellow ranch hands as well. "*Danke.*" He bundled Cade's clothes along with his own and started toward the shower block. Svensen was coming out as he entered, the towel wrapped around his waist threatening to slide off completely as he rubbed his hair with another.

"Enjoy your shower, Heller." His voice was loud enough to announce Erick's destination to half the ranch, and the wink he gave as he turned to the bunkhouse made Erick wonder if that was his intention.

Erick shook his head and dropped the bundle of clothes on the bench. So far Cade had been correct about the other hands' reaction to their—Erick wasn't sure what to call it even in his own thoughts. *Their relationship*, he hoped, though he wasn't sure Cade would consider it the same when he had only ever referred to physical intimacies, not emotions. For now he would just enjoy the time they could spend together and consider himself blessed.

He had just started to undress when Cade walked in, tugging off the bandanna around his neck. It caught on the beads in his braid for a moment before he got it free, making Erick smile. The grim line of his lips softened when he looked up and saw Erick. "Let me do that?" he asked. "Payne is on the warpath and I don't know when we'll next have five minutes, much less an hour, to ourselves. Let me take advantage of the time we have now?"

Perhaps that was the answer to Erick's question. Pushing thoughts of the future aside, he determined to appreciate the moment and stepped close enough for Cade to reach him. "Only if I can return the favor," he murmured, opening the buttons of Cade's shirt. Moments later they were both naked beneath the cool water, and Erick drew Cade into his arms and into the kiss he had longed for all day.

Cade went easily into Erick's embrace, resting against him as he ran his hands over as much of Erick's skin as he could reach. He seemed especially interested in the breadth of Erick's shoulders—why, Erick wasn't sure, when they were nothing compared to Cade's—and to the damp curls of hair on his chest. He licked across Erick's lips, tempting his tongue out to play.

Not that it took much coaxing for Erick to explore Cade's mouth, not when Cade's tongue tangled with his to return every caress. Erick let his hands wander where they would before settling over the firm curves of Cade's buttocks. Holding Cade against him, he drew his mouth along Cade's jaw, the prickle of stubble beneath the water's slickness shooting straight to Erick's groin. He pulled Cade to fit more tightly against him, gasping when their erections aligned against each other.

Cade rocked his hips in time with the movement of their kisses, keeping the pace slow despite the heat rising between them. Each time Erick tried to speed things along, whether the kiss or the frottage, Cade reined them in, until Erick finally broke and pulled back to gasp, "More. *Bitte.*"

Cade nipped at Erick's lower lip and spun him so Erick was facing into the water with Cade a line of heat along his back. He shifted to slot his cock into Erick's crease, the tip bumping the back of his balls. He settled one hand low and heavy on Erick's belly, holding him in place. The other he wrapped around Erick's aching erection. "I'm going to make you feel *so* good," he whispered in Erick's ear. "Keep your legs nice and tight. I won't take your ass for the first time in the shower when we're rushed, but I'm going to fuck you just the same."

Erick bit back the groan that tried to escape at the slow drag of Cade's hand along his cock and the press of Cade's erection against his balls. He arched back, trying to mold against Cade's skin, locking his legs to give Cade more friction to rub against, but it wasn't enough. "Want to touch you." He twisted his head, but he couldn't reach Cade's lips. "Need to kiss you."

Cade wrapped around him even more tightly, carding his fingers through the hair on Erick's chest and bringing his mouth within reach, although the angle was awkward. "You took such good care of me yesterday in the barn. Let me return the favor." He punctuated his request with a thrust of his hips that dragged the head of his cock over Erick's entrance and a twist of his wrist at the top of his stroke so his fingernail caught the delicate tendon, making Erick gasp and writhe in his arms. "That's it, darlin'. Sing for me."

"Cade." Between gasping breaths and wet, clumsy kisses, Erick rocked between Cade's hand and his cock, groaning his name. "Cade, *ja*, please, more, Cade, more…." He could only hope it was as good for Cade as he chased his release. The head of Cade's cock nudged his entrance again and Erick was gone, lost in a flood of pleasure. He leaned back against Cade, his legs suddenly boneless as he spent himself over Cade's hand.

A moment later Cade tensed and shook behind him and wet heat coated his skin as Cade bit his shoulder to muffle his groan. Cade stayed where he was for a few heartbeats, keeping them both steady, then slowly he pulled back until he could get a hand between them. He worked a finger down Erick's crease and across his hole, making him shiver. "So sensitive," he murmured. "I'm gonna have so much fun with you when we have the time and privacy to really explore. Ever had anyone open you up with his tongue?"

The image was enough to make Erick's cock twitch again. He twisted in Cade's arms and seized his mouth, trying to imagine what it would feel like, imagining his head buried between Cade's cheeks, licking and sucking and—"We have to ride into town. The things I want to do to you"—the things he wanted Cade to do to him—"we need privacy for."

"You like that idea," Cade said around a low chuckle. "Good, because I like doing it." He teased around Erick's rim a little more. "I'm going to love doing it to you. And then you're going to tell me everything else you like having done to you or have always wanted a lover to do and I'm going to do every one of them until you can't move without feeling me in every inch of your body. I'm going to treat you like you've never been treated before."

Erick wanted to pull Cade to the ground and take him up on his sinful promises then and there, but the small part of his brain that was still rational held him back. Another part of him wanted to tell Cade how he ached for more than just physical pleasure, but that would be an even greater mistake, when that was all Cade was offering. He would take that and be grateful. Not knowing how to respond without revealing too much, he allowed himself one more kiss before drawing back to reach for a towel. "The next time Javier needs supplies, I will ask to escort him. I can tell Payne I need to return the books Miss Dawson lent me, and that you need to accompany me to select new ones."

"He'll agree to that because he'll want an extra gun or two on the supplies anyway." Cade still sounded breathless. It made Erick want to kiss him again, but they had been in the shower a long time and they were not the only ones who needed it. The dinner bell rang, settling the question. Cade grabbed his own towel and dried off quickly before pulling his clothes on just as fast and claiming a final quick kiss. "Let's eat. And then after dinner, we can do another reading lesson so we really can return those books to Miss Dawson."

"Perhaps we can progress beyond the letter E this time." Erick pulled down his shirt cuffs and started toward the dinner tables.

"No promises," Cade said with a smirk.

CHAPTER TWENTY-FOUR

"Webster!"

Payne's voice cracked in the humid air. Cade stopped on his way to join the line for dinner, grumbling inwardly at having to wait even another minute to see if Erick and Matt were back from their shift on the range. Cade knew he couldn't always be the one to work with Erick, but having Erick ride off this morning while Cade was stuck on guard duty had burned.

"We're missing cattle," Payne began bluntly. "Maybe they just got a wild hair and wandered off, or they coulda found a patch of locoweed and made themselves sick, or some of those JR bushwhackers mighta rustled them, I don't know. But it's more than I'm willing to lose without an explanation. You're the best tracker we have. I need you to find as many of them as you can and bring them back to the main herd."

Cade bit back a grin Payne wouldn't understand. "I'll do my best, but that's a big task for one man, if we're talking about more than a dozen head. It's keeping them together while still tracking the others."

Payne gave him a dry look. "And I suppose you have an opinion on who you should take with you?"

"Well, since you asked...." Cade shot him a grin. "The very first time he rode out with me, Heller helped me stop a stampede. He might look like a greenhorn still, but he's got more skills than his appearance suggests."

"If it keeps the two of you from getting up to trouble in my barn, I might consider it."

"I wouldn't call it trouble, exactly...." Cade refused to blush, refused to feel in any way guilty for jumping Erick in the stable when he'd found him working there shirtless a little over a week ago. "... but it would give Heller more experience than just a day or night on the range does."

"And of course you're the best one to teach him." Payne waved his hand dismissively. "The two of you leave in the morning. Take enough supplies for two weeks. With the size of Wellspring, finding a hundred cows on the land we don't graze on could take that long. If you haven't found the strays by then, you won't find them."

Cade nodded to acknowledge the orders and forced himself not to run off in search of Erick to share the good news. Two weeks. Two whole weeks alone on the range in the most isolated portions of Wellspring.

Two weeks of riding side by side, sleeping next to each other at night, with no one to interrupt or wonder what they were doing.

It sounded better than anything he'd be likely to find outside the eternal hunting grounds.

Erick wasn't in the bunkhouse, so Cade resigned himself to joining the line for dinner and sharing his news with an audience. Usually they went down to the spring after dinner, but with all the preparations they'd need to finish to leave tomorrow like Payne wanted, they wouldn't have that moment of privacy tonight.

He didn't have to tell anyone else he'd convinced Payne to send Erick along so they'd have some time together. He could simply say Payne had given him the orders to pass on to Erick. Everyone else might see through him, but most of them would let it ride. He just had to avoid Burke at dinner.

"Thanks, Javier," he said as the cook filled his plate. "Have you seen Erick?"

"No, he hasn't come through yet, although I did see Matt, so I'm sure he's around somewhere," Javier replied.

Cade frowned and went to sit with Chel and Svenson. At least Svenson wouldn't give him shit about heading out with Erick in the morning.

"Where's your shadow, *louveteau*?" Chel asked.

"I don't know," Cade replied. "He should be here soon."

A few minutes later, Erick joined them, his damp hair and pink cheeks evidence that he'd stopped to shower and change clothes after his shift on the range. Cade couldn't help but regret that he wouldn't have another chance to join him before they'd have to leave tomorrow.

"Any problems?" he asked once Erick sat and greeted everyone.

"A quiet day. It is good to work with more of the men and get to know them better." Cade might have envied the hands working with Erick, except that he was about to have him all to himself for two wonderful weeks.

"Yeah, Chiles is great. He's been here about a year, bounced around a bit before that, always leaving when yet another outfit didn't treat him good because he's black. I think he about cried when he first laid eyes on Payne," Cade said. "Kinda like the rest of us, not fitting in anywhere until we washed up here."

"Speak for yourself," Chel said airily. "I fit in anywhere I go."

Cade gave her a dismissive wave and focused back on Erick. "Payne grabbed me just before dinner. He has a job for us."

"Gathering more mustangs?" Erick didn't seem excited at the prospect. "I had hoped to spend more time working the herd before having another batch of horses to train."

Cade could feel the grin spreading across his face, but he didn't care. "No, he wants us to hunt down some stray cattle. Since you did such a good job with the ones that tried to get away when we worked together."

Erick flushed and shook his head. "I only followed your lead. But I look forward to another day to ride with you."

Both Svensen and Chel laughed. At Erick's puzzled expression, Olav explained, "If they are not to be found where we usually let them graze, it could be quite a lengthy search."

"Payne's given us two weeks," Cade said. "That'll give us time to check the backcountry if they've wandered there."

"And if JR hasn't rustled them," Chel said with a frown. "Be careful, both of you."

"You know I always am," he told her gently. And while he wouldn't say it out loud, he had Erick to look out for—and come home to—so he had more reason than ever to watch his back. "We'll have to skip our reading lesson tonight so we can get everything together and leave at first light."

He just had to figure out how to fit two weeks' worth of supplies into their saddlebags and still have room for their book and a pot of something slick. If he had two weeks alone with Erick, he wanted to take advantage of it.

"What must I prepare?" Erick asked.

"A change of clothes and food, mostly. There are a couple of spots we should be able to clean up where we'll be heading." Cade spent a moment imagining Erick naked under the waterfall before forcing his mind back to the matter at hand. "And your weapons, in case they haven't just wandered off."

"You can help me make sure I have everything after we finish eating," Erick said with a small smile, the one that *did things* to Cade's insides.

"Sure can," he drawled to cover the heat in his belly and probably on his face. At least the hotter, longer May days had tanned his skin enough to hopefully hide any visible blush.

Chel rolled her eyes at him, but he ignored her in favor of Javier's delicious dinner. They'd be back to jerky and beans tomorrow.

"THIS IS almost like the trip from Galveston," Erick said as they prepared the turkey Cade had brought down to augment their store of tinned beans and jerky.

"Except we aren't wasting all that time we could have been together," Cade said, sliding an arm around Erick's shoulder.

Erick leaned into the embrace. "And I am not as sore from having to become accustomed to a new horse and saddle."

"You should have said something." Cade squeezed Erick's shoulder. "We could have taken more breaks or had shorter days on our way to Austin."

"But then we would not have been in time to hear Reichardt's threats," Erick reminded him. "And while it might have been an easier adjustment for me, it would have been more of a struggle for Wellspring, and I cannot wish for that."

"No, I suppose not," Cade agreed. He poked at the meat in the skillet. "This looks done. We can smoke the rest while we're eating and it'll stay good for a few days while we travel."

"Should we have seen any cattle by now?" Erick asked.

"Depends on when they took off. They mighta been gone for days before Payne realized they were missing. And Wellspring has a lot of ground to cover. They coulda made quite a distance if they had a mind to. Not that anyone knows what goes through a cow's mind."

"You do not think that JR hands made off with them?"

Cade scowled. "I wouldn't put it past them, but we've kept a pretty close watch. Someone would have spotted it if they were brazen enough to rustle that many head all at once."

Erick nodded and speared a piece of meat out of the pan Cade had pulled off the fire and set on the ground in front of them. "So we will wander around hoping we find them?"

"Not quite," Cade said with a chuckle. "Wherever they went, they'll have left tracks. It hasn't rained much since the last big storm we had, so they shouldn't have been washed away. If we're lucky, they'll be all together and easier to track. If not, we may have to keep the ones we find together as we look for the rest. We'll just have to see when we find their trail."

"It sounds like quite the challenge."

Cade shrugged. "My family taught me to read the land, but yeah, it's a lot of ground to cover, hoping to find a sign."

They ate in comfortable silence for a few minutes. "I am sorry we did not bring the primers with us, but I would not risk them coming to harm when Miss Dawson was kind enough to lend them to us," Erick said when they had finished. "I brought a notebook and pencils should you wish to practice your letters."

"Practice my—" Cade laughed. "Did you seriously think I'd have the patience to practice my letters when I finally have you all to myself?"

"Practice makes perfect," Erick said with a quirk of his lips. Cade's answering grin made clear that he understood exactly what kind of practice Erick meant.

He tackled Erick back onto the ground and nuzzled below the collar of his shirt. "Drives me crazy," he murmured against Erick's skin. "Sleeves rolled down, shirt buttoned up, all prim and proper, when I know what's hiding underneath." He popped the top two buttons and rubbed his face against the hair that covered Erick's chest. Erick didn't really understand the fascination, but Cade was clearly fascinated.

Erick caught the beaded braid that tickled his skin and gently tugged Cade up until he could claim his lips. "Not everyone turns golden in the sun as you do," he countered, dropping kisses along Cade's cheek until he reached his ear. "Staying covered is preferable to burning, no?"

"At least no one else gets to see you all unbuttoned and rolled up," Cade growled when Erick nipped his ear.

Erick shuddered as the sound vibrated through Cade's chest above him and spread his legs a little so Cade could settle between them. He doubted the wisdom of disrobing completely out in the open like this, especially with the infernal bugs that had arrived with the summer heat, but even with layers of clothes between them, Cade's weight pressing him into the ground made him hope he would eventually get his desire. He ran his hands down the back of Cade's shirt to his finely toned buttocks and grabbed hold. "No one but you."

Cade kissed him, the deep, fierce kiss that felt as though he couldn't get enough of Erick's taste, and rocked his hips into Erick's. More than willing to take what Cade was giving, Erick gasped when Cade drew back. "We should bank the fire and move this to the bedrolls," Cade said, his voice sounding as ragged as Erick felt.

"Surely it is too warm to bury ourselves in bedding." Perversely, Erick felt the loss of Cade's warmth as he rose to his feet. "Perhaps we can arrange them side by side?"

Cade banked the fire quickly, so the embers would still be burning in the morning but without the risk of sparks, and turned to Erick. "I have a better idea." He spread his bedroll out flat, making a bed large enough for two. "Let me have yours."

When Erick handed it to him, he spread it on top of the first. "A little extra padding, just in case."

Erick would take all the extra padding he could since he fully planned to feel Cade on top of him tonight. He sat on the doubled bedroll and tugged off his boots. That was as far as he planned to disrobe on his own—he'd leave the decision of how much more to take off to Cade. Lying back, he folded his arms behind his head and smiled at Cade. "Let us practice, then."

Four days later, Cade found what he'd been searching for since they left Wellspring: hoofprints going away from the mess left by a full herd. "Here," he called to Erick. "They went this way."

Erick rode to where Cade had stopped Nahnia and peered at the ground before looking back at Cade. "What do you see that I do not?"

"Tracks," Cade said. "Hoofprints leading away from the herd." He pointed toward the bluffs that ran along the southern edge of Wellspring's land. "Those bluffs are treacherous, full of blind canyons and dry gullies that flood when we get a heavy rain. We generally don't run cattle on that section of the ranch unless we have no other choice."

They also hid Cade's favorite spot on the entire ranch. If his luck held, the missing cows had found the one watering hole in those hills. If not, they'd be finding carcasses instead.

"Could you not fence that section off?" Erick asked.

"I mean, I suppose we could, but it would be miles of fence line we'd then have to maintain. For the most part, the herd don't wander that way because there's not a lot of water, which means not a lot of grazing, but obviously the runaways weren't that smart."

It hadn't rained recently, so the tracks could be anywhere from a few days to three weeks old, but Cade didn't think Payne would have waited that long to send someone after the missing cows. Not with everything going on with the JR. No tracker caught every sign, but Cade didn't see anything to indicate the cows had been driven toward the bluffs—no horseshoe prints, nothing but cloven prints even outside the main trail, so a herd of mustangs (or band of Comanche) hadn't come through to startle them either. Whatever wild hair had gotten into the herd, Cade was pretty sure it was natural, not human.

The farther the trail led south, the more Cade's anticipation grew. If the tracks didn't veer off, they would lead straight to the waterfall where he'd imagined taking Erick since the day they met. He hadn't dared to hope they'd get there so quickly, especially not with JR's hands pressing them from all sides.

By late afternoon, Cade had stopped worrying about following the tracks and simply turned Nahnia toward the waterfall. They'd find the cows on the way or they'd find them there, he was sure, because the tracks made a beeline for the bluff where he could see the occasional glisten of light off water. "Do you see that?" he asked Erick, pointing toward the falls. "We'll make camp there tonight. The cattle should be there, but even if they aren't for some reason, we can clean up a bit, refill our canteens, and rest before searching more."

"I will look forward to the rest," Erick said. "Zephyr is not accustomed to such uneven ground. Perhaps one of the mustangs would have been less fractious, though I suppose it is best he become acclimated to it. He will not always be riding over flat rangeland."

"For sure," Cade said. "There's more rough terrain than flat rangeland around here, with the bluffs in the south and the hill country to the west. And if you went southwest, you'd end up in the desert, so that's not any better."

"I have hopes I may prove myself worthy enough to accompany you on the drive to bring the herd to market," Erick confessed. "I must demonstrate to Payne that I can do more than train horses."

"He didn't argue me bringing you with me on this roundup." *Much,* Cade added silently. "You have almost three months to convince him. That shouldn't be too hard."

"So long as he continues to include me on the range rotation, I will improve. I have learned much from each of the hands I have shared shifts with. They each have such different backgrounds and skills, and are most generous to instruct me."

They'd better have been sticking to the skills of a cowboy, Cade thought direly. If any of them had tried to instruct him on anything more personal…. Cade stopped himself. That thought wasn't fair to Erick. No, they hadn't made any overt promises, but they spent every moment together they could, and that was all Cade could ask, given the rotations on the range that they couldn't control.

"If you want, I could teach you how to use my bow."

Erick smiled. "I doubt I could match your proficiency even with much practice, but perhaps you could share your skill with a whip? It was most useful in redirecting the runaways when we rode together."

Cade set aside the image of pressing himself along Erick's back to help him learn how to hold and draw the bow, for the moment anyway. Maybe after the drive, when things were quieter and the weather kept the herd closer to home, he'd bring it back up. But Erick was right. In the short term, learning to use the bullwhip would be more useful. "When we get to the waterfall," he suggested. "You don't want to clip Zephyr with it by mistake while you're learning."

He shot Erick a mischievous grin. "Race you!"

Cade bent low over Nahnia's neck and gave the pony his head, his hat falling off in the breeze of his pace, only its cord keeping it from flying away. Despite Zephyr's longer stride, Cade pulled to a halt a length ahead of Erick, laughing.

"Considering you know this land and I do not, I am not certain that was a fair contest," Erick protested, though his eyes were sparkling. "It is as well we did not wager on the result."

Cade threw a leg over Nahnia's neck, slid to the ground, and prowled toward Zephyr's side, his eyes fixed on Erick's face. He didn't want to misread the situation and make Erick uncomfortable, but at the same time…. "What? You'd deny me a kiss for winning?"

Erick dismounted gracefully and raised a hand to cup Cade's jaw. "I would never deny you a kiss." He leaned forward to brush his mouth against Cade's, and Cade couldn't resist pulling him closer and sliding his tongue between Erick's lips.

Heat rose between them as it always did the moment they touched, and Cade saw no reason to resist, running his hands down Erick's back to cup his ass and snugging his leg up against Erick's balls so he was riding Cade's thigh. He released Erick's mouth to nip along his jaw toward his ear. "Maybe more than just a kiss?" He nibbled on Erick's earlobe.

"Perhaps after you demonstrate your prowess with the bullwhip, you could be persuaded to demonstrate your prowess in… other areas?" Erick was altogether too composed in Cade's opinion, but they had only a few hours of daylight left, and they didn't need the sun for the "other prowess" Erick was hinting at.

He stole another kiss before he stepped back, just to prove he could, intending to leave Erick as hopelessly turned on as Cade himself was, just from the kiss and the promise of things to come. He turned back to Nahnia and grabbed his whip from the saddle. Turning as he shook it out, he looked around the glen for suitable targets. He couldn't show off his skill without something to aim at.

The leaves of the scrub oak would work. "Three strikes, three oak leaves," he told Erick. Erick's gaze followed his hand as he flicked the whip once, a crack echoing back from the bluff as he caught the stem of a leaf with the tip of the whip and separated it from the tree. A second crack, a second leaf. He shot Erick a cocky grin and sent the tip of the whip skyward to pluck a leaf almost from the top of the tree.

"Is there anything you do not excel at?" Erick asked, shaking his head. "You must show me the way of it, though do not expect me to match your talent."

"Reading," Cade replied. "And writing. I don't excel at those." He recoiled the whip and handed it to Erick. "And it's not hard if what you're trying to do is get the whip to crack so the sound helps drive the cattle where you want them to go. Let the tail drop, bend your elbow to flick it behind you, then bring your arm forward sharply. The whip will do the rest."

Erick shifted the whip's handle in his palm a few times until he found a grip he seemed comfortable with. He swung the tail back and forth, then bent his elbow and swung the whip forward quickly, generating a respectable *crack*. He smiled warmly at Cade and cracked the tail a few more times before offering the handle back to him. "I see I must acquire one of these for myself. Though this skill is far easier to master than reading and writing. Do not denigrate your advancement in that regard. You have shown much proficiency already, and will only improve more with further practice."

Cade flushed at the praise—and at the memory of everything else they had done during their reading lessons. "You can find a whip at Miss Hart's mercantile," he said hoarsely, wondering if they could get back to the "other prowess" Erick had mentioned earlier now that he'd shown Erick how to use the whip. "Next time we go into town to get more books. Do you want to keep practicing while I make camp?"

"I do not suppose I shall need to match your accuracy, since the goal is not to strike the cattle but only maneuver them. I would prefer to assist you in setting up camp and preparing our meal." Erick glanced over his shoulder to the west. "We may still have an hour or more of daylight before we retire for the night, should you wish to practice… your letters."

Cade's pulse quickened along with his cock, because he'd heard that pause, and he was going to follow up on the promise in those heavy words. "Come on, then. Let me show you my favorite place on earth."

He led Erick around the bend in the bluffs to where they could see the waterfall and pool at its base. With the relatively low rainfall, the waterfall wasn't running hard, but it was still a steady flow, certainly enough that they could stand underneath it for a quick shower. And the pool at the base had enough water for a soak if they felt like it. The cool water would be refreshing after the heat of the day.

Erick took Cade's hand, twining their fingers. "I can see why this place is special to you. You are fortunate to have found such an oasis of beauty and peacefulness, and I am honored that you would share it with me."

There wasn't much Cade *wouldn't* share with Erick, given the chance, although he wasn't sure Erick was ready to hear that yet. He wasn't sure he was ready to say it. "I've been dreaming about bringing you here since the day we met." He could admit that because it was about sex, not emotions. "About stripping you out of your suit and finding out what was underneath."

"You have seen it now," Erick said with a shrug. "I find what is beneath your work garb far more alluring."

Cade stripped without hesitation and reached for Erick's buttons. "You're all flushed. We should cool off, don't you think?"

Erick's gaze slid over Cade's body like a caress before he shed his own clothing, folding it and setting on a rock clear of the fall's spray. "Seeing you unclothed is not likely to cool me off."

"The water would," Cade said, though he made no move to step into the pool or beneath the falls. He traced a finger from the base of Erick's neck down his chest to just below his navel. "Or I could get you even sweatier first."

"Even the coolest water would not temper my desire for you," Erick murmured, his body proving the truth of his statement. He nudged Cade in the direction of the falls, startling a yelp from him when the water, still cold from its underground source, splashed over them.

Cade pulled Erick beneath the water with him, then turned, keeping his hands on Erick's arms until they were back to front, Erick's arms around Cade, holding him close. Cade ground back against Erick, his cock a hard, hot line against Cade's ass. "Gonna bend me over the rocks and fuck me?"

Erick rutted against Cade, mouthing a string of kisses up his throat. "As tempting as it sounds, I have not the supplies nor the patience to prepare you." He turned Cade in his arms and sank gracefully to his knees. It was Cade's turn to yelp when Erick opened his lips around him, the warmth of his mouth a vivid contrast to the cool water showering over them.

He cradled Erick's head in his hands, caressing rather than guiding him, as Erick licked and sucked and generally did everything he could to drive Cade out of his mind. When Erick flicked his tongue over the slit, Cade almost lost it right there. He grabbed at Erick's hair. "Too much," he gasped. "Too fast."

A wicked grin was the only response Erick made as he gathered Cade's sac in one cool palm, his other hand pushing his ass closer, taking him deeper. Cade threw back his head and surrendered to the inevitable, shuddering as Erick swallowed around him. "Most refreshing," Erick said as he sat back on his heels and wiped the water from his eyes.

Cade's stomach did a slow roll at the idea that Erick had found getting him off refreshing, but he pushed it aside to focus on returning some of the pleasure Erick had lavished on him. He pulled on Erick's hands until he stood, then flipped them around so Erick leaned against the rocks. "My turn."

Erick pulled him into a kiss, the taste of himself on Erick's tongue whetting Cade's hunger. He lingered over the kiss, his own body sated. He was definitely going to get his mouth on Erick before long, but he didn't have to rush to do it, not when Erick seemed as lost in the kiss as Cade was.

When Erick bucked restlessly against him, Cade took it as a sign to get moving. He reluctantly released Erick's mouth to nibble his way down his neck, the salt of his sweat mixing with the slightly mineral flavor of the water. He licked at Erick's nipples until they hardened beneath his tongue. He might have stayed there longer, but Erick bit off a groan and pressed down on Cade's shoulders. Cade nipped once more, in gentle retaliation, before dropping to the ground. Erick's hard cock stood at attention, and Cade gave in to the desire to taste. He had wanted to get his mouth on Erick since… well, since they met if he was honest about it. Definitely since the first time they'd had sex.

Erick was heavy on his tongue as Cade drew him deeper, thick and leaking. He swallowed around the head, dragging another groan and a babble of incomprehensible words from Erick. Cade pulled back with a grin. "You sound so good." He gave the slit a quick lick. "You taste even better."

"Cade…," Erick rasped, burrowing his fingers into Cade's hair to push his head back down. Not that Cade needed the encouragement to swallow Erick down again. The garbled sounds grew in intensity until Erick stiffened and spasmed against him, and Cade drank him in, not releasing him until Erick's hand on his shoulder drew him away.

Licking his lips, Cade looked up to see Erick red-faced, his eyes downcast. "My apologies," he murmured, stroking Cade's hair. "I should not have pawed at you so."

Cade pushed to his feet and tipped Erick's chin up so their eyes met. "Paw at me all you want." Erick's expression didn't change so Cade leaned in and kissed him softly. "I grew up in a very different world than the one you did. There was no shame attached to sex with the Comanche, as long as both partners were willing. I *want* to know how good I'm making you feel."

"You make me feel things I have never felt before." Erick lowered his head, but raised it again a moment later. "I hope I am bringing you the same pleasure."

Cade reveled in the thrill of Erick's admission as he brought Erick's hand to his cock, which had tried valiantly to harden again while he was sucking Erick. "More than I thought possible."

"I as well." A gust of breeze wafted through the air, making Erick shiver. "Perhaps we should dress to prepare dinner. We have still cattle to find, after all. It would not do for us to fall sick and have to return to Payne without them."

Cade wasn't worried about falling sick. Once they were out of the water, the May heat would warm them back up quickly, but he let Erick retreat from the intensity of the moment. He gathered his dirty clothes to wash in the pool and let dry overnight and dug in his saddlebags for his clean set. He had just started to pull on his pants when he heard the distinctive lowing of cattle.

He shot Erick a grin. "I think the cattle have found us."

CHAPTER TWENTY-FIVE

CADE SHIFTED in the saddle as he and Erick rode shotgun on either side of the wagon Javier drove toward Eldorado. He scanned the horizon automatically, but they hadn't seen any sign of JR riders since crossing off of Wellspring land, and his thoughts, like his gaze, kept slipping back to Erick. After returning with the missing cattle, they had finally managed to finish the first of the books from Miss Dawson, at Erick's insistence. Despite the tension in the air, Cade couldn't completely smother the grin that rose to his lips at the memory.

"No, Cade, we should at least look at the book," Erick insisted.

"Why?" Cade asked, angling for a kiss. "I can think of much better ways to spend our time. Can't you?"

"Because I do not care to lie to Miss Dawson about your progress, or exchange this for a more advanced book you cannot read." He opened the book to the letter F—a frog, Cade could tell from the picture—and gave Cade a smoldering glance through his lashes. "Perhaps there is another way to solve this impasse. For each page you are able to spell out, I will allow one kiss."

Cade stumbled his way through the spelling more because he was too distracted by thinking about where he could kiss Erick than because he didn't recognize the letters, but in the end, he managed it and claimed his kiss—on the lips to start. By the time they got to L—a lamb, and really, silent letters should not be allowed—he'd gotten them both out of their shirts and kissed his way down Erick's chest to his waistband.

"I can see I should have defined kisses more clearly." Cade took pride in the hint of a tremor in Erick's voice.

"You didn't say anything about where I could kiss you," Cade countered as he turned to the next page. "Moon. M-O-O-N, moon." He nuzzled beneath the buckle of Erick's belt, swirling his tongue around the indentation of his navel, making Erick shiver.

"We are fortunate to have a full moon tonight. We will need its light for you to finish at this rate." Erick's voice was stern, but his eyes

crinkled in the secret smile Cade loved. "And I am not certain that can be considered a kiss."

"Then I'll just have to try again," Cade said as he flipped the buckle loose and closed his lips over the puckered skin. He licked and nibbled as Erick squirmed, making sure to keep his lips in contact with Erick's skin the whole time. "Was that better?" he asked when he finally lifted his head.

"I suppose that must be classified as a kiss," Erick conceded, his voice a bit deeper. He tapped the next page. "Now, apply yourself as thoroughly to your study of the alphabet."

Cade slid his hands beneath Erick, palming his ass through his thick pants. "I'd much rather study you. I have some promises to keep. You wouldn't want me to break my word, would you?" He traced Erick's crease with his finger. "Nest. N-E-S-T. I could make you feel so good, Erick."

The book page fluttered as Erick turned it, another telltale reaction. Erick could pretend to be unmoved, but Cade knew it was a game, one he was determined to win. "I am certain you could, but we have an objective to complete first. Focus, please."

"I didn't get my kiss," Cade insisted. "I spelled nest, so I get a kiss." He looked up at Erick for confirmation and approval. Yes, it was a game, but he needed to know Erick was still playing.

Erick's eyes twinkled as he inclined his head. The game was on, then. "We did agree." He leaned forward and brushed his lips lightly over Cade's. "There is your kiss. Now, proceed."

Cade rolled his eyes at the boring kiss but turned his attention to the owl, the pear, the queen—that was a hard one—and the rock and worked his way back down Erick's chest after each one. At snake, he grinned wickedly. "S-N-A-K-E." He plucked open the buttons on Erick's trousers, slid his hand inside, and drew out Erick's cock. Without breaking eye contact, he bent and dropped a feather-light kiss on the very tip.

He was sure that would break Erick's control, but though his grip tightened on the book, his voice remained even as he turned another page. "A clever analogy. Though I fear there is no comparing it with a tree."

"I could compare you to a tree," Cade said. "I would climb you like one if you'd let me." He thought about climbing into Erick's lap and riding him into oblivion again, but he wanted Erick to break and admit

he wanted it first. So he looked back at the page and spelled out "T-R-E-E" before kissing Erick's shaft.

With tongue this time.

Erick grasped Cade's shoulder, but rather than pulling him forward, he eased him back. "Six letters, Cade. Perhaps you could complete them before the moon sets as well as the sun."

"Or I could finish you instead," Cade replied, but he flipped the page and stumbled through spelling out umbrella—another sucking kiss to Erick's shaft—vase—a nibble at the base of his cock—and water—a nuzzle to his balls—but the next one stumped him.

"What the hell is that?" He pointed at the picture, frowning as if whoever had written the book were intentionally cock-blocking him.

Erick frowned too. "Xylophone. It is a kind of musical instrument. I am surprised it was chosen to illustrate a child's alphabet, but there are not many words that begin with X, even in German." He met Cade's frustrated gaze. "Can you read out the letters? Since it is such a long word, perhaps we may allow two kisses in compensation."

With that kind of motivation, Cade dragged his thoughts away from his aching cock and back to the letters on the page. He read them out and, when Erick nodded confirmation, took his first kiss from Erick's lips and his second by sucking Erick's balls into his mouth.

What? It was a hard word. He deserved a reward.

Erick seemed to agree, if his cut-off moan was any indication.

"Two more words," he rasped, trailing his fingers along Cade's jaw. "You have done so well. Let us finish now."

"Y-A-R-N," Cade spelled, preening beneath the attention. He pressed a kiss to Erick's inner thigh for that one, not because he didn't want to lean deeper and lick across his hole, but because if he did, he wouldn't stop, and he still had one more word. He flipped the page. "Z-O-O." Another word he didn't know, but he could sound it out. "Zoo?"

"Yes, it's—" Cade didn't care. He was tempted to toss the book aside, but Erick would fuss if he did that. Instead he plucked it from Erick's hand and set it aside carefully as he kissed Erick deeply and thoroughly while bearing him down to the ground. When Erick relaxed beneath him, Cade released Erick's mouth and dove for his groin again, taking Erick's cock as far down his throat as he could.

"It seems—unfair—" Erick gasped "—for you to have worked so hard and I alone reap the reward." He raised himself up on his elbows. "Turn about so I may please you as well."

Cade didn't need to be told twice. He scrambled around, unfastening his pants as he went, and when Erick took him into his mouth, he thought he'd died and gone to heaven. Determined to take Erick with him, he slid a finger in his mouth alongside Erick's cock to wet it and reached between Erick's cheeks to scrape across his hole. Erick jerked and moaned eagerly, adding to Cade's determination to lavish all the pleasure he possibly could on him. Erick hadn't said anything, but Cade was starting to suspect he hadn't had enough of it in his past. Cade couldn't change that, but he could damn well make sure Erick had a lifetime of it to look forward to!

"Pleasant thoughts?" Erick's voice broke Cade from his reverie, the glint in his eyes suggesting that he knew exactly what Cade was thinking about. He drew Zephyr closer, even though Javier's attention seemed focused on the road ahead of them. "I regret we will not be able to spend the night in town."

Cade regretted it too, but he shrugged. "If we didn't need supplies, Payne wouldn't even let us go into town. There's no reason for Javier to stay the night, and we can't let him drive the wagon back to Wellspring on his own."

"We will have other chances," Erick said. "Or other reading lessons."

Another lesson like the last one would kill Cade for sure, but he wasn't going to tell Erick that. Instead he licked his lips. "I'll have to think of other ways to kiss you, then. I wouldn't want to get predictable."

He didn't say it aloud with Javier within earshot, but he was going to get his mouth on Erick's ass at the next possible opportunity.

That made Erick laugh out loud. "You are anything but predictable, Cade. But perhaps for our next lesson it will be my turn to reward you."

As far as Cade was concerned, getting to rim Erick would be more than enough reward, but he kept that thought to himself. "I'm sure we can come to a satisfactory arrangement."

A cloud of dust on the horizon drew his attention. "How about we pick up the pace a bit, Trujillo?" he called to Javier. "The sooner we get off JR land, the happier I'll be."

Javier raised a hand in acknowledgment and snapped the reins over the team's backs. Riders could cover ground faster than a wagon and team, but the wagon was empty and the riders far enough off that they should be able to reach the border of JR's rangeland before having to face a confrontation.

He hoped.

Erick pulled his rifle from its saddle holster as the JR hands gained on them, his gaze moving between the riders and Cade. "Not unless they fire first," he confirmed, "but we will defend ourselves."

"Let's hope it doesn't come to that," Cade said as Javier slapped the reins against the team's rumps again. He hadn't seen Javier load the seven-barreled Nock gun, a family heirloom stolen off a Royal Navy ship that attacked his grandfather's vessel as he emigrated to Mexico, into the wagon before they left, but it would go a long way toward evening the odds if it came to a fight. Except they were on JR land and it would be their word against Reichardt's and Lutz would take Reichardt's side and then they'd all be fucked—and not in the lovely, cock up the ass kind of way. He looped Nahnia's reins around the saddle horn and set an arrow to his bowstring. They'd have to stop and reload rifles. He could keep shooting until he ran out of arrows.

"I'd rather not find myself in the middle of a shootout," Javier called over his shoulder as he urged the team to its limits. "How much farther until we're off JR land?"

"Just past that dry creek bed up ahead." Cade gauged the wagon's speed against the distance the riders had gained on them. They just might make it. "Course, that assumes they won't shoot even if we're off their property."

"Aren't you just full of joy and optimism?" Javier retorted. He drove the team toward the creek bed. Cade winced as the wheels bounced along the rutted trail and hoped the axle would hold. Shouts echoed from behind them as the draft horses crossed the creek bed, but no shots. Cade spared a second's thought to be grateful Burke had made the axle. For all his faults, he was a damn good blacksmith. Cade should probably remember to tell him that at some point. As soon as they were clear, Cade risked a glance back to see Carter and a couple of others Cade didn't recognize, guns in hand but none of them aimed. Carter shouted something after them, but distance and the noise from the wagon kept

Cade from hearing the details of the threat. Cade didn't need the words to know they were threats. What else would Carter be spouting?

"Keep going, but I think we're safe," he told Javier and Erick.

"Is there another route to the ranch that does not cross JR land?" Erick returned his rifle to its holster as Carter and the others wheeled their horses and rode away. "It will be harder to outrun them once the wagon is weighed down with supplies."

"A few," Cade answered, frowning. "But going around to the north would take a few days, and from what we heard in Austin, Ulrich could give us the same hard time about crossing the Bar U. You seen how rough the terrain to the south is. The wagon couldn't clear it, especially loaded." He hooked his bow back onto Nahnia's saddle. "Telling Lutz about this will be as productive as milking a bull, but we should do it anyway, just so it's on record."

"Like his records aren't as crooked as the rest of him," Javier said, "but you're right. If we don't at least try to report it, then we don't have any proof of what happened."

"Now who's full of joy and optimism?" Cade joked, but his comment did nothing to lighten the mood. It was just as well he and Erick wouldn't get to spend the night in town. The confrontation with the JR hands had sucked all pleasure out of the day. He wouldn't be able to relax until they were all safely back at Wellspring.

Chapter Twenty-Six

They maintained a tense, watchful silence the rest of the way to town, but they didn't see any signs of JR men following them or of any other danger, not that Cade let down his guard. Lutz might pretend otherwise, but Eldorado was a JR town as surely as if it were on JR land. Oh, the townspeople didn't all feel that way. Most of them probably didn't, when it came down to it, but they didn't have the wherewithal to stand up to Reichardt as long as he had Lutz in his pocket.

When they got to town, they hitched the wagon in front of Miz Hart's mercantile and left Javier to fill their order while he and Erick went in search of Miz Dawson.

She was in the middle of a lesson with a group of children ranging from toddlers to teens, if Cade was any judge, so they stood in the back of the classroom until she finished. Cade was surprised by how much of what was printed on the chalkboard he was able to understand. Seemed Erick was a better teacher than either of them realized.

"Mr. Heller, Mr. Webster," she greeted them after sending the children outside to play. "I hope the books you borrowed proved helpful?"

Erick nodded with a small smile as he handed them back to her. "We found them most… effective. We are ready for something a bit more advanced, I think."

"In that case, here are the primers." Miz Dawson showed them a stack of books, "and if you think those are not advanced enough, here are the readers I use after the children finish with the primers."

"We're not getting to town too often at the moment," Cade said. "Could we take one of each, and maybe even one after? So we don't have to make the trip again right away."

"Of course," she said. "I'm happy to lend you as many as you want. I only wish my students were as excited about learning their letters."

Cade hoped his cheeks weren't as red as they felt at the thought of exactly how Erick had motivated him.

"Cade is most dedicated to our lessons," Erick agreed dryly. "I thank you for sharing your resources with us."

They found Javier waiting for them outside when they'd taken their leave. "Lizzie is putting our order together, but we have some time to kill before it will be ready to load on the wagon. Let's check for mail and see if Lutz's in his office so we can waste our time reporting the JR crew's harassment."

Cade rolled his eyes but followed Javier to the sheriff's office cum post office. They picked up the mail, but Lutz's desk was empty. "He's probably in the saloon," Tatum, the postmaster who doubled as Lutz's deputy, offered with a twist of his lips. "He usually is, this time of day."

Just what they needed. Then again, maybe if they told him what happened in front of witnesses, it would be harder for him to deny knowing about it later. If they ever found an impartial person to listen to both sides of the story, anyway. Laughter and the tinny sound of the out-of-tune piano poured from the doors of the saloon as they approached. Nothing out of the ordinary, but Cade couldn't help wishing he hadn't left his bow secured to Nahnia's saddle. He tried not to carry it in town. The townspeople didn't need any additional reminders of his unconventional upbringing. But he was better with his bow than with his pistol, faster, and right now every sense he had was jangling, leaving him on edge.

The saloon wasn't especially crowded, not surprising this early in the afternoon. Jock, the blacksmith, was eating a plate of bacon and eggs at the bar, washing it down with a mug of beer and chatting with one of the Meier brothers about the first child he and his wife Sofía were expecting. Lutz was deep in conversation with—no surprise there—the JR foreman, Frank Sanders, a half-empty bottle of whiskey on the table between them.

"JR's men have been out of line," Cade said with a glare at Sanders. "They've fired at our hands on Wellspring land and threatened our passing over JR land to get into town."

"Anybody dead?" Lutz took a sip of his whiskey. "If not, don't bother me. What's the matter, is Wellspring too weak to take care of itself since old man Roarke died?"

"Well, that won't be a problem much longer," Sanders drawled. "I feel almost guilty, staying here enjoying drinks with you, but Carter deserves a chance to prove himself." He downed his shot with a sigh of satisfaction. "Miz Roarke has been so reluctant to consider Mr. Reichardt's suit that he's decided to take more, shall we say, direct action."

"What the hell does that mean?" Cade demanded as Lutz chuckled and raised his glass in a toast.

"By the end of the night she'll either have agreed to Reichardt's proposal or, well. Let's just say I'm not sure anyone would have her after the hands are done passing her around. Probably the best thing that could happen to the bitch."

Cade was ready to flatten him for that, but Erick got there first, his punch knocking Sanders out of his seat onto the floor. "You demean an honorable woman with your scurrilous implications," he growled, casting a withering glare at Lutz before turning his back on them both. "I think we should return to Wellspring with all haste."

Before Cade could agree, Sanders levered himself to his feet and reached for his pistol. Cade scrambled for his own gun but Sanders fired before he could draw it, the shot knocking Erick to his knees.

A shout tore from Cade's throat as he dropped to the ground at Erick's side. Blood pulsed from the hole in his back, staining his chambray shirt bright red. The memory of Pahayoko falling from his horse with a similar wound flashed through Cade's mind, stealing what little breath he still had. He couldn't let history repeat itself. Erick groaned, struggling to push himself up, his arm trembling with effort. "Warn them," he rasped, his voice breaking as his elbow buckled and he collapsed, unconscious.

Cade leaned his full weight onto the wound, trying to slow the bleeding. He hadn't been able to save his brother when the cavalry gunned him down, but he would be damned if he let Erick die. The cries of fear and distress from the other patrons echoed around him without registering as more than sound. He had eyes only for the labored rise and fall of Erick's back. As long as he could see that, Erick was still alive.

"Here." Javier pressed a folded kerchief into Cade's hands. "Use this."

Cade pressed the pad against the wound and turned to meet Sanders's gaze. "You're a dead man."

"Watch yourself, Webster," Lutz blustered, but Cade ignored him as he pushed to his feet.

"Cade!" Javier's voice cut through the rising anger that colored his vision. "Erick needs a doctor *now* if he's going to survive, and I can't get him there by myself."

Cade shook himself free of the rage threatening to consume him. Killing Sanders could wait. Erick had to come first. He bent again to find Javier holding the pad he'd just pressed against Erick's back. When

Javier rose, he saw the cloth was already soaked with blood. "Keep pressure on the wound," Javier said as he lifted Erick over his shoulder.

Even pressing as hard as he could, blood seeped through the pad and trailed in rivulets down Cade's arm. How could Erick possibly survive this? His vision darkened around him, the red haze of blood all he could see, until Javier staggered up the steps to Dr. Lillard's surgery and kicked open the door.

"We have an emergency here!" Javier shouted. Lillard hurried out from a back room, grimacing as Javier laid Erick on the examination table. "He's been shot."

"In the back?" Lillard looked horrified as he peeled the blood-soaked pad away, though Cade couldn't tell if it was by the wound or the cowardice behind it.

"Sanders," Javier spat out, just as disgusted.

"Can you save him?" Cade would deal with Sanders later—there was nowhere on earth he'd be safe from Cade's vengeance—but Erick had to survive first.

Lillard cut away Erick's shirt, shaking his head. "I'd have to operate to get the bullet out, and if it's pierced a lung or nicked his heart, there's not much I can do."

Before Cade could insist that he couldn't let Erick die, a young woman and man hurried into the surgery. "We saw someone carried in from the street," the woman said in a lilting accent. "What can I do to help? No, Tim, you know blood makes you queasy," she added, trying to push her companion back from the table.

"Lucy and Tim O'Neill are new in town. They've opened an apothecary next door," the doctor explained. "Lucy, get my surgical tools ready, please. O'Neill, I'll need ether to keep him anesthetized. Triple the usual amount—this will be a lengthy surgery, if he doesn't die on us first." He rolled up his sleeves and began to pump water at the sink to wash his hands.

O'Neill nodded, seeming relieved to have something to do that would take him out of the surgery. "Yes, sir."

Javier tried to herd Cade toward the door after O'Neill, but Cade stood his ground. "Webster, let the doc do his job."

"No," Cade protested. "I have to stay. I have to be here if…." He couldn't get the words out. He'd lost so much in his life. He couldn't bear to lose Erick too.

"Come on, Cade." Javier guided him out of the surgery, shutting out the sight of Lucy O'Neill laying down a variety of gruesome-looking tools for Lillard to use to cut into Erick's back. "You have to warn Wellspring."

"No, I can't leave Erick! I—"

"Cade," Javier said sharply. "Pull it together. You're a better rider than I'll ever be, and they have to be warned. I'll stay right here and I won't let anyone get to Erick, but you being here won't change whether he lives or dies right now, and you warning Wellspring could make that difference for all our friends. For Michele."

And she was the one person Cade loved enough to leave Erick's side for. "Fuck," he muttered. "You won't let Sanders get a second chance at him?"

"I swear," Javier said. "I'll get my gun from the wagon, and I won't let anyone other than you come through that door. Now, go!"

Cade cast one more glance toward the surgery where Lillard was preparing to fight for Erick's life. He ached for a moment of privacy to give Erick one last kiss, but asking for it would give away their secret and take the doctor away from Erick's side when time was critical—for both of them. He turned and bolted for Nahnia, driving his heels into the horse's sides as soon as his ass hit the saddle. They raced down the dusty streets and out of town. He blamed the wind in his face for the tears that blurred his vision and wet his cheeks. Cade briefly considered crossing through JR land, since Sanders's threats made it sound like everyone would be focused on attacking Wellspring, but if he had the timing wrong, he'd end up wounded or dead with no backup, and that wouldn't help anyone. He'd have to take the southern road and hope he could get there in time.

Chapter Twenty-Seven

Cade couldn't have described the race back to Wellspring if his life depended on it, his focus on pushing Nahnia and himself to their limits in his haste to get back before it was too late—for Wellspring, for Chel, for Kit and Mac and the rest of his friends. For the life he'd almost started to believe he and Erick could build together. He crossed out of the foothills and onto Wellspring property as the sun started to set. Sanders had implied the attack would come as night fell, probably hoping they'd be less alert or at least less able to see anyone coming under the cover of darkness, which gave him a matter of minutes. He drew his pistol from his belt and fired into the air, hoping someone would hear and the sound would put them on alert enough that they'd be ready if he couldn't get there in time, especially the riders out on the range.

A horse approached, and Cade had his pistol drawn before he recognized the rider as Jesse Beaufort. He couldn't waste time explaining the threat more than once, so he waved Beaufort back. "Get everyone together," he gasped, pulling air into his lungs. Beaufort took one look at his and Nahnia's state and didn't ask any questions, just wheeled around and raced back in the direction he'd come from.

Payne was on the porch of the main house, rifle in hand, when Cade pulled up and slid from Nahnia's saddle. At least half the hands clustered around the steps, with more running up every second. "JR," Cade ground out. "They're planning to attack tonight. We have to be ready for them."

Chel pushed through the men to his side. "Javier and Erick?"

"Sanders shot Erick." The words cut like knives, all the more since Cade knew Erick might already be dead. "We brought him to Dr. Lillard, and Javier stayed with him, but…."

"He's strong, *petit loup*," Michele said as curses rung out from the rest of the hands. Payne looked as grim as Cade had ever seen him, which was saying something, given everything the man had lived through before coming to Wellspring. "If anyone can pull through, it's him."

Cade tried to take comfort in her words, but with his hands still covered in Erick's blood, comfort was beyond him. "Miz Roarke, it's you they're after as much as anything else."

"Of course it is," she spat. "They won't find me easy pickings."

"They won't find Wellspring easy pickings," Payne added. "Logan, you have the most experience with a full-scale assault. How do we stop them?"

"And how do we keep Lutz from throwing us all in jail on made-up charges even if we do?" Svensen added.

"We need a lawman we can trust," Matt said bitterly. "I just wish I knew where to find one."

"There's a US Marshal in San Angelo," Cade replied, "but how do we get him here? If we can even convince them to pay any mind to what Reichardt's doing? We need every gun we have and a dozen more as it is."

"I'll go," Mac offered quietly. "I'm getting better, but I don't trust my aim yet. If someone is going to ride for San Angelo, it should be me."

Kit gave Mac a hard look, but Mac stared back without flinching. "If you're going, now's the time, before the fighting starts."

Mac nodded sharply and took a step toward the barn, but Kit caught his hand and spun him back into a fierce kiss. "Ride hard and don't look back. No matter what you hear, don't stop."

"Yes, Captain," Mac said. Cade heard the undercurrents in his voice that, before Erick, he wouldn't have understood. Then Mac was gone into the barn, and a short minute later the sound of hoofbeats indicated his departure.

Kit watched him go for a moment, then tore his attention back to Payne. "There isn't anywhere on the rangeland we can hide to pick them off. Best we can hope for is darkness and the element of surprise. Did anyone see you ride off?" he asked Cade.

"I didn't see anyone," Cade answered. "Lutz and Sanders were still in the saloon, and he's the only JR man I saw in town. He said something about giving Carter a chance to prove himself, so it will probably be Adam leading the attack."

"Let him come," Chel purred, stroking the hilt of the knife in her belt. "He's mine."

"Not if anyone else has a bead on him first," Kit cautioned. "We have to stop them by any means possible. We can't let personal scores get in the way."

Chel grumbled at that, but she didn't argue. Cade could sympathize. He wanted Sanders on the business end of an arrow so badly he could taste it, but Kit was right. "We'll be outnumbered and probably outgunned, especially at first, but no matter how many guns they bring, they can only carry so much shot. And they don't know the lay of the land like we do. Those are our advantages, so use them. Shoot to kill, stay behind cover so you aren't an easy target, and make for damn sure you're shooting at JR hands and not at each other."

"Cade's right," Kit said. "We want to sow chaos wherever possible, anything to keep them guessing."

"Buildings can be rebuilt. Livestock can be replaced," Miz Roarke interrupted. "Your lives can't be. If saving those means sacrificing the barn, the bunkhouse, even the main house, do it. We may not be the biggest or richest spread in the area, but we can afford to rebuild as long as we have the people to rebuild for."

Payne cut through the murmur of agreement. "Beaufort, find Quinn and Walsh and bring them back in if you can. I won't risk JR catching them by surprise just to keep a watch on the herd. Chiles, wake up anyone who's still sleeping and get them armed. I want every hand ready to blow JR's men to hell."

"Speaking of blowing things to hell…." Burke stepped forward. "I may be able to throw together some grenades to surprise our guests. They won't be pretty, but they'll bring them down." Burke had been an ordnance officer during the war, Cade remembered, so it wasn't surprising that he knew his way around explosives.

"I'll take any advantage we can get," Payne said.

"Just don't blow yourself or anything else up in the process," Kit added.

"You wound me." Burke mimed being shot, but no one laughed at his antics the way they usually did. Burke scowled and stalked toward the smithy as everyone else scattered to their assigned tasks or to gather weapons and ammunition for the coming fight.

Cade strode toward the bunkhouse, Chel on his heels. He tossed his gun belt on his bunk and stripped down, heedless of her presence. He pulled his buckskins from his trunk and on and then painted his face with careful deliberation the way his Comanche brothers had taught him.

"Cade," Chel said, but he ignored her. He would defend Wellspring, but the moment that fight was done, he was going hunting. He had a score to settle with Sanders now, and nothing would stop him from finishing it… tonight.

"Tutaatu Isa," she tried instead.

"What?" he snapped.

"When you go after Sanders, I'm coming with you."

"This is my fight," he started.

"And I'll let you fight it, but you need someone to watch your back."

Cade flinched. Sanders had managed to shoot Erick in the back even with Cade watching.

"You won't do Erick any good if you get yourself killed," she added.

"Just drop it," Cade ground out. "We've got to get through the night first." He filled the empty bullet loops on his gun belt and buckled it around his waist—he might prefer his bow, but in this fight he'd use every weapon he had. After adding a few throwing knives, he checked his arrows, filled the quiver, and slung it over his shoulder. Last he picked up his bow.

He stalked back out of the bunkhouse and headed toward the windmill behind the main house. He'd climbed the first two supports when Payne barked, "What the hell are you doing, Webster?"

"Lookout," he replied. "It's the tallest structure around. It'll give me the best sightlines to pick off JR assholes."

"And the least cover when they start shooting back," Payne replied.

"They can't aim worth shit," Cade said as he continued to climb.

"Don't get yourself killed. I ain't explaining that to Heller," Payne said with a frown. Cade just kept climbing. To have Payne's acceptance was a gift without price, but the words only underscored Erick's absence and the reason for it. He couldn't let himself dwell on that now. Once the JR attack was stopped, he'd head back to Erick as fast as Nahnia could carry him. Erick just had to survive until then. He had to.

Yeah, definitely the best vantage point around, Cade decided when he reached the top. He settled onto a crossbeam and considered the blades. There was enough wind to set clouds scudding over the moon, which would reduce visibility even more, but wolves see best at twilight. He could already spot a few pinpricks of light moving over the plain— the JR men must be carrying torches. *All the better to pick them off.* He swung the metal head around and jammed one of his knives into the gears to keep it from turning. He could shoot between the blades, and they'd give him some cover, at least until any of the JR hands passed him. And he didn't plan to let that happen.

As the riders drew closer, lights went out in the main house, the bunkhouse, and last of all in Burke's smithy, leaving the landscape in near darkness. Carter knew most of the ranch would be asleep by now and must think he'd be catching them unaware. He'd soon learn differently. Cade fit an arrow to his bow and settled in to wait for them to ride into range.

Shots rang out in the distance, and Cade cursed under his breath. Even he couldn't see well enough in the darkness to know who had fired out on the range and whether they'd hit anything, but Beaufort hadn't made it back in with Quinn and Walsh yet. He'd just have to pray they were safe and get revenge if they weren't.

The flickering lights moved slowly toward them, and Cade whistled to alert the others. Chel whistled back. The clatter of hooves caught Cade's attention. "Hold your fire," he yelled as he recognized Beaufort's horse even in the low light.

Quinn followed close behind him, Walsh's lax form cradled in the saddle in front of him. "Shot his horse out from under him," Beaufort called softly, letting Quinn ride past him to the main house. "Probably a few cracked ribs and a slug in his thigh, but he should make it. We took out the shooter, but they'll have heard the gunshots. Won't be long now."

Cade nodded grimly. Quinn must have handed Walsh off to Miz Roarke inside, because he thundered up to rejoin Beaufort and ride back toward the oncoming attackers.

That wasn't the plan, but what the hell, he'd go with it. He pulled back on his bow, the fletching a familiar tickle against his cheek, and waited for the first of the JR riders to come into range. The moment they did, he loosed the arrow and watched in satisfaction as the figure fell from the saddle, his torch hitting the ground and sputtering out. He grabbed another arrow and fired again, determined to keep as many of them as possible from even reaching the others.

Beaufort and Quinn had peeled off to either side of the oncoming riders, shooting from the darkness at anything carrying a torch. Cade had never had a high opinion of the hands JR hired on, but it took an embarrassing number of them falling before the rest realized the torches made them a target. By then the first men reached the outbuildings, and one of them was sharp enough to toss his torch into the hayloft. The dry feed kindled quickly, and Cade gave a thought toward anything trapped inside.

"Let it burn," Payne shouted. "The horses are already in the paddock." One of the JR men fired toward the sound of his voice and dropped a second later when Payne's rifle cartridge split his head open.

Cade looked away from the fire, not wanting the light to mess with his night vision. Without the torches to pinpoint his targets, he'd have to work harder to locate them in the darkness, waiting for the flash from the muzzles of their guns as they fired, but he'd learned patience as well as the art of war with the Comanche, and the JR crew had made it personal. He wouldn't be letting a single one of these bastards get away with attacking his home.

Burke had worked his usual magic, and bombs exploded with irregular blasts, each one taking out a knot of attackers and sowing chaos in their wake, but Cade wasn't counting on them, because he didn't know how many Burke had made or where he'd set them. He put an arrow in the eye of a man who was trying to flank Kit's position and turned back to surveying the battle as a whole.

They'd managed to get the JR hands off their horses, which took away their speed, but it also made them harder to spot. At least the Wellspring hands were sticking to the plan and staying in their hideouts so anyone moving around was someone Cade could shoot. He just hoped it stayed that way. If the JR men lit more buildings on fire, that might change.

The cloud that had been obscuring the moon drifted to let a sliver of light break free, enough for Cade to spot Chel race from her hiding place and leap onto one of the attackers. It had to be Carter—she wouldn't give up her advantage for anyone else. She kicked the gun from his hand and slashed one of her knives across his throat. "*Meurs, salaud,*" she called as he fell heavily to the ground.

That was enough for one of the JR hands to target her. Before Cade could fire, Burke dashed out of nowhere and threw himself at Chel, knocking her to the ground. Cade brought the man down with an arrow through the eye, but Burke fell too, blood pouring from his head.

Shit! Ned could be a pain in the ass, but Cade had always considered him a friend. To lose him now was one more black mark against the JR attackers, as if Cade had needed another reason to wipe them from the face of the earth. Chel dragged Burke toward the bunkhouse, though

Cade had slim hope he'd survived. Even if Ned had gotten on Cade's last nerve at times, he was a good man who'd given his life protecting Chel. He added another score to his tally to revenge.

The handful of remaining JR men, once they realized Carter had fallen, didn't seem inclined to press the fight. Cade picked off as many as he could as they hightailed it off Wellspring property. *Take that, fuckers.*

Once he was sure they were gone and not coming back, he dropped to the ground and raced toward the bunkhouse. As he did, he heard Payne calling for everyone to check in. He shouted his own okay, but he didn't stop. He needed to see Chel for himself, pay his respects to Ned, and get back to town.

"He's alive," Chel said as soon as Cade crossed the threshold into the bunkhouse. "He's a fucking idiot, but he's alive."

Cade sagged against the doorframe, relief flooding him that at least one of his friends had made it. Now he could only pray Erick would be as lucky. "How?"

Chel brushed Ned's bloody hair back with a gentle hand. "It just grazed him."

"You're right. He's an idiot," Cade said with a shake of his head. He came closer to examine the wound, but while Ned didn't stir, Cade could see him breathing easily, and head wounds always bled more than anywhere else. "And I owe him your life."

"I'll bandage him up while you make sure we got everyone," Chel offered. Cade nodded and left her to work.

Though he begrudged every minute that kept him from riding back to town and Erick, Cade scouted the grounds to salvage his arrows when he heard a low groan. Not wanting to take a chance if it wasn't a Wellspring hand, he nocked an arrow and approached cautiously. As he got closer, he saw it was one of Reichardt's men. "Collier, isn't it?" he asked when it was clear the man posed no threat. A bullet had shattered his right shoulder, the gun limp in his hand.

"Fuck off, squaw," Collier protested.

"Is that any way to talk to a man who could put an arrow in your face?" Cade dragged Collier to his feet by his undamaged shoulder and back toward the barn, where Kit was overseeing the hands dousing the fire's embers. Cade couldn't judge how much of the building was salvageable. Still, it was one building, not the whole ranch in flames.

Wellspring was safe, for himself, for his friends, for his future. Erick just had to survive to see it.

Kit grinned when he spotted them. "We'll patch him up once we're sure this is out. At least we can prove to Lutz that we didn't kill everyone who attacked us."

Cade handed Collier off. "Get him to Lutz when you can. I don't have time to wait for you."

"Be careful" was all Kit said.

Cade nodded sharply and whistled for Nahnia. He swung onto the horse's back and dug his heels into Nahnia's side. As he wheeled him toward town, he heard another set of hoofbeats and glanced over his shoulder to see Chel right behind him. He faced forward again and rode on. She could keep up or not. He wasn't waiting, even for her.

Chapter Twenty-Eight

If anything, the return to Eldorado was even more tense than the ride to Wellspring had been. Then he'd been able to force aside thoughts of Erick by focusing on the danger bearing down on his friends. Now, while he knew things could still go badly if Mac wasn't able to reach the marshal in San Angelo or if that marshal was just as corrupt as Lutz, his only real thought was for Erick and whether he'd survived the night. Sanders was a dead man either way, but if Erick died, Cade would make Sanders pay for it before killing him.

Cade decided to chance riding back across JR land rather than the more treacherous southern route. He was pretty sure Reichardt had sent most of his men in the attack on Wellspring. Even if some had remained or returned, the risk of their spotting two riders in the dark was worth taking if it got him to Erick faster.

He could only pray, to his birth parents' God or his adoptive parents' Great Spirit or any other power that might be listening, that Erick had survived. The part of him that had watched cavalry soldiers gun down his Comanche brother argued that Erick's wound was fatal, that he couldn't survive after all the blood he'd lost, but he wouldn't let himself believe that.

"Erick is strong," Chel called to him, as if she could read his thoughts. "He has you to hold on for."

Cade just dug his heels harder into Nahnia's flanks and sped on.

The sun was rising as they hit the edge of Eldorado. Cade reined Nahnia in at Dr. Lillard's office and slid down. Exhaustion pulled at him, but he forced his knees to hold and braced himself to deal with whatever awaited him inside.

"You ready?" Chel asked.

Cade nodded and pretended it was the truth. He rapped on the door and waited.

"Who is it?" Javier called through the door.

"Chel and Cade." He hoped Javier still being on guard was a good sign. If Erick were dead, Javier wouldn't be worried about Sanders coming to finish the job.

"Webster!" As Javier was opening the door to the surgery, Sanders stumbled out of the saloon with Lutz on his heels. "I was hoping Carter would save me the trouble of having to shoot you too."

"Sorry to disappoint you, Frank, but Chel here slit Adam's throat while he and his men were attacking Wellspring." Cade drew an arrow and ran the fletching through his fingers, while Chel gave Sanders a wicked smile. "Reichardt may not be happy when he hears you sat here drinking while we were kicking JR's ass."

The shouting brought Javier outside, cradling his massive gun in his arms. Several other patrons staggered out of the saloon, followed by the Meier brothers, and Lizzie Hart stood outside the door of the mercantile. That was fine with Cade; he didn't need an audience but it wouldn't stop him either.

"Erick's in bad shape, but he's still alive," Javier murmured as he came to stand alongside Cade and Chel.

Sanders drew his pistol and took aim toward the three of them, but there was no question who he was gunning for. Cade dove to the side, taking cover behind a horse trough as Sanders fired. The shot went wide, but Cade wasn't taking chances on being as lucky a second time. He fit the arrow to the bow's string and aimed at Sanders. As he drew back his arm, a second shot rang out, followed by the explosive retort of Javier's Nock gun.

Cade watched Lutz sink to the ground, trying to hold his guts in, but he swallowed down the bile that rose in his throat at the sight. He could get sick later. Sanders took another shot that set chips of rock flying from the trough—how had he survived this long with such lousy aim?—and that was all Cade could take. He rose up on his knees and fired, his arrow hitting Sanders in the eye. Too quick a death for him, but he wouldn't be shooting anyone in the back ever again.

A couple of people applauded, but Cade ignored them. He burned with the need to take Sanders's scalp so he would never be reincarnated to make someone else's life hell, but half the townsfolk already thought he was a savage. *He'd* never shot anyone in the back, but that vengeance was denied him. He just needed to see Erick.

The gunshots had drawn Tatum out of the sheriff's office. He looked sick when he saw what Javier's gun had left of Lutz and Cade's arrow sprouting from Sanders's face, but he drew his Colt as he walked toward them. "I don't want any trouble, but I'm going to have to take you in."

"It was self-defense!" Chel protested, knives in hand. "Sanders fired at us first, and so did Lutz."

Several people in the crowd that had gathered called out their agreement, but Tatum didn't back down. "There are two men dead. I didn't see it happen, so we'll just have to send for a judge and let a trial sort things out."

"MacRae rode to San Angelo before the JR attack to find a marshal who wasn't being paid off by Reichardt." Chel didn't look happy, but she sheathed her knives as she glanced at first Cade and then Javier. "Maybe it would be safest for you to go with Tatum until he gets here. At least it would keep any other JR hands from gunning for you."

"I'll take my chances," Cade insisted. "I need to see Erick."

"I don't want to fire on you, but I will if you don't come with me." Tatum wasn't under JR's thumb, as far as Cade knew, but that was probably because Reichardt hadn't needed anyone but Lutz to do his dirty work.

"Maybe we should go with him." Javier looked green as he handed his gun to Chel. "One shootout was more than enough for me."

"I won't let anything happen to Erick," Chel promised Cade. "Right now you haven't done anything illegal, but if you don't go with Tatum, it'll make things harder when Mac and the new marshal get here."

Cade looked back at Tatum, weighed his chances of getting to Erick before Tatum shot him, considered the likelihood of Erick getting hurt worse in the ensuing scuffle, and decided this wasn't a fight he could win.

He gave a last, longing look toward the door to Doc Lillard's clinic, aching at how close Erick was while still being so far out of reach. Javier's words were little consolation when all Cade wanted was to hold Erick's hand, feel his heart beating, however weakly, watch his chest rise and fall. Maybe kiss him, even though he wouldn't be aware of it, if no one was around to see. He swallowed all that down, keeping his face impassive as his brothers had taught him. Fucking Tatum thinking he was the fucking sheriff now that Lutz was gone. Who'd gone and elected him anyway?

"Whatever." He stalked ahead of Tatum toward the sheriff's office at the other end of the street. He might be going, but he wasn't going to pretend he was under arrest. He hadn't done a damn thing wrong.

"I'll need your weapons," Tatum said when they entered the office. Cade handed him his bow and the quiver of arrows from his back, then unstrapped his gun belt and handed that over too. He still had a knife in one of the seams of his leathers, but Tatum didn't seem ready to search him and Cade wasn't about to offer it up.

"I gave my gun to Michele." Javier held out his arms to show he didn't have any other weapons. Tatum prodded them into the building's one cell and turned the lock, then set the bow, quiver, and gun belt against the far wall.

"If anything happens to my bow, I'm taking it out of your hide," Cade growled. Tatum must have felt braver with inch-thick bars between them, because he just rolled his eyes and settled in behind the postmaster's desk.

The cell had two flimsy cots with chamber pots beneath them and nothing else. "Tell me about Erick," Cade demanded as soon as they'd sat down, facing away from Tatum.

"It's not a pretty story," Javier said grimly. "Remember that he's still alive, and it gets more likely he'll recover with each passing hour."

Cade hadn't expected it to be anything but horrifying, but to have Javier lay it out so bluntly made it even harder to sit in that cell instead of breaking out and going to Erick's side. "Tell me," he repeated.

"Doc Lillard worked on him for hours," Javier said. "He had to open him up pretty deep to find the bullet, and the way it was lodged, he had to cut from the front to get it out. It punctured a lung and shattered a few ribs."

Bile rose in Cade's throat at the thought of Erick's strong chest torn open from behind and cut open from the front. He knew the damage a bullet could do, but he hadn't expected it to be this bad.

"Once he had the bullet out, he did something to patch up the lung and stitched Erick back up. He used some kind of suction thing to get the air back in Erick's lung, but he'd lost so much blood by then that Lillard didn't think he'd make it."

Much of the explanation went over Cade's head. "But you said he's still alive." His voice sounded desperate to his own ears.

Javier gave him a sympathetic look and nodded. "He is, I promise. Or at least he was when you arrived. I asked the doc if there was some way I could give him some of my blood. Doc said it was risky, that it was as likely to kill him as it was to help. We figured since chances were he wouldn't make it unless we tried, it was worth the risk."

Cade reached out to squeeze Javier's hand. Fuck, he'd known things were bad, but he'd hoped…. He didn't know why he'd expected anything less, not after seeing what the bullet had done to Pahayoko, but a part of him had hoped it wasn't as bad as it had seemed. "You didn't have to do that, but thank you."

Javier shrugged. "I don't know him as well as I'd like, but Erick seems like a good man. And Doc said there wasn't any risk to me unless he took too much. So we did it, and Doc said it seemed to help. At least it didn't make things any worse. Doc is keeping him sedated so he doesn't move around and tear the stitches open. The biggest risk now is if the wound gets infected. So all we can do is wait."

"Fucking Sanders," Cade muttered, wishing desperately he could wait by Erick's side, no matter the outcome. "If Erick dies, I'm going to find a way to drag Sanders back to life just so I can kill him again. Slowly this time." If he got out of here before they buried the body, he'd be taking that scalp after all.

Javier stretched out on the cot, hands behind his head. "We may as well try to get some sleep. No telling how long it will take MacRae to get back here, if he's even able to convince another marshal to come with him."

Despite his exhaustion, Cade felt too keyed up to sleep, but he followed Javier's example and lay down on the hard cot. He hoped Mac was successful, because if he wasn't, Cade would need to start planning a jailbreak.

Chapter Twenty-Nine

THE FIRST time Erick awoke, the pain piercing through his chest was so agonizing that he welcomed sinking back into blissful oblivion.

The next time he woke, the pain was still there, but it felt as though all his senses were muted. He could hear voices nearby but couldn't tell if one of them was Cade's. He struggled to open his eyes but wasn't able to force the lids apart. He drew in a breath to call Cade's name when the pain lanced through him so sharply that though he fought against it this time, he again lapsed into unconsciousness.

The third time he woke, it was to the sensation of fingers twined with his. His eyelids felt crusted together, but he was finally able to pry them open, only to find not Cade but Michele sitting beside him. He blinked, but the image didn't change. He didn't remember much after being shot, but he remembered urging Cade to warn Wellspring of the JR attack. Michele had been at Wellspring, so if she was here, at least some of Wellspring's hands had survived. But if Cade wasn't here, did that mean…? The thought was too dreadful to even finish. He drew a shallow breath, just enough to rasp out "Cade?"

"He's safe." Michele squeezed his hand and brushed the hair back from his forehead gently. "He killed Sanders, though, and Javier killed Lutz, after they both shot at us first, so Tatum has them cooling their heels in jail until Mac gets here with a new marshal. He'll be thrilled to know you're awake. When the doctor gets back to check on you, I'll go tell him."

"He got to Wellspring in time?" His chest burned when he spoke, but he needed to know his friends had survived.

"Of course he did," she said, her fondness clear in her voice. "He would have killed himself and his horse getting there before he let us down. You know that."

"How many hurt?" He couldn't ask if anyone had died. How quickly he'd come to care for these men and women who'd been strangers only months before.

"Walsh took a bullet in one leg and cracked some ribs, and a bullet grazed Burke's head, but they were the worst of it, from what I saw before we rode back to check on you," Michele reported. "The ranch took some damage from both fire and bullets, but buildings can be replaced. You just focus on getting well."

Erick was sure the conflict had been worse than Michele was telling him, but before he could press her for more details, a stranger he could only assume was Dr. Lillard entered the room, a cautious smile on his face.

"I'm glad to see you awake. I've been cutting back the anesthetics, but I wasn't sure how long it would take for them to clear your body. You're very lucky to be alive, Mr. Heller," he said.

Michele stood and moved toward the door. "I'll give Cade and Javier the good news. Don't do anything stupid to set back your recovery or you'll answer to me."

"Your girl's very devoted." The doctor pulled aside the bed sheet to check the bandages covering Erick's chest. "She's barely left your side since she got here, except when Reverend Smithson came to pray over you."

"She's not—" Erick's voice broke as the doctor peeled away the bandage and pain stabbed through his torso. Maybe it was better to let him and the rest of the town believe what they wanted.

The pounding of hooves on the street outside drew the doctor's attention away from Erick's injuries, and he stepped to the open window. "It's that MacRae fellow, and it looks like there's a marshal with him," Lillard said.

Erick didn't sigh, though relief flooded through him. Hopefully this marshal would be more honest than the last lawman and Cade would be out of jail soon.

CADE ROSE to his feet when the door swung open and Mac stalked in, followed by a tall man with short brown hair and a US Marshal's badge. "What the hell are you doing in there, Cade?" Mac demanded.

Next to him, Javier stood as well.

"And Javier?" Mac added. "Tatum, where's Lutz and what the hell is going on?"

"Lutz's dead," Tatum said with a grimace. "Trujillo blew him away with that big-ass gun of his. And Webster put an arrow through Frank Sanders's eye. That's what the hell they're doing here."

"Tell them the rest, Tatum," Javier insisted. "Lutz and Sanders both opened fire on us first. And that's after Sanders shot Erick Heller in the back. There are plenty of witnesses to both, if you'd had the stones to ask anyone."

"I'm a postmaster, not a lawman," Tatum protested.

"Well, I am a lawman," the man with MacRae said. "US Marshal Jonas Parnell. Gentlemen, I'm afraid I'll have to ask you to stay here a bit longer until I can get to the bottom of this, but if what you're saying is true, I won't see any cause to charge you."

"Get to the bottom of it fast," Cade demanded. "I need to see if Erick's still alive."

Parnell looked at Tatum. "Where is this Erick now?"

"In Dr. Lillard's surgery, just down Main Street," Tatum replied.

Parnell pursed his lips, but before he could reply, the door opened again to admit Chel. "About time you got here, MacRae," she groused. "Cade, Erick is awake and asking for you."

"Then I believe that is where I should start," Parnell said. "Since he is the most wounded party in all of this, barring the dead men, he can tell me his side of the story, and we can begin the process of uncovering the truth." He tipped his hat in Chel's direction. "Ma'am."

She rolled her eyes at Parnell and turned to glare at Tatum.

"I'll show you where the surgery is, Marshal," Tatum offered.

Cade snickered. Tatum was a fool, leaving them alone with Chel and Mac. Although the new marshal seemed like a decent man, so Cade wouldn't break out just yet.

Parnell glanced Cade's way, like he knew what Cade was thinking. "You'd better stay here, Tatum. MacRae can show me where the surgery is."

Cade's opinion of the man rose another few notches. At least he wasn't an idiot like Tatum, and he had to hope he wasn't as crooked as Lutz.

DR. LILLARD had just finished putting Erick through a round of torture as he examined the wounds on his back and chest, had him breathe in and out as strongly and as long as he could, and rebandaged him, when the door opened. Having it be Cade would be a fitting reward for his suffering, but instead it was MacRae with another man Erick didn't recognize.

"Heller, this is Marshal Parnell," MacRae said. "I told him about all the shit Lutz was pulling with the JR, and he agreed to come check things out."

"And I understand Sheriff Lutz is dead, so I need to gather information on my own," the marshal said. "I thought I'd start with you."

"I didn't see what happened to Lutz, but if Cade and Javier said they acted in self-defense, I know they're telling the truth," Erick said. It hurt to speak, but he had to convince this new lawman to set Cade and Javier free. He tried to sit up, but Dr. Lillard eased him back into bed.

"He's recuperating from a life-threatening injury," Dr. Lillard insisted. "He needs to rest, so be quick about it."

"Can you tell me what happened before you were shot?" Parnell asked.

"We'd come into town to pick up the week's supplies," Erick began, speaking slowly. He and Cade had hoped to spend the night away from prying eyes at Wellspring before the threats from the JR hands escalated, but he wasn't about to volunteer that. "We decided to stop at the Meiers' for some refreshment while Miss Hart prepared our order. Lutz was there, along with Frank Sanders, the foreman of the JR ranch." He stopped to draw a shallow breath, fighting to suppress the expression of pain it caused. "Sanders said he was sorry we'd miss the excitement. He made it clear that JR hands intended to attack Wellspring to seize the ranch's water access."

"Because Miz Roarke wouldn't agree to marry JR's owner," MacRae added. "Reichardt couldn't get the ranch the easy way, so he decided to take it by force."

"And Sheriff Lutz heard this?" Parnell asked.

"He all but drank a toast to JR's success," Erick said. "Then Sanders made a vulgar insult regarding Mrs. Roarke. I will not repeat it, but I admit I struck him, hard enough to knock him down."

"Good for you, Heller," MacRae said. "I've wanted to knock the sneer off that jackal's face since the first time I met him."

"Since the company was no longer congenial, we decided to return to the mercantile," Erick continued. "Sanders shot me as we were walking away. I'm afraid I do not recall much after that."

Parnell turned to Dr. Lillard. "Not to doubt Mr. Heller's word, but is his wound consistent with his story?"

"Was he shot in the back, do you mean?" Dr. Lillard asked acerbically. "Yes, absolutely. The bullet entered between his shoulder blades, hit his lung, and barely missed his heart. And while I couldn't leave my patient this morning to see the gunfight that resulted in Lutz's and Sanders's deaths, I heard the shouting, which included Sanders threatening to finish Webster off since Carter hadn't done it, and heard them shoot before Webster and Trujillo."

"How do you know they shot first?" Parnell asked.

"Because Trujillo uses a seven-barrel Nock shotgun that makes a very distinctive roar," Lillard explained. "Any other shots were fired before Webster did."

"A gunslinger, is he?" Parnell asked with a frown.

"Not quite," Erick said. "He uses a bow."

"Although he's as good or better than any gunslinger you're likely to meet," MacRae added.

Parnell raised his eyebrows but let it go. "So as far as you are aware, Mr. Trujillo and Mr. Webster acted only in self-defense."

"Yes," Dr. Lillard said. "And good riddance to the other two. I have their bodies in back if you'd like to take a look at them."

"Perhaps later. Thank you for your information, gentlemen," Parnell said. "I believe my next step should be to speak with the— Meiers, was it?"

"They run the Lone Star. Best saloon in town," MacRae said. "Only saloon in town, actually. I'd be happy to show you the way. I might even buy you a drink."

"Trying to influence my decision?" Parnell asked with a wry smile.

"I won't need to. After everyone tells you the same story, only an idiot would keep Javier and Cade locked up."

CADE ROUSED from a light doze when the door to the sheriff's office opened again and the marshal entered, Mac one step behind him, a grin on his face. That boded well.

"Mr. Webster, Mr. Trujillo, you are free to go," Parnell announced. "Everyone I spoke with agreed you only defended yourselves against an unprovoked attack." He pulled the ring of keys from the hook on the wall above Tatum's desk and opened the door to the cell.

Javier was saying something polite to the marshal, but Cade didn't have the patience for it. He bolted the second the door opened, needing to see Erick for himself. Sure, Chel had spent the past few hours assuring him Erick was alive and even awake, but until he could see that with his own eyes, he wouldn't completely believe it.

He barreled his way through the townspeople going about their business and crashed through the door to Dr. Lillard's surgery.

"Slow down, boy," Dr. Lillard scolded. "Where's the fire?"

"No fire." Cade panted for breath. "I just need to see Erick."

"He's resting at the moment," the doctor said. "Speaking with the marshal tired him out more than he'd like to admit. It's going to take quite some time to build his stamina back up to where it was before."

"I'll be sure he takes it easy," Cade assured him, though he privately thought Erick would try to be back on his feet far sooner than Dr. Lillard would like. "We need him back at Wellspring." *I need him back.*

"Well, you can go sit with him 'til he wakes up. Do him good to see someone besides that girl of his."

"Girl?" Cade had to smother a laugh when he realized the doctor was talking about Chel. "I hope he won't be too disappointed that it's just me."

Dr. Lillard clapped him on the back. "I'm sure he'll be glad you're out of jail. Just don't wear him out."

"I won't," Cade promised as he headed toward the room the doctor indicated with a wave of his hand. He walked in on silent feet, glad he wore his moccasins and not heavy boots, even if Lizzie Hart had brought a change of clothes for him and Javier after their first day in lockup. Erick needed his rest and Cade didn't want to disturb him. He just needed to *see*. He trusted Chel—of course he did—but he trusted his own eyes more. Once he'd seen for himself that Erick was still alive, he could let go of the fear and tension that still hadn't left him.

With the curtains pulled, the room was dim, but Cade didn't need more light to see Erick on the bed, pale against the white sheets, his chest rising and falling slightly in the rhythm of his fitful breathing. Cade collapsed into the chair next to the bed, catching himself in time to keep from making a noise that might wake Erick. He was alive. Barely, maybe, but he was alive. Cade buried his face in his hands to muffle the sob that threatened to choke him.

Erick was alive.

He took a deep breath and then another one, forcing down the bile that rose in his throat. Sanders hadn't succeeded. Erick was going to live.

CHAPTER THIRTY

ON THE bed, Erick stirred, although Cade knew he hadn't made any sound. He reached out but stopped short of touching Erick's hand, not wanting to wake him if he was only shifting in his sleep. Warmth radiated from Erick's skin, another layer of reassurance, not the fever heat that would've indicated more problems, but the safe warmth of a healthy body. Okay, as healthy as someone could be with a bullet hole in him.

He studied Erick's face instead. His skin was pale beneath the little bit of tan he'd managed to acquire from working outdoors, his forehead furrowed, creases drawing his mouth into a frown. His hair was tousled against the pillow beneath his head, and knowing the care Erick took with his appearance even when wearing work clothes, he couldn't stop himself from reaching a hand out to gently smooth it down.

Erick's eyelids fluttered, and his brow furrowed even more as they parted, giving Cade a glimpse of clouded blue eyes. "Cade?" he rasped, as if it hurt him to speak,

Cade grasped his hand and squeezed it gently. "Yeah, I'm here. Parnell let me and Javier go." He leaned forward to drop a kiss on Erick's forehead. "You're not allowed to die on me, understand?" he ordered, his own voice nearly as rough as Erick's.

"I'll do my best," Erick answered dryly, "as long as you stop trying to get yourself killed too."

"Hey, Sanders shot at me first! Not that I wasn't going to kill him anyway for what he did to you."

Erick sighed. "Michele told me what happened. I'm sorry I didn't get to see you wearing your buckskins." He caught the thin beaded braid of Cade's hair and tugged it lightly. "Come over here."

Cade leaned in to kiss Erick, but before he could mate their lips, Erick frowned and moved his hand to rub at Cade's temple. "What do you have on your face?"

"War paint," Cade replied bashfully. "I wiped off what I could, but I didn't exactly have a bath, much less a mirror, to clean up in jail."

Erick traced the paint with his fingers. "I am sure Dr. Lillard will have a way for you to wash up later." He drew a labored breath. "One day you must let me see you in your Comanche garb. But now, give me a kiss."

That was a request Cade would gladly grant. Erick's lips were dry and he had to break away far too soon to draw in another ragged breath, but it was still the best kiss Cade had ever gotten. He planned on getting a lot more of them as soon as they had the guarantee of privacy.

A rap on the door forced Cade to draw back. He rested his hand on the hilt of his knife, ready to throw at a moment's notice. He hoped the threat had passed, with Sanders and Lutz dead and Parnell seeming to believe their side of the story, but he wasn't about to take chances with Erick's safety just yet. Javier stuck his head in the door, shaggy after several days in jail. "Michele, Mac, and I are heading back to Wellspring. They need the supplies we came into town to get before"—Javier glanced at Erick with a wince—"before things went to hell, and after nearly a week of Beaufort's cooking, Payne will be even more bad-tempered than usual."

Cade chuckled a little at the image. "I'm staying here until I know for sure there's no one coming to finish what Sanders started. Payne will just have to do without me for a few more days."

"I think we can manage," Javier said, "though we'll miss both of you. Erick, you keep getting better, you hear?"

"I shall endeavor to do so," Erick replied with a strained smile. Javier returned it and started to leave.

"Javier," Cade called. "Be careful. Even with the fight and Parnell, Reichardt is still out there, and we don't know how many hands the JR has left."

"Actually, Parnell offered to go with us," Javier said. "He wants to see what happened at Wellspring for himself."

That sounded good to Cade, as long as Reichardt didn't have them all killed as they crossed JR land to get to Wellspring, but he kept that thought to himself. "Ride safe," he said instead.

Chel cuffed Javier to step aside so she could enter the room. "Erick, I hope you'll be well enough to come back to Wellspring by the time we make the next supply run." Her gaze slid over to Cade. "Don't do anything stupid enough to get thrown back into jail before then."

"Not planning on leaving Erick's side," Cade asserted. Though at some point he'd have to retrieve his weapons and his leathers from the sheriff's office. Only for Erick would he have left his bow behind.

"I'll keep him safe from himself," Erick assured Chel in a rough voice.

"That's it. You all quit ganging up on me and get out of here so Erick can get some sleep." When Erick tried to protest, Cade silenced him with a gentle kiss as Javier and Chel took their leave. "The more you rest, the sooner you'll heal. I have plans for you that Reichardt's stupid attack interrupted. And trust me, you'll need all your strength to keep up."

"I look forward to it," Erick said. He looked like he wanted to say more, but a yawn interrupted him, which turned into a grimace.

"Sleep." Cade settled in to keep watch.

"Take a breath for me, Mr. Heller, as deep as you can without coughing," Dr. Lillard said two days later. "I want to see how your lung is healing."

Erick shot Cade a quelling look where he hovered nearby. He wouldn't ever get stronger if he didn't push himself, but Cade didn't want him to lift so much as a finger. Erick inhaled slowly because he seemed able to get more air that way than if he gulped it in, but even with that, he could only take in half what he could have before Sanders cravenly shot him in the back.

"Excellent," Lillard said as Erick exhaled just as slowly. "You're making better progress than I'd hoped. Lungs are tricky things. We know so little about them, you see. Now, let's get you on your feet. Lying in bed all day isn't good for you either. The wound has closed almost completely, so as long as you're careful, you can start building your strength back up."

That sounded wonderful to Erick; he was tired of simply lying in bed, even if he'd begun to sit up to eat. He swung his legs over the side and tried to push to his feet, only to have his knees buckle under him. Cade was at his side in an instant to steady him before he could drop back onto the mattress.

"Are you sure he's ready to be out of bed?" Cade asked sharply.

"I'm fine." Erick took as deep a breath as he could and stiffened his legs. With Cade hovering at his side, he took a few shuffling steps, only making it as far as the door to his room before he had to catch hold of the frame to hold himself up, his breath rasping.

Dr. Lillard nodded toward the chair at his bedside. "To start, let's just have you sit here for a bit. You can eat your meals there, and tomorrow we can start having you take short walks."

It took Erick a humiliating long time to catch his breath enough to speak. "How long… before I am back to my full strength?"

Dr. Lillard frowned. "Truthfully, you may always see some aftereffects. I had to remove the bottom lobe of your lung. There are breathing exercises that will help restore some of your lung capacity, but only time will tell how much that will be. I've only had to perform this type of surgery once before, during the war, and unfortunately that soldier succumbed to sepsis. But conditions here are much more aseptic than a field hospital. I should be able to remove your stitches within another week, but I'd recommend at least another six weeks of reduced activity before you attempt anything as strenuous as riding a horse."

Cade blanched and leaned against the far wall, looking as near to fainting as Erick had ever seen him, whether at the thought of the surgery or at how near Erick had come to dying, Erick didn't know. "Is there still a risk of sepsis?" Cade asked after clearing his throat twice.

"No, we passed that worry several days ago," Lillard said. "Now we just have to let the wound finish healing and build Erick's strength back up, however far that ends up being. The biggest issue there, as you'll have seen with your friend MacRae, is getting discouraged and giving up. Recovery won't happen in a straight line. There will be good days and bad days. You didn't lose a limb the way he did, but that makes it harder in a way. You won't have that visible reminder to slow down and give yourself time to heal."

"I did not travel from Prussia to Texas to give up," Erick said with what he hoped was a reassuring smile at Cade. "Teach me these breathing exercises so I can begin to regain my potency." Cade snickered, as Erick hoped he would. No matter how much effort or time it took, he would become the man Cade had fallen in love with again. Anything less was simply not acceptable.

CADE TIPPED his face up to absorb the warmth of the morning sun and stretched his legs to rest on the porch rail. Too many days spent inside always left him feeling like his skin didn't fit right, but this morning Doc Lillard had decided Erick could walk as far as the porch of his office and rest there while he did his breathing exercises. In the time they had been sitting there, half the town, it seemed, had stopped to check on Erick and thank Cade for shooting Sanders and Lutz. Cade had made sure to tell them Javier had killed Lutz, although Cade would have if Javier hadn't, so maybe it wasn't worth correcting them. Still, credit where credit was due and all that.

"Erick," Miz Hart exclaimed, sailing up to where they sat, "you are looking much better than the last time I saw you. I'm glad to see Webster is taking good care of you."

"Ma'am." Cade touched the brim of his hat politely.

He let the flow of words wash over him as Miz Hart caught Erick up on all the town chatter, which seemed to mostly consist of admiration for the new marshal. He'd have to warn Burke when he made it back to Wellspring. The blacksmith had grown overconfident in his courtship of the independent shopkeeper, but it sounded as if he might have actual competition for once.

Speaking of the new marshal…. Cade sat up slowly, dropping his feet to the ground as he watched Marshal Parnell ride into town leading a posse of riders and in the middle, a wagon holding several trussed-up men, including…. Hot damn, he'd actually done it. He'd gone and arrested Reichardt.

"Marshal, if you're a drinking man, I'll buy you the best whiskey the Meiers have to offer," he hollered over the noise of the wagon wheels and the clomp of the horses' hooves.

That met with a jeer from one of the men in the wagon—Collier, who was obviously recovering more quickly from his gunshot wound than Erick had—but the marshal only tipped his hat. "Just doing my job, Webster," he called back. "Good to see you out of bed, Heller. Miss Hart."

"Marshal," she replied with a genteel nod and a slight blush. Oh yeah, Burke had competition, all right.

"What will become of the JR now that Reichardt is in custody?" Miz Hart asked when Parnell and his prisoners had ridden on.

"Well, nothing immediately," Cade said. "He'll have to stand trial—"

"Everyone in the tavern heard Sanders announce that Reichardt wanted Carter to lead the raid to prove himself," Erick said. Cade hid a flinch at the reminder of what Sanders had done next. Erick was alive and getting stronger every day. "So he clearly had knowledge of what would happen, even if he had not planned it himself."

"Payne must have turned Jim Collier over to the marshal when he visited Wellspring. One of the JR hands, wounded in the attack," he added for Erick's benefit. "I bet he's been happy to claim he was only following Reichardt's orders. Not that he wouldn't say anything to save his own miserable skin, but that will back up what the Meiers and Jock and the others heard. And if Reichardt's convicted, well, hanging's too good for him but it's probably all we can hope for."

"If Reichardt has any relatives, they don't live in the area." Though she wasn't a gossip herself, Miz Hart seemed to hear all the local news, hearsay, and chitchat. "It may take some time to track that down. And if there is anyone, they might not be interested in running a ranch in the middle of Texas."

"I bet Miz Roarke wouldn't mind picking up some JR property," Cade said. "Especially if it meant we could stay on Wellspring land all the way into town."

"With Reichardt and most of his men gone, there may be no one left to manage the estate," Erick added. "There will be cattle and horses that need to be seen to, especially before winter comes."

"Winters in Texas probably aren't like the ones you're used to," Cade said with a smile. "But you're right. The stock can graze awhile longer, but they'll run out of feed and supplies before long, and I don't see any hands sticking around if they aren't getting paid."

"I am sure Payne is already making plans." It was clear from Erick's voice how eager he was to return to Wellspring as soon as Doc Lillard would release him.

"Plans that'll have us busier than ever," Cade said with a groan. They were already shorthanded. If they added land and livestock from the JR, that would make it even worse. And it's not like they could trust any of the men left from the JR outfit, even if Parnell didn't arrest all of them or if any of them didn't stand trial or weren't found guilty. Cade sure wouldn't sleep at night with any of them in the bunkhouse with him!

And yeah, he hoped he and Erick wouldn't be in the bunkhouse forever, but he had arrangements to make before that could happen, and he couldn't get started on those until they could return to Wellspring and he was sure Erick was back on his feet.

"If Mrs. Roarke is indeed hiring, especially with a new marshal in town and the threat posed by Reichardt lifted, I suspect she'll find it easier to sign people on than she has in the past," Lizzie said. "I'll put the word out as soon as she gives me the go-ahead."

"We'll bring it up when we get back, if Payne doesn't say something before then." Payne seldom came into town, not wanting to draw any more attention to his unorthodox role as Wellspring foreman, but this might be enough to draw him out.

Chapter Thirty-One

"There." Dr. Lillard removed the last of the stitches from Erick's chest. "I'm afraid you'll always have some hellacious scars, but I'll give you some cream to rub into them to keep the skin from tightening up."

Erick flexed his arms and smiled. There was some pull, but much less now that the stitches were removed, and he could exercise to get his range of motion back. "Thank you, Doctor, for all your care, though I hope you will forgive me for saying I wish to never experience it again."

"Just don't try to do too much too fast," Lillard warned as Erick pulled on the shirt Lizzie had insisted on giving him to replace the one ruined when he was shot. "I don't want to see you back here any more than you do. And that means no riding for at least another month."

Erick didn't meet Cade's gaze, determined not to betray the thoughts running through his head at just what kind of riding he would like to do. Knowing Cade, it would be weeks before he would be allowed such liberties again. His lover was even more of a worrier than the doctor. Today, though, he would only be sitting in the buckboard as Javier drove it back to Wellspring with the week's supplies from the mercantile, and even then, he expected to be coddled within an inch of his life. "I will be careful."

"Tim O'Neill made this to help you with your breathing exercises." Dr. Lillard held up a glass jar with a tube and mouthpiece attached. "He calls it a spirometer. The jar has a feather inside. Inhale as deeply as possible, then blow into the mouthpiece and keep the feather in the air as long as you can."

It was harder than it sounded to keep the feather floating for more than a few seconds, and Erick was gasping for breath after his first attempt, his mending ribs aching. "I want you to use it at least four times a day, ten breaths each time," Dr. Lillard instructed. "The more you use it, the sooner your lung will expand and strengthen."

Erick wasn't looking forward to the discomfort, but he'd endure it to regain the stamina he'd lost.

Cade hovered at his elbow as he walked outside to the boardwalk. "Cade, I'm fine," he murmured.

"But you weren't," Cade replied just as softly.

"No, but I'm getting better every day," Erick reminded him.

"And you should continue to do so," Dr. Lillard confirmed. "Just listen to your body. When you're tired, rest. Add new activities gradually. And keep doing your breathing exercises. I'd like to check up on you in a few months, just to be sure everything is still going well."

"We'll see you the next time we come into town," Erick promised, all but dragging Cade away from the surgery. "Come on, we need to pick up the horses." Even if he wasn't able to ride yet, he was looking forward to seeing Zephyr again.

After confirming that Erick was well enough to return to Wellspring, Javier had dropped Michele off at the stables before continuing to pick up the week's supply order from the mercantile. The walk from Dr. Lillard's office wasn't far, but Erick didn't have a chance to get out of breath. Every few steps, it seemed, someone stopped him to congratulate him on his recovery or wish him well.

Jock Murphy and Michele were waiting outside the stables when they arrived. Nahnia was saddled for Michele to ride on the way back to Wellspring, but Erick didn't trust anyone else but Cade to handle Zephyr. The big stallion snorted and tossed his head as Erick approached. Cade had to catch his halter before he could butt Erick in the chest.

"Easy, my friend." Erick stroked Zephyr's silky nose. "Today I cannot ride you the way we are accustomed to doing, but we will go for a long run again before too long, I promise." He cut Cade off before he could say it. "Not for at least a month, I know. But for today, you must let us tie you to the wagon so we can go home to Wellspring. You will do that, will you not?"

He'd offered to let Cade ride Zephyr as he had often enough on the journey from Galveston, but Cade had insisted on riding in the buckboard with him. Erick could only hope Cade would have less time to coddle him once they returned to the ranch.

Zephyr snorted, but the sound of Erick's voice was enough to calm him and when Javier arrived with the supplies, Erick was able to tie his lead rope to the side of the buckboard, far enough away from the draft horses that he wouldn't bother them even if he decided to act up on the way home. And if it got bad enough, Erick or Cade could reach the rope from the back of the wagon and release the tie, setting the horse free. Michele would have to chase him on Nahnia if they did that, but it would be better than watching him injure himself.

Once they got Zephyr situated, Cade climbed into the wagon and settled himself in a nest of blankets and pillows, then gestured for Erick to join him. "Oh for heaven's sake," Erick muttered when he saw it.

"The road is rough," Javier said. "This will provide some protection."

"Let us make you as comfortable as we can, Erick," Michele added. "The other choice is another week or more as Doc Lillard's guest before you get to come home."

"Yeah, get these two out of my barn, especially the big one," Jock said with a grin. "Let him eat Wellspring's oats, not mine. Though the next time I see him, I expect you to be riding him again."

"You can be sure of it." Erick clambered into the back of the wagon, smiling at Javier but ignoring his offered hand. When he tried to settle beside Cade, strong arms drew him into an embrace, his back to Cade's chest before he could voice a protest.

"Just let me enjoy holding you," Cade murmured into his ear. "I haven't had my arms around you for weeks."

Erick could admit—to himself at least—that it felt good to be held as the wagon rolled out of the barn and along the rutted street. Cade's body and the blankets and pillows provided some cushion against the jolts of the road, making the ride less agony than it would otherwise have been, but nothing could make it comfortable. Worse, inhaling the dust raised by the wagon wheels on the arid trail aggravated his throat and caused racking coughs. Cade's suggestion to tie his kerchief over his nose and mouth did little to make breathing any easier. Erick gritted his teeth and dug his fingers into his thighs and reminded himself that his own bed awaited him at the other end of the journey.

Less than an hour into the trip, Cade called out to Javier. "Erick needs a break. Just for a few minutes."

"I'm fine," Erick tried to say, but Cade hushed him.

Javier pulled the horses to a stop and jumped down. "I'm sorry, Erick, but there's not a lot I can do about the state of the road."

"I know." Erick breathed easier now that he wasn't being jostled almost constantly. "Let me rest for a short time and we can go on."

"We should have stayed in town," Cade fretted.

"It is worth it to be going home." Cade's arms tightened around him, and Erick marveled how in a few months, Wellspring felt more of a home than his estate in Prussia ever had.

Michele climbed down from Nahnia and reached into the wagon to hand Erick one of the pillows that made up the nest. "Try holding this against your chest," she suggested. "The pressure helps some women cope with cramping."

To his surprise, Erick found that clutching the pillow to his chest did help ease the worst of his pain from the jostling and coughing. Cade had Javier stop once more to let him rest before they finally reached the boundary of Wellspring land.

MacRae was riding the border line, and when he saw the wagon approaching, he let out a whoop and set his horse racing toward the big house. By the time Javier pulled up in front of the porch, every hand on the ranch seemed to have gathered together.

"Hoss!" Burke pushed through the crowd to the back of the wagon. "What's this bullshit I hear about you letting Sanders shoot you in the back? You're supposed to be smarter than that."

"Burke," Cade growled, but Erick just smiled. After almost a month in Eldorado and nearly dying, he welcomed even Burke's bravado.

"I made the mistake of crediting him with basic human decency," Erick replied. "It's a mistake I will not have to worry about making again since Cade killed him."

"About damn time someone did," Burke said. "Let's get you out of that wagon. Can you walk? Do you need a chair with wheels? A pulley to get you in and out of bed? Although with Webster's arms, he can probably lift you."

"I can manage on my own, thank you." Erick pushed up to stand, taking a breath before climbing carefully to the ground. Cade hopped down beside him, standing close enough to catch him if he wobbled, but Erick locked his knees and stood straight as one by one the hands ambled up to shake his hand or clap him on the shoulder to welcome him back.

"Why don't you come sit on the porch?" Grace asked after an especially enthusiastic buffet from Svensen nearly sent him to the ground. Grateful for the chance to get off his feet, Erick sank into one of the wicker chairs and accepted the glass of sweet tea she handed him.

"Yeah, that way Kit can help me unload the supplies instead of lollygagging with his boyfriend," Javier said. MacRae flipped him off, but Logan flushed and helped lift the cartons of groceries out of the wagon.

"I'll come back once I get the horses settled." Cade untied Zephyr and followed Michele and Nahnia toward the stables.

"How are you?" Grace asked when everyone had scattered and returned to their jobs. "Tell me the truth."

"As if I would dare to tell you anything else," Erick replied with a tired smile.

She looked at him steadily until he sighed. "I am weak as a newborn kitten, in a great deal of pain, and under strict orders to rest and recover for at least another month, but I am no longer at death's door."

"Well, you won't be able to rest and recover in the bunkhouse. You'll stay here in the guest room," Grace said with a decided nod.

"I cannot put you out in such a way," Erick protested. "I will sleep with the other men as I always have."

Grace flushed a charming pink. "I know that you were shot because you knocked Frank Sanders to the ground over what he said about me. Giving you a peaceful place to recuperate is the least I can do when you were hurt coming to my defense."

"I did no more than any man would have done upon hearing such slanders."

"It speaks to the man you are that you believe that," Grace said with a shake of her head. "But I will not take no for an answer. You will stay here until you are fully recovered."

"Yeah," said Cade, coming to join them on the porch. "You'll rest much better if you don't have to listen to Svensen snoring and Beaufort farting all night."

Payne strode up from the direction of the barn and gave Erick a long, steady once-over. "Nice of you to join us, Heller. Had enough of lazing about in town?"

"The scenery there left something to be desired," Erick replied in the same tone of voice, "though I did appreciate the break from work. Then again, according to Dr. Lillard, I have another month at least before I can return to my regular labors. I shall have to find other ways to be useful until then."

"You'll sit your ass in that chair and do exactly what the doctor says until then, that's what you'll do," Payne snapped. "And not a damn thing more, if I have to sit on you myself to make sure of it."

Erick raised his eyebrows. He'd known he had Payne's grudging respect, but he hadn't realized the man's regard had grown to such a degree. "If you say so, though I am sure there are things I can do to help Grace with the accounts and such without taxing myself unduly."

"In time, perhaps," Grace said. She met Payne's challenging stare evenly. "Not until he is up to it, but I could use his help in calculating our available funds, should any of the JR's land or assets become available."

Payne dropped a kiss on Grace's hair. "You'll do things your own damn way and have us all dancing to your tune and liking it, as always. Just remember the man almost died," he grumbled.

"I won't let her forget," Cade muttered at Erick's side.

"As if I would," Grace said with a huff. "And it is accounting, not hard labor. The worst he would have to worry about is a paper cut. Men. Really!"

"He looks like a stiff wind would blow him over," Payne said. "Webster, get his things from the bunkhouse. As for you," he fixed Erick with a glare, "you can sit here until Trujillo makes a goddamn edible dinner—damn fool idiot, getting thrown into jail and making us eat swill—and then your sorry ass is going to bed if I have to make Webster carry you there. Since he hasn't seen fit to do his damn job around here either."

Cade just grinned at Payne's insults and trotted off toward the bunkhouse. Erick wouldn't object to sleeping on a real feather bed again—the straw mattress in the bunkhouse was no longer a hardship to sleep on, but a softer mattress would be much easier on his scars. But he did object to being separated from Cade for as much as another month. Not that they had any privacy in the bunkhouse, but they'd been able to find other places to be alone. Between Grace and Payne, he doubted he'd be able to leave the house for more than the shortest of walks.

Chapter Thirty-Two

Cade returned a few minutes later with Erick's saddlebags, which he carried inside at Grace's direction and set at the foot of a simple wrought iron bed. Grace, at least, didn't seem inclined to confine Erick to the chair or the bed, allowing him to follow Cade to the guest room and back to the porch. Cade hesitated like he wanted to stay, but he had been absent from his duties for as long as Erick had, without the same justification, and so finally he excused himself with the promise to see Erick at dinner.

"Close your eyes and rest if you need to," Grace said.

"I have rested enough for a year," Erick grumbled. "Tell me what has happened while I was not here. I saw that the new marshal arrested Reichardt."

"He came out here a couple of days after he arrived in town," Grace replied, "asked a lot of questions, poked around the barn and other buildings the JR hands shot up. We handed Collier over and he squealed like a stuck pig. After that, the marshal deputized pretty much everyone in sight, rode straight to Reichardt's house, and you know the rest. He'll have to send for a judge before Reichardt can stand trial, but with all the witnesses, that's a formality at best."

"And if he is found guilty, what will happen to him? I have read stories of 'frontier justice,' so it pleases me that he will receive a fair trial. Everyone deserves that, even blackguards such as Reichardt." While Erick could understand Cade's thirst for revenge—he would feel the same, had Cade been shot instead—he could wish Sanders were still alive to stand trial beside his leader.

"If he's convicted, he'll hang." Grace seemed unperturbed at the prospect, but it had been her property and safety, and that of the hands she employed, that Reichardt had threatened. "He's lucky he hasn't already been strung up. Parnell told us that he'd talked to some of the other smaller ranchers outside of town, and we're not the only ones Reichardt was threatening. He wanted to take over as much land as he could grab."

Erick shifted in the chair, trying to find a more comfortable position, and winced as the movement pulled at his healing muscles. Grace noticed and rose from her seat. "Come on. Let's get you inside so you can rest. We can look at the accounts later."

"I am fine," Erick tried to insist, but Grace ignored him and helped him to his feet.

"Does Reichardt have an heir?" he asked as Grace herded him back to the guest room where he had left his things earlier.

"Not around here. I suppose he could have family back east somewhere, but I never heard him mention anyone. If he has a will, we'll find out that way. If not, it'll be a land grab, and I want to know how much we can afford to acquire. I want direct access to Eldorado without having to pass over someone else's property, if nothing else. Now, you rest until dinner. We can look at the books tomorrow. It'll take at least a week for a judge to arrive, so we have time."

As much as he wanted to protest that he'd spent more than enough time in bed since the shooting, Erick had to admit at least to himself that the ride from town had been more taxing than he'd expected. He lowered himself onto the bed, and Grace spread the sheet folded at the foot over him before closing the door softly behind her. He didn't realize he'd closed his eyes until Grace was knocking at the door. Judging by the lengthening shadows outside the window, he'd slept away several hours.

"Trujillo made stew." Grace carried in a tray holding a steaming bowl, a thick slab of cornbread and, to Erick's surprise, a glass of red wine. At his raised eyebrow, Grace shrugged. "It will help build your blood back up."

"I could have joined the rest of the hands," Erick protested. He'd been looking forward to spending mealtime with Cade and the rest of the outfit. It would even be worth putting up with Burke's attempts at humor.

"Webster said the doctor told you not to try to do too much too soon." Grace set the tray at the bedside table and handed Erick a napkin. At least she didn't try to assist him as he sat up or, worse yet, offer to help him eat. He was perfectly capable of feeding himself. "Enjoy your dinner. I'll come back later to pick up the dishes."

Erick sighed. He'd hoped to be able to resume at least some of his duties once he was back at Wellspring, but Grace was proving to be as much of a nursemaid as Dr. Lillard.

The food was delicious as always, and he had forgotten how much he enjoyed a glass of wine after months of water and the occasional beer, but Erick had grown used to having company with his meals, and eating alone held no appeal. In Prussia, it had been a fairly common occurrence, but he seldom had to do so since arriving in America, and it was not a change he wanted made permanent. He reminded himself it was only until he was stronger, and that the fastest way to make that happen was to rest and eat Javier's good food now, but he still resented the isolation. In town, he'd had Cade's company at least.

Movement at the window interrupted his silent grumbling.

Cade stuck his head through the wooden opening and then a moment later shimmied inside. Erick lifted an eyebrow as he waited for an explanation, not that he wasn't glad of Cade's presence. Cade shrugged and ducked his head. "I missed you, but Miz Roarke would've glared at me and told me to let you rest if I'd tried to come in the regular way. I'll leave before she comes back, I promise, but I had to see you."

"Come here." Erick shifted to one side and patted the mattress beside him. The bedroom didn't have a chair, but he'd want Cade close to him in any case. The bed dipped beneath Cade's weight, and Erick let his head drop forward to rest on Cade's shoulder. "I have missed you also. I fear we will have far less time to spend together than if I were back in the bunkhouse."

"Everyone at dinner was asking about you and says to tell you to hurry up and get better. Burke even offered to let you have the bottom bunk so you wouldn't have to climb up to the top bed. Though I wouldn't be in any hurry to give up this comfortable mattress if I were you." Cade bounced, making Erick smile. "Just imagine what we could get up to on a bed like this."

Erick could imagine all too easily, and were it not for the pain that persisted in his back, he would slide down even now and urge Cade above him to take advantage. Or perhaps not *right now* given that Grace and Payne were surely eating dinner in the kitchen not far away, but soon. Just now, his body would not allow for such vigorous activity. Soon, though, as soon as he was able, he would find the time and the privacy to seal the promises he and Cade had been poised to make to one another before the situation with the JR had come to a head. "Do not tempt me with things I cannot yet have."

"Hey." Cade lifted Erick's head to press a gentle kiss to his lips. "I didn't mean to make you feel bad. Just the opposite. I've been laid up before, and I know how frustrating it can be. I was hoping you'd laugh and tell me to ask you again in a month when you were all healed up. For now, it's enough just to be here with you and get to kiss you. I couldn't even do that in town for fear of being interrupted."

He suited actions to words and kissed Erick again, just as tenderly, though Erick could taste the heat behind it, as if Cade wanted more nearly as much as Erick did. But even breathing a little more deeply through his nose to accommodate the kiss made his chest hurt, and he pulled back regretfully. "I *will* get better and when I do, we will both find our pleasure together." He rested his forehead against Cade's, drawing in his warm breath. "And it will take less than a month, I promise you."

The door swung open, forestalling any reply Cade might have made. He yelped and jumped up as if burned, backing toward the open window. Erick turned to stare at Grace, who stood in the doorway, looking torn between trying to appear stern and breaking into laughter. "Oh, for Christ's sake, Webster," she said with a sigh, "next time use the door like a civilized person? If anyone understands having to hide your relationship in public, it's me. Just remember that Erick was shot recently and very nearly died. So let him get some sleep. If I find out you spent the night in here, I will be very displeased." She gathered the empty dishes and stopped in the doorway to look back at both of them. "*Very* displeased."

"I suppose we should consider ourselves fortunate it was Grace who caught us and not Payne." Erick ran a hand through his hair and willed his racing heart to calm. "I can only imagine what he would have to say to us."

"He'd probably tell us to keep it in our pants if we didn't want to lose it." Cade ambled back to the bed and gave Erick another long, slow kiss. "And since I have plans involving your cock and my ass—or my cock and your ass if you prefer—I'm going back to the bunkhouse. Sleep well, love."

The warmth that spread through Erick's chest at that easy admission had nothing to do with his wounds. He could only answer in kind. "And you, *mein Lieber*." Erick raised an eyebrow when Cade threw a leg over the window ledge. "Didn't Grace request you to use the door?"

"And risk running into Payne? Not a chance, not tonight anyway." He winked at Erick and disappeared.

Erick had started to doze again when a rustling near the window caught his attention. Dusk had fallen and he hadn't lit the lamp in his room, leaving it in near darkness. Surely Cade wasn't returning? By the time his eyes acclimated to the dim light, a small orange body hopped up onto the bed. "Biscuit? What brings you here? I'm sorry I didn't come out to the barn to visit you and the horses."

The cat bumped its head against Erick's hand. Bemused, Erick stroked between Biscuit's ears as it circled a few times and finally settled against Erick's side. Erick closed his eyes and drifted back to sleep to the sound of Biscuit's rumbling purr.

Chapter Thirty-Three

Erick awoke the next day feeling much better for having slept on a soft bed and convinced Grace to let him sit at the kitchen table for breakfast.

"Burke has a list of all the supplies we need for the repairs," Payne said with a nod when Erick joined him and Grace. "Trujillo can give the list to Miss Hart when he goes into town to get this week's order, and we can pick them up when they're ready. The biggest portion of it will be lumber to replace the parts of the barn and bunkhouse that were shot up or burned. We have those big oaks that came down in the spring that we haven't chopped up yet. We could haul them into town and have Graff mill them for us. That would save on the cost of lumber, especially if we want extra for that other project we talked about."

Erick contented himself with eating and let the conversation flow around him. He was no construction expert, to know what would be needed for the repairs, but even his untrained eye had picked out the damage done to the buildings during the firefight. While the temperatures had not begun to drop, winter would arrive eventually, even if Cade assured him it would not be as harsh as the winters Erick was accustomed to in Prussia. It would be in everyone's best interest to have the repairs done before then.

"I'll get some of the boys to hitch the oxen to the trees and drag them into town," Grace said. "I doubt they'd fit even in the big wagon."

"How big are those trees?" Erick asked in surprise. He knew how heavy a load they'd hauled in the wagon on the way back from Galveston.

"Too damn big," Payne replied. "And there are six of them. That's the real problem. The horses could handle one or two, but I don't want to be dragging our asses back and forth to town six times to get them there, even if we don't have to worry about JR assholes fucking with us anymore. We had one hell of a storm not long before you and Webster got back this spring. We're lucky all we lost were those trees. That kind of weather, buildings go flying."

"I remember that storm," Erick said, "or one much like it. It seemed as if the sky had turned green. And Cade said something about a… twister?"

"That's the one," Payne confirmed.

"A twister—a tornado—is when the wind spins back on itself," Grace explained, twirling her finger to demonstrate. "It can level an entire town in a matter of seconds. Zeke is right. We were lucky to only lose a few trees. We had talked about using them for firewood this winter, but we wouldn't go through that much wood in three winters. Having Graff mill them for lumber makes much more sense. Now, I need some help with the ledgers, and then a short walk down to the barn before lunch to see the mustangs will do you good. And now that the threat from the JR has passed, we can see about bringing some more down from the wild herd for you to work with when you're well again."

"I could start getting them used to being around people again," Erick began.

"Not until you're fast enough on your feet to get out of the way if one of them takes exception to you being there," Payne all but roared. "We just got you back. We're not taking the chance of losing you again."

The outburst silenced any protest Erick might have made. He would have expected such sentiments from Cade, but to hear them from Payne, of all people, made him feel that he had not only found friends at Wellspring but, as Cade had often claimed them, a family as well.

"I can walk to the barn to visit the horses before joining the others for lunch," Erick proposed. Before either Payne or Grace could counter him, he added, "Eating lunch with the other hands will allow me to rest before returning to the house. Dr. Lillard prescribed walking every day as a way to increase my stamina."

"I have better things to do than watch your scrawny ass all day," Payne grumbled. He carried his plate to the sink and bent to kiss Grace before heading to the door. "So I better not find you passed out somewhere."

Grace shot Payne an amused glance before turning her own intimidating stare on Erick. "I know you want to be well again. Just remember that you won't get there by pushing yourself into a relapse. And it won't be Zeke or me you'll have to explain yourself to if that happens. It will be Webster, and I know you don't want that. He's had enough death and disappointment in his life. He doesn't need more."

Perhaps it shouldn't surprise Erick that Grace knew at least some of Cade's history. That understanding and caring for each man and woman who worked there was what made Wellspring such a special place. "I have no intention of adding to it, I promise you. Now, let us take a look at those ledgers."

ERICK SUSPECTED that Grace did not truly need his help with her accounts, since he found no issues with the recent entries he reviewed, but it filled the time before he could reasonably leave to walk toward the kitchen where Javier would be serving lunch. He stopped in the barn along the way to visit the mustangs he'd been training. Maybe it was his imagination, but they seemed happy to see him, or at least happy to lip up the sugar cubes he'd filched from Grace's breakfast table. Rosy in particular nudged at his shoulder as if asking to be taken from the paddock and ridden.

"I'm sorry I cannot give you the attention you deserve," he told the paint, stroking her nose. "You are as eager to be put to work as I am, it seems. Soon, I hope." With a final pat to her neck, he continued on to the kitchen, where Javier was already starting to dish out plates of tamales and beans.

"Good to see you up and about, Erick," Javier said as he handed Erick a plate. "Do you need anything added to this week's order? I'm going into town tomorrow."

Had his recuperation progressed more, Erick might be riding to town with Javier himself. He would like to find something for Cade, but he could not ask Javier when he didn't know what gift would be enough to demonstrate how much Cade's loving care meant to him. "Perhaps a new pair of dungarees to replace the ones I was wearing when I was shot. I doubt even Miss Annie will be able to make them fit to be worn again," he replied.

"I'm sure Miss Hart has just the thing," Javier said. "I'll add it to the list. Let me know if you think of anything else."

Erick nodded and moved on so others could get their food. He made his way slowly to the table where MacRae and Logan sat. Cade was nowhere to be seen, so Erick figured he was on the range with Michele and the other hands who were absent from the meal.

"Should you be up so soon, Erick?" Logan asked solicitously.

"Don't listen to Kit," MacRae countered. "He's a mother hen. Erick knows what he's capable of doing."

"I am under strict orders from Payne not to collapse somewhere," Erick replied. MacRae at least would understand how much he chafed at his body's weakness and how soon he needed to carry his own weight again. "I will be resting more once I have finished lunch."

"Hoss!" The shouted nickname was almost enough to make Erick wish he'd stayed in bed. Still, he'd learned that Burke's abrasive manner hid a caring heart he would be embarrassed to reveal. "You're looking better than you did yesterday. Was it Miz Roarke's feather bed or Javi's good cooking that made the difference?"

"The bed in the *spare* room is quite comfortable, but most of all, it was being home," Erick replied honestly. "Even knowing the new marshal had arrived, it was difficult for me to relax fully in town."

"You need not fear for your safety here," Svensen assured him as he took a seat. "The threat is gone, but even were it not, we would defend you as we so recently defended our home."

"I know," Erick said. He gave thanks again that at Wellspring he had found not only a home, but a family who cared for him. "It is what allowed me to sleep last night. I have a long recovery ahead of me still, but the doctor assures me I will get there in time. I will just need everyone's patience until then."

"They'll give it." The glare MacRae leveled at the others made clear the threat that backed up his words, but Erick knew it wouldn't be needed. He'd seen them all with MacRae himself.

True to his word, when lunch was finished and the other hands returned to their chores, Erick made his way back to the house. He was more tired than he'd hoped to be from such a short excursion, but he resisted Grace's suggestion that he lie down and instead seated himself in one of the wicker chairs on the porch. For a time he occupied himself performing the breathing exercises Dr. Lillard had prescribed for him, using the device Tim O'Neill had constructed until it felt he had no air left. He repeated the process again and again until his chest muscles ached. It took far too long for his breathing to return to normal when he'd finished, but only by pushing himself would he regain his endurance, and he was determined to do so as quickly as possible.

Sitting idle did not suit him, and he wondered if he could find some reading material to keep himself occupied. About the only aspect of his former life he truly missed was his library, but he had brought only a few much-loved books with him to America. Perhaps he could ask Javier to bring back some newspapers on his next trip into town. That reminded him of borrowing the primers from Miss Dawson to help Cade learn his letters, a memory that proved his libido seemed to be recovering at a faster pace than the rest of his body. It was not something he chose to indulge while anyone who might pass by the porch could view the effect it had on him. He would have to see if there were saddles and bridles that needed mending on his next trip to the barn, or perhaps he could help Javier chop vegetables. Anything to make the time pass more quickly.

Erick hoped Cade would be back from whatever task he'd been assigned to by dinnertime, but neither he nor Michele joined the rest of the hands. From Matt Chiles, Erick learned that Cade had volunteered to take over his shift on the range to make up for the ones he'd missed staying in town. Given how long that had been, between the days he'd spent in jail before Parnell released him and the time he'd stayed with Erick while he recuperated, Erick wondered whether he'd see Cade again for the rest of the month.

Cade still hadn't returned by the time Erick finished eating, although he noticed Javier setting aside two plates, so the cook clearly expected Cade and Michele to return that night rather than staying out on the range. Erick wanted to wait, to see Cade before he retired for the night. He dared not hope for a kiss in front of the other hands, but even a brush of Cade's hand over his shoulder would let him sleep more easily. He had already pushed himself harder than he'd been able to under Dr. Lillard's watchful eye, though, and his energy was flagging. He sat on the porch as long as he could, but the third time his chin dropped to his chest and he jerked awake, the sudden movement pulling at his injuries, he submitted reluctantly to the inevitable and went to the bedroom to rest. Perhaps not taking a nap that afternoon had been a mistake after all.

He stripped down to his undergarment and climbed into bed, only the thin sheet covering him in deference to the heat of the day, which hadn't yet broken—and might not, given how little breeze came in the open window. Before he could nod off again, a tap sounded at the door. He pulled the sheet up to cover his bare chest in case it was Grace coming to check on him, but it was Cade who poked his head through the crack in the door.

Weariness giving way to elation, Erick let the sheet fall back to his waist and reached for Cade. "I was afraid I wouldn't get to see you today."

"I'm sorry. We got back as soon as we could, but we had a calf caught in a thicket near the creek, and we had to get her loose," Cade explained as he came farther into the room. He'd changed out of his dusty clothes and washed quickly—very quickly if the damp smear on his neck was any indication—before coming to the main house, so Erick patted the bed next to him.

"I missed you," Erick admitted. Cade claimed his mouth in a gentle kiss, but Erick wanted—needed—more, proof that Cade was truly here with him and not another of the erotic daydreams he'd struggled against all day. He traced his tongue along the seam of Cade's lips, slipping inside when Cade gasped. Tangling a hand into Cade's hair, he drew his head closer, plundering Cade's mouth until he had to pull back to draw a breath. His chest ached, but it was worth the pain to taste Cade again.

"I missed you too," Cade said. "If I thought I could get away with it, I'd stay right here until you're well again, but Miz Roarke would fire me if Payne didn't do it first, and it's not fair to the others. But never think for a minute that I want to be away from you." He ran his fingers from Erick's shoulder down his arm to tangle with Erick's own and squeezed gently. "I want *you* in every way."

Cade's words eased his heart. Even diminished as he was—and he *would* recover his full strength—Cade still desired him. "Come, stay with me as long as you can." He drew Cade beside him on the bed, though Cade made him wait to kick off his boots before taking him into his arms. "I was thinking of you this afternoon," he said as Cade nuzzled his neck. "About how much I enjoyed teaching you the alphabet." The memory alone had stirred him, but with Cade's body firm against him, his scent of sweat and horse and leather tickling his nose, he couldn't stop himself from pressing his hips forward, hungry for more contact.

Cade closed one big hand over Erick's flank, holding him in place. "I kinda enjoyed it myself," he replied against Erick's lips. "Lie still and stay quiet. We don't want Miz Roarke coming to see what's going on." With that, Cade captured Erick's mouth in a torrid kiss, though the touch of his hand stayed gentle as he moved it up to stroke the bare skin of Erick's torso, teasing through the dusting of hair but avoiding his scar. The careful caress ignited sparks that flared through Erick's chest and down to his cock. He gasped into the kiss and gave himself over to the magic Cade wove with his hands and mouth.

Slowly, so slowly it made Erick want to scream, Cade moved his hand lower until he encountered fabric. Erick started to lift his hips, to allow Cade to push his undergarment out of the way, but Cade kept him immobile and caressed him through the cloth instead.

As wonderful as it felt, Erick needed to feel Cade under his hands as well, to see his face flushed with the same pleasure Cade was lavishing on him. He had never been able to find satisfaction unless he could share it with his partner. Sliding a palm beneath the placket of Cade's shirt, he paused to play over a peaked nipple before gliding down the taut plane of Cade's abdomen. When he reached the barrier of Cade's belt, he rucked the shirt free from the waistband, eager for the press of Cade's bare skin against his.

Cade sucked his belly in, giving Erick enough space to loosen the buckle on his belt and work the buttons free of their holes, though the motion pulled at his healing muscles. He ignored the discomfort and went back to the more pleasant task of reacquainting himself with the feel of Cade's skin beneath his palms. Cade shifted on the bed to ease the angle on Erick's arm and slipped his hand between Erick's legs to cradle his sac. "Feel good, sweetheart?" he murmured.

"Better if I can feel more of you." Erick tried to pull Cade's shirt over his head, too impatient to even work open the buttons, but Cade again stilled his hands.

"Miz Roarke might be ready to kick me out any minute. We can't risk getting naked." He rolled Erick's sac in his palm, swallowing Erick's groan in another kiss. Erick shifted against him restlessly, his cock jumping in a plea for Cade's touch. Before he could succumb to the bliss his body craved, he tried to work a hand into Cade's jeans to return the caress, but the angle he twisted into wrenched at his healing wounds and he cried out as pain shot through his chest, stealing his breath.

Cade released him immediately and drew back as if scalded. "Fuck, what did I do? I'm sorry, Erick!"

Erick tried to shake his head, but that hurt almost as much as twisting his arm had done. "Not your fault," he managed to get out through gritted teeth. "Stay."

Cade sat back down on the bed, but he didn't touch Erick again as he rode out the flare of pain. When it finally passed, Erick sagged against the pillows. "It would seem my appetites have outstripped my abilities."

Cade gave him a pointed look. "What does that mean?"

Erick sighed. "It means that no matter how much I want you, I am not recovered enough to act upon it. Yet," he added when Cade's jaw tightened.

"You don't need to do anything but lie there and let me take care of you."

"I am not so selfish as to take what I cannot give in return." He could never repay the generosity of Cade's lovemaking with anything but its match. Erick silenced Cade's protest with a kiss. "As much as it pains me to admit, I fear Dr. Lillard was correct. I still have more healing to endure before I am strong enough for what we both want."

Cade pouted a little. "It's not like you're asking me to do something I hate. I guarantee I'd get off from sucking you dry. No selfishness involved."

Erick cupped Cade's cheek in his hand. "But I am selfish enough to wish to offer the same pleasure to you." Cade looked as though he wanted to argue further, but Erick didn't know how much time they had left before Grace's patience ran out. "Please, just let me hold you. That is enough to suffice me for another day."

Cade subsided against him and rested his arm gently across Erick's belly. "When you're well enough to walk down to the spring, I'm getting my mouth on you again, no more arguments," he whispered against Erick's neck.

"Nor would I present any, as long as I can offer you the same." He settled Cade's head on his shoulder and played his fingers through the long hair, letting the peacefulness of the moment settle into his frame.

Chapter Thirty-Four

OVER THE next weeks, Erick's days settled into a routine. In the mornings, after breakfasting with Grace and Payne (and he felt honored that they trusted him enough to display even the small tokens of affection they allowed before him), he worked on the ranch accounts, entering whatever amounts Javier or Burke had expended and updating the herd records with births or cullings and those head identified for sale in the upcoming drive to market. He also worked with Grace to determine how much they could make available from savings and working capital to bid on Reichardt's assets. At midday he would walk to the kitchens to join the other hands for lunch. If he was fortunate, Cade would be among them, though too often he was out on the range, making up the shifts he'd missed. After eating, Erick returned to the ranch house, sitting on the porch to perform his breathing exercises and engage himself with whatever busy work Payne had managed to find for him that day before joining the rest of the hands again for the evening meal.

When Cade was present for dinner, they would walk together back to the ranch house. Those few hours they could share before Cade needed to return to the bunkhouse were precious to Erick, and he begrudged every night Cade spent on the range until he was fit enough to join him again.

And then word came that a judge had arrived in town and Reichardt's trial would begin the next day. Grace, Payne, Javier, and Cade would all be called to stand witness.

"I can go," Erick asserted.

"And set your recovery back days or weeks?" Cade replied. "Why?"

"Because Reichardt tried to destroy Wellspring, and he deserves to pay for that," Erick said.

"Yes, he does," Grace agreed. "And he will, but he didn't shoot you or have anything to do with you being shot, not directly, so what would you add to the trial that we can't say just as clearly? What could you add to the trial that would justify the cost to your recovery?"

"I heard the threats he made in Austin before I ever came to Wellspring," Erick insisted.

"So did I," Cade countered. "We can tell the judge we have another witness who can't testify in person because he was shot by Reichardt's foreman. If he thinks it's necessary, we can come back and get a written statement from you to confirm it." He laid a hand on Erick's shoulder and squeezed gently. "I know how much the trip from town cost you. I don't want to see you go through that again, twice, when there's more than enough evidence to convict Reichardt without you."

"And if you think I'm driving the goddamn wagon all the way to town and back just to give your pampered ass a seat, you're sorely mistaken," Payne growled. "Can't keep out of trouble when you're there anyway."

Erick wanted to protest that he could ride with them, but the thought of controlling even one of the ranch horses, let alone Zephyr, on the hours-long journey was enough to silence him. "I will write up my statement tonight so you can present it to the judge." Despite Cade's confidence, he could only hope it would be enough.

"If the judge needs more than your written statement, we'll send someone for you," Grace promised. "We all know you'd be there if you could, but it isn't worth the risk to you if it isn't going to make a difference to the outcome of the trial."

Erick nodded once more and slumped into his chair as Grace and Payne withdrew to the parlor, leaving him and Cade alone in the kitchen. "Come on," Cade said. "Let's go for a walk."

"Where?" Erick asked morosely.

"Anywhere you feel up to," Cade replied. "The barn, the shooting range, the creek. Just somewhere that isn't here. It'll make you feel better."

It would make him feel better to attend Reichardt's trial, but unless the judge was willing to delay it by some weeks, that wouldn't happen, so Erick would have to make the best of it. "I am not sure I can make it all the way to the creek and back, as much as I would relish the coolness of the shade."

Cade pursed his lips for a moment. "Here's a thought. It's late enough everyone is probably done in the showers by now. We could go stand under the water in there. That would help cool us off."

"Sharing a shower with you would do nothing to cool me off," Erick said with a crooked smile, remembering when he'd said something similar before making love at Cade's waterfall. "But after weeks of nothing but sponge baths, I would enjoy being able to cleanse myself fully. A shave would not go amiss either."

"I'll be happy to help with that." Cade's answering grin was positively wicked. He held out a hand, and they walked slowly to the deserted shower block. Cade ducked into the bunkhouse and returned seconds later with Erick's straight razor, soap, and two towels.

It was foolish to feel awkward undressing before Cade, but Erick still hesitated before removing his undergarments. His physique had never matched Cade's muscular frame, but now jagged scars marred him both back and front. Cade had seen them, of course, but Erick couldn't help feeling vulnerable at being so completely bared.

Cade came to stand at Erick's back, his body a line of heat, even in the humid summer night, but Erick didn't pull away. His presence was a welcome comfort and silent protection. Instead he leaned back and let Cade take his weight. Cade nuzzled Erick's neck and spread his hands over Erick's shoulders, tracing across Erick's collarbones before resting his fingers at the top of the scar. He shifted enough to wrap one arm low around Erick's waist, his half hard cock nestling gently along the seam of Erick's ass. Erick gasped and resisted the urge to spread his legs, to bend forward, to beg. They had neither the privacy nor the supplies for what he wanted, nor had he recovered enough to withstand the pummeling that would surely follow, but oh how he wanted!

As if sensing his desires, Cade nipped his earlobe. "Soon, sweetheart," he drawled. "Tonight, though, we're just going to step under the spray and cool off." He ran his hand down to Erick's swiftly filling cock. "Unless you've changed your mind about letting me take care of you?"

The temptation to fall to his knees and take Cade into his mouth was strong, but Erick knew he didn't yet have the breath to manage the feat. "Not until I can take care of you too," he insisted, hoping Cade would not press the issue. He wasn't sure he had the strength of will to continue to fight what they both wanted.

Cade rubbed against Erick. "You'd be taking care of me, believe me, but we'll wait as long as you want."

Erick sighed and took a step forward into the cool water. "What I want is unfortunately not the same as what my body is ready for." He turned and cradled Cade's cheek in his palm. "Do not doubt my desire for you, now or ever."

"I know," Cade said. "Let's get you clean and us both cooled off." He stepped under the water next to Erick, brushing against him lightly enough to have been an accident were it not for the mischievous smile he tossed over his shoulder as he bent to retrieve the cake of soap. He worked it into a lather and smoothed the foam over Erick's face. "Sit. It will be easier for me to shave you that way."

Erick eased down onto the wooden bench, his breath catching in his throat as Cade steadied his head with one hand, the other drawing the razor carefully down his cheek. Erick had always considered shaving a routine necessity, but in Cade's hands it became an act of intimacy, each pass of the blade over his skin a caress.

Cade felt it too, if the way his blue-green eyes darkened was any indication. He rinsed the razor and returned to begin shaving the other side. "If this feels half as good to you as it does to me, we might have to make a habit of it."

"I have never found it so before." Erick swallowed when Cade gently tilted his head back before plying the razor over the tender flesh of his chin and throat. "But it feels good any way you touch me."

"I'm glad." Cade set the razor aside and ran the tips of his fingers over the freshly shaved skin. "Close your eyes now."

When Erick did, Cade sluiced water over his face, washing away the remnants of soap. "There. As smooth as the day I met you."

"On that day I would not have dared to do this." Erick reached up to cradle Cade's head between his hands and draw him into a kiss. "You have taken such care of me, from that day to this."

"I wish you'd dared. We might have figured things out faster if you had. As for taking care of you, I'll do whatever it takes to help you get back on your feet again." He urged Erick to stand and moved behind him to begin washing his back. "Don't complain," he added before Erick could do just that. "You can't reach your own back right now, and I won't have you hurting yourself trying. Let me help you, okay?"

The gentle press of Cade's palms eased aches Erick hadn't acknowledged even to himself. He leaned into Cade's strength and turned his head to brush his lips against Cade's jaw. "I do not mean to fight you. But you must allow me to regain what I have lost, if I am ever to become worthy of you again."

"Wor—" Cade stammered to a stop. "Erick, is that what you think? That being shot somehow means you aren't worthy of me? What the hell? You survived something that should have killed you! If either of us should be worried about being worthy, it's me." He set the soap down and kissed Erick long and slow and deep. "I love you so much. I'm no good with words, not in English and not in Comanche. Maybe it comes from bouncing back and forth between languages when I was a kid. Or maybe it's just me. But I love you. I don't care if you never get any stronger than you are right now. You're all I want. All I'll ever want." He stopped and took a breath, then another. "Tomorrow I have to go to town with Payne and Miz Roarke for the trial, but when that's over and I come back, I will fix this."

Erick's heart swelled at Cade's declaration. He knew Cade cared for him. No one took such care with another person if they didn't, but hearing the words aloud with such force and surety erased any remaining doubts. Still, he could not let Cade believe he was anything less than the amazing man he was. "How can you doubt your own worthiness?" he countered. "You survived a childhood that would have broken a lesser man. You are strong and capable and resourceful—everything I hoped to prove myself to be in starting a new life. I am proud and humbled to have won your regard—your love." He shook his head. "There is nothing you need to fix. If I sometimes fear I will never regain my full strength again, all I have and all I am belong to you."

"When you spend ten years listening to men call you 'squaw' or worse because a tribe of Comanche were kind enough to take you in, it's easy to start doubting yourself," Cade admitted. "Still, they are as much or more a part of me as the white man's world. Wellspring is the only place I've found since leaving the tribe that has welcomed all sides of me."

"Why did you leave?" Erick had wondered since the first time Cade mentioned his family, but the moment had never been right. Now, after all this time, he finally felt like he could ask.

"The Army actively tried to find and rescue children 'captured by Indians'," Cade explained in a bitter voice. "They saw a white youth riding with a Comanche and shot first instead of asking questions. They killed one of my brothers, shot him clean in the back, never mind that we were trying to flee, not fight. I couldn't stay after that, not when my presence put the rest of my family at risk."

Of course Cade would sacrifice his own happiness for the safety of his adoptive family. Erick could only be grateful that fate had brought them both together from such separate worlds.

"When I decided to come to America, I scarce dared dream of finding a haven as accepting as Wellspring." Erick picked up the soap and ran the lather over Cade's chest. "Nor a man as perfect as you." He placed a finger against Cade's lips before he could speak. "You are perfect for me. I wish only to become once more the man you deserve."

"You *are* the man I deserve," Cade replied. "But there's no point in arguing over it." He ran the soap over Erick's chest in turn. "I can think of other things I'd rather do instead."

Chapter Thirty-Five

Cade shifted uncomfortably on the pew in the church turned courtroom. He'd changed into his cleanest outfit in the back room of Miz Hart's mercantile once they got to Eldorado, and now he had to resist the urge to tug at the collar of his shirt where the bolo tie he wore left him feeling like he was about to choke. Reichardt sat on the other side of the center aisle, looking as disdainful and superior as always, making Cade wonder if he knew something they didn't. Nothing Carter could have told him of Wellspring's secrets would change his guilt, but it might sway the judge in his favor, not to mention how at least some of the townsfolk might react to hearing what was accepted at Wellspring. Carter hadn't known about Payne and Miz Roarke, but he might have told Reichardt about Kit and Mac. If he couldn't save his own skin, he'd revel in taking Wellspring down with him.

"All rise. This court is called to order," Marshal Parnell said from the front of the room. "The Honorable Judge Samuel Martin Morrison presiding."

A gray-haired man in black robes walked into the room and took a seat behind the large desk that had been moved into the sanctuary. He appeared serious and no-nonsense to Cade, but what did he know about legal proceedings and trials and, fuck, he should have insisted on driving the buckboard so Erick could be here. He would've been much better at this than Cade would be.

Once the judge was seated, everyone else returned to their places and the marshal outlined the charges against Reichardt: attempted murder, attempted theft, bribing a US Marshal, and the list went on, half of which Cade didn't understand, but the longer he spoke, the more serious the judge's expression grew.

"Mr. Reichardt, how do you plead?" the judge asked.

"Not guilty, of course," Reichardt said haughtily. Cade resisted the urge to snort.

The judge sighed. "Very well. Marshal, present your evidence."

"Mr. Payne, if you would take the stand?" Marshal Parnell asked.

"You'd take the word of a—"

"Mr. Reichardt, there will be no insults in my court," the judge interrupted. "You will have your turn to speak, but I will hear the testimony of anyone Marshal Parnell calls as a witness, is that understood?"

Cade relaxed a little for the first time since he'd left Wellspring. Maybe things would be all right after all.

The judge stood with a flutter of his robes. "Before we begin, let me make it clear that I expect everyone giving testimony today to swear to tell the truth and nothing but the truth. If there is anyone who isn't prepared to agree to this, let him or her leave this courtroom now." No one moved. "Very well, then consider yourselves all bound by this oath. Now let's proceed. Mr. Payne, was it?"

Payne rose and walked to the seat beside the judge's desk. "Ezekiel Payne, foreman of the Wellspring Ranch. And you'd best believe everything I tell you will be the truth."

Cade smothered a smile. At least Payne hadn't started swearing yet.

"Mr. Payne, please tell the court what occurred on the evening of May twenty-eight of this year."

"We had just finished feeding the hands when Webster"—he gestured to where Cade sat—"returned from town riding hell-bent for leather. He'd heard word from the JR's foreman, Frank Sanders, that Reichardt had ordered his hands to take over Wellspring. We barely had time to arm everyone and take cover before the attack started."

"I'll speak with Mr. Webster later, but for now, why would the defendant try to take over Wellspring Ranch? He owns a much larger spread of his own, does he not?"

Payne snorted. "Water," he replied succinctly. "Well, and greed. There's a spring on Wellspring property. It feeds a creek that runs onto the JR ranch and eventually joins the bigger stream that runs through town. If we get a bad drought, the creek can run dry on JR land, but the spring itself never runs dry. Oh, it may not give a lot of water, but there's always enough to get us through the summer. We don't have any dams on the creek, no holding pens, nothing to divert it, just what nature provides, so it's not like we're hoarding water or keeping it from flowing downstream. But Reichardt wanted control of the spring. He tried years ago, before Miz Roarke married her husband—the land was her father's, you see—-but old man Wells turned him down, and he's been sniffing around her skirts again ever since Roarke died. If you want my opinion, he got tired of her telling him no and decided to try to take it by force."

Reichardt scowled and looked as if he was about to speak, but a glare from the judge silenced him.

"So what happened when the JR hands arrived?"

"They expected to take us by surprise, so they rode straight in. The sun had gone down by then and there wasn't much of a moon, and they were carrying torches." Payne grinned. "Made it easy for us to know where to shoot. One of them tossed a torch into the barn, but by then we'd already brought most of them down. We had a few men injured, but no one killed, luckily. Can't say the same for the JR hands. The rest hightailed it off like the cowards they were, but we did catch hold of one of them—Collier. Turned him over to the marshal when he came to look into what happened."

The judge looked at the marshal, who nodded. "He's in a jail cell for the moment, Your Honor. We'll bring him over when you're ready to speak to him."

"Did you see Mr. Reichardt himself during the attack?" the judge asked Payne.

"No, that would require him to do his own dirty work," Payne replied, "and as anyone in town will tell you, Reichardt won't do anything he can pay or force someone else to do for him. Goddamn coward. But everyone in town heard Sanders say Reichardt had ordered the attack, so whether he was there or not, he's the one behind it."

"But you weren't in town that night, so you didn't hear it, is that correct?" the judge asked.

"No, I didn't hear it, but I didn't need to, not this time. I've seen and heard more than enough other threats to know how it all added up," Payne replied. "And other people did, so you can ask them."

"Don't worry, I will. Thank you, Mr. Payne."

Payne nodded and returned to his seat. "Mrs. Roarke," Marshal Parnell said.

Miz Roarke rose and took the seat Payne had just vacated. "Mrs. Roarke is the owner of Wellspring Ranch," Parnell told the judge.

"Rather unusual out here," the judge observed.

"My grandfather settled here," Miz Roarke said. "I grew up on the ranch, but my parents only had me, so when my father died, the ranch passed to me and my husband. He died last year, thrown from a horse. And so it came back to me."

"My condolences, ma'am," the judge said kindly. Cade kept his thoughts to himself. Roarke hadn't been a bad sort in the way Reichardt was, but he knew Miz Roarke was happier now with Payne than she'd ever been before. "Tell me about your relationship with Mr. Reichardt."

"He owns the neighboring ranch. Our families have known each other since he came to Eldorado. As my foreman told you, he approached my father years ago, but my father refused the match. A few months ago, after my husband died, he and his late foreman came to visit me and he offered marriage again. I refused as it hasn't even been a year, and when I did so, he told me I'd regret turning him down."

"Did anyone else hear him say that?" the judge asked.

"Two of my men were with me," Miz Roarke replied. "Sgt. MacRae and Mr. Heller. Mr. Heller isn't able to be here in person as he's recovering from being shot in the back by Reichardt's late foreman, Frank Sanders, after Heller defended me in the saloon here in town. But Heller's written an account of everything he's seen or heard that he thinks might be relevant to the proceedings, if you wish to look at it. Sgt. MacRae will be here tomorrow if you need to speak with him. We could only bring so many of the outfit at a time without leaving the herd untended."

"Thank you, Mrs. Roarke." The judge offered her a kindly smile as Parnell escorted her back to her seat.

Parnell called for Javier Trujillo next. Javier explained how they'd come into town for supplies and decided to wait in the saloon while the order was being pulled together.

"When we got there, Sheriff Lutz was drinking at a table with Frank Sanders. Webster told Lutz about the harassment we'd been experiencing from the JR crew—firing at our hands on Wellspring land, trying to stop us from crossing their land to get into town. Lutz said not to bother him unless somebody was dead."

A murmur rose among the spectators, though Cade didn't know why they seemed surprised. Everyone knew Reichardt had bought and paid for Lutz.

The judge brought his fist down on the desk. "Quiet! Please continue, Mr. Trujillo."

"Lutz asked if Wellspring was too weak to take care of its own problems, and Sanders said we wouldn't have to worry about that much longer." When the judge raised a questioning eyebrow, Javier added, "Sanders said since Miz Roarke kept refusing Reichardt's offer, he was going to take more direct action. By sending Adam Carter and a bunch of men to take over Wellspring."

"And it was clear this was at Mr. Reichardt's orders?" the judge prompted.

"Absolutely," Javier confirmed. "Sanders said by the end of the night she would either agree to Reichardt's proposal or—" He glanced apologetically at Miz Roarke. "—that she'd be passed around between the JR hands until no one would have her."

Cade wanted to smash the lecherous expression off Reichardt's face. "Tell them what happened next," he shouted as he jumped to his feet. "Tell them how Erick Heller punched Sanders in the face, and Sanders shot him in the back. And Lutz didn't raise a hand against him."

The judge pounded on the desk again for order. "Neither Mr. Sanders nor Mr. Lutz are on trial here today."

"Because they're both dead," Cade muttered.

"Webster, you'll get your chance to speak next," Parnell said. "Please take your seat so I don't have to remove you from the courtroom until it's your turn."

Cade subsided grudgingly because he didn't want to get kicked out. Erick would never let him hear the end of it if he caused that much of a scene, no matter how justified Cade felt it was. When the mutterings in the courtroom had died down, the judge turned back to Javier. "What *did* happen then?"

"Pretty much what Webster said. Heller defended Miz Roarke. Because he was the fastest, mind. Any one of Wellspring's outfit would have done the same. Well, most of us would have gone for our guns instead of fists, but we'd have defended her, one way or another. But Heller knocked Sanders down and walked out. Sanders shot him in the back, and Lutz did nothing. Dr. Lillard managed to save Heller, and I stayed to stand guard while Webster rode like hell to warn Wellspring. I can't tell you anything about the attack itself since I was here in town the whole time, but what I do know is what I heard in town before it all started, which I already shared, and that's that Reichardt ordered the attack, even if he didn't participate."

"Thank you, Mr. Trujillo," the judge said. "All right, Mr. Webster. Let's hear what you have to say."

Cade messed with his tie and reminded himself he'd survived far worse than this as he walked up to take the seat the others had vacated. "Now, what did you see or hear that night?"

"With all due respect, Your Honor, it started before that," Cade said. "It goes back at least to mid-March. Miz Roarke sent me to Galveston this spring on an errand, and on my way back, Heller and I stopped in Austin for a night to rest and pick up some supplies to get us the rest of the way home. The next morning, we overheard Reichardt talking to Otto Ulrich, another rancher in the area, about Miz Roarke and how she was a problem. Reichardt said the simplest solution would be to marry her because then it wouldn't matter what she thought because the land—and the water—would be under his control. And in a few years, after she'd given him an heir, no one would think twice if she had an unfortunate accident. Ulrich asked what he'd do if she refused to marry him, and he said there were other ways of getting what he wanted. Heller and I didn't hear anything else, but we didn't stick around either. We had to get back to warn Miz Roarke, not that I thought she'd give Reichardt the time of day."

A sudden thought struck him. "It does make me wonder, though. Roarke had been working with mustangs his whole life. Everybody has bad days, but now I wonder if his accident wasn't so much of an accident after all."

"You'll never prove it, boy," Reichardt spat. "You can't prove any of this. It's all hearsay and gossip."

"If enough people all saw or heard the same thing, Mr. Reichardt, it stops being hearsay or gossip, and becomes evidence," the judge said. "And while facts about the death of Mr. Roarke might be hard to come by, I've certainly heard plenty of testimony of other crimes already. Now, Mr. Webster, you overheard the conversation in Austin and came home to warn your employer. What happened then?"

Leaving out everything between himself and Erick, Cade took the judge through the events of the months since—the harassment by JR hands, the threats, the mounting tension, and finally Erick getting shot and the harrowing ride through growing darkness to warn Wellspring before the nighttime attack. "And when it was over, I came back to town to make sure Heller had survived and to confront Sanders. You can ask anyone in town. Sanders shot at me first. I killed him in self-defense."

"You don't need to defend yourself to me." Judge Morrison nodded his dismissal. Cade hightailed it back to his seat, loosening his tie enough to pull open his collar. He only hoped he'd been convincing enough.

"Your Honor, I'll need to fetch Jim Collier from the lockup, if you'll grant me a few minutes," Parnell asked.

"Let's take a twenty-minute recess so the marshal can produce his next witness," the judge agreed. "In the meantime, can someone show me where I can get a beer in this town?"

Chapter Thirty-Six

Billy Meier was swift to offer to escort Judge Morrison to the Lone Star. Cade sagged in his seat as soon as the judge left the building. "Fuck, I don't know if this is going well or not."

"We have plenty of witnesses on our side," Javier said.

"Hearsay and gossip." Payne scowled. "Reichardt's right, we don't have any hard proof. It's our word against his, just like it's always been."

"But a lot more of us against one of him," Miz Roarke said. "The judge seemed receptive to that. But we'll just have to wait and see."

"Collier's testimony should be pretty damning," Javier said hopefully. "He told Parnell they attacked on Reichardt's orders."

But when the JR hand was sworn in, he kept glancing at Reichardt, whose glare was hard enough to cut glass.

"Mr. Collier, you took part in the attack on Wellspring. On whose orders were you acting?" Parnell asked.

"Adam Carter was the one who took us out there." Collier glanced at Reichardt, then down at his shackled hands.

"Mr. Carter was killed during the attack," Parnell explained to the judge. "And whose orders was Carter acting on?"

"Sanders's, I guess." Collier spoke with a bit more confidence. "He was the foreman, after all."

"Mr. Collier, you told me earlier you acted on Mr. Reichardt's orders," Parnell declared. "Were you lying then, or now?"

"Well, I never heard Mr. Reichardt give no orders," Collier said. Reichardt smiled, obviously pleased at the answer.

"But Mr. Sanders wouldn't have the authority to order an attack on Wellspring, would he?" Parnell pressed. "An order like that would have to come from Mr. Reichardt."

"Mr. Reichardt never talked to us hands himself." Collier shrugged. "We got our orders from Sanders and Carter. You'd have to ask them where they got them from." He grinned. "Oh, except how they're dead."

"That's enough sass from you." The judge frowned. "Do you have anything else to add?"

"If Mr. Reichardt goes free, will I too?" Collier asked hopefully.

"Considering you were caught red-handed trespassing and shooting up Wellspring property, the answer to that is no," Parnell answered. "Come on, back to jail with you."

"Marshal Parnell, do you have any other witnesses to call?" the judge asked when Parnell returned.

"One more, Your Honor," Parnell said. "Otto Ulrich."

A babble of shocked voices broke out. Cade hadn't seen the other rancher in the crowd, but he'd apparently arrived at some point, walking up to the witness chair from the back of the church.

"What the hell?" Reichardt snarled, his face red with rage.

"We may have been friends, but I'm not about to hang with you," Ulrich replied. Reichardt continued to fume as Ulrich related the conversation Cade and Erick had overheard in Austin. He made tracks out of the building as soon as the judge excused him.

"That was my last witness, Your Honor," Parnell said when the door closed behind Ulrich's back, "though I do have a written statement from Mr. Heller, who is not well enough yet to make the trip back into town, confirming everything Mr. Webster and Mr. Ulrich have said."

The judge glanced over Erick's statement and set it beside him on the desk. "Very well, then. Mr. Reichardt, do you have any evidence you wish to present in your defense?"

Reichardt stood, smiling broadly, though to Cade his casual attitude seemed a bit forced. Still, Cade supposed he'd gotten so used to having Lutz in his pocket that he didn't realize Parnell and Judge Morrison were a different class of men. "Well, Your Honor, unfortunately most of the men I would have called as witnesses are dead, gunned down by Wellspring in an unprovoked attack."

"Excuse me," Parnell interrupted, "but most of your men were killed on Wellspring property, by men—and women," he added with an apologetic smile to Miz Roarke, "who had every right to defend their land against trespassers."

"What right does Wellspring have to hoard the water other ranches need to survive?" Reichardt countered. "If Mrs. Roarke would stop acting like an emotional female and listen to reason, all this unpleasantness could have been avoided."

"Mrs. Roarke," Judge Morrison asked, "would it be possible to ride out and see the spring and creek in question? It's been a fairly dry summer this year, so I'd be able to see the situation for myself. Not that using water on land that's been in your family for generations gives Mr. Reichardt a right to harass your employees, much less attack you outright, but it would help me understand his supposed grievance and give me a chance to speak with your employees who weren't able to be here today."

"This is highly unusual, Your Honor," Marshal Parnell began.

"One of the benefits of age and position, my boy, is the right to be unusual when it suits me," the judge replied. "It won't hurt anything to delay my judgment by another day or two, and if it makes it a fairer one for everyone involved, then all the better. Would that be agreeable to you, Mrs. Roarke?"

"Of course, Your Honor," Miz Roarke said. "Although I can't promise how well we'll eat tonight. Trujillo is our usual cook, and he's been here in town all day. His assistant is less proficient."

"Inedible slop," Payne muttered next to Cade.

"I can ride ahead and get something ready," Javier offered.

"I'll go with him," Cade said, "if the rest of you want to stay and ride back with the judge. If you're finished with us, Your Honor?"

"Yes, you're dismissed," Judge Morrison said.

Cade only stopped himself from bolting from the church by sheer force of will. The moment they were free of the building, he tore the tie from around his neck and opened half the buttons on his shirt. "Let's get the hell out of here," he said to Javier.

They made their way back to the mercantile where they'd left their horses, since Jock was one of the spectators in the crowd. Cade swung up onto Nahnia's back and only barely resisted the urge to spur him into a gallop, anything to get away from the oppressive feeling of the trial and the layer of filth that seemed to cling to him after being around Reichardt all day. Only the knowledge that Javier and his horse couldn't keep up held him back. Granted, with the JR decimated and Reichardt in jail, Javier would probably be fine on the ride back, but Chel would never forgive Cade if he rode off and something happened.

They made it back to Wellspring in good time, even at the slower pace set by Javier's gelding, and everyone clamored around them, demanding to know how the trial had gone.

"Let Cade tell you," Javier roared. "I've got to get dinner going. The judge is coming to talk to Erick and to see the spring for himself."

And just like that, Cade found himself the center of attention once more. At least this time it was just his friends staring at him, not a room full of people he only sort of knew and barely trusted. Before he could do more than take a breath, Erick was there, not touching him, just at his side, and all the tension bled out of him. "Let's go somewhere in the shade and I'll tell you all about it," Cade said with a cocky grin.

CADE WASN'T sure what the judge gained by riding out to the source of the spring, though he seemed impressed by the orderliness of the Wellspring buildings and the demeanor of its hands. Not that any of them dared to approach him. He, Miz Roarke, and Erick ate dinner together in the main house, so Cade didn't get to hear what Erick told him, though he knew it would only back up his own testimony. If nothing else, it would let Erick feel that he'd done his part to build the case against Reichardt, and Cade knew how much that meant to him.

He didn't know how Reichardt could have mentioned anything he might suspect about Wellspring to the judge without everyone knowing about it, but he couldn't stop the tension from mounting at the base of his skull the longer the judge was there. They were careful when outsiders were around, but any mistake could cost them all dearly.

He'd taken his dinner plate—meat loaf and mashed potatoes, and Cade was amazed that Javier had managed to throw it together so quickly—and chosen an empty table, looking to put all the pieces together the way he hoped the judge would to determine Reichardt's guilt, when Burke dropped down into the seat beside him.

"You're looking awfully glum, Wolf Boy," Burke said. "Javier said it went well today. So what's raised your hackles?"

"It's still our word against his," Cade said. "Ulrich confirming their discussion in Austin was a surprise, but Collier's the only person who could have said outright that Reichardt gave the order, and he claimed it came from Carter by way of Sanders, who are both dead. Now, granted, who else could have told them to attack us except Reichardt, but that's not evidence."

"None of that," Burke said. "The judge is in there now with Miz Roarke and Hoss. If anyone is going to convince him of what's really going on, it's the two of them, so get rid of that long face. Reichardt's going to get what's coming to him, and we're going to be free of him for good."

"I never took you for an optimist," Cade said.

"I'm not. I'm about as pessimistic as they come, but this is one time even I recognize a good thing when I see it," Burke said. "So finish this delicious dinner Javi whipped up for us and when the judge is done in there, sneak your man off somewhere to celebrate. Because if it weren't for the two of you, we wouldn't have known what was coming to be prepared to fight them off."

Payne dropped a plate beside Cade's and straddled the bench. "Judge Morrison decided it's too late to ride back to town. He's staying the night, so I'll be taking Heller's bed in the bunkhouse." Burke started to speak but Payne quelled him with a scowl. "And if anyone suggests that isn't my usual bunk in the judge's hearing, they'll spend the next month on night duty."

"What about Erick?" Cade asked. The only parts of the inside of Miz Roarke's home he'd seen were the front parlor and the guest room Erick was recuperating in. Surely the judge wouldn't put Erick out of his bed?

"There's a daybed in the sewing room. Grace says Heller tried to insist on moving out of the guest room to sleep there, but the judge wouldn't hear of it. Seemed real impressed with what Heller had to say."

That didn't surprise Cade—Erick could talk the birds out of the trees if he put his mind to it. "I hope that's enough to convince the judge that Reichardt's guilty."

"We'll know tomorrow," Payne said. "The judge told Grace he was ready to announce his verdict."

"Already?" Cade said. "I thought it would take… I don't know… days, at least. Maybe weeks."

Payne shrugged. "He says he's heard everything he needs to hear. And really, what is there to figure out?" It seemed whatever he'd overheard from Judge Morrison had eased his earlier skepticism. "Reichardt's guilty as hell, and everyone knows it. The only reason he wasn't strung up years ago is because he paid off Lutz. Parnell and Morrison are cut from a different cloth entirely. I don't know if Parnell will stay, but Eldorado will be a damn sight better for it if he does."

Cade tried to imagine a life where he didn't have to constantly worry about the threat of the JR or some other outfit trying to steal their land or their water or pressure Miz Roarke into something she didn't want. A life where going into town didn't mean watching his back the whole time, his hand on the butt of his pistol or the fletching of an arrow.

Where he could actually get a room at the Lone Star and spend the night with Erick instead of ending up with a bullet in Erick's back and a wild ride back to Wellspring in the hope of warning his friends before they were all killed.

"I think you might be right about that," he said. "If he doesn't stay, maybe we can find someone like him to be the new sheriff in town instead."

"Hell, with Reichardt gone, maybe you should run for sheriff, Wolfie," Burke said.

"Oh hell no," Cade protested. Talk about the last job he'd possibly want….

"Not that he couldn't do it, but he'd have as much chance of being elected as I would," Payne snorted. "Logan, now, there's somebody the townsfolk would get behind."

Cade thought Erick would make a great sheriff, but his being foreign-born was probably as much of a strike against him as being "colored" or "raised by Indians" to too many townsfolk. "Before we try to solve all Eldorado's problems, let's be sure Reichardt gets convicted first."

"I doubt that will be a problem," Erick said from behind Cade. Cade jumped up from his seat and made room for Erick on the bench.

"Did the judge say something?" Cade asked.

"Not directly. He would not be so indiscreet," Erick replied, "but he had read my statement, so he did not seem surprised by what I reiterated at dinner. Indeed he seemed almost to concur with it, as if it confirmed what he already knew, which says to me that he believes Reichardt is guilty."

"Good," Payne said. "I want this done. I have a ranch to run and cattle to drive to the railhead in a few weeks. I don't have time for this bullshit to drag on. Webster, take Heller for a walk. I need him fit for the saddle before we ride for Abilene. I can't have him lazing around here doing nothing."

"You are no more eager for me to be fit than I am." Erick rose to his feet.

"Damn it, with the judge at Miz Roarke's and Payne in the bunkhouse, there's nowhere we'll have any privacy. Unless you need another shower?" Cade asked as they walked away.

"Perhaps we can walk to the creek," Erick suggested. When Cade grinned, he added, "For nothing more than resting on the swing, I fear, if I am to have the strength to walk back again."

"It's a start." Cade swung their clasped hands between them. "We'll have you fit for the saddle again before you know it."

Chapter Thirty-Seven

The next morning Cade sat once again in the church turned courtroom, waiting for Judge Morrison to arrive and declare Reichardt's fate. While he hadn't managed to convince Erick to make love at the creek the night before, they had spent a very pleasant hour kissing on the swing before walking back slowly in the deepening twilight, and Cade looked forward to another walk tonight. First, though, they had to get through whatever the rest of the day held.

Parnell arrived a few minutes later with Reichardt in handcuffs. He called the gathered crowd to order for Judge Morrison to make his entrance. The judge droned on for several minutes about the charges and the evidence, all of which Cade had lived. Finally, he turned to Reichardt.

"Johann Reichardt, I find you guilty of the charges against you. You are sentenced to hang by the neck until dead. You will be taken to Fort Concho, where your sentence will be carried out immediately," the judge declared. "If you have a will or any final wishes, advise the court of them at this time."

Reichardt's eyes grew wide, and his mouth opened and closed a few times, but no words came out.

Judge Morrison nodded sharply. "Marshal, you have your orders. In the absence of any will, all property belonging to Reichardt will be auctioned off in one week's time. I will remain in town to preside over the affair. I assume there's a room I can rent for that time?"

Parnell dragged a struggling Reichardt out of the church as the townspeople began to cheer. Cade slumped back into the pew. It was done.

They'd done it.

They'd won. Without any of their secrets coming to light. Reichardt was in chains on his way to the gallows, all his property about to be auctioned off to the highest bidder or bidders. Cade wouldn't be one of those people, but Miz Roarke might be, at least enough to guarantee direct access to town.

It almost seemed too easy, but Cade wasn't one to look a gift horse in the mouth.

"Go on," Miz Roarke said softly. "Payne and I will likely be stuck here all day, possibly longer with the auction and all. Head back to the ranch and let the others know the outcome. And Cade?"

He paused in standing to meet her kind smile. "Ma'am?"

"I don't expect we'll be back tonight."

He touched a finger to the brim of his hat. "Ma'am."

"And Webster?" Payne added. "Don't break any furniture."

CADE WASN'T sure he'd made better time riding back to Wellspring the night of the attack. There was no longer a reason to avoid crossing over JR land, though he kept a wary eye out anyway. He didn't think any of the remaining hands, if there were any, would care enough to avenge Reichardt's arrest, let alone his conviction once they learned of it, but he wasn't about to take any chances. Not when he had the prospect of a night alone with Erick to look forward to.

Chiles was patrolling the fence line when Cade reached the border of Wellspring land. He gave him the good news, then galloped to spread the word to the rest of the hands.

He barely waited for Nahnia to halt before he vaulted to the ground, his gaze fixed on Erick seated on the porch of the ranch house, looking good enough to eat. Of course he always looked that good to Cade, but that did nothing to diminish the pulse of anticipation that hummed beneath the surface of his skin. Tonight was theirs.

"You're back earlier than I expected," Erick said when Cade bounded up the steps to the porch. Cade grabbed Erick's hands to pull him up and danced him around. All the way back in Galveston, he had imagined dancing with Erick. The circumstances didn't resemble his fantasy, but the reality of Erick in his arms was far more erotic than his imagination. And knowing what other news he had to share only made it better.

Erick laughed at his antics. "I take it the verdict went in our favor?"

"Judge Morrison found Reichardt guilty on all counts. Parnell is taking him to Fort Concho to hang," Cade said. Heart pounding, he met Erick's eyes and delivered the rest of his news. "And Miz Roarke and Payne are staying in town until at least tomorrow." He leaned in and stole a kiss, pulse picking up even more when Erick returned it in spades. "Payne told us not to break any furniture."

Erick turned a most becoming shade of scarlet. "I doubt I am capable of anything active enough that it would break a spiderweb at the moment, much less any furniture."

"Maybe not," Cade said, "but that's not the point. The point is that I can stay the night *with their blessing*. We can sleep in the same bed for once, even if we do nothing but sleep. For one night, it can be just us." And if he hoped he could persuade Erick to do more than just sleep, that was between him and his gods. For now, he'd settle for this.

Javier cooked up a special dinner—roast pork with green beans and creamy, cheesy grits—to celebrate the news of Reichardt's conviction, and Burke broke out a bottle of his home-brewed hootch to toast the verdict. Cade shared his friends' need to celebrate, but the desire to be alone with Erick was stronger. Each time Erick's leg brushed his beneath the table, each time Erick leaned against him or bumped his shoulder, Cade wanted to say to hell with them and spirit Erick away. He forced himself to be patient, to wait until Burke's liquor had made the rounds a few times before he stood and drew Erick with him toward the house. If anyone noticed, no one saw fit to comment on it.

"I have been most diligent in performing my breathing exercises," Erick said when Cade closed the bedroom door behind them. "I should have enough stamina to… return the pleasure you have offered me."

Cade caught Erick's hands in his own and brought them to his lips. If Erick had made that offer the night before down at the creek, he'd have jumped at it, but now, here, in a real bedroom, in a real house, with the prospect of an entire night ahead of them, he wanted… not something different, because he wanted exactly what Erick was offering—he wasn't dead, was he?—but more. "Glad to hear that, because I intend to offer you every pleasure you could imagine and more, but tonight there's no rush. I don't know what tomorrow or next week or next month will bring. I don't know if we'll ever be able to arrange our own place like Kit and Mac have. So tonight, I want it all. Will you do that with me? Will you share that with me?"

"I will share all I have and all I am with you." Erick raised Cade's hand to his lips in turn. "I wish only that I had more to offer."

"You have yourself. That's all I want." He cupped Erick's jaw in one hand to angle his head for a kiss and slid his other hand inside the collar of Erick's shirt to trace the skin of his neck and shoulder. Erick's lips parted beneath his, letting him in. Cade resisted the urge to plunder, keeping the kiss tender, though he swept his tongue in to taste and claim.

Erick's tongue met his, parrying Cade's sweetly as Erick staked his own claim for long moments before having to draw in a breath. Cade reveled in the knowledge that Erick wanted this as much as he did, that he was Erick's as Erick was his. Erick worked open the buttons of Cade's shirt and pulled it free from his waistband. "We have no threat of Grace coming to send you back to the bunkhouse tonight." He pushed the fabric easily down Cade's arms, his grip steady now in a way Cade had missed since his injury.

"Finally being able to get naked with you is one of the things I looked forward to the whole ride back," Cade admitted as he dropped his shirt to the floor and reached for Erick's buttons. He undid them and parted the fabric but left the shirt hanging on Erick's shoulders, his hands resting against Erick's ribs. The tips of his fingers brushed against the scar on Erick's chest, unsure of where the limits were. "Is this okay?"

Erick shrugged free of his own shirt and drew Cade closer. "I have looked forward to this also." Cade had felt the touch of their chests before this, but it was more intense now, the rasp of scar tissue reminding him of how close he had come to losing Erick completely, and how strong Erick was. He spared a moment to give silent thanks for Erick's survival and recovery. Cade slid his hands gently down Erick's sides, careful not to press too firmly, but Erick caught his shoulders and dragged them together. "Let me feel you."

"Any way you want." Cade backed Erick toward the bed. He urged Erick to sit and knelt to pull off Erick's boots. While he was on his knees, he took the opportunity to nuzzle Erick's inseam, but he wanted more than a quick blowjob tonight if Erick was strong enough for it. They'd had sex before, of course, but it had always been quick, almost furtive, all about physical release without the open acknowledgment of everything that lay between them. He wanted more than that now. With the gift of time and privacy Miz Roarke had given them, he wanted everything Erick had to give and to give all that he was in return. When Erick gasped softly, Cade grinned and unfastened the placket of Erick's pants. "Let's get these off and get in bed. We can decide what we want from there."

"I want to feel all of you. I want to feel you...." He lifted his hips to let Cade slide his jeans and undergarments away, revealing his still strong thighs and rigid erection. He tugged Cade to his feet so he could unbuckle his belt, the brush of his knuckles against Cade's aching cock setting off sparks behind his eyelids as they closed despite him at the sensation. Erick worked him free of the rest of his clothes and caught Cade's mouth in a deep, heated kiss, letting Cade tumble him to the mattress.

Cade followed Erick down onto the bed but supported his weight on his elbows as he hovered over Erick. The last thing he wanted to do was cause Erick any pain or do anything that might force him to change his mind about making love with Cade that night. And if Cade understood him correctly…. His cock throbbed at the thought of sinking into Erick's ass, but he wouldn't do it if he thought it would hurt Erick. They'd waited this long. They would have other chances. He could be satisfied with getting his hands and mouth on Erick's body again and having Erick touch him in return.

Erick leaned up until he could reach Cade's lips for another deep kiss. He was breathing a bit roughly when he finally pulled away, but then Cade was feeling pretty breathless himself.

"In the life I left behind…." Erick hesitated, his cheeks pinkening the way Cade always found adorable. "Because of my place in society, the expectation was always that I would take the… dominant role." He lifted his head to meet Cade's gaze, his own eyes dark and wide. "I would feel you inside me."

Well, shit. Cade hadn't misunderstood, but he also hadn't understood at all. He opened his mouth to ask if Erick was sure, but no, he knew his lover better than that. Erick had asked, which meant he was sure, so Cade had only one decision to make: how he was going to fulfill Erick's request.

Cade grinned, feeling downright wolfish. "Just lie back, darlin'," he drawled. "I'm going to take such good care of you."

"Of that I have no doubt." Erick nodded toward the bedside table. "The cream Dr. Lillard gave me to use on the scars should serve…."

"I'll get there, but we won't need that just yet." He pressed Erick's shoulders gently back to the mattress, nuzzling down the curve of his neck to the hollow of his throat. Erick hummed his approval as Cade dragged his thumbs over Erick's pebbled nipples. "Yeah, let me hear you. There's no one here to know or care how loud we get." He nipped at one of the tight points, winning a groan before he soothed the tiny ache with a swipe of his tongue and treated the other side of Erick's chest to the same attentions.

They had this one, golden night to themselves, and then who knew when they'd next have this kind of privacy, so Cade took his time, licking and sucking at Erick's nipples until they were both red and swollen and Erick was arching beneath him at every touch of his lips. He pressed a single, tender kiss to the healing scar tissue and licked his way lower, along the lines of muscle bisecting Erick's belly.

"I will not last if you take me in your mouth," Erick gasped.

Cade lifted his head and smirked at Erick. "As much fun as that sounds, I promised you something else tonight, and I intend to keep that promise." He dropped a quick kiss to the overheated shaft, already slick with fluid, and resisted the impulse to taste. His own cock ached like a sore tooth, but he ignored it in favor of urging Erick to spread his legs so he could kneel between them.

He stopped for a moment and simply stared, humbled by the trust Erick was placing in him, allowing him to play like this. Somehow, through some twist of fate, they had ended up here, both of them alive against the odds, in bed together. As much as he longed for Erick, Cade knew in his soul this was more than just the joining of their bodies. This was the start of the rest of their lives. He ran his fingers up the inside of Erick's thigh, stopping short of his balls. Erick shifted, spreading his legs wider. Cade slid his hand beneath Erick's thigh and lifted so his knee bent, opening more space. He turned his head and pressed a kiss to the patch of skin there; then, bracing one elbow next to Erick's hip, he kissed his way down the inside of Erick's thigh until he reached his groin. The smell of Erick's desire surrounded him, making him feel as intoxicated as he'd ever been, and he paused to rub his face against Erick's sac, reveling in the heat and scent and masculinity.

Above him, Erick gasped and squirmed, making Cade smile. He shifted to balance his weight so he had his hands free to angle Erick's hips to give him access to his target. His Comanche brothers had not named him Wolf for nothing, and the scent of Erick's arousal drew him to this target as unerringly as any other, his tongue circling the puckered, untouched flesh.

"Cade," Erick rasped, and Cade would never get enough of hearing his name in that pleading tone. For a moment he resented anyone else who had ever seen Erick like this. *But,* he told himself, *no one had ever loved Erick this way—no one had ever loved Erick at all*. He had the rest of their lives to fix that.

He licked and sucked and nipped until Erick was writhing beneath him before working his tongue into the furled entrance. It was a damn good thing Payne and Miz Roarke were gone, because the cry that wrung from Erick might have been heard all the way to the bunkhouse.

Cade's chest swelled with pride at being able to bring his lover such pleasure. Determined to wrest as many similar sounds from Erick as he could before the night was over, he pressed closer and thrust his tongue in again, a little deeper each time, a hint and a tease of what was to come. He wanted Erick wet and loose and desperate for him even before he slid a first finger inside to stretch him. Erick's taste and smell drove Cade wild, but he reined in his desire to focus on Erick's pleasure first.

Erick bucked against his mouth, riding his tongue the way Cade fully intended Erick to ride his cock before the night was over. Cade tensed his tongue and met Erick's movements with little thrusts and sucks of his own until Erick's feet were kicking restlessly and his hands were scrabbling in the sheets for something to hold onto.

"Cade, please…." Erick's voice was hoarse and broken and had never sounded more beautiful to Cade's ears. "I ache… I need you now."

Cade nearly ignored the plea, so lost in the joy of getting to ravish Erick this way, but the need to finally sink into his hot depths outweighed even that. With one last swipe of his tongue, Cade knelt up and reached for the pot of salve. "Not until I'm sure you're ready for me." He dragged his index finger through the thick cream and rubbed it around Erick's wet hole before slowly easing it inside. "How does that feel, darlin'?"

"I have had my fingers inside me before," Erick said a bit testily. "More!"

"Oh, you're going to be one of those, are you?" Cade crooked his finger to coat the passage. He was going to come back to the image of Erick with his fingers in his own ass. Maybe even get Erick to demonstrate some night. Some *other* night. "Trying to steer the wagon even when you're not holding the reins."

"I am happy to leave you the reins so long as you move at a proper pace." Erick bucked his hips to drive Cade's finger deeper. "I can take more."

Cade slid out and slicked up a second finger before working them both inside. "Yes, but have you felt this?" He swiped a fingertip over the bundle of nerves that made Erick curse in German. Oh, that was going to be his new goal—to make Erick lose his English. He rubbed over the sensitive bump until Erick was clenching around him. "So tight—you're going to feel so good squeezing around my cock."

"Yes," Erick gasped. "I want to feel that. Now."

Cade spread his fingers, judging the give of the muscle, but however ready Erick thought he was, Cade wasn't satisfied. Besides, he was having too much fun making Erick gasp and squirm and curse. Anything to drive Erick even wilder than he already was. "Soon," he promised as he spread more cream around Erick's entrance and pressed a third finger against his hole. Erick froze and cursed at the stretch, proving Cade right. As good as it would feel to simply sink into Erick's hot depths, it wouldn't feel good to Erick, which meant exercising his patience a little while longer. He rubbed his thumb over the patch of skin between Erick's sac and his entrance, massaging his sweet spot from the outside until the constriction released enough that he could get three fingers inside. Finding the little bump again, he worked it from both directions, milking it relentlessly. "Sing for me, my sweet," he murmured in Comanche.

"Cade, *mein Lieber… bitte, bitte….*" Erick was starting to sound frantic. Cade wasn't sure how much longer he could hold off himself. His cock throbbed each time Erick clenched around his fingers. Erick keened as he drew his fingers out, driving Cade mad with the sound. As much as he wanted to just push inside that slick heat, his weight might be too much for Erick's still-healing body to bear. Shifting to one side of the mattress, he rolled onto his back and smeared what was left of the cream over his leaking shaft.

"Erick, kneel up over me," he urged. "It will be easier on you this way, and you can take me inside as slowly as you need to."

Erick bent down to seize Cade's mouth in a needy, demanding kiss before straddling his hips. Cade reached back, dragging his cock up and down the crease between Erick's cheeks, biting his lips at the need to let Erick take control. He wanted nothing more than to roll Erick to his back and drive into him, but he had to let Erick do this at his own pace. When Erick's hand closed over his own, he slid his palms around to brace Erick's hips, hoping he would be able to last long enough for Erick to take him inside.

He and Erick cried out together when Erick thrust down, taking all of Cade in one strong push. Erick let out a ragged breath, not moving for a long moment, while Cade struggled not to give in to the insistent, exquisite pressure.

Cade caressed Erick's flanks as tension mounted between them. He had to give Erick the time he needed to adjust to Cade's presence inside him, no matter that it had been Erick's choice to take him in so quickly, but fuck, he didn't know how much longer he could stay still. After what seemed like hours, Erick shifted a little, though it only ratcheted the tension higher as Cade fought to lie there and let Erick explore.

Finally Erick rose up onto his knees, beginning to move more freely. Cade rocked his hips to meet Erick's downward thrust and shot his lover a sly grin. "Ride me, cowboy."

"Ah, now you do not complain that I take the reins?" Erick pushed down and circled his hips, raising a smug eyebrow when it made Cade gasp.

"When I'm not worried about this"—Cade ran his fingers over Erick's scar—"causing you pain, I'll flip you over and mount you as hard and fast as any stallion, but until then, you set the pace."

Erick leaned onto his elbow, bracketing Cade's chest so he could tweak at Cade's nipples. "This is… so much more than I ever dreamed. It is good for you?"

Cade sat up enough that he could capture Erick's lips with his own. He never wanted to hear such doubt in Erick's voice again, not in relation to them. "It is everything I could have hoped for and more," Cade promised when he broke the kiss. "That you are here with me at all, much less that you would let me be the first to touch you this way…. You are a gift beyond price, one I will spend the rest of my life cherishing if you will let me."

He didn't know what he'd do if Erick said no, but since Erick leaned forward to kiss him and picked up a rolling rhythm with his hips that had Cade struggling to keep up, he hoped that was a yes. He dropped back onto his elbows, the better to brace himself so he could match Erick's gait. When Erick reached for his own cock, though, Cade slid the rest of the way to his back so he could bat Erick's hand aside and replace it with his own. *He* wanted to be the one to lavish pleasure on his lover tonight. He might not be able to swear yet that Erick would never have to take care of himself again, but not while Cade was right there in bed with him. He bent his knees, planted his feet, and thrust harder, determined to push Erick over the edge before giving in himself. "What do you need?"

"The head," Erick grunted. "Your thumb."

Cade swiped his thumb over the slick tip of Erick's cock and through the slit. Erick threw his head back with a shout, every muscle in his body going tense as release swept through him. The exquisite pressure on Cade's cock stole the last of his control and he followed Erick over the edge into oblivion.

Erick gasped and panted roughly as he lifted enough to let Cade slide out and nestle beside him. Cade wondered if it still hurt Erick to breathe, but he didn't want to break the tender mood by asking.

"Now I am claimed." Erick lay with his head pillowed on Cade's shoulder, drawing patterns through the streaks of milky fluid on Cade's chest and stomach.

"I'd say you claimed me too." He lifted Erick's hand to his lips and sucked his fingers clean. "Anyway, you've been mine since the moment I saw you on the dock in Galveston. You just didn't realize it right away."

"I scarce dared to hope such a strong, capable man would return my regard." Erick raised his chin until he could reach Cade's lips. "You were everything I wanted and everything I dreamed to become."

Humbled, Cade returned the kiss with all the emotion swelling inside him. When Erick broke the kiss to lay his head on Cade's shoulder again, Cade said, "You don't need to become me to belong here. You've carved out your own place, which is better than trying to fill someone else's boots. But as for the rest, you have me. For as long as you want me, I'm yours."

He stopped short of asking for a declaration in return, not because he doubted Erick's feelings but because making such a commitment without observing the rituals he had grown up with seemed wrong. Still, now that Reichardt was dealt with and Erick was on the mend, he'd see to things as quickly as he could, because having tasted a hint of what life with Erick could be like, he did not want to go back to the way things were before.

Erick spooned into Cade, an arm around his waist and a leg over his, and pressed a kiss to the side of Cade's neck. "And I am yours," he murmured sleepily. Cade listened as Erick's breathing, still a little uneven from the exertion or the injury, slowed and deepened before letting his own eyes fall closed. They'd both need their rest for what he had planned when they woke up.

Chapter Thirty-Eight

"With what we acquired from the JR auction last month, we should be able to double the number of head we send to Abilene compared to what we sent to Sedalia last year." Grace glanced at Erick, who nodded confirmation.

"Auction" was a bit of a misnomer, from what Erick had heard. Once it was confirmed that Reichardt had not left a will and had no known relatives to inherit, Judge Morrison had called a meeting with all the ranchers whose land bordered the JR's. He rolled out a map Marshal Parnell had provided and turned to Grace. "As the most aggrieved party, it's only fitting to give you first choice of the property available."

Erick had helped Grace pore over Wellspring's assets in the week after the trial, using what they estimated was a fair cost per acre to determine how much she could afford to offer. It meant stripping the ranch's savings, but it was a risk Grace and Payne were willing to take to ensure passage to Eldorado without leaving Wellspring property. The cost per acre Judge Morrison quoted, though, was less than half what they had estimated. Grace was able to almost double Wellspring's total acreage. After that, the judge turned to the two smaller ranchers who abutted the JR, each of whom purchased adjacent parcels. Finally, he offered what was left to Ulrich.

Along with the land, Wellspring had acquired an equal proportion of the JR's assets, including cattle, horses, and supplies. Wellspring's hands had spent the past several weeks inspecting the new herd, replacing the JR brand with Wellspring's, and culling the stock that was ready to sell.

"If we can get them there," Payne grumbled, arms crossed in front of him in a gesture Erick had come to recognize during his convalescence. "Twice as many cattle with no extra hands and my best set of eyes missing for three weeks now on some godforsaken errand he didn't even bother to tell me about."

Not that Cade had told Erick any more. A week after their night together, a wonderful week in which they'd taken every opportunity they could steal to be together (and to make love whenever and wherever they could), word arrived that Judge Morrison had set a date for the auction of the JR's property. Erick didn't know why, but the news left Cade uncharacteristically quiet and thoughtful. The next day, he'd told Erick he had some personal business to attend to that would require him leaving the ranch. It was clear from his demeanor that he hadn't wanted to talk about it, and Erick hadn't felt it was his place to push for answers Cade clearly didn't want to give. Cade had promised to return as soon as he could, but that had been three weeks ago, and Erick couldn't help but worry as he lay in his lonely bed at night. He'd seen for himself on the trip from Galveston the kind of dangers Cade might face, from weather to bad terrain to dangerous animals, not to mention JR hands looking for revenge. And Cade had no one to watch his back.

"And I don't care what Marshal Parnell says," Payne continued. "I ain't convinced those JR fuckers are gone for good, so don't give me any shit about how many hands I plan to leave behind."

"Who's left?" Grace countered. "Carter, Sanders, and Reichardt are all dead, and without them, the others are just leaderless cowpokes. Sure, maybe they bought into Reichardt's bullshit, but they don't have the brains or the resources to do anything without someone backing them up. And most of those didn't stick around, as you well know since you've been all over the old JR homestead. More than once."

The survivors who'd taken part in the raid on Wellspring had managed to disappear after Reichardt's conviction with the exception of Collier, who would be serving twenty years hard labor, despite his argument that he was only following orders. Erick suspected few other JR hands wanted to work for a woman and a black man. No loss, since he wouldn't want to work alongside such bigots. "Braddock and Freeman seem to be good, solid hands," he said, though they could use another dozen like them.

"Becca Spencer has been talking with Michele," Grace warned. "She grew up on a ranch, but Reichardt never let her work anywhere but the kitchen. You can expect her to be asking to ride the herd soon."

"Annie Dawson also," Erick added. "She is capable of much more than washing laundry."

"When you get back from Abilene, you'll need to build another bunkhouse for the women," Grace told Payne with a smile.

"Four when I could use forty," Payne retorted.

"Don't exaggerate," Grace scolded. "I'd settle for half that, male or female."

"And a bunkhouse for women. What's this world coming to?" He grinned when he said it, or maybe it was a grimace. Erick could never be sure. His expression turned grim when he continued, "I'll need at least ten hands to wrangle that many cattle if we have any hope of holding them together on the trail to Abilene. And that won't leave you enough to work the herd that's left."

"We've done more with less before," Grace said with a philosophical shrug that didn't seem to mollify Payne in the least.

"Oh, and still no Webster. You really don't know where he went or when he'll be back, Heller? I don't like the idea of doing the drive without him. He reads the land better than any cowboy I ever seen, which I need with the new route. I wanted to leave August 1st, and we've already missed that by more than a week. We can't afford to leave any later than August 15th. We got to make it to Abilene before the weather turns up north."

Erick suppressed a sigh and shook his head. Payne had made it clear it would take at least three months to drive the herd the six hundred miles to the railhead in Kansas, where the cattle would be shipped to the slaughterhouses and packing plants in St. Louis and Chicago. "He said he had business to attend to and would be back as soon as he could." Three weeks didn't feel like "soon" to Erick, but if Cade's business was in Austin or, worse yet, back in Galveston, it could easily take him that long or more. Even without the wagon slowing him down, he and Nahnia could only cover so much distance in a day. Their one week together, with the rest of the hands doing their best to announce their presence before walking in on them in the barn or the shower or the bunkhouse as Cade had once laughingly told him they'd done for Kit and Mac, only made Erick's loneliness worse, since now he had more than just his hopes and imagination to reinforce what he was missing. Michele did her best to keep him company when he wasn't working with Grace, reassuring him that whatever Cade's business was, it must be important if he was willing to leave Erick to deal with it. Still, Erick couldn't help feeling as if he'd been abandoned. Zephyr was as strong and swift as any mustang. Surely Erick could have accompanied Cade, whatever his errand.

"He has another week," Payne said. "Then we leave without him and he'll have to hold down the fort here instead of leading the drive to Abilene."

Erick wasn't sure what he was supposed to do with that information. He had no way of contacting Cade or affecting his return in any other way. "He'll be back when he can" was the only thing he had to offer.

Payne looked like he wanted to argue more, but Grace silenced him with a glance. Erick tried to convey his appreciation through his smile. He was worried enough for all of them. He didn't need Payne's harangues to remind him of how long Cade had been gone and all the things that could go wrong.

TWO DAYS later, Erick had just sat down to lunch with Grace when he spotted a cloud of dust down the road leading to Wellspring. (He'd spent every moment he was outside watching the road, hoping to see Cade riding back.) As it drew nearer, it resolved into three riders, one of them Marshal Parnell, accompanied by two strangers, women from the looks of their apparel.

"Mrs. Roarke," Parnell greeted when they came to a halt. "These women rode into town asking for directions to Wellspring, so I offered to show them the way."

"We are looking for Jesse Beaufort," the older of the two added.

"He's out with the herd," Grace answered. "I can send someone to fetch him." She nodded to Luke Quinn, who took off for the stables. "We were just about to have lunch, if you'd like to join us."

The three dismounted and hitched their mounts to the porch rail before sitting down at the table. "My name is Li Mei Zhou, and this is my… ward, Alice Smith. Beaufort wrote to us some time ago describing Wellspring in such glowing terms that we hoped you might be in need of hands."

Grace looked as if one of her prayers had been answered. "You'll have to pass muster with our foreman, but if he agrees, we can definitely find a place for you." She gestured to Javier, who dished up three more bowls of chili and set them before the newcomers. "Can I ask how you know Beaufort?"

Alice giggled, and Li Mei shot her a stern glance. "We met in San Francisco. My husband and I emigrated from China to purchase land to start a ranch. Beaufort had wandered into an area of town that was… less than hospitable for strangers."

"Anyone not Chinese, she means." Beaufort strode to the table and pulled Li Mei into a quick hug. "I was looking for a drink and stumbled into the middle of some kind of gang tussle. She saved my ass. You wouldn't think it to look at her, but she's quite a fighter."

"And Beaufort proved to be quite a good ranch hand, until his wanderlust grew to be too much for him."

"What brings you to Wellspring?" Beaufort straddled the bench next to her.

"Sentiment against Chinese has been growing in California," Le Mei said, her expression stern. "We were vandalized several times—cattle slaughtered, fires started—and the law turned a blind eye. When my husband was killed confronting a rustler, I decided to find somewhere more accepting to start anew. Beaufort's description made Wellspring sound like such a place."

"After you dealt with the rustler, I assume," Beaufort said dryly. "I'm sorry to hear about Ang. He was a good man."

"Beaufort," Payne barked from across the yard as he strode toward their table, "what's this I hear about you bringing home strays? That's Webster's job."

Erick hid the wince at the mention of his missing lover. No, not missing, just absent. Cade would be back with an explanation and a tale of high adventure to rival any in Erick's beloved books. He just had to be patient.

"Not strays, boss," Beaufort replied easily. "Old friends, including the woman who saved my life years ago. Li Mei, this is Zeke Payne, foreman of Wellspring, Payne, this is Li Mei Zhou and her ward. She's the best damn street fighter you'll ever meet."

Payne looked around the open ranch. "You see any streets around here? I need people who can handle cattle and a gun."

Beaufort smirked at Li Mei and handed her his pistol. She examined the barrel for a moment before emptying all six rounds into the bole of the big live oak tree on the opposite side of the yard. Erick didn't have Cade's vision, but he suspected they'd find the bullets all in one spot.

"Is that good enough for you?" Li Mei asked calmly.

"Well, shit. Webster might have some competition when he gets back."

"Li Mei ran the ranch with her husband," Beaufort added. "What she doesn't know about cattle isn't worth knowing."

"What about you?" Payne snapped at the younger woman. "You a sharpshooter too?"

"Not like Li Mei, but I can defend myself if I need to." Alice met Payne's gaze squarely, not cowed by his brusque manner. "I'd much rather work with horses than cattle, though."

"Heller's in charge of the horses around here." Erick blinked at the sudden promotion. "Take her to the barn and see what she's got. You, saddle up." He pointed at Li Mei. "Let's see if Beaufort's just blowing smoke out his ass."

"After they've finished eating," Grace interjected. "They've just gotten here, and you will not make a poor hostess out of me, Ezekiel Payne, not even for two new hands. And you too. You haven't had lunch either. Sit."

Payne subsided with a glare that bore no real heat as Javier brought him a bowl. He grumbled under his breath but ate the whole thing like he was starving. No one went hungry at Wellspring, but Erick had wondered more than once about how Payne had ended up at Wellspring and what his life might have been like before he arrived. He often ate like someone who had known hardship, more than what life at Wellspring could explain away.

When Payne finished, he pushed the bowl back and stared pointedly until Li Mei and Alice emptied their meals. Grace nodded her okay, murmuring something as Payne stalked past her that sounded suspiciously like "women's bunkhouse."

"Another damn building. I'm a rancher, not a carpenter," Payne muttered as he stalked away. Li Mei rose with a grace Erick recognized from his days of fencing and pugilism and swung onto her horse's back with the ease of an experienced equestrian. Whatever tests Payne had devised for her, Erick had no doubt she'd pass them with flying colors. He turned to the younger woman. "If you have finished, I can introduce you to some of the mustangs we are preparing as mounts for the outfit."

Alice turned to Marshal Parnell with a smile. "Thank you for seeing us here, Marshal."

"My pleasure, Miss Smith," he replied with an answering smile. "You'll be in good hands here."

"You may want to bring your horse into the barn," Erick suggested as she rose. "If your… companion… is as good as Beaufort says, I'm sure the two of you will be staying."

Alice must have heard the hesitation in his voice. "Oh, let Li Mei hear you call her my companion!" she said with a grin. "Most people assume she's my mother or aunt, but we're not related. Not by blood anyway, though she sort of adopted me after she caught me picking her pocket."

"That sounds like a story worth hearing," Erick said as they led Alice's horse into a vacant stall.

"I was abandoned in front of an orphanage as an infant." Alice unsaddled her horse with the ease of experience before patting the bay's nose and shutting the stall door behind her. "I ran away when I turned twelve and lived on the streets, stealing food and picking pockets to survive. I picked the wrong person when I tried it on Li Mei—or the right person, I guess. She saw something worth saving in me and took me back to the ranch with her."

Though Erick didn't say it aloud, Cade had done much the same with him, not that he'd had to resort to picking pockets. "You will be the latest in a line of newcomers to Wellspring, all who came here because they had nowhere else to go, and all who have found there is nowhere else they wish to be."

He led her out the back to the paddock where the mustangs grazed aimlessly. Rosy came up to him immediately. He rubbed her nose before she could butt him with it. "This one is Rosy. The others have yet to be named as I had to stop working with them eight weeks ago, although I hope to have a new batch to train after the cattle drive."

"Why'd you stop?" Alice asked. "They need consistency if they're going to make progress."

"I am aware, but being shot and nearly dying makes riding any horse inadvisable, much less riding ones that are still new to a saddle or bridle."

"Now *that* sounds like a story worth hearing," Alice countered.

"Perhaps, but not today." Erick didn't want to relive that experience, even though he was finally beginning to feel recovered. *Enough to take part in the cattle drive*, he insisted to himself, even if he had to ride on the chuck wagon with Javier. He just had to convince Payne that he had the stamina to accompany them. *To accompany Cade.* Assuming he made it back to Wellspring before they had to leave.

Shaking off the worrisome doubts, he opened the gate to the paddock. He'd gotten the mustangs ready for riding before the ill-fated trip to town, but they hadn't been handled since and might well have fallen back into bad habits. "Have you trained horses before?"

"Not a lot of wild horses roaming the streets of San Francisco, but Li Mei let me work with the ones on the ranch, and she says I have a way with them." Alice followed him inside the paddock. The mustangs, except for Rosy, took off for the far side of the field.

"See if she will let you approach her."

Alice held her hand out and started toward the little mare. Rosy shied away at first but Alice didn't give up, circling around and crooning to her until Rosy relented and let Alice get close enough to pat her withers. "There's a good girl," she murmured. "You've forgotten how to be around people again, haven't you? That's okay, though. I forget how to do that sometimes too."

The words tugged at Erick's heart. What must it have been like for the girl, abandoned as a baby and then on the streets alone so young? At least Cade had his Comanche family to care for him. That was in the past, though. She was here now, and that was what mattered. She would carve out her own place just as he had done.

"Bring her over here and let us see if she will take a saddle."

Alice led her to the paddock fence and clipped her halter to a lead rope tied there. Rosy shook her head but didn't fight the rope beyond that. "Easy, *Kleine,*" Erick soothed. "You are safe here." He pointed out the tack room to Alice and waited while she fetched a saddle, blanket, and bridle.

Rosy quivered as Alice set the blanket on her back but she accepted the saddle, even when Alice tightened the girth.

"You have an apt touch," Erick complimented. "Slip her bridle on and you can try riding her if you would like."

Alice beamed as she fitted the bridle over Rosy's ears and then eased into the saddle, crooning to the paint under her breath. Rosy shook her head once but didn't buck or strain under the weight, though Alice was much slighter than Erick. He unclipped the halter from the lead rope, and Alice guided Rosy in an easy walk around the paddock.

"What a sweetheart you are!" Alice murmured to Rosy as she dismounted. Erick watched as she removed the saddle and bridle and rubbed the horse down. He offered a carrot from the bunch Lizzie provided him in every supply run, and Rosy took it from Alice readily.

The sound of hoofbeats in the stable yard heralded the return of Payne and Li Mei. Alice took the reins from Li Mei's horse after she hopped from the saddle, and after a nod from Erick, she led them into the barn to find another vacant stall.

"She any good?" Payne asked as he swung his leg over the saddle horn and dropped to his feet.

"Since I am now in charge of the horses, I say yes. She handled her own horse well and managed to saddle and ride Rosy. I would feel confident leaving the horses in her care." Payne raised an eyebrow but didn't rise to the opening Erick gave him. "What is your opinion of Li Mei Zhou?"

Payne tossed the reins of his horse to Erick. "Eh, she'll do." Coming from Payne, that was practically effusive praise. "Now we just need another couple dozen like them before the damn cattle drive starts in five days."

That was a problem for which Erick had no solution.

Chapter Thirty-Nine

Four days later Erick was perched atop a fence, ticking off a count as Logan and MacRae drove cattle marked for sale into the near pasture where, the day after tomorrow, Payne would be leading them on the months-long drive to Abilene. One more day for Cade to return, and Erick was steeling himself to accept that he might not make it. *In time*, he insisted to himself. He might not make it back in time to join the cattle drive. Erick refused to accept that something might have happened to keep Cade from returning at all.

A shout rose from the direction of the main house, and Luke Quinn came running up along the fence line. "Erick!" he shouted. "Kit, Mac, c'mon, you won't believe this!"

Erick swung down from the fence and followed Quinn toward the house, looking up the road, but Quinn pointed in the opposite direction, into the bluffs behind the house. At the crest of the hill, a figure on horseback was silhouetted against the bright sky. A moment later a second figure appeared, one Erick knew intimately. A third figure joined them, and then, to Erick's surprise and confusion, the crack of a whip echoed over the valley and a string of mustangs started down the hill. The two unknown figures stayed where they were, but Cade spurred Nahnia and galloped ahead of the mustangs down into the valley… toward Erick.

He heard Kit and Mac dismount behind him, heard the shouts as other hands came running, but Erick's gaze was locked on Cade as he rode forward until he came to a stop before Erick. Cade, dressed in the buckskins Erick had never seen him wear, a beaded headband circling his forehead, feathers plaited into the braids at each temple rather than the single beaded braid he usually wore, a wolf's tail hanging from his waist. This was the child who had grown to manhood among the Comanche, who had shaped him as much if not more than his birth parents. This was Tutaatu Isa. Erick couldn't take his eyes off him.

Grace and Payne made their way to Erick's side as Cade slid from Nahnia's back but didn't come any closer. "What the hell is this, Webster?" Payne barked.

Cade held Erick's gaze as he answered Payne, as if he couldn't force his eyes away either. This was the side of Cade that Erick hadn't seen before, the upbringing that had shaped him into the man he loved. "You're shorthanded since picking up the land and cattle from the JR. My Comanche brother and his band are troubled by the cavalry raids on their people. In exchange for space to pitch their tipis, they're willing to work for Wellspring."

"And do they know anything about working cattle?"

Cade grinned, still watching Erick as if he were afraid he'd disappear. "They stampede bison to hunt down the weakest of the herd. I think they can handle our longhorns."

Payne rubbed his chin. "There's the land along the creek we cleared the trees from… they could set up camp there."

"And they'll be paid the same wage as any other hands," Grace added.

"I never doubted it," Cade replied. He whistled sharply and the figures still silhouetted atop the hill started down, two becoming three becoming twenty, not only braves but women and children. Most of them lingered on the edge of the paddock, but one man rode directly to Cade's side before sliding off the back of his pony. Cade spoke to him in what must have been Comanche, and the man nodded.

"This is my brother, Nocona," Cade said. "He speaks for his band."

"I accept your terms," he said in a deep voice, inclining his head to both Grace and Payne.

"You speak English?" Payne asked. "That'll make things a damn sight easier."

"Nocona and I grew up together. He taught me Comanche and I taught him English." Cade shrugged. "Some of the others know a little, but they'll learn quick enough."

"It is, sadly, a white man's world we live in," Nocona said to Payne. "Speaking English is one way to protect the people who place their trust in me."

"It might be a white man's world out there," Payne said, "but in case Webster didn't tell you, Wellspring's owned by a woman and run by her and a black man. Everybody's welcome here."

"Of course I mentioned it," Cade squawked. "How do you think I persuaded them to come back with me?"

"My wife convinced me to accept his offer," Nocona replied. "Tatsinuupi, will you join us?"

A heavily pregnant woman with a toddler clinging to her skirt made her way slowly through the milling horses to their side.

"Cade Webster!" Grace scolded. "The first order of business should have been getting your sister-in-law and niece somewhere comfortable!" She turned to Tatsinuupi. "Come sit down." She guided her to one of the mess tables before glaring at Payne and Nocona as well. "Men, really!"

"Thank you, ma'am," Tatsinuupi said, her voice much more hesitant and accented than Nocona's. "I am well. But it will be good to be settled in one place when our child comes."

Payne turned his scowl back to the horses. "I didn't send you out for more mustangs, Webster."

"They ain't for you." Cade rubbed the back of his neck. The gesture brought a smile to Erick's face. Cade took a deep breath and indicated the mustangs, now masterfully controlled by the remaining members of Nocona's tribe. "They're for Erick."

That broke Erick out of the spell Cade's return had cast on him. "For me?"

Nocona said something in Comanche that made Cade throw his head back in laughter. He took a step closer to Erick, still smiling. "Erick, this is Nocona, my brother. Nocona, this is Erick."

Erick bowed slightly, not sure of the tribe's customs.

"My brother speaks highly of you, Erick Heller. It is an honor to meet you."

"The honor is mine," Erick insisted. "Were it not for you and your family, I would never have had the chance to meet Cade, and for that, I will be forever in your debt."

Nocona shook his head. "We do not speak of debt among brothers. The bond of family is too strong for such notions."

Erick could only be grateful Cade had found such a family. "But the horses?"

"I'm sorry there aren't more, but I had to get back before the drive started, and this was as many as I could find," Cade said in a rush.

"More?" Erick asked. "Cade, I do not understand."

Cade flushed and rubbed at his neck again. "In Comanche tradition, when a brave finds the one he wants to share his life with, he offers a gift of horses to prove how highly he values his beloved. If he is accepted, the two share a tipi together for the rest of their days." He held out his hands. "Erick Heller, will you join your life with mine?"

Erick stepped forward and took Cade's hands, his breath caught in his throat. He had spoken similar vows in Prussia, a public declaration devoid of any real emotion. This was the connection he had longed for all his life but never dared to dream could become real, much less in the light of day. The best he had hoped for was a life in the shadows with a lover he could never claim. Here, though, now, in this place, among these friends, he could give voice to his heart, offering Cade the same commitment Cade was offering him. He had to swallow twice before he could answer. "I fear I have no tipi to offer. Would a cabin suffice?"

"A cabin?" Cade repeated. "What cabin?"

Nocona elbowed him, forcing a grunt from Cade.

"Of course a cabin would suffice," Cade said with a shake of his head. "But what cabin?"

A smile spread over Erick's face at the thought of everything they'd accomplished in less than a month. "If the cabin meets with your approval, then yes, Cade Webster, it would be my joy to spend the rest of our days together." He wasn't sure who moved first, but suddenly he had Cade in his arms, their lips meeting in a slow, reverent kiss to seal their promises.

A whoop broke them apart. "Shit, did Wolf Boy and Hoss just get married?"

"Shut up, Burke." Michele cuffed his head, then moved to pull them both into a hug. "I'm very happy for the two of you."

Cade beamed at Michele before leaning in to whisper "What cabin?" in her ear.

"I will show you," Erick promised, "but first you need to show Nocona where he and his friends can set up their tipis, and I need to get my wedding present settled so they don't escape."

"I'll show them where to make camp," Michele offered. "Cade, you can help Erick with the horses. If you don't make it to dinner, I'll save you both a plate."

"Such a happy occasion calls for a celebration!" Svensen shouted.

"I had a special dinner planned for tomorrow, before we hit the trail." Javier grinned at them both. "I'll just move it up a night."

Chapter Forty

Cade tore his gaze from Erick's beloved face to take in the joyful expressions on the faces of his family—both his families: the Comanche one who had saved his life when he was orphaned, and the one at Wellspring who had been his salvation as he learned to live again in the white man's world. He had imagined once or twice finding a way to bring the two families together, but he'd always dismissed it as a pipe dream, not something he could actually have. Like everything else since meeting Erick, it hadn't been as far out of reach as he'd feared.

And yet, as happy as it made him to see Chel, the sister of his heart, wrap a supportive arm around Tatsinuupi, his sister-in-law, as she guided her and Nocona toward the field where they could set up their camp, as much joy as Olav's calls for a celebration and Javier's promise of a feast brought him, he needed Erick most of all. "Let's get the horses settled."

Erick smiled. "Trust me?"

"Always."

"Alice?" Erick called. A woman Cade didn't know separated from the crowd.

"Cade, this is Alice Smith. Payne hired her a few days ago to help with the horses. If it won't break any taboos, we can leave them with her and I can show you the cabin where I hope we will spend our lives together."

Cade probably should have insisted he and Erick secure his gift themselves, but somehow in the weeks he'd been gone, Erick had managed to find, build, conjure out of thin air a cabin for them. A place of their own where they wouldn't have to worry about who was around or whether they'd be interrupted. "Nice to meet you, Alice. Watch out for the sorrel mare. She bites. Show me this cabin, Erick."

Erick threaded his fingers between Cade's as he led him along a path between the main house and Javier's kitchen. "When Payne had the trees from the creek milled to repair the damage the JR attack did to the barn, there was wood left over. Grace and Payne asked if the hands would be willing to use it to erect another cabin." Erick's voice was tinged with pride and a hint of wonder. "Everyone offered to help, even if Payne grumbled about taking time away from getting the herd ready. Anyone who wasn't actively working with the cattle pitched in when they could."

The building Erick stopped in front of was a simple affair, similar in size to the foreman's cabin Payne had given to Kit and Mac. A shingled roof stretched over a porch that ran along the front, and several steps led up to the slatted door. Cade stared at it in wonder at how much had been accomplished in such a short time as Erick continued. "Payne said the space below the floor will allow a breeze to blow through to cool it during the summer, and also help keep it dry in case of flash floods."

Erick opened the door into a single spacious room. "Olav appointed himself as construction foreman—he helped build his parents' house in Sweden." Cade turned slowly, gratitude welling within him as the magnitude of what Erick had arranged dawned on him. Cade had mentioned in passing as they lay in Erick's sickbed that he wasn't sure if they'd ever have a cabin of their own, and without even knowing where Cade had gone or why, Erick had made that dream a reality. "Kit laid the stones for the fireplace," Erick continued. The hearth already had logs ready for a fire, and a metal tripod holding a pot hung over it. "Javier contributed the pot so we could make coffee whenever we wish. Matt built the table and chairs, and Jesse installed the sink and pump for water." The other side of the room was filled with a large bed, complete with carved wooden headboard, side tables, and armoire. "Grace insisted on gifting us the bedroom furniture. She said it was only right, since sending you to Galveston to pick up its replacement is what led to our meeting." He squeezed Cade's hand and dropped a kiss on his lips. "For which I am forever grateful." Cade drew his head down for a longer kiss, fully intending to spread Erick out across the bed at the earliest opportunity. "Michele commissioned the bedspread from the quilters at Reverend Smithson's church."

Cade chuckled. "That must have been an interesting conversation."

"Lizzie contributed the rug and curtains, but best of all is this." He swept aside the curtain from a window at the back of the house. "Ned has built us our own private shower. He said it would keep us from scandalizing the other hands in the communal shower."

Cade took in the cabin, the shower, the contributions large and small from his friends and the town, and knew he was the richest man in the world. "A Comanche couple has two things they share: their horses and their home. I grew up in a tipi with Nocona and Pahayoko and our parents. When I left the tribe, I mostly slept rough with just a bedroll, other than a few months I spent with a different outfit before I came to Wellspring, where I moved into the bunkhouse. I've never had a home of my own. I never really believed I would. And then I met you and things that had seemed impossible suddenly became possible. And now you've gone and given me a home."

He swallowed down the emotions threatening to choke him and pulled Erick into his arms. Their bodies fit together like they had been carved from the same stone, separated into two pieces but only complete when slotted back as one. "Nocona asked me if I was sure when I told him about you, about how you'd left your life in Europe to come here. He wasn't sure if someone from such a different life could be happy with a simple cowboy, much less one who had grown up among the Comanche, but I told him you weren't like that. That you didn't need a big house or fancy clothes, that you would understand and accept my gift the way any Comanche would, even if I had to explain it to you first. That we would figure out a place to live and a way to be together even if the white man's world doesn't accept our love."

"*Mein Lieber*," Erick murmured against Cade's neck.

"*Kamakuna*." Cade brushed his lips over the top of Erick's head as he spoke. "Wanna try out our new shower? I've been riding hard and living rough for the past few weeks. I'm dusty and sweaty and I'm sure I stink."

Erick raised his head, a wicked glitter in his eyes. "We would only need to shower again after, if we do not wish everyone at dinner to know what we have been doing."

"I think they'd guess anyway—" Cade gasped as Erick nestled his head against his neck again, nipping down hard. "We did just get married, even if no one but my Comanche family recognizes it."

"And Burke," Erick said dryly. "More importantly, *I* recognize it. I never dared to dream of even a lover to call my own. To have this life with you now is a gift beyond price." Erick soothed the bite with his tongue before moving lower, parting the thong that held the beaded tunic closed. "You do not know how many times I have imagined you like this…."

Cade arched so he straddled Erick's thigh and ground down against it. "Hard and desperate for you?"

Erick shifted enough for Cade to feel his answering hardness. "Even more magnificent than I imagined." He slid his hands under the buckskin, making Cade shiver. "Michele described you confronting Sanders and Lutz, and all I could see was you dressed like this, claiming your heritage."

"Not exactly like this," Cade admitted. "I wasn't wearing these clothes that day. My mother gave these to me when I became an adult in the eyes of the tribe. I've worn them three times since then—when we laid my mother to rest, when I stood witness as Nocona gave his betrothal gift to Tatsinuupi, and today, when I brought home the horses for you. Sanders and Lutz didn't deserve the honor, but marrying you? I couldn't have done it any other way."

"I would have you in any clothes, or none at all." He unfastened the tie from around Cade's waist, setting the tail aside reverently before drawing the tunic over his head. "The wolf for which you are named?"

"Yes, a gray wolf," Cade replied as he started on the buttons of Erick's shirt. "I found the pelt less than an hour before I found Nocona and his band. I claimed the tail as a sign that my totem approved of my quest."

Erick shrugged out of his shirt and knelt to nip and lick at Cade's chest. His nipples tightened, drawing Erick's attentions until they were hard and glistening. Cade shivered, though the cabin was warm and Erick's breath was hot against his damp skin. He nuzzled lower, following the trail of hair that arrowed down beneath Cade's leggings.

Cade tore at the leather tie holding up his leggings and pushed them off, grateful for the soft moccasins that slipped off his feet easily. He grabbed Erick and pulled him back up to standing so he could strip him the rest of the way as well. He ran one finger down the line of the scar on Erick's chest. "No more pain?"

Erick shook his head.

"Then tell me what you want. Anything you want. Let me make your dreams come true."

"I want you." Erick wrapped a hand around Cade's cock, smearing the droplet of fluid over the head. "In me, around me, over me, until all I smell, all I taste, all I feel, all I am is you."

"It will be my genuine pleasure," Cade growled as he backed Erick toward the bed. The mattress gave easily between their combined weight— feathers, Cade thought distantly, even more of a gift than he'd realized—as he laid Erick down on the quilt and stretched out next to him. He traced the line of Erick's collarbone with one finger, reveling in the freedom to be together without fear of interruption or shame, of being *allowed* to love this man for the rest of his life, even if the only people who knew it were the family he'd built for himself on the ranch. The feast that was Erick's body tempted him far more than any spread Javier could put together, and he fully intended to savor every last inch.

"*Küss mich*," Erick murmured. Cade grinned and bent his head to mate their lips in a tender kiss. Erick tasted of coffee, despite it being some hours after breakfast. He must have filled a flask and sipped out of it over the course of the morning.

He pulled back so he could stare down into Erick's blue eyes, deep with emotion and desire. "I love you, kuhmapu." He had never dreamed he would find a man among the Comanche or in the white man's world who would accept him as he was, who he could call his husband.

"And I you." Erick caught one of Cade's braids in his fingers, drawing him down gently until their mouths mated again. Erick opened to him so sweetly, so fully, and Cade gave thanks to the gods of both his birth parents and his adoptive parents that he had been blessed to find this man, the perfect match promised to him in his spirit quest.

Erick shifted beneath him, and Cade eased up on his elbows enough to allow Erick to reach into the drawer of one of the bedside tables and draw out a tub of salve. "Mac's housewarming gift," he explained with a smile. "He told me he made an especially large batch just for us."

Cade laughed and buried his face in Erick's neck. "I don't know whether to thank him or shoot him."

"Thank him," Erick replied dryly. "Definitely thank him."

Cade took the tub and set it within easy reach, but as much as he ached to sink into Erick, he had been dreaming of this moment for months, and he wouldn't be rushed, not even by Erick. "I have quite a few people to thank, it seems." He kissed Erick more deeply, letting his hunger seep into the contact as he claimed Erick's mouth. Erick responded in kind, his tongue dueling with Cade's until Cade pulled away, panting hard. He mouthed his way down Erick's neck until he reached the line of paler skin usually covered by Erick's shirt. Then he latched on and sucked hard, drawing a mark to the surface, the first of many he intended to leave before they left the bed. Erick was *his* now.

Erick arched up beneath him, the hard length of his cock hot against Cade's. "*Mein Gott*, I missed you," he groaned as Cade latched onto a peaked nipple. "You should not have stayed away so long."

Cade raised his head, rubbing a thumb over the wet nub. "It took longer than I hoped to find Nocona's camp. And then I had to find enough mustangs to make you a proper gift."

"He said something to you that made you laugh." Erick ran a hand down Cade's back to squeeze his ass. The way their cocks slid against each other was almost enough to make him forget the answer to Erick's question.

"He told me that, having met you, he understood why I insisted on so many horses." He kissed his way down Erick's abdomen and sucked another bruise to the surface in the crease where hip joined thigh. "And then he told me to be careful neither of us were too sore to ride tomorrow."

Erick bucked up against his mouth, and Cade lost all will to resist. He angled his head and took Erick in his mouth, the hard length pressing all the way to the back of his throat. He hummed and swallowed around the flared tip. Erick thrust into the contact, but Cade rode out the movement. When Erick subsided, Cade pinned his hips to the mattress and set out to drive his new husband wild.

The groans and guttural German words Cade couldn't understand were proof that he was succeeding. They were driving Cade pretty wild too, and he wrapped a hand around the base of his cock and squeezed. Erick wanted Cade inside him, so he couldn't let himself come yet. But there was no reason Erick couldn't come first. He sucked harder, dragging his tongue up and down and around, using his other hand to cup Erick's sac in his palm. Just when he thought he'd tipped Erick over the edge, Erick pulled away, shaking.

"Inside me." He threaded his fingers into Cade's hair and drew him upward, taking his mouth in a hard, needy kiss. "I've been so empty with you gone. Want to feel all of you inside me, even if I can't ride tomorrow."

It would take a stronger man than Cade Webster to deny that request. He fumbled for the tub of salve and coated his fingers generously. As desperately as Erick was kissing him, Cade didn't know how long he would let Cade spend stretching him, and if he couldn't get Erick loose, at least he could get him slick. He pressed lightly at Erick's hole, expecting resistance but found none. "Erick?"

"I have been waiting for your return." Erick's voice broke on the words as Cade found his sweet spot and teased it mercilessly. "At night as I lay in my lonely bed, I imagined this moment, and I wanted to be ready for it. For you."

The image of Erick fingering himself each night so he would require less preparation now nearly did Cade in. He gritted his teeth against the need to come and added a second finger. When Erick arched against him with a breathless "please, more," Cade gave up. He moved between Erick's legs, swiped a handful of salve over his own aching erection, and lined himself up with Erick's entrance. Gaze fixed on Erick's face, he sank slowly into Erick's hot depths, alert for any sign of discomfort, but Erick's body welcomed him in like a missing piece that needed only this moment to make them both whole again. When he could go no deeper, he leaned down for another kiss.

Erick rocked beneath him, the ridge of his scar brushing over Cade's nipple. Erick had said it didn't hurt anymore, but Cade wasn't going to take any chances. He slid an arm beneath Erick's back and pushed up until he was sitting on his heels, drawing Erick with him. "Take what you need," he murmured against Erick's ear.

"Only you," Erick answered. Bracing his arms over Cade's shoulders, he rode him as expertly as any of the mustangs he'd tamed. Erick was beautiful like this, masterful even as he yielded, and Cade once again gave thanks for finding the man so perfect for him in every way.

"Can you come like this?" he asked when Erick released his mouth to draw in a ragged breath. "Come on my cock?"

Erick shifted, changing the angle of his hips slightly, and murmured, "If you make me. Fuck me harder, *mein Herz*."

Cade surged up to meet each downward slide of Erick's hips, their bodies slapping together with all the urgency they'd held in check until now. Erick's thighs trembled on either side of Cade's, but he didn't slow his pace, and Cade met him thrust for thrust. With a sharp cry, Erick threw his head back as he tightened around Cade and spattered both their stomachs with the proof of his pleasure. Cade braced Erick's hips and fucked up into him as he rode out the aftershocks. When Erick sagged in his arms, Cade urged him onto his back. He started to withdraw, but Erick wrapped his legs around Cade's hips. "In me, remember?"

Cade rested his forehead against Erick's shoulder as he pounded his release into Erick's willing body. He collapsed onto Erick's chest and rolled to the side so as not to put his weight on the scar.

"There is no pain, and no tightness when I breathe, even when you are stealing my breath." Erick nestled against Cade's side, wrapping an arm over his chest and a leg over his thigh. "I am healed."

"Healed enough to try out Ned's gift?" Cade smirked. "Since he gave us free rein to do all the things we couldn't do in the common shower."

"We should refresh ourselves before dinner," Erick agreed, though he made no move to let Cade rise. "I hesitated to comment before, but you are a bit… pungent."

Cade poked Erick in the side, startling a laugh from him. "I did suggest we shower before we tried out the bed," Cade reminded him. "You're the one who couldn't wait."

"You made no complaint at the time." Erick dropped a kiss on Cade's neck. "But I will be pleased to help wash you now. It would not do to be late to Javier's special supper."

"I'd just as soon miss supper altogether." Cade turned his head enough to brush against Erick's lips. "You realize this is the last time we'll be able to sleep in a proper bed for months, once we leave for Abilene. We should take advantage of it." Erick didn't answer, and Cade drew back enough to meet his eyes. "What's wrong?"

"Payne has not named who will accompany him on the drive. He may feel I am not yet strong enough, or skilled enough." Erick shook his head. "I would not be parted from you again so soon, for so long."

Cade kissed Erick as thoroughly as he could, determined to dispel any doubts in Erick's mind. When Erick went pliant beneath him, Cade lifted his head. "First, Payne never announces who's doing the drive until the last minute, so the delay has nothing to do with you. Second, you are more than strong and skilled enough to help, and he'd be a fool to leave you behind. But if somehow he decides you aren't going, then I'll trade out with someone else who's staying behind. I'm not indispensable. They can get the herd to Abilene without me just fine. Payne's fair, though, and he's not as insensitive as he pretends to be. He won't separate couples for more than a shift or two without a damn good reason."

"And if he thinks my injury or my ability to help Grace with the accounting are good enough reasons?"

"Then I'll stay behind too. It's not like I *enjoy* spending months on the road behind a herd of cattle kicking up dust and doing their damnedest to get themselves lost or killed," Cade replied. "It's part of the job and I do it because it's expected, but I wouldn't be upset if we stayed behind."

"Payne said you read the land better than any cowboy he has ever seen. Now that you have returned, he will not want to leave without you."

Cade flushed at the compliment. He always did his best, but it felt good to know someone thought that highly of him, especially someone as stingy with praise as Payne. "If he's stupid enough not to see how valuable you are, he'll have to go without me. And Payne's not that stupid." He shared another long, slow kiss with Erick before levering himself up. "Now, let's go check out Ned's shower."

Chapter Forty-One

THE SOUND of the dinner bell broke Cade and Erick out of the lazy mood they'd settled into after their shower, tender kisses and soft caresses rather than the wild urgency of their earlier lovemaking. Erick hadn't slept well between his healing injury and his worry for Cade the whole time Cade had been gone, and Cade admitted to sleeping with one eye open until he met up with Nocona's tribe and only sleeping fitfully even then. "Nocona says I've gone soft," he'd confided.

Erick ran his hands over Cade's hard ass and muscular thighs. "He is clearly mistaken."

Cade laughed at that. "He doesn't know me the way you do."

"It pleases me that no one knows you the way I do." Erick twined his fingers in Cade's as they headed toward the mess tables.

A chorus of cheers and catcalls greeted them, but even that couldn't disrupt Erick's spirits. "Enough already," Kit stood and shouted in what must have been his Army captain's voice. After one more wolf whistle from Burke and a glare from Kit, the hands returned to eating.

True to her promise, Michele had saved plates for them, loaded with smoked brisket, pinto beans, potato salad, jalapeño bread, and greens with bacon. Erick took one bite and groaned in pleasure. "This is delicious, Javier."

"It's the traditional last night before the drive meal. Would have been better if Cade hadn't messed up my plans. We'll be eating jerky for dinner tomorrow." Javier grinned at Cade. "You couldn't have waited one more day to come back?"

"Not even for your smoked brisket," Cade replied easily. "As good as it is, finally getting Erick to marry me is better. Although I know you. We won't be eating jerky for dinner tomorrow or any other night."

The food at Wellspring was very different from what Erick had grown up with, spicier, earthier, and often with unfamiliar ingredients, but while the dishes were exotic to his Prussian palate, he wouldn't trade them for the bland dishes from his former home for anything, even without taking everything else he'd gained into consideration.

Michele joined them, sitting close enough to Javier that their legs were surely touching beneath the table. Erick couldn't help the smile that brought as Cade reached across the table and squeezed her hand. "Thank you, all of you really, for the cabin. It's perfect."

"I do know you, *petit loup*," she teased. "I think I'm capable of decorating a one-room cabin to suit you."

Cade shook his head. "It's more than that. It's the fact that everyone contributed in some way. You saw me in the months after I first left my tribe. You know how lost I was." He took Erick's hand in his other hand. "I'm not lost anymore."

"We have both found our home." Erick could not have imagined, when he took ship for America, that he would find not only a way to leave his past behind but work with real meaning, friends who accepted him as he was, and a man who loved him as much as Erick loved him back. He swallowed past the emotion that threatened to choke him and then realized he no longer had to hide behind a stoic facade. He caught Cade's other hand and brought it to his lips, smiling at his friends. "I am truly blessed."

"You did not tell me the food would be this good when you told me we could eat with the rest of the outfit, manusu naru."

"Not that nickname again, Nocona," Cade protested.

"What does it mean?" Erick asked.

"Wild child," Cade replied before Nocona could.

"He was very uncivilized when we found him," Nocona added primly. He took a bite of his dinner. "Tatsinuupi has already declared she will never cook again."

"She may change her mind when Javier isn't here," Cade replied with a chuckle. "He'll go with the hands who drive the herd to Abilene, and no one else cooks nearly as well as he does."

"Perhaps, but in how many other ranches would we even be allowed at the table?"

"Wellspring is special," Erick said.

"Tutaatu Isa told me this was so, but it is only now that I am seeing how very true that is."

Payne rose from his seat at one of the other tables. "Now that we're all back"—he glared at Cade, who ignored him in favor of leaning into Erick's shoulder—"we'll leave for Abilene the day after tomorrow. Trujillo, you're in charge of provisions. Make sure the chuckwagon has enough for the road there. We can resupply for the trip back after we sell the herd. Burke, as much as it pains me, you're riding shotgun. We can't afford to have an axle break and not be able to fix it."

"You know you'd be lost without me," Burke preened. "The rest of you will just have to miss me while I'm gone."

"Yeah, miss you like dysentery," someone called out to raucous laughter.

Erick's mood turned suddenly sour. He'd counted on riding in the chuckwagon with Javier if Payne didn't choose him as one of the trail hands. Now that option was closed to him.

Payne turned his eye on Burke, who subsided but continued to murmur under his breath to Javier. "The rest of the trail crew will consist of Webster, Logan, MacRae, Svensen, Bessette, Chiles, Beaufort—"

"At least we won't have to suffer through Jesse's cooking for the next three months!" someone called out.

"I'll keep you fed while they're gone—this year." Becca Spencer stood and stared down Payne. "Next year I'll be joining him on the drive."

Grace, seated at Payne's side, laughed. It was hard to hear over the chatter at Becca's announcement, but it sounded like she repeated "women's bunkhouse."

Payne scowled and raised his hand for quiet. "Braddock, Quinn, Walsh."

Erick's heart fell. Those were the ten hands Payne had said he'd need. Cade squeezed his hand and started to speak, but Erick shook his head. There was no way he would let Cade refuse to take part in the drive.

"And Heller will wrangle the remuda," Payne finished.

Erick's gaze flew from Payne to Cade, almost afraid to hope. "I—I do not know that word," he admitted, stunned. Did it mean he was going on the drive?

"It means the string of horses we take with us," Cade explained. "We need at least two horses per hand to let them switch off, plus extras in case any of them run off or get hurt."

"Told you you were in charge of the horses," Payne rumbled. "'Less you don't want to come along."

"No, of course I will come," Erick stammered.

"Damn straight you will," Cade whispered. "I have some promises to keep still before we ride out."

Erick frowned for a minute, trying to remember any unkept promises between them. Then it came back to him, the night they'd spent together in Grace's house before Cade went to find his brother and his betrothal gift. "I'll flip you over and mount you as hard and fast as any stallion," Cade had said. It hadn't happened that night because of his injuries nor this afternoon as they'd sealed their vows face-to-face. Tonight, though....

"We do have two more nights in the cabin," Erick agreed slowly.

"Yeah, enjoy that soft bed and that private shower while you can," Ned crowed. "You'll be sleeping on the ground and wishing for a stream to wash up in soon enough."

"Shut up, Burke," Cade growled. "He dealt with all that on the way from Galveston. He's tougher than you think."

Erick thought of the naif who'd stepped off the steamer from Bremen, fortunate enough to meet a man with tanned skin and sun-bleached hair brushing his shoulders, a thin braid interwoven with colorful beads at one temple. And how much that man had taught him and given him.

"Of course I am," Erick asserted. "I am a cowboy."

Authors' Notes

WE'VE TRIED to keep the information in the story as accurate to the period as possible, especially when it comes to the treatment following Erick's shooting.

One of the first pulmonary lobectomies was recorded in 1821. By the Civil War, it was a risky but not uncommon treatment for chest wounds. The first recorded blood transfusions date to the 1650s, though they were not used regularly until the early 1800s. Since blood types were not identified until 1900, there were real risks of an incompatible blood type killing the recipient. Luckily Javier seems to have been a universal donor. A form of spirometer was invented in the 1840s as a way to measure lung capacity. Dr. Lillard may have been a bit advanced in prescribing its use to help Erick's recovery.

Cade's adoption by the Comanche was not an isolated incident. The most famous "Indian captive" of the time was Cynthia Ann Parker. She was taken at age nine following an attack on a Texas fort in 1836 and spent the next twenty-four years living with the Comanche. She married a tribal chief and bore three children before being "rescued" by Texas Rangers in 1860. She never readapted to white life and tried several times to return to her Comanche family, unsuccessfully, before her death in 1871. Her son Quanah Parker was one of the last Comanche tribal leaders.

Keep reading for an excerpt from
Checkmate
by Nicki Bennett and Ariel Tachna

Sɪʀ Lᴏᴡᴇʟʟ St. Denys stood in the shadows of the dank alley outside the seedy tavern in Madrid, waiting impatiently for his contact. He searched the face of each person who passed, but none gave the gray-haired man a second look. That suited St. Denys fine. The last thing he wanted was to be recognized here, in this setting, except by the man he was supposed to meet. Teodoro Ciéza de Vivar had been recommended to him as a sword for hire, a mercenary with enough honor to complete the job, but not so much as would prove troublesome. With that thought in mind, St. Denys had worked out the perfect story to get the swordsman to go along with his plan.

Movement at the corner of his eye caught his attention. A man stood at the entrance to the alley, clothed in dark leather over a paler linen shirt despite the heat. The brim of his hat was wide and slightly tattered, and he wore a sword at one hip and a dagger tucked in his belt on the other. As the man approached, St. Denys took note of the thick moustache that obscured his upper lip and the expressionless brown eyes that pierced even the deepest of shadows for any threat. St. Denys's eyes lingered appreciatively on the breadth of the shoulders revealed by the leather jerkin, the trim waist, the narrow hips and long, long legs, a frown marring his face only when he reached the battered, mended boots. With a regretful shrug, the Englishman stepped out of the shadows. "Ciéza de Vivar?"

Teodoro Ciéza de Vivar had been watching the older man for some time before he was ready to approach him. His finances were always uneven, and the coin for this job, if he decided to take it, would be most welcome, but he had enough in hand at the moment that he could afford to decline the offer should it come to that. He did not always have the luxury to be so discriminating, though there were some undertakings to which nothing could compel him to agree, but this did not feel like one of them. Teodoro had learned that observing his would-be employers could often reveal to him whether he would agree to their task, even before hearing the details or the terms. His instincts told him that this richly dressed, silver-haired gentleman would at least be worth hearing out. "I am Ciéza de Vivar," he replied. "And you?"

"St. Denys," the noble said with a courtly bow, seeing no reason to admit his title to the swordsman. It would likely only raise his price. "Lowell St. Denys. I'm hoping you can help me, señor. My friend is most distressed at his son's behavior."

"Shall we take some refreshment while you tell me of it?" Teodoro inclined his head toward the tavern—surely not the type of place his prospective employer would normally frequent, but even if he chose to decline the job, he could at least get a decent bottle of wine from the meeting.

St. Denys frowned a little, not accustomed to such common taverns, but he understood the game. He would buy the mercenary food and drink in exchange for being heard. The rest was up to his powers of persuasion. "I would be pleased to dine with you," he said magnanimously. "Lead the way."

Teodoro had met enough men of a certain type at this tavern that the serving girl knew to seat them at a quiet table against the back wall. Declining his prospective employer's offer of a meal—he would have St. Denys's measure first—Teodoro asked her to bring a bottle of their best vintage, then settled in his chair, stretching his long legs and turning his attention back to the Englishman. "Why is your friend not here to see me himself, if he is so concerned about his son?"

"He is still in England," St. Denys explained. "His son was supposed to return from the Continent last month. Instead, he has run off with his... friend... and refuses to return home." In another place, St. Denys would not have minced words, but he had seen the burnings in the town square the week before; the Inquisition had no mercy on sodomites. Still, he was well experienced in concealing his own inclinations and would not hesitate to play upon the mercenary's undoubted prejudice in that regard, if it would gain St. Denys what he sought. "His father asked me to approach him as an old friend of the family, but the boy will not be swayed. So his father requested that I employ whatever means necessary to separate him from the current bad influence in his life and return him to England at once. Thus my message to you."

"So the boy is not being held against his will?" Teodoro asked, frowning. "Is he of age?" The original message had implied that the lad in question had been kidnapped, but St. Denys was describing a spoiled runaway. If the boy was unwilling to return, Teodoro's task would be that much harder—and his fee that much higher, he decided as he waited for a response.

"He is twenty-three," St. Denys replied, "but his father retains control of his purse and his future until he is twenty-five, so it remains his father's decision what he should be doing. If after that, he chooses to consort with… men like Hawkins, that will be his choice. For now, his father insists that he come home."

There was a moment's pause as the serving maid brought their wine, poured them each a glassful, and set the bottle in the middle of the table. After raising his goblet to his companion in a silent toast, Teodoro took an appreciative swallow, letting the flavor of the rich red wine mellow his mood. "So I will be fighting both the… friend, and the youth himself?" he mused. "That will make the task more difficult, especially since I expect the father wishes them both unharmed."

"Hawkins is unimportant," St. Denys declared with a wave of his hand. "He is the reason the boy has neglected his duties in the first place. But I will increase your pay by half for dealing with him. All that matters is bringing Blackwood to me unharmed so that I can get him home where he belongs."

Teodoro's well-developed sense of self-preservation made him immediately suspicious of anyone to whom price was no object. Still, St. Denys met his eyes steadily, and what harm could there be in returning a young man to his own father? "Where can I find this Hawkins and… Blackwood, was it?"

"Christian Blackwood, and they are in Valencia," St. Denys replied. "He seems to think that by not returning to England, he can avoid his father's disapproval. I am quite sure you can reach him faster than I would be able to get there to hire someone local."

"It will take me some days to ride that far," Teodoro calculated. "And no guarantee the young man and his… friend… will not be gone by the time I arrive."

"You can be there in nine days if you ride hard," St. Denys countered. "If they have left by the time you get there, follow them. The boy's father will pay you well to make sure he recovers his son."

Teodoro fingered the end of his moustache, his thoughts troubled. The easy way St. Denys countered his every objection only strengthened his distrust. Still, the man was paying well—too well, his judgment told him, but he would be a fool to refuse to profit from the foreigner's ignorance. "I will take your commission," he declared. "How will I recognize Blackwood when I get to Valencia?"

"He should be quite easy to pick out of a crowd," St. Denys assured him. "He's reasonably tall—about your height, I think—with blue eyes and blond curls long enough to brush his shoulders. Hawkins is tall— very tall—dark-haired, but also obviously English. None of the swarthy skin so common in Spain."

"And what should I do with the young man once I find him?" Teodoro inquired.

"Bring him back to Madrid," St. Denys instructed, his face carefully calm, only adding to Teodoro's unease. "I will make sure he returns to his father from here." He reached in his pocket and withdrew a purse. "Here is the first installment of your fee. I will have the rest for you when you bring me the boy."

Teodoro opened the purse and let the coins spill into his hand. As he expected, they were gold—enough to satisfy his obligations and some to spare. Pushing aside the misgivings he could not afford to indulge, he nodded shortly. "If all goes well, we should return within three weeks," he said. "I will send word to you when we arrive." After draining his goblet, he stood, his blade settling at his hip. "Until then, Your Mercy."

St. Denys watched the mercenary disappear out the door and leaned back against the wall of the inn, his eyes closing. Close. He was so close. Surely this time his plan would succeed.

TEODORO CLIMBED the stairs to his rooms in the upper level of the parochial residence of *la iglesia de San Pedro*—rooms he occupied at the insistence of his son's uncle, though as often as he had needed to leave the boy in the priest's care during his early years, there had been little choice but to accept. He found Esteban where he had left him, practicing his letters at the small table that served them as desk and dinner table as well, when he could afford to put food on it. "Fetch my saddlebags," he said. "I have a commission, one that will take me out of town for several weeks. Don Inocencio will see to you while I am gone."

Esteban was full of questions, but he knew better than to ask for answers his guardian was unlikely to give him. "*Sí*, Teo," he replied, rising from his seat and then putting the items Teodoro was likely to need in the pouches. He returned with the bags and offered them to Teodoro. "Be careful," he added unnecessarily.

"Stay out of trouble while I am gone," Teodoro countered. Esteban was at the age, no longer a child but not quite yet a man, when he was most ripe to get into any kind of scrape, but there was no way Teodoro could take him along on a journey where speed was of the essence—even if he could afford to hire a second horse. Reminded of his change in finances, Teodoro took the Englishman's purse from his belt and tossed one of the gold coins to Esteban. "That should keep you fed while I am gone. I don't want to find you've used it on anything but food when I return!"

"What else would I spend it on?" Esteban asked innocently, pocketing the coin with a bland stare.

Teodoro lifted an eyebrow, his dark eyes kindling until Esteban blushed and dropped his own. "You might buy a new shirt," he observed. "You've nearly outgrown that one."

"Food, and a new shirt," Esteban agreed, cursing himself for the blush that gave him away. "Anything else will wait until you return, Teo, I promise."

Teodoro nodded, ruffling Esteban's dark hair before dropping his hand to the hilt of his blade. He ran a checklist in his head—his sword, the *daga izquierda* tucked into his belt, the smaller dagger hidden in the top of one of his boots. Sighing to himself, he crossed to the small armoire in his bedroom and took out the box containing his pistol. It was a weapon he disliked, preferring the grace and elegance of the rapier, but his gut told him this affair was one in which he would need every advantage he could get. After pouring powder and shot into a small pouch, he moved the dagger to the back of his belt, tucked the pistol in its place, and gathered up his saddlebags.

"Three weeks, Esteban," he said as he headed toward the door. "Expect my return sometime after that." He did not mention what would happen should he not return—he no longer needed to.

"Be careful," Esteban said again, softly this time, as he watched his guardian, the only father he had ever known, disappear out the door.

Growing up in Chicago, NICKI BENNETT spent every Saturday at the central library, losing herself in the world of books. A voracious reader, she eventually found it difficult to find enough of the kind of stories she liked to read and decided to start writing them herself.

Email: nickibennett1@gmail.com
Facebook: www.facebook.com/100011754789784

ARIEL TACHNA is a polyglot linguaphile with a passion for travel, yarn, orchids, and romance. She has explored 45 states and 15 countries. The rich history and culture of France, the flavors and scents of India, and the sunrise over Machu Picchu in particular have left indelible impressions and show up regularly in her writing. Her passion for yarn has resulted in an overflowing stash and more projects than she'll probably finish in a lifetime, but that has yet to stop her from buying more. Her orchid collection has outgrown her office and spilled over into the rest of her house (much to her family's dismay), but that hasn't stopped her from adding to her collection or from resuscitating any unhappy ones she finds.

When she isn't writing, knitting, or poking at her orchids, she spends her time marveling at her two kids, who never cease to amaze her with their capacity for love and acceptance and sports—they certainly didn't get that from her!—and their refusal to accept injustice of any kind—she hopes they got that from her.

Visit Ariel:
Website: www.arieltachna.com
Facebook: www.facebook.com/ArielTachna
Email: arieltachna@gmail.com

Rocky Road To Love

Nicki Bennett and Ariel Tachna

When Mason gets caught in a blizzard on his way home for Christmas and ends up in a snowdrift, the outlook is grim—until a handsome trucker appears, offering shelter, companionship, and a tow in the morning.

Tate has never been anyone's idea of a hero. He's been on the road most of his adult life, with few ties to people and even fewer to any particular place. Now, after one steamy night in the cab of his truck, all that changes. Suddenly he has a sweet, intelligent guy who can't get enough of him, who invites him to spend New Year's with his family… who already feels like home. But Tate's job keeps him on the road for weeks at a time. Can he really build something permanent?

NiCKi BENNETT ♥
♥ ARiEL TACHNA

THE
ESCAPE
ARTiST

Health issues have kept Scott Calligan in quarantine since the start of the pandemic. But when a wandering dog is nearly hit by a car in front of his house, he can't help but come to its rescue—even if he's more of a cat person.

Max's owner, Brandon Richards, represents everything Scott has kept himself safe from. Once he picks up the runaway, Scott doesn't expect he'll see either of them again.

It seems Max has other ideas….

EXPLORING LIMITS

Exploring Limits: Book One

NICKI BENNETT
ARIEL TACHNA

Exploring Limits: Book One

We could always share him....

After failing to capture the attention of their bicurious costar singlehandedly, Kit and Devon team up to seduce Jonathan, who plays King Arthur in the new miniseries Camelot.

The chemistry between the three actors is off the charts, and it brings out the adventurous side in all of them. Things heat up in the bedroom as the trio explores the pleasures of dominance, submission, bondage, toys, and anything else they can find to get the most out of their secret time together.

But a gay ménage presents problems without easy solutions—especially as they work closely together on set. For their threesome to survive and evolve into a true committed relationship, they'll all have to test their physical and emotional limits.

OUT
of
BOUNDS

NICKI BENNETT
AND
ARIEL TACHNA

Exploring Limits: Book One

We could always share him....

After failing to capture the attention of their bicurious costar singlehandedly, Kit and Devon team up to seduce Jonathan, who plays King Arthur in the new miniseries Camelot.

The chemistry between the three actors is off the charts, and it brings out the adventurous side in all of them. Things heat up in the bedroom as the trio explores the pleasures of dominance, submission, bondage, toys, and anything else they can find to get the most out of their secret time together.

But a gay ménage presents problems without easy solutions—especially as they work closely together on set. For their threesome to survive and evolve into a true committed relationship, they'll all have to test their physical and emotional limits.

OUT AND ABOUT

OUT
of
BOUNDS

NICKI BENNETT
AND
ARIEL TACHNA

An Out and About Novel

Out and About: No commitments, just fun.

Liam Gruene and his best friend, Kate Weaver, start Out and About to give LGBTQ singles fun, safe, stress-free events where they can meet other LGBTQ singles. Liam hopes—but doesn't really expect—to meet someone for himself in the process.

Erik Jansen moved to Houston a few months ago after a bad breakup. Since his move, he's thrown himself into work at the expense of a social life. When Liam withdraws funds managed by Erik's firm to finance his new venture, it brings Out and About to his attention and he thinks what the hell. It can't be any worse than trying to meet someone at any of the gay clubs and bars around the city.

Erik and Liam hit it off right away, but Erik can't forget that Liam is a client and Out and About is Liam's job. Erik has an ironclad rule against mixing business and pleasure, and that puts Liam firmly out of bounds.

UNDER THE SKIN

NICKI BENNETT
AND ARIEL TACHNA

Police detective Patrick Flaherty has no illusions about Russian mobster Alexei Boczar, but that doesn't stop his fascination with the bodyguard to one of the most ruthless families in Chicago's growing Eastern European crime community. From the moment Patrick meets Alexei's eyes over the body of another Russian mobster, Alexei is a thorn in Patrick's side, refusing to cooperate with the police and turning all of Patrick's questions back on him. Alexei's hard-as-nails persona whets Patrick's professional determination to get the information he's sure the gangster is hiding, while personally Patrick just wants to get his hands on Alexei's hard body.

The tattoos marking Alexei's skin tell the story of his criminal past, but the more Patrick learns about Alexei, the more he wants to know, until he finds himself over his head in a relationship that might cost him his job and could well cost Alexei his life. Alexei is equally fascinated by Patrick's willingness to overlook his past and even his present associations, but he has secrets of his own that could drive a wedge between them forever.

Police detective Patrick Flaherty has no illusions about Russian mobster Alexei Boczar, but that doesn't stop his fascination with the bodyguard to one of the most ruthless families in Chicago's growing Eastern European crime community. From the moment Patrick meets Alexei's eyes over the body of another Russian mobster, Alexei is a thorn in Patrick's side, refusing to cooperate with the police and turning all of Patrick's questions back on him. Alexei's hard-as-nails persona whets Patrick's professional determination to get the information he's sure the gangster is hiding, while personally Patrick just wants to get his hands on Alexei's hard body.

The tattoos marking Alexei's skin tell the story of his criminal past, but the more Patrick learns about Alexei, the more he wants to know, until he finds himself over his head in a relationship that might cost him his job and could well cost Alexei his life. Alexei is equally fascinated by Patrick's willingness to overlook his past and even his present associations, but he has secrets of his own that could drive a wedge between them forever.

FOR **MORE**
OF THE
BEST
GAY
ROMANCE

www.ingramcontent.com/pod-product-compliance
Lightning Source LLC
Chambersburg PA
CBHW060240100726
47907CB00003B/713